C.B. HAIGH

THE PRICE OF KNOWING

A POWERS OF INFLUENCE NOVEL

Knowing the only way is half the Battle! Then Taking the First Step Requires Courage!

THE PRICE OF KNOWING

A POWERS OF INFLUENCE NOVEL
BOOK II

© 2012 Added Touch Publication

Printed in the U.S.A.

Second Edition Printing 2016

ISBN-13: 978-1541252097 (Added Touch Publications)

ISBN-10: 1541252098

Cover Design by: ExpertSubjects

This book is protected by copyright laws of the United States of America. Any reproduction or unauthorized use of the material or artwork contained herein is prohibited without the express written consent of Added Touch Publications.

For my children, nephews, nieces, and all those who struggle to find their feet. May you always see the light within yourself, even when it feels like the darkness completely surrounds you. For that light will help you find your way.

"To be or not to be?' That is not the question. What is the question? The question is not one of being, but of becoming. *'To become more or not to become more'* This is the question faced by each intelligence in our universe."
— Truman G. Madsen, *Eternal Man*

"Knowledge is power, and power is strength. Every soul is worthy of fighting for. Learn your weaknesses, rise above them, and find the strength within to fight for your soul."
—C.B. Haight

PRELUDE

Virginia May 1732

Considering her fragile cargo, Merilynn pushed the horse as hard as she dared down the well-beaten path. She knew to hasten any more would defeat her purpose to protect her precious cargo. Suddenly, the wagon's wheel struck a rock, jolting the precious cargo, and a whimper of protest came from one of the two infants. She gritted her teeth, knowing she could not afford to stop.

Her instinct urged her to hurry faster, but Merilynn forced herself to pull back on the reins. She did not want the jostling wagon to hurt the boys. Even worse, if her pursuers were close and the infants cried out too loudly, it would ruin everything.

It was difficult to control her emotions. Her heart was weighed down by the loss of her friend, and she worried about the future of the innocent babes in her care. Merilynn reminded herself that her actions would keep them safe, as she felt moisture gather in her eyes.

Leaving Lyndell, the infants' mother and one of her truest friends, behind to face the angry villagers only hours after she brought these precious twins into the world was indeed the hardest thing Merilynn had ever done. Her thoughts screamed at the injustice, and she fervently wished she could go back and save her friend from her coming fate. But her mind knew better, so she stayed the course set in motion months before.

Lyndell herself had made this plan even as the babies grew within her. She knew the events would occur as they had. Lyndell's gift of foresight had shown her that this would happen, and this forewarning is why Merilynn, trusting in her friend's abilities, rushed with all haste to save Lyndell's sons. Saving the babies was all that mattered.

Finally, after far too much time, Merilynn spotted Rowena, the other woman in their treasured circle, near the small creek. *I made it,* she thought, looking over her shoulder to ensure no one pursued her.

Rowena sat upon her bay mare as it pranced around in a circle. Upon hearing the coming wagon, the mare looked and acted as nervous as Rowena felt. Her nervousness ebbed slightly when she spotted Merilynn, the only friend left to her. She understood the feelings of foreboding she felt these last days.

As soon as Merilynn reached the creek she drew back on the reigns, effectively halting her horse. Rowena dismounted and began to hurriedly unhook the wagon. Rowena also knew the urgency of their task and moved with clear purpose.

"Lyndell will not be coming," Merilynn said in a voice thick with the emotion. She leaped down from her seat on the wagon to join her friend.

Offering no reply, Rowena concentrated on the task before her.

After a moment of hushed silence, Merilynn narrowed her eyes. "You knew!" she accused.

As a champion for the weak, Merilynn was vivid and lively when happy, colorful and funny when the mood struck her. She was also quick to anger. Her moods often flashed through her like lighting—there one second, and SNAP, gone the next. Most of all though, she was loyal and strong.

Whereas Rowena, soft and timid, though brave in her own way, was not as verbal as Merilynn. She was logical and plotted out each thought before committing to it. She was the quiet, calm person of reason in their trio. As such, Rowena simply nodded, still choosing not to speak.

"How could you not tell me? Why?" she sputtered. "We could have stopped this. It is not right. She should at least get to care for one of her sons. This is a pure injustice!"

Rowena stopped before she began packing Merilynn's mare with a saddle and let go of a weary, grief-filled sigh. She tried to pull in the pain, but their sister was lost to them. The loss of such a cherished friend cut deep within her soul. Lyndell always held Rowena and Merilynn close to her. She had held them all together. But no more. The knot that kept them tightly bound had been loosened by death.

Lyndell had been strong and stubborn, mature and loving. She was giving and forgiving. She was, and always would be, a part of a whole—their whole. Without her, they felt broken. *After today we will be broken*, she thought sadly. They were all so different...raised differently, taught differently, loved differently, and yet...the strength of their bond had been stronger than any sisterhood of blood or birth, and it had been stolen from them in one fell swoop of fate.

As Rowena reflected on this tragedy, she looked at her friend with glistening tears and understanding in her eyes. Finally, in a soft tone she answered, "Things don't always make sense. It is not for us to question the wisdom of a higher power. This course of events must be fated, which means we must see it through. There is little choice left to us."

Merilynn bristled at Rowena's faith. She couldn't understand it, and as much as she wanted to, she could not replicate it in her own heart. "How can you of all people believe that? You—who has suffered so greatly?"

Rowena stood still and looked down at the trampled grass at her feet to compose her thoughts. With her red hair blowing softly in the light spring breeze and her sea green eyes full of sorrow, she looked deep into Merilynn's soft brown eyes. "Because I have to," she whispered, choking on each syllable.

"I did not mean to cut at your already bleeding heart. My heart is heavy and grieves at the loss of Lyndell," Merilynn replied softly as guilt dampened the anger.

"It is not only the loss of Lyndell that cuts you so deeply, it is anger at the circumstance. I agree wholeheartedly that it should not be like this. We should not fear for our lives because of who we are by birth. There is no justice in it, but it simply is. No ranting or screaming, cursing or stomping will change what has happened when the sun rose this day. From this day forward all we can do is honor her sacrifice and keep our promise to protect the babes."

As if they understood, a soft, infant cry pulled them both from the current conversation and the overwhelming grief surrounding them. Rowena closed her eyes at the sound of it, and a fragile piece of her broke.

Her thoughts flashed to the sound of her own infant's cries. The ten-month old son she had ironically lost only days before to the fever, along with her husband, the only man likely to understand and embrace her gifts. The pain was so great within her. Her husband knew of this plan and had agreed to join her in her efforts before he had taken ill, but now she would be alone in this endeavor.

Merilynn gently squeezed Rowena's shoulder, offering reassurance. "They need to be fed."

"I'll see to it," Rowena replied, barely above a whisper. Slowly, she walked over and scooped one of the tiny, squalling babies into her arms, and she looked into his abnormally golden eyes. She knew her earlier words to be true. Things did happen for a reason. For the first time in many days, Rowena smiled.

She looked back to a busy Merilynn. "They are important," she proclaimed. "As Lyndell foretold. You can feel it, can you not? I can feel it. What we do this day will change many lives." Merilynn stopped working but did not face Rowena, who continued, "And she is not lost to us as you believe. We will forever have a piece of her right here with her sons. She would never leave us. Lyndell will forever and always be a part of our lives." As she finished, Rowena looked down once more to the fussing, hungry baby who had already suffered so much. She would do anything to protect him, even if it meant sacrificing her very life.

Hearing the heartfelt proclamation went a long way to tempering Merilynn. *Maybe these events were meant to happen after all,* Merilynn thought, as she watched Rowena kiss the infant tenderly on his tiny brow. With the loss of her own son and loving husband, Rowena had become sad and broken. Here, Merilynn realized, was a chance for Rowena to heal.

This realization filled her with love and optimism, and it was something she would forever remember. Seeing the hope and faith in her friend was something she knew must be passed on to any who could learn it, and she promised herself she would make sure to teach it to Lyndell's son. Merilynn promised herself that even when her temper snapped, she would always strive to remember this lesson of love, forgiveness, and the odd circle of fate taught to her by the gentlest person she knew.

Her lips turned up just a fraction. Even while grieving for one friend, she rejoiced for another. Clearing her throat, she interrupted Rowena's ponderings by saying, "That child Lyndell named Jarrett, after her father. He is the eldest of the two. The other is Cade, named after the boy's father." Merilynn waited another heartbeat, not wanting to ruin the emotional moment for her friend. Though, after a time she knew she had to. "We must not tarry any longer. If they suspect, even in the smallest way, that the boys are alive, they will not be far behind."

Nodding her agreement, Rowena promptly nursed each child, changed their rags, and swaddled them once more. Meanwhile, Merilynn finished saddling her horse with the spare saddle she brought and burdened the horses even more with the supplies they would need.

As the day-old infants slept, Rowena used a long piece of fabric to secure Cade to Merilynn's body for easier travel. Merilynn then helped Rowena do the same with Jarrett.

Rowena's heart warmed. The minute she laid eyes on him, Rowena forged an instant connection with the first of Lyndell's twins. It seemed as if fate would have a hand in deciding which child would go with her. They did not discuss the matter of who would take which child, but Rowena knew deep in her heart that this was the right way of it.

After finishing all of the necessary tasks, they looked at each other for another short span of time. Neither of them wanted to be the first to speak as things came to an end.

"Should we stay together, at least until you can find a wet nurse?" Rowena questioned, finally breaking the silence.

"No, it is too risky. I am sure I can find somebody before this small supply runs out. Though I abhor it, I plan to purchase a slave to help. That would ensure secrecy, and I can give her a better life than most would."

Rowena nodded slowly. Neither of the two women wanted to part company yet. They knew it would very likely be the last time they would ever see each other. Merilynn's eyes shimmered with unshed tears, and Rowena could feel the heaviness of despair weighing on her chest. Merilynn wiped at a rogue tear that escaped, and though Rowena swore she had shed all the tears her body could in this last week, more of them slipped past her guard.

Suddenly, a peaceful breeze picked up, blowing toward them as it rolled across the spring grass at their feet. The green blades danced and swayed in the wind like waves on the water. The long hair on both women floated up softly with the cooler air currents and tickled their fair skin. The horses nickered and whinnied, then calmed, as the breeze floated over them.

Both women felt warmth and comfort creep into their saddened souls. They both acutely felt the warm tingling sensation in direct contrast with the chill morning air. Closing their eyes, they absorbed the power of it, while praying silently that they could do the right things for these helpless babies unfairly left to their care.

When the strange breeze abated, Merilynn whispered, "We best be on our way."

"I know," Rowena replied with equal reverence.

They embraced one another as best they could considering the tiny, sleeping infants between them. Still whispering, Rowena said, "Blessed be, sister of my heart."

"Blessed be," choked Merilynn.

Minding their bundles, they slowly mounted their horses. With one last, longing look at each other, the tie binding them together fell away, and the two friends departed, each taking a different path toward destiny.

CHAPTER I

He somehow knew he was dreaming, but he couldn't make it stop. Jarrett was a boy again in Colonial Pennsylvania, and felt small and young. He had been ill for almost an entire week. Jarrett's bones ached, and his skin burned with fever as chills wracked his body. Rowena kept tending to him fretfully, placing cool rags on his brow, only to change them right away due to his burning fever. In the beginning, Rowena tried to get him to eat, but his stomach revolted each time she presented him with any food. He could barely hold down anything as simple as water.

No healer could be found, and no one near the small Pennsylvania settlement knew what plagued the small boy.

After six terrible days and five restless nights of painful suffering and frantic worry, one bright full moon changed everything for them both.

That night, as the moon rose to its peak taking the sun's place in the cloudless sky, Jarrett's young legs suddenly cracked. He released an ear-splitting scream that echoed through the still night. Incomprehensible pain ripped through him. Then he felt several sharp pops originate in his spine. With each agonizing jerk of his

~ 8 ~

body, he could feel the bones realigning themselves one by one. Against all odds, Jarrett remained conscious throughout the entire harrowing event as his young body betrayed him.

He would forever remember the excruciating shift of that first agonizing change. Sweat dripped from his pores, and he panted frantically through pain and panic. He thought he would surely die at any minute. Terror would have overtaken him if not for the pain that occupied his thoughts.

Rowena surprised him by calmly slipping a thick wooden stick between his teeth to bite down on to cope with the searing pain. And bite he did.

With quick, hurried breathing he grunted and growled past the wooden bit between his teeth. Suddenly, Jarrett's jaw began to elongate. His teeth lengthened and sharpened into deadly weapons. He easily snapped the thick piece of wood that he held in the canine-like jaw as if it was no more than a small, dry twig.

His clothing tore free of his body as he shifted, and his ribcage snapped and moved. Thick black hair sprouted from his feverish skin until it covered the whole of his body. His young, human cries and grunts became animalistic yelps and growls.

When it was finally and blessedly over, Jarrett stood before Rowena in their sparse home on four furry legs.

Jarrett panted and whimpered in confusion, cowering like a whipped dog. His hands and feet had become padded paws. Skin was covered by a sleek black fur, and his frightened and confused mind felt foreign. Jarrett could feel instinctive, animal-like impulses. He wanted to run, to hunt, to howl. He no longer felt like Jarrett the twelve-year-old boy, he was an animal, a monster, a myth.

His young, prepubescent mind fought against the animal urges as best he could. She tried to reassure him. Still able to hear Rowena and understand her every word, Jarrett tried to talk back, but instead, a whimpering yelp came from his muzzle.

Rowena startled, back peddling away. Despite her knowledge that this day could eventually occur, centuries of fear and superstition were difficult to overcome in a single life-changing moment. She looked unsure and slightly afraid of the young, black wolf he'd become. Uncertainty of what to expect from him in this state kept her from rushing to him.

She had no way of knowing if he could understand her or if he would abruptly become violent. When she looked carefully at his almond-shaped eyes, she could see him. His eyes were still the same golden eyes of the young boy she raised these past years. She kept her voice calm and continued to offer him soothing reassurance.

Jarrett tipped his head and whined like a small, lost puppy. His wolf's ears could hear more than his human ears. Hearing things he had never before noticed, the cacophony of several different sounds frightened him even further. He could hear the crickets outside as if they were right next to him, and the rustle of trees as the wind blew through them was amplified.

He understood his senses had been muted, diminished, until now. He sniffed the air and realized Rowena's scent seemed different too—stronger, sweeter maybe. Jarrett could also smell something else. An odd, tangy flavored aroma floated around her. The instinct in his animal-like mind recognized it as the smell of fear. Regardless of how calm she sounded, she was afraid, afraid of him.

Her fear of him made Jarrett fight harder for control, and yet fear rushed through him as well. He did not understand this irrevocable change from boy to demon. He could not understand the deep, pressing need to run through the forest, nor his sudden unexplained anger.

She stayed with him the whole night, trying to calm him with soft lullabies. Not once, but twice Rowena bravely tried reaching out to him tenderly. She wanted to give him any comfort she could offer.

Deep in his heart Jarrett wanted her comforting and motherly contact, but for unknown reasons, he snapped at her both times, baring his sharp teeth and snarling. While his child-like mind screamed for him to trust her, every instinct within the animal tingled. The enmity between man and beast came as natural as the need to breathe.

He cowered in the corner, and she could only sit, cautiously watching him. After long hours, the night finally passed. The sunlight began peeking over the hills, allowing the soft, grey light to peek in through the windows. His body painfully betrayed him once more, this time shifting and twisting him back into a frightened young boy.

Beyond exhausted, and beaten down by the painful changes, Jarrett passed out halfway through his morning transformation.

Grateful he survived the night, Rowena never left his side. She gently lifted Jarrett's unconscious, naked body back onto his straw mattress and tucked the blankets around him to ward away the chill morning air. Then she waited while he slept. She stroked his shaggy black hair away from his face and hummed lightly, trying to ease his troubled dreams.

Though he slept, he sensed her there, and in his unconscious thoughts, Jarrett heard her soft prayers that his change would not always inflict so much pain upon him. Watching him endure so much was unbearable. She prayed she had done as well as Lyndell would have if she had been here. Most of all, Rowena prayed Jarrett could cope with the truth when he awoke.

But he didn't. That afternoon when Jarrett's eyes opened, and before the foggy cloud of sleep cleared away, she embraced him fiercely and cried with relief. She bustled around and got bread and butter, hoping he could finally eat. As he ate his bread in quick, hungry bites, Rowena tried to explain.

She did her very best to explain his parentage. She told him of the great sacrifice his real mother made all those years ago and of his twin brother whom he would never meet. Her tale was so sordid and horrific his twelve-year-old mind refused to believe her. He protested her words as lies, yelling and fighting against her. His

~ 11 ~

experience the night before mattered little that day, and because of fear, Jarrett denied the truth.

The next night when he did not change, he convinced himself it was nothing more than a dream, a fever induced hallucination. *She must be wrong,* he thought. *Werewolves are no more than tales to frighten children.* "It is not real!" he insisted aloud.

He went on in denial for weeks. Until it happened all over again the next month—the sickness, the excruciating pain, the change from boy to wolf.

Even worse, something else began to happen. After the third change, an unexplained excitement coursed through his veins. Jarrett could not contain the urges that burned through him. He ran from Rowena and their home howling into the darkness. He leaped and bounded through the woods, and the speed at which his new form could run created a thrill that pumped through his heart. As he ran, he easily lost track of his worried human thoughts and fears. He embraced the wolf and the sensations that were part of it becoming a young hunter of the night.

The air was filled with the scent of prey around him, and he felt the urge to chase, to kill. Catching a rabbit, he tore into its flesh and consumed the animal raw. The fresh warm meat, the crunch of small bones, and the salty tang of blood in his mouth felt right, good even. The next morning, the violent memory of what he'd done made him ill, and he despised what he was becoming.

By the fourth month, Jarrett could feel the differences in his human body as well. He grew taller than anyone his age. Broader too, boasting sharpened and defined muscles on every part of his body. He got faster, stronger. His senses were much keener. His temper became shorter.

Anger at his circumstance clouded his thoughts. He could never go back to being the clueless boy he'd been before. He could barely tolerate the company of boys his own age, or company of any kind for that matter. He became reclusive and avoided contact with people entirely.

The Price of Knowing

He felt his animal urges constantly, not only on the nights of a full moon. As each day drew nearer to that fateful night, he could sense it, feel it. As the moon cycled each month, and each day passed, he had a harder time controlling his urge to change. His body wanted to bring forth the monster, and while the pain of doing so was becoming more bearable, it was increasingly difficult to subdue his volatile nature.

Even though she didn't voice it to him, Jarrett could see the fear on Rowena's face. She knew they would have to leave and told him as much by explaining that people were becoming much too suspicious. She made prompt plans to leave their home, but things exploded before they could get away.

Four days before the next full moon, Rowena and Jarrett went into town to trade for goods they would need to make their impromptu trip. He knew she risked having him with her because she needed help carrying their stores. While crossing the center of the town square, Jarrett's sensitive ears pricked. "Witch whore," a man whispered as they passed.

His short fuse ignited like dry brush to flame. Fiery anger burned through him. Jarrett turned sharply on the speaker, and an animalistic growl rumbled past his lips.

Rowena's hand went to her mouth in fear. She closed her eyes slowly, hoping no one noticed his slip. They had. His growl was so primal and unnatural that people murmured and whispered, while a brave few moved closer to verify what was seen.

"Demon eyes! The boy has the eyes of a demon!" a woman cried out in fear.

"He is possessed!" another woman shouted.

Rowena turned, dropped her goods, and moved to calm Jarrett with soft, quiet words. She hoped to defuse the tenuous situation. To her dismay, it only made things worse. As Jarrett straightened his boyish frame at her words, another woman in the crowd cried out, "Tis true. She's a witch. She controls the beast with her powers!"

~ 13 ~

The town preacher came forth. "She has summoned a demon from the darkest chasms of Hell!"

Shocked commotion rippled through the small crowd. More people moved in as the whispers spread from one person to the next. The buzzing crowd, closing in on them, only fed Jarrett's uncontrollable urges for violence. With little hope left, Rowena tried to pull Jarrett away and run, but strong hands seized her harshly.

As the brutal hands grabbed her and pulled her away from him, Jarrett struggled fiercely to control his urge to kill. All that existed for him in that moment was a red haze of rage.

The mob began shouting for her to burn and die, cries escalating quickly. They threw her to the ground. Rocks and sticks flew from hate-filled fists. The projectiles battered against them both, but Jarrett was past feeling any of it.

One rock smacked Rowena on her head above her brow, cutting it open. She couldn't hold back her cry of pain, and she looked to him with tears in her soft eyes. Even through the chaos Jarrett could tell she believed that this was the end for them. He felt the burn as his own eyes began to change and smolder once more. Only this time, it was no flicker of light that dissipated. They glowed with eager violence. The demon they believed him to be was surfacing.

"No!" she cried out pleadingly. "Jarrett, no! I'm fine!"

Despite being a young boy, it took two strong men to hold him fast. He snarled and snapped. His eyes glowed, frightening any who looked upon them. The noise in the crowd shifted from accusation and judgment to cries of fear and shock.

Jarrett's actions were making matters worse, but he could not find the will to rein in his temper. Despite what anyone there believed, he tried desperately to make it stop. Deep within, the boy behind the monster cried out, desperate to stop the beast from taking over. The entire crowd was about to discover the monster he harbored within.

Skin tingled. Bones burned. The need to shift coursed through him. He never yet transformed on any night other than that of the

The Price of Knowing

full moon, much less the middle of the day, but Jarrett knew it was coming. "Jarrett!" Rowena cried out to him. He jerked his rage-filled expression in her direction.

With ragged breathing, he looked at her and saw her sad, pleading eyes beg him silently to find control. He tried. Heaven knows he tried. The boy continued screaming from within, wanting it to stop, but that voice never came from his lips. Instead, an audible snarl came forth. He felt his muscles quiver as the beginnings of the change rippled through him. Even in his hazed state he knew she didn't want this for him, but there was no judgment in her eyes, only acceptance. He wasn't yet strong enough to make it stop, and they both knew it.

Taking a risk, Rowena chanted softly, trying to use her craft to cast a spell of sleep to calm him. A burly man jerked Rowena up violently when he heard her soft words. "There'll be no callin' your demon to save ye," he told her snidely. The snapping motion of his violent shaking broke her concentration, and along with it, the final threads of the fragile control for which Jarrett struggled so fiercely to hold on to.

He was beyond caring about anything other than Rowena. The animal instinct to kill and protect rushed through him.

He lunged forward with unnatural strength, ripping free of his captors. Jarrett felt the prickling of the fur underneath his skin, and he felt the saliva build in his mouth where he knew long, sharp teeth would soon grow.

He almost made it to her before four men toppled him. They took turns kicking and battering him. All of them screamed and yelled while they beat him into unconsciousness, unknowingly keeping him from fully making the change that would ensure his immediate death—or more likely, theirs.

~ 15 ~

CHAPTER 2

New York, NY

"Jarrett!" the woman urged on a whisper. Her soft voice haunted his dreams, calling for him to wake.

The dark images of the dream turned off as if someone had flipped a switch. Jarrett's eyes snapped open. His heart rapped hard against his chest. The memories of the past were raw and fresh in his mind. They pressed down on him heavily, but he knew that wasn't what woke him.

Acting on instinct and using his lightning-fast reflexes, Jarrett rolled to the left, spun off the bed, landed easily on his feet, and crouched to face his attacker. He barely missed being skewered through the heart by a long, wicked dagger. The sleek, shiny blade glinted in the dim moonlight as its wielder lifted it from the mattress where he had lain a second before.

His preternatural eyes penetrated the shadows of his room, and he looked down the length of the blade to see who his assassin was. On the opposite side of his bed stood a tall, thin woman. A thick floral odor permeated his senses as soon as she entered his room. Her sickly, sweet odor and the soft dreamy whisper in his memories

~ 16 ~

became his saving grace. He drew in the scent of her again and smelled a hint of *other*. She was not all human, as she appeared.

Demon. The woman was definitely part demon.

Demons carried a specific fungal-like scent that was unmistakable, even if it was diluted. Half-demons were common enough in his world and often easily dealt with. In fact, most humans dealt with them every day without realizing it. More often than not, they looked completely normal.

Then again, so did he. But death could often look normal until it came knocking on your door.

His sensitive eyes assessed his would-be assassin. The woman's spiked, blond hair looked white in the dim light and matched her pale, almost translucent skin perfectly. Her ears boasted several small hoops and studs, beginning at her lobes and climbing their way up to the elfin-like tips. She wore a long, shiny, white jacket over a tight, low-cut green dress that left little to the imagination. The picture wasn't a good one. Years of tapping into the dark side of magic drained her body of its beauty long ago and left her skin withered and her eyes cold. If misused, magic could drain the body much like drugs. He had seen the look before.

Jarrett rolled his eyes at his circumstance. He knew she was one of The Faction's mindless lackeys. She was the first in what would likely be a long line of them. He'd run out of time.

Looking into his animalistic eyes with her cold, grayish orbs, and holding the wicked blade she had almost killed him with, they considered each other.

He'd heard of her before. They were in the same business of bounty hunting for The Faction, but Jarrett couldn't recall her name. Not that it really mattered. Her name was as unimportant to him as she was.

Her thin, angular eyebrows lifted in mock surprise. "You are good. I guess I'll have to earn my money tonight." Her voice was low and throaty from too many cigarettes over the years. "You're not bad looking either. Too bad."

~ 17 ~

"How'd you get lucky enough to draw the short straw?" he questioned, his tone almost amused.

She tilted her head. "Draw?" she chortled. "There was no need to draw. We've all been called out for you. Such is the consequence of betrayal. Although, I'm glad I got here first."

Jarrett shrugged. Her words didn't tell him anything that he didn't already know. Using The Faction's commonly used mantra, *first come, first served,* to suit him, Jarrett replied, "First to come, first to die. The order of who dies hardly matters to me."

Her brows drew together angrily, and her mouth pinched into a tight slit. She spun the intricate dagger around with proficient ease as she considered his words with less care than she probably should have.

"Tell me," she questioned as if genuinely curious, "in the interest of self-preservation, what did you do to have him calling us all out to take you down?"

"Don't worry, you won't live long enough to be able to make the same mistake." Moving swiftly, he leaped over the large bed that separated them only to meet empty space.

Jarrett didn't bother to scan the darkened room with his superior sight. He identified where she was right away. Not only could he smell her pungent perfume, but his hunter's instincts were with him. He could feel her and sense her nervousness

She stood in the back corner of his sparsely furnished room. He immediately knew she was using magic to enhance her speed. Otherwise she would already be dead in his grasp. Her cold, gray eyes stared back at him with a lifelessness he'd seen often. It happened to all who lived like her, on the hard edge of life with The Faction.

He didn't rush her though. Jarrett knew how to play this game. In fact, he was an expert. He had learned over the many years of his life that patience was the key. In surviving or in battle, Jarrett never made any moves unless it brought purpose to his own designs.

He also knew people The Faction recruited always made mistakes. Whether through stupidity, overconfidence, or greed, the reasoning didn't matter. It was these mistakes that he, as the Hunter, capitalized on—costing many their very lives.

He held his position in the middle of his room and waited patiently for the witch's blunder. He adjusted his neck to display his annoyance. "If you leave, I might let you live," he rasped in a low voice that promised death.

She shrank back slightly from him. His deadly orbs penetrated the darkness with an eerie and unsettling glow. The moonlight clung to the bare skin of his muscled chest and glinted off a green gem that hung from his neck. The sight of him was disarming. The moonlight that shone on his form welcomed him within the night's dark embrace as if it existed solely for him.

Shaking off the eerie mood, she reminded herself that she had dealt with killers and fighters her whole life. Her skills were unsurpassed—evident in the fact that she was still alive today. Straightening her shoulders, she sauntered forward a couple of steps on her spiked, high-heeled boots. The sound of her heels clicking on the polished wooden floor beneath her echoed ominously through the silence.

She gave Jarrett a coy look, then spoke low, trying to make her words sound sultry, "Sweetie, I've played with many of your kind before and lived to tell the tale. You'll be no different."

As Jarrett predicted she would, the witch made her first mistake. She assumed him to be like any other bounty. He arched one of his dark brows.

"Did you come to kill me, or did you come to talk me to death?"

Something about the way Jarrett stood there, completely relaxed, gazing steadily at her, made the tiny hairs on the back of her neck stand on end. Suddenly, she realized this man wouldn't be like any of her past assignments. His corded muscles weren't even tense in the slightest. He didn't look ready for battle. His easy tone and relaxed demeanor hinted at his comfort level with the current situation.

"Who are you?" she uttered, not even realizing she said the words out loud. She took a cautious step back, squinting in slight confusion.

Jarrett grinned devilishly. His excited eyes flickered red. He knew she may no longer be so glad she got here first. *Mistake number two,* he thought. *Hesitation.* Jarrett understood that knowing your opponent was really the first rule of hunting. Rule two, make your play and complete your kill. Hesitation was a death sentence.

It was all he needed. Really, one mistake was enough. Two, of course, was better.

Using the witch's ignorance and new-found fear against her, Jarrett made his move. His body flew forward. He held the half-demon witch in his grasp before she could even blink her eyes. Barely any sound was made as he whipped her around with unnatural strength, forcing her against his body.

He underestimated her though, something Jarrett rarely did. She was not without a trick or two of her own. She was, after all, half-demon. With practiced skill, she aimed her dagger behind her and plunged the shining blade deep into his lower right side. But the odd angle of her attack caused her to lose her grip on the dagger.

Her effort and speed with the weapon impressed him. It was a trait he would have normally appreciated, except the blade in question was currently embedded deep in his side.

The burn he felt surrounding the offending metal told him that the blade must be silver. So, she did know at least a little bit about him. The intense, fiery sensation coursing through his blood, caused by the cursed metal for any of his kind, was a distinctive and unforgettable pain that would get worse fast. The silver would infect his blood and hinder his natural ability to heal.

While Jarrett stood still, growling from the sharp, intense pain running through the entire right side of his body, she stomped the heel of her boot down as hard as she could, stabbing into his left foot. Though caught off guard, and in severe pain, Jarrett didn't release his grip on the scrawny woman. If anything, he tightened it. He sensed her surprise.

The witch ground her spiked heel in harder and made an unsuccessful attempt to grab the protruding dagger. He dodged it, and despite her fierce struggling to gain freedom from his bruising grip, he held her firm. He wrapped his left hand around her fragile neck and pinned her arms down with his other arm while trying to decide what he wanted to do—kill her or leave her unconscious.

Abruptly, she went still, and Jarrett heard her whispered chanting. Knowing her intent, and also knowing the unpredictability of magic all too well, his decision was made for him. He knew if he let her go she would come back. They always came back. *End it,* he told himself.

A strange sort of disappointment coursed through him. He felt none of his usual satisfaction. She'd killed many before and deserved to die, but he was sick of it all, tired of the game. He grew weary of it decades ago. But it always seemed to follow him no matter what he did. *How many will I have to kill to buy my freedom?* he wondered.

He knew she would be still until the spell was cast. Keeping a firm grip on her neck, he released her captive arms. Jarrett didn't even flinch as he reached down and viciously yanked the offending blade free from his body. The ease in which he did the gruesome act would lead anyone watching to believe that he just removed a thorn from his finger instead of the dagger from his bleeding side. Crimson blood flowed freely from the fresh wound. Jarrett gritted his teeth against the pain and lifted the blood-covered blade before his eyes.

He ignored her quiet chanting and focused his attention on the finely crafted silver weapon. It was only mere seconds, but to him, it seemed to play out in long, slow minutes. Shaking off his strange melancholy, Jarrett waited patiently for her to finish every delicate syllable. When she did, he felt the slight distortion in the air around him as the spell tried to take effect. He tightened his grip on her neck, cutting off her precious air flow. He heard her struggle to gasp and felt desperation fill her.

Fear made its way through her cold and evil veins. He could smell it and felt her panic rise. Her spell didn't work on him of course, and he was sure the demon-witch must have never seen such a thing before. People can often fight effects of paralyzing magic, but it takes them several minutes to do so.

He, on the other hand, was immune.

She shivered. He knew she understood that he wasn't affected in the slightest way by her spell. Because of her error, she would die.

He tilted his head toward the ceiling, and closing his eyes, he let the hated demon within him rise. Though his body made no change, his senses heightened. He took in a deep draw of the rich, fear-scented pheromones. "Tell me," he said, mimicking her earlier words, his voice a growling whisper in her ear, "what did you plan to do if this went badly?"

She couldn't answer, due to his painful grip on her throat. Chills raced over her, and she renewed her struggle to get free. *Rule three*, he thought, *always plan a contingency*.

With an almost casual movement, Jarrett flipped the blade, caught it, and buried it with deadly precision deep into her breastbone. He spun her around to face him, and looking right into her wide, shocked eyes, he said, "Because it just did."

Jarrett let the body fall and inspected his side. Pressing his hand to the injury, he winced slightly from the sensitive wound and cursed himself for being so slow. Ever since his encounter with Cade, Jarrett seemed to have lost his edge. This happened to be the second time someone almost got the drop on him, and the first time, in many years, he found himself wounded so severely. It made him wonder what could be happening to him and if he could fix it before it was too late.

The Price of Knowing

His memories plagued him regularly. It was an annoyance he'd never allowed himself—at least not since he'd been a boy. He'd forced those painful images deep down long ago, burying them under his fury. That's where he wanted to keep them, and unless he could find a way to push them back, the nightmare of his past would continue distracting him.

Jarrett could only figure his recent encounter with the woman named Collett was the cause of his unwanted recollection of the long-forgotten images. It was a cruel irony that the woman in question was currently shacked up with his estranged brother, Cade. She was also the same woman who forced him from his burning home as a boy centuries ago.

No, Jarrett thought to himself, *not forgotten, but repressed.* He knew he could never forget anything about Rowena. Even if the curse of his life lasted 1,000 years, he would never forget.

Sweat dotted his forehead, and he cursed again. The infection from the silver was spreading already. He grabbed a hand-towel from the bathroom, pressed it firmly to the stab wound, and tied it there with one of his belts. He winced at the applied pressure. Then he dressed quickly, threw a few belongings into a black duffel, and left without looking back. It wasn't the first time he'd left everything to start over.

He didn't know where he would end up, and he didn't have a clue how to get out of his latest predicament. It wasn't like anyone he knew could, or even would, help him. Fortunately, his contingency had always been in place. He'd hired strong people long ago to watch over his substantial assets, such as his club, so he knew he had time to figure it out.

And if he didn't—*Well,* Jarrett mused glumly, *maybe the world would be better off without The Hunter.*

CHAPTER 3

Cody grunted as his tormentor landed another heavy fist to his ribs. The chains holding his hands high above his head, straining his shoulders to painful limits, rattled and clinked as his body moved with the impact. His toes barely touched the floor, but not enough to offer any relief to his aching arms.

The man who controlled the strings to the puppet doing all the punching asked, "Now then, tell me again why you left?" His unearthly voice was soft, yet it grated and chilled Cody as it echoed in the empty warehouse.

Cody closed his eyes in frustration. There would be no correct answer here. He could not win. He'd told them the story three times already. Over and over again he had related what he'd learned while forced to spy on Cade Werren and Rederrick Williams.

His master was desperate to get his hands on the woman, Collett. She currently resided with Cade under the protection of The Brotherhood, an organization built to help protect those with supernatural abilities. They made a habit out of frustrating The

Faction's plans, and thereby frustrating his master, The Faction's creator.

Rederrick and Cade had taken Cody into their group a couple years ago, not knowing that he had already been recruited by The Faction.

Desperate, between screams and moans Cody began to recount the details of his time spent in Rederrick's home once again. He explained again about Thanksgiving Day, when he sat across from Collett at dinner, he saw the apprehension on her face. He panted through pain as he told his leader about overhearing everyone in the house talk about Collett's ability to delve into their personal minds and feelings. He knew it was only a matter of time until she knew the truth.

"I told you," he pled, knowing that silence would only make matters worse. "She would have figured it out. Then Cade would have killed me on the spot."

"What makes you think I won't give you the very same treatment for your cowardice?"

He felt another painful blow connect with his stomach. Cody groaned pitifully in response as he tried to draw his legs up in reflex, but the strain on his arms wouldn't allow it.

"Come on man!" he groaned. "Wouldn't it have been worse if they found me out? I can't help it if she can sense thoughts. How'd you expect me to work with that?"

"You idiot! Her talent is not so simple. You were there to understand their plans and find a way to get her here, and now I have nothing!" shrieked Niall, the man in command of The Faction.

His outburst startled not only Cody, but the thug using him as a punching bag. Neither man ever saw their master less than completely level headed.

He recomposed himself and straightened his perfectly groomed suit. He stepped forward into the light to stare into Cody's blue eyes with his empty, silvery orbs. If Cody didn't know any better, he would have assumed the man blind. It was an assumption that he knew could get a man killed.

Niall pinched his thin lips together, and his eyebrows drew together as if he were considering a puzzle. Then he nodded to the thug, and the heavy, thick-armed man answered the gesture with another solid blow to Cody's already bruised body. Cody coughed and gasped as his breath left him again.

"No matter. You've given me something at least. You are certain then that she can't remember who she is?"

"I swear it. She has short, vague flashes here and there, but has no real understanding of anything in her past. She doesn't even know about you," Cody insisted hopefully. For some unknown reason, even knowing it would cause him more pain if they found out, he held back the information of how Collett had been coming into her powers.

"What else have you learned?"

Cody felt a small amount of his tension ease. His ability allowed him to know Niall believed him.

"I'm pretty sure she's fallen for that guy, Cade, and he loves her. Also, they keep her under close guard at Rederrick's home in Colorado." When Niall scowled, Cody added promptly, "but I have the security codes."

"Continue," Niall bade.

"Cade doesn't know why I left. He probably believes I'm dead. I left the same night a fire started. Finnawick called to check in, and when I was on the phone someone attacked me. When I came to, everything was in chaos. I figured it was one of your guys, so I just got out of the way. I could…"

His words trailed off as a small, skinny woman with dark hair and angled features hurried into the derelict warehouse. She bustled over to Niall on her stiletto heels that matched her fashionable business suit. She was dressed to perfection, as Niall insisted of all the cronies close to him. Cody watched as she whispered to Niall frantically. Then she pulled a sheet of paper out of a manila folder.

The harsh light glinted off the image, and even through his swollen eyes, Cody immediately recognized the man in the picture. "If you already knew who Cade is, what did you need me for?" Even as he said it he regretted it, because Niall's attention came back to him.

He looked up sharply from the paper he examined. "Cade?" he questioned with interest.

"Yeah, Cade. He goes by Cade Werren."

"Are you telling me that this man," Niall held up the fuzzy picture, "is Cade Werren, leader of that ridicules Brotherhood?"

The tone of Niall's voice made Cody nervous. He squinted his swollen eyes to get a better look of the picture in Niall's hand. The picture seemed to be a sort of security footage with poor resolution, but it still looked like Cade. The man in the picture wore dark glasses, and his hair was longer, but Cody was almost certain it was him.

"Well, yeah, it looks like him except . . ." Cody said hesitantly, "the hair is longer. This must be an older picture."

Niall considered Cody's words carefully, not exactly sure what it meant. Then his thin lips spread into a wide, sinister smile as he reflected on the possibilities of Cody's assumption. "Well done," he mumbled while he looked at the picture once more. Of course, no one in the room believed he congratulated them. His comment was clearly directed to a person unknown. "Well done!" he said again, almost cheerfully.

Holding his breath, Cody waited, hoping the information would gain his freedom. He didn't even really know why he got mixed up with these people in the first place. How could something so simple go so wrong? It started with gambling debts, and then the ugly man named Finnawick learned of his ability when he talked them out of collecting on the debts. Now he found himself in so deep he couldn't see a way out.

For as long as he could remember, Cody could somehow sense when other people lied. As he got older, he discovered that he could

~ 27 ~

easily use those feelings in reverse. He'd used that talent to convince people of almost anything. The problem evolved when those skills didn't seem to work on Finnawick or Niall. He tried once to use his natural persuasion against Finnawick, and Finnawick had played him like a fiddle.

He didn't really want to hurt Rederrick or Cade. They were pretty nice, and the people they worked with trusted him, despite the fact that they knew of his ability. Trust became a feeling people rarely felt around him—at least not for long anyway. Cade barely knew Cody, but he'd always been fair to him. They were even training him in all manner of things, something Finnawick or Niall would have never done. However, Cody could see no way out of this without betraying The Brotherhood. *It was no big deal*, he told himself. *I've done it before. What is the difference really?*

There was a difference though, and subconsciously Cody knew it. But what were his choices—give Niall what he wanted and live, or refuse him and die? In the past, the decision would have been easy. Self-preservation always came first to him. Cody learned to take care of himself before anyone else early in life. As a young boy, he learned how often people lied, especially his own father. Nobody was ever honest. His musings did little to comfort him. Logic told him it was either him or The Brotherhood, but for the first time, both choices weighed heavily on him, and neither prospect seemed appealing.

Niall's cool voice broke Cody's reverie, "Cody, once again you have proven your worth. I'll let you live, but you must learn the consequence of disobeying me. The price of failure is indeed high." He nodded once again to the thick armed brute who continued beating him long after Niall left the room.

As each brutal blow inflicted more pain on his already battered body, Cody began to wonder if it wouldn't have been better to die instead. He knew better than to try and use his ability to escape his punishment. It would only make matters worse. So he took every painful punch as if he was once more a boy, and hoped he would find oblivion soon.

After Jarrett paid cash to the drowsy clerk and checked into the dingy motel, he walked down to his assigned room, slid the key into the lock, and opened the door. He took a quick scan of the rundown space. The sagging double bed sat in the middle of the room with a dresser straight across from it, leaving a narrow pathway to the small bathroom. What may have once been white walls had become yellow from too many years of nicotine-users smoking within the confines of the room and too little maintenance. A very outdated television which, Jarrett assumed probably didn't even work, was secured to the dresser. Not that he cared. He never watched much TV, and he didn't intend to start today.

With a grumble of acceptance, Jarrett shut the door, threw his duffel on the bed, and headed to the bathroom for a quick shower. His side burned, and he could feel his body fighting to heal the wound. Stripping off his clothes, he turned the shower on. Soon, he saw steam begin to gather and stepped under the spray. He closed his eyes when he felt the sting of water slide over the garish slice in his side. Jarrett leaned his head forward, resting it against the shower wall, while the water poured over him.

"Damn, I'm tired," he mused.

He thought killing the imp Finnawick would have bought more time, but he realized he should've known better. He had killed Finnawick out of necessity to save Jeffery's mother and keep him away from Cade and Collett. However, the action was like leading a moth to flame. It had been a pure act of defiance. He just couldn't stand to let the smelly bastard keep breathing after he kidnapped the sorcerer's mom.

It wasn't the first time he killed one of Niall's lap dogs. Though, considering his predicament, it may be one of the last.

After a long time of letting the water slide down over his aching, fevered body, he felt the water temperature change. Clearing his mind, he washed and exited the shower. He dried off carefully with the thin, economy-sized towel offered by the motel, then strode over to his bag on the bed.

He pulled out the first aid supplies he'd grabbed as an afterthought and looked at the needle and thread. Then scowling, he examined his side. He knew it would require too much effort and decided not to bother sewing it closed, convincing himself it wouldn't matter. He was likely to be attacked again soon, and the stitches wouldn't stay closed in a fight.

Instead, he packed the slowly leaking wound with gauze and tape, pulled on his shorts, and flicked out the lights as he went to bed. Reaching over, he pulled the recovered dagger from his bag. He twisted and turned it in his fingers while wondering how he ever let the witch get the better of him. He reminded himself he would have to step up his game.

The blade of the dagger showed a few nicks here and there—each mark telling a story about the weapon's use. He laid the weapon down at his side and thought about who and what would be coming for him next. He knew things were only going to get worse. Letting his thoughts drift, Jarrett closed his eyes and sought sleep, knowing the next days, maybe even months, would promise little of it.

"Demon child!"

Their horrible words still echoed in his mind and pierced Jarrett's heavy, guilt-filled heart. They were out there watching, preventing any possible chance of escape. The twelve-year-old Jarrett didn't care. He didn't want to escape. He only wanted to save Rowena. He knew they waited to hear Rowena's and his last dying screams as the fire claimed their bodies and sent their unclean souls back to Hell.

Unclean soul. He heard those terrible words at the trial. These past days were a horrific nightmare. They were both subjected to unspeakable tortures, all in the interest of finding the truth.

Jarrett could still see the sad, broken look in Rowena's green eyes as they examined her. Holy men looked over every inch of her, trying to find the marks of Satan. Even at twelve, he understood all of it happened because of what he was.

Rowena could have probably survived if she had lied and let them have him. He'd begged her to do that very thing. At night, when they were locked up and alone, she begged him to focus, to induce his change, and escape. Neither of them relented to the other's wishes.

When the ministers found him guilty of demon possession, they took him to the village square, tore his shirt from his back, and lashed him repeatedly. Jarrett took the beating without complaint, and few watched closely enough to see the pain and torment in his expression. Deep down, Jarrett hoped the preacher would be successful in, "...beating the monster out of him," as he promised.

Every lash cut through his skin like a burning knife, tearing flesh with each stripe. Rowena screamed for him. She begged them to stop with tears streaming down her cheeks. She tried, unsuccessfully, to free herself from her bonds, and even pleaded with the people watching to release him.

Even after several lashings, he refused to scream or yell out. The crowd murmured about the unnatural way a mere boy withstood the severe beating. They gossiped about their surety of his parentage, and he heard every painful murmur and whisper. The worst part was that he believed them.

After finishing with him, the men turned on Rowena. They tied her to a post and stoned her in front of Jarrett's eyes. The minister quoted scripture with frenzied excitement, and with every word, provoked and rallied the crowd even more. Jarrett looked at him;

C.B. Haight

the promise of death was clear in his eyes. In his heart, he vowed if he ever escaped this hellish torture, he would kill that man first.

When a stone struck her head and knocked Rowena unconscious, it all became too much for his volatile temper to bear. Jarrett lost control. He growled and snarled. His fingers changed. Sharp, deadly claws grew from every tip. Not questioning small mercies, he cut his rope bonds and ran to Rowena to shield her with his own body.

The stunned crowd gasped. Without realizing it, long black fur had begun to sprout from his back, and his teeth were sharpening into white points meant for tearing and shredding. Partially changed, the small boy looked very much like the demon they accused him of being.

Panic spread throughout the crowd, and after shocked silence dissipated and murmurs began, the minister shouted, "They must be cleansed by fire! Let holy flame reclaim their bodies and send their unclean souls back to Satan. They and all they have touched must be cleansed from the earth."

Then, several men seized them. Jarrett fought with every ounce of strength he possessed. Rowena remained unconscious throughout the entire ordeal. The crowd took them to their tiny home and violently threw Rowena on her bed. Then, as a precaution against his changing form, the blacksmith used heavy chains to bind his hands and feet. After shackling Jarrett, they left both of them inside as they boarded windows and blocked the door. He heard their cries for vindication when they put flame to tinder.

Now all he could do was sit inside his own home. The place that once gave him comfort would serve as his coffin. Guilt consumed him, and despair took over as he awaited death. Even at twelve years of age, Jarrett was unbothered by the prospect of his coming demise. He accepted it—almost welcomed it—knowing death would end his torment. However, he treasured Rowena's life, and anguish that he could not save her consumed him.

His lungs burned, and each coughing fit incited painful spasms down his back where he had stoically taken each of the flesh-striping lashes. The raw and swollen wounds on his back were beginning to close. He could feel the uncomfortable crawling sensation as the skin tightened and pulled together, staunching the flow of blood that trickled from the open sores. It didn't matter though. He was sure he would not be able to heal from the fire.

Jarrett's vision began to dim from lack of oxygen. As he accepted fate and gave up any hope of saving Rowena, he twisted and saw movement. He looked up and surprise covered his features upon seeing her. His worry over life and death flew from his mind as he could focus on nothing else but how beautiful she was. Her long, blond hair glowed with a soft, golden light that shimmered in the harsh, red light of the fire. The black haze made by the smoke drifted around her ethereally. He couldn't look away from her mystic blue eyes, and feelings of calmness and warmth began to cascade over him.

He blinked and thought it must be a dream, or he must be dead already. As if she knew his thoughts, she put a finger to her lips to hush any questions he wished to ask. Then, using magic, she released his shackles.

Seeing her power, he felt hope rise within. He coughed out, "Ro...Rowe...Save her..." His hacking made it difficult to get the words out.

The blond woman shook her head sadly and moved to help him rise.

"No!" he insisted. "Not ...me."

The woman put a hand on his defiant shoulder, and he suddenly felt calm. "Be still," she encouraged, and there was quiet authority in her tone.

Grabbing his arm, she urgently began pulling him toward the blocked window. Jarrett dug in his feet, stopping her. "Rowena!" he said firmly.

"I cannot," she said with regret.

"I won't go." He shouted, "Save her!"

"I cannot."

Jarrett's desperation rose. "Not me. Save her. Please!" he pleaded. For the first time in several months, Jarrett felt like a little boy. Tears slipped from his golden eyes.

A sad expression covered her face. She turned and repeated quietly, "I cannot do as you ask."

She stretched out her hand toward the window. Bright, bluish light came forth. It encompassed them, and forced Jarrett to close his eyes against it. When the light dissipated, Jarrett looked forward, and he could see the window was gone. In its place stood a blank, white space. He looked to her in shock, He was unable to comprehend such magic.

She was strong, too. Against his will, she yanked him forward, pulling him into the white void, and he found himself stepping out into the woods. Jarrett turned around to get his bearings. When he whipped his head around toward the north, he saw the black smoke, and recognized where they were.

They were miles from his burning home, the home with Rowena still inside. He fell to his knees and gave into the guilt and despair. He let go an agonized wail that turned into a mournful howl, and he began pounding the ground with his fists in frustration and anger. A long time passed before Jarrett remembered he was not alone.

He rounded on his rescuer. "You should have saved her!" he accused.

She only looked upon him with sad, blue eyes.

"Say something!" he screamed at her.

"You are my purpose in being here. I could not interfere with Rowena's fate."

He was shocked. "Her fate? I caused this fate! I made this fate for her!"

"No, Jarrett you did not. Rowena chose her own path, and therefore created her own fate. She understood the sacrifice she made and what it may cost to save your soul the day she spirited you

away as a baby. It is hard to understand why we are given a certain path, but we must persevere and continue along to the very end. Otherwise, temptation seeks us, and we might become lost in the darkness. Rowena knew this. She knew she could not control the will of others—only her own choices and reactions. One day, you will understand this."

Jarrett didn't want to understand. He needed Rowena back, and he wanted to be normal. He wished so desperately for everything to be as it had been months before. Seething and needing someone to blame, he charged at her, wanting to take out his anger on this strange woman. Only, she disappeared in front of his very eyes.

"I HATE YOU!" he yelled out at nothing. "When next we meet, I will kill you! Do you hear me? I will kill you!"

Then the broken boy once again fell to his knees and sobbed for the loss of the only mother he ever knew—the only person he believed would ever love a demon such as him. While in the shadows, darkness waited.

CHAPTER 4

Collett woke breathing hard. Her chest felt heavy, and her stomach rolled. Every second of the dream felt so real, and her heart screamed out for the small child all over again. She had endured the tragic images several times since her encounter with Jarrett, and she heard his promised shout of lasting hatred reverberate through her soul each time.

Except he hadn't killed her, and they all knew he could have.

None could blame him, she thought, and felt shivers crawl down her spine. *If only I could remember.* Every time the dream came to her, she tried to recall why she wouldn't save the woman, why she'd let an innocent die. The event seemed clearer each time, and still she had no explanation for her actions.

That fateful night broke a child's heart, and because she felt each feeling of his as sharply as if they were her own, she knew it remained broken.

She wiped at the tears on her face, composed herself, and realized something was wrong. It only took a minute to identify what felt out of place. When she reached over to the other side of the bed, her hand didn't make contact with Cade. The sheets next to her were cold, so he must have been up for a while. Rising, she grabbed her robe off of the bed post where she had slung it earlier and headed downstairs.

Cade stood in the parlor of his friend Rederrick's home and looked out the oversized window at the snow-covered ground. The frozen crystals from yesterday's heavy storm sparkled as moonbeams reflected off the white-blanketed earth. The night sky was free of clouds, and stars twinkled in the vast blackness that was a direct contrast to the icy landscape. However, the soft winter beauty happened to be wasted on the stoic man staring through the glass.

She could see the shadow of his reflection in the window and sensed his thoughts were dark and heavy. With his arms folded over his chest and a deep scowl on his face, he was too lost in his inner ponderings to notice the winter landscape. A soft glow, coming from the nearby Christmas tree lights, fell over his strong features, and she felt her heart tighten with both love and concern.

She entered the room as quietly as possible so as not to disturb him, but Cade's sensitive hearing picked up her soft footfalls as she came toward him. She covered the distance between them, and in a gesture so natural it seemed they'd always been together, he reached out and pulled her to him. She snuggled into his warm embrace, rested her head against his chest, and wrapped her slender arms around his waist.

She remained quiet, simply offering him silent companionship. She could feel his brooding temperament even stronger with the contact. Sensing his emotions was easier than it had been when they first met. She suspected it was a result of their deepening connection.

After a few minutes, she observed quietly, "You're thinking about him again." Cade's brow furrowed further, and he blew out an exasperated breath.

C.B. Haight

Collett pulled back slightly. She untangled her arms and put a hand on his chest and felt his heartbeat beneath her fingers. She tipped her head up to meet his eyes. "You're worried about him."

"Jarrett can take care of himself," Cade grumbled. "I'm more worried about Cody. We still have no idea what happened to him. I can't figure it out. Then there's the note. . ."

"All right then, I'm worried for him—worried for them both," she admitted. "Go Cade. Go and try to find him—it's time. He's had a few days to think. Maybe Jarrett can tell you something about Cody too."

Pulling away and giving her a stern look, he said sharply, "We've been over this."

"Cade, it's not as if there's no one here to protect me. Besides that, I could go with you."

"I don't want you within a hundred miles of him."

Narrowing her eyes, she admonished, "You judge him so harshly." Silence followed her statement as each considered the other's argument. Frustrated, Cade roughly pulled his fingers through his hair.

"He hasn't given me a reason not to," he said weakly.

"Really? *Nothing*?" she questioned gently. Her words held no incrimination, but Cade felt it all the same. They both knew that recent events showed Jarrett was not the enemy Cade thought him to be.

"What do you want from me, Collett?" he asked earnestly.

"I want you to find peace with your brother, and I want you to try and understand."

"I don't know if I can," he muttered.

"It's never been easy for him—not like it is for you. What you two are, I mean," she stated softly, knowing in her heart it was true. Cade stood quietly again with a pensive expression. When it became obvious he wouldn't reply, she added, "Most of all, I want you to do what makes you happy."

"Being with you makes me happy," he replied as he reverently cupped her cheek in his hand. She leaned into his touch, and he bent down and kissed her tenderly. Having just found her, he couldn't stand the idea of leaving for anything, or anyone, for that matter. "You're all I need," he promised.

He saw the light in her eyes, but at the same time, he heard the serious tone in her voice. "I know I make you happy, but your relationship with Jarrett makes you unhappy. It eats away at you a little each day. Eventually, our happiness won't be enough to sustain you."

"You're all I'll ever need. You're my life," Cade insisted.

Looking deeply into his eyes and thinking of the memories she relived earlier, Collett tried to help him understand. "Cade, we have been so blessed to find each other. You have been equally lucky to have people like Rederrick, Cynda, and their family to lift you up and embrace you as one of their own." Sighing, she turned in his arms to view the scenery. He embraced her from behind as she continued, "What of Jarrett? Will you leave him to fight The Faction alone? I'm not sure you understand how it really feels to be completely alone. I do, and it's a scary feeling. You can be surrounded by people on all sides, and still be utterly and desperately alone. I felt that from him. He's not happy, Cade."

"He doesn't want my help," Cade protested. She knew that was true too, but there was something nagging at her—an urgency in her belly she couldn't explain.

Twisting her head around, she reached back and brushed her fingers over the nape of his neck, sending shivers through him. "No, he doesn't want help, but he does need it. He'll see that eventually." The words were said for herself as much for him.

Cade considered her words, and his resolve wavered slightly. "I wouldn't know how to find him, even if I wanted to."

"Look out there at the sky. A moment ago, you didn't see a single star because you weren't looking at them. And if you look even more carefully, you can see a few of them are dimmer than the rest—barely noticeable among the others. You only have to make the effort, and there they are as if they are waiting for you." She sighed again. "It's been a long day. I'm going back up to bed. Are you coming?"

Feeling slightly off balance, he mumbled, "I'll be there shortly. Don't wait up for me."

"I love you, Cade, and I'm sure you'll think of something."

He turned and kissed her forehead affectionately. "I love you too." Cade then watched as his new wife strolled from the room. *My wife*, he thought. He never figured he would get to say the word wife again. After the disaster with his first marriage, Cade swore he would never bring that kind of pain to any other woman again.

Everything had changed so fast. He met Collett when she was being hunted by The Faction, and their relationship bloomed in days. Then Jarrett, who had been ordered to kill Collett, kidnapped her and whisked her away into the mountains of Colorado. When Cade realized he couldn't live without her, his life turned around quickly.

Maybe he did owe Jarrett for that. If Jarrett and the other members of the Faction hadn't been hunting her, he might never have met her, and her kidnapping bound them together in ways he never could have predicted.

The vague images of Collett's past were still few and far between, but she tapped into Jarrett's memories the night he took her and saw herself in a shared event from both of their lives.

She remained reluctant to tell Cade everything she remembered, and he could admit that bothered him a little. However, she did tell him how she helped Jarrett as a young boy on a horrible day of his life. It was confusing and crazy, but it meant that she was somehow older than the werewolf brothers. How much older was yet to be decided, but she had excitedly explained that it all made sense to her.

"Don't you see? I did remember Juliet—her clothes, her hair, are real. She was real."

The Price of Knowing

Juliet, her sister, had been Collett's first returning memory, but she originally disbelieved it because of the dated images. Seeing Jarrett's memories, Collett understood why Juliet had looked so different in her mind.

The thought of her enthusiasm still brought a smile to his face. He recalled how her eyes sparkled and her smile lit her whole features when she told him that his immortality no longer mattered between them.

Cade grasped at the opportunity so swiftly that they were both still adjusting to it. He asked her right then to marry him, and after she accepted his abrupt proposal with teary eyes, he pushed for a quick wedding. As far as they knew, there was no need to postpone it for her family. She felt sure there was no one.

He would have been content to find a judge and marry her that minute, but Cynda, Rederrick's wise wife, insisted on a proper wedding. Cynda, Rederrick, and Jenny helped put together a small, but beautiful, wedding in less than a week.

Cade knew he would never forget how special those extra touches had made that day for both of them. Cynda's insistence was all well worth it when he watched Collett enter the room. His bride looked flawless, and the image of her standing with him, making vows to each other, would remain with him no matter how many centuries he lived. Not even a week had passed yet, and he sometimes wondered if he would wake and find it was all a dream.

Cade thought nothing would ever destroy the happiness he felt that day. Then, that night, Jeffery, the sorcerer, showed up, and he knew he'd been wrong.

Cade reached into his pocket and pulled out the folded, worn letter that Jeffery delivered to him. He kept it with him every day. He'd read it at least twenty times, and he still remained unsure about what to do. He opened it once more and read the manly script.

Cade,

Once again you've gotten yourself mixed up in another lost cause. Thanks for dragging me along for the ride. Hope to see you in another hundred years. I hope your friends can handle what's coming. This will only get worse. Just a heads up—your woman is in the center of it, but I don't know why. They want her dead. Keep her close and figure it out, then you may even live to make puppies.

Don't be an idiot and come looking for me. You've got bigger problems. Besides, that ship has sailed. Don't bother looking for that kid you kept around either, he's not what you thought. Use Jeffery if you can or get rid of him, makes no difference to me.

Jarrett

After reading the letter again, Cade let out an exasperated breath. He was worried about Jarrett. He didn't say it specifically in the letter, but Cade knew Jarrett was on the run. Cade could read between the lines, and what's more, he knew how The Faction operated. Jarrett would be on the run because he had let Collett live. It hadn't been Cade's interference that changed his mind, either. Before Cade had even arrived to save Collett, Jarrett had made the choice to keep her alive, a fact Cade missed until it was almost too late.

Cade could picture his brother gasping for breath when he'd almost killed him out of anger. No, not anger, rage. His feelings in that encounter had been unbridled rage. He'd never experienced the like of it before. If not for Collett's interference, his brother's blood would have forever stained his hands, a possible outcome he was not proud of.

Cade wondered what had stayed Jarrett's hand that night. He wasn't a compassionate person, and the last Cade knew, Jarrett had a respected position within The Faction. Jarrett was angry and vicious, and the whole incident still made little sense to him. Even after endlessly pestering Collett about it, she remained closed-mouthed regarding Jarrett's thoughts. She insisted Jarrett deserved privacy, and none of the flashes she'd seen related to their current problems. She only gave him cryptic comments like, "He is hurting, Cade," or, "I don't really understand it all myself."

It didn't matter really. Regardless of the why, Jarrett still failed to do the job, and failure was not an acceptable outcome when employed by The Faction. Even though Cade already knew that, Jeffery clarified the situation when he explained how Jarrett saved his mother.

Jarrett not only failed The Faction—he betrayed them.

When Jeffery first showed up on his wedding day, Cade felt murderous thoughts leap to the forefront of his mind. He wanted, with every fiber of his being, to do nothing more than repay the wicked sorcerer for all he did to Cynda and Collett shortly before coming to them. He almost killed Cynda in his pursuit to capture Collett for The Faction. If not for Selena's quiet interference, Jeffery would most likely be dead and lying at the bottom of the river where the attack was initiated, instead of bunking with a watchful Nate downstairs.

The fact that Jeffery still refrained from disappearing, when they all knew he could, and his eagerness to please them all, currently kept him alive. Well, that and the part where Collett delved into him and read his thoughts and emotions. She reassured them all of his new intentions. Cade was skeptical of Jeffery's loyalties. He knew how a desperate person could turn when faced with life or death. When it came to Collett's safety, he would continue to be cautious no matter what. So far though, Jeffery continued to comply with all of the restrictions they gave him.

Realistically, Cade knew the problems wouldn't end just because Jarrett had a change of heart. But to have it thrown in his face, on his wedding day no less, still aggravated him. A growl of frustration rumbled past his lips. He roughly crumpled the letter and moved to throw it in the trash. Balling up his fist tightly, he thought about his brother.

Jarrett's right, I do have bigger problems. I don't have time to worry about him, Cade thought. *Besides, how is it my fault he got involved? It's not! It's Jarrett's fault. He shouldn't have mixed with The Faction in the first place.*

"It's your own fault," he muttered aloud to himself, his voice sounding odd in the silent room. His grip relaxed, and looking down at his hand, he lifted the crumpled paper. He didn't understand why, but he pulled it open again, carefully refolded it, and put his only connection to his twin back in his pocket.

He felt a sudden need to vent his frustrations. If Jarrett was there, Cade probably would have been beating him to a pulp. As it was, he would have to settle for a run. He stomped out of the house, stripped his clothes, and contorted his body. Bones cracked, and his skin tingled as long black fur sprouted over it. He changed into a large black wolf—far larger than any in the forest. Leaving his clothes behind on the front porch, he took off.

It was extremely aggravating to him that he couldn't let loose and really run. He wanted so badly to feel the rush of wind through his fur as he darted in and out of trees, or to hear small animals scatter as he rushed by their homes. No, he couldn't even have that. He was stuck racing across the grounds close by, over and over again, like some sort of caged animal. The confinement wore on him almost as much as his inner conflict.

He couldn't risk going too far in case someone from The Faction made a surprise appearance in their ongoing search for Collett. He would never risk Collett's life because of selfish desires. For the very same reason, he couldn't go and help Jarrett or find Cody. He was only one man, and he couldn't be everywhere at once. It remained an impossible situation, and Cade was left running circles.

After a long time, he gave up on trying to exert himself into exhaustion. It likely wouldn't work anyway. Taking one more sweep of the grounds, making sure all was quiet, he passed by the area where Jarrett had, such a short time ago, lit the fire to draw him away from Collett.

Snow covered the charred ground, but Cade could still smell the smoky scent of burnt earth and wood. Even with the element of surprise, Jarrett hadn't killed him that night. Sparing his life was not something Cade had figured Jarrett would do. When they had separated all those years before, Cade had expected them to forever be enemies. He reflected on that day so long ago when he learned about Jarrett's allegiance to The Faction.

"I cannot be like you, Cade. I refuse to help these people. I won't sacrifice myself for their idiotic causes. I do what I think is best and damn them. These people you want to save are the very same people that would gladly watch you burn, throwing kindling on the fire, if they ever found out about the real you. Think about if they ever learn your secret."

"You can't do this! It's not right, and you know it. You do not have to be like them. You are better than they are. Come with me. We can leave this place. We don't have to be a part of it," Cade pled.

"You're right. I am *better. We* are *better than every one of them! Don't you see that? This is not our fight. I will not subjugate myself to any ruler, not even this one and his ideals. Eventually, this will end like it always does, and I intend to profit from it in the meantime. Their laws don't have to apply to us. Why is it you cannot see the possibilities?"*

With a broken heart, Cade replied somberly, "Because I cannot be like you either." With conviction in his voice, he continued, "I believe in laws and justice. I believe in mankind! I believe in their capacity for good. I believe in this war, and I believe in hope for a better way."

"Then you are a fool," Jarrett snapped.

"Better a fool than a monster."

Jarrett's expression changed so quickly it startled Cade. His eyes filled with hate. "We are to be enemies then."

"I can't let you do this."

"When next we meet, it will be in battle."

"So be it," Cade uttered as he dejectedly turned his back and walked away, knowing things would never be the same between them.

Cade stared absently at the spot for a long time as the memory came to him. Then shaking his animal head to push the memory away, and feeling defeated, he trudged back to the house.

He reached the front porch, changed back to a man, and dressed. Making his way to the security room hidden just off the den, he accessed the entrance behind a goofy picture of Rederrick holding a fish. He listened for the click permitting his entrance and went inside.

"Not your watch," he heard Rederrick say before he was fully inside.

"Couldn't sleep," Cade replied.

"How would you know? You haven't tried," Rederrick said with a slight chuckle.

Cade ignored him and changed the subject, "Any news?"

"Nothing, but I've spread the word," Rederrick said more seriously. "I've also left a message for Rory to look into it. He'll make contact with us if he can."

Cade nodded and swung one of the black and chrome chairs around to straddle it. He watched Rederrick shuffle through stacks of paperwork from his law office.

"Something else you wanted?" Rederrick inquired knowingly after a suitable amount of time passed.

"What would you do?" Cade asked. Knowing what Cade was referring to, Rederrick leaned back in his chair and carefully considered the question.

"I can't tell you what to do, Cade."

"I'm not asking you to. I want to know what you would do if it was your brother."

Rederrick gave a slight nod of assent and replied, "If it were me, I guess I would first decide who I thought was in the most danger. Then I would figure out if my help could tip the scales. I

~ 46 ~

know for sure I would never leave Cynda unprotected and vulnerable."

"That's what I keep telling her," Cade asserted, relieved that Rederrick understood.

"But is she?" Rederrick probed.

Narrowing his eyes and tilting his head in confusion, Cade responded, "Is she what?"

"Unprotected. Look around, Cade. Do you honestly believe Collett is vulnerable or unprotected?" He held up his hand to stop Cade from answering and stated, "For that matter, if you do, it's not like we couldn't call in some help—for either job. Although, my guess is that Jarrett would probably kill anyone but you."

Cade rested his chin on his folded arms that lay across the back of the chair and contemplated Rederrick's advice. His words were reasonable, but it still left Cade conflicted.

The room fell quiet again for a time, and Rederrick continued to shuffle papers while glimpsing back to the camera feeds periodically. He knew Cade needed to weigh things in his head. "I do know one thing I wouldn't be doing if I were you," he offered after a few minutes.

Cade lifted his head, "What's that?"

"I wouldn't be down here brooding, in the company of a surly old man, if I knew my new wife was in bed upstairs waiting for me to join her."

Cade smiled for the first time in hours and replied, "Trying to get rid of me?"

"No, simply telling you what I would do if I were you."

"Then I guess I'll just have to take your advice and be on my way," Cade replied. Standing, he pushed the chair back to the table smoothly. "Goodnight old man."

Rederrick glared at him because of the old man remark, but they both knew it was meaningless. As Cade made it to the door, Rederrick said, "No matter what happens, we'll support your decision."

C.B. Haight

"I know," he replied over his shoulder. It was something he never doubted. No matter what, as his family, they would have his back.

Hours later, Cade lay in his darkened room on his back with Collett snuggled against him. Her head rested on his bare chest, and her golden hair fanned out against his skin. He absently stroked her soft locks as she slept peacefully, and he continued thinking about his options.

It was well past four in the morning. He knew dawn would not be far off, but he still couldn't shut his troubled thoughts away long enough to find the comfort of sleep. Rederrick's suggestion to call in help wasn't a bad one, but he couldn't bear to leave Collett. The very idea of being away and the possibility of something happening tightened his gut and burned through him. He wondered if he could send someone to find Jarrett and make sure he was okay, but the errant thought vanished before it fully formed when he realized Rederrick was right. Jarrett would more than likely kill anyone he didn't know on a regular day, let alone when he was on the run.

Realizing he would have to be the one to go, Cade wondered about Collett's safety. He didn't want her near his twin. Though he worried about Jarrett's predicament, their relationship was definitely not one of trust. Jarrett could change his mind at any time and take Collett to The Faction.

More than one hundred years ago, when the brothers were together for a short time, Cade learned that Jarrett was a volatile creature. His temper was swift, his rampages deadly. That was not a situation he dared to put Collett in. Plus, taking her along would make her visible to any Faction members looking for Jarrett. He knew there would still be a significant number of them searching for her. He didn't need to gift wrap her for them. Since Thanksgiving, things here had been fairly quiet. There was no need to invite trouble.

Therefore, he concluded again that to help Jarrett he would have to leave Collett, and the mere thought of it pressed against his heart.

Why does everything have to be so difficult? he wondered to himself. After all this deliberation, Cade's eyes began to drift closed. As his mind finally began to float on the edge of sleep, he heard Collett moan slightly and stir next to him.

She often dreamed these days. So much so, that lately she rarely slept without shifting and making odd noises. Without even opening his eyes he knew she was only dreaming again. Cade absently brushed her hair, trying to soothe her back into a deeper sleep. She quit stirring and snuggled into him more, and he relaxed once again. Then she said something that caused his eyes to pop wide open, bringing him back to full alertness.

"Jarrett," she murmured. Cade pulled away in a knee jerk reaction. The shock of hearing his brother's name while she snuggled up to him radiated through him. It felt like a vicious punch to the gut. Then, her elbow suddenly shot out, literally punching his gut as she reached for something invisible. "Wake up!" she pled.

Cade put an arm on her shoulder and tried to turn her to him. "I am awake," he insisted firmly, with annoyance lacing his tone.

As if she couldn't hear him, Collett rolled and smacked him again, this time connecting with his jaw. "He is coming! Jarrett, you have to wake up." Her words were urgent, agitated.

Still a little confused, Cade sat up and pulled Collett with him. He looked at her, seeing her eyes were open, but he knew right away she couldn't see him. She was in a trance-like state, seeing images far way. A tingling of fear, for her and for his brother, worked its way up his spine. He could see the desperation in her expression.

"Jarrett, he is at the door. You have to wake up—please!" she begged, more quietly this time, but her fear was compelling.

Helpless, Cade could only listen and watch her frantic actions. He didn't understand exactly what was happening, but was familiar enough with supernatural events such as this. He tried to remain calm. Still, his heart was pounding as he felt the warning in her voice pull at him.

C.B. Haight

She looked back as if looking for an enemy. "Good, now move! Hurry, the window!" she commanded as she put a hand on Cade's cheek as if trying to turn his head to see the window in question. Then, suddenly, her body jumped, as if in fear. Collett, grabbing her side and crying out, her eyes fluttered a few times before she opened them. Tears welled in those blue depths, and Cade knew she was no longer staring at his unseen brother.

"Oh no!" she whispered, and sobbing, she fell into his arms.

CHAPTER 5

"*Jarrett, he is at the door! You have to wake up—please!*"

Jarrett heard the desperate, pleading words in his head and opened his eyes, but he felt drugged, heavy. Cursing, he knew the infection was spreading too fast and fought against the feeling. He sensed the flutter of something against his cheeks and, through his haze, heard the urgent whispering of a woman's voice, *"Good, now move! The window!"*

He wasn't quick enough. The door slammed open with a crashing sound, and the hinges gave way under the force. The battered wood thudded to the floor.

Startled, Jarrett jerked up and felt the burning pain in his side as the wound stretched. He didn't have the time or the inclination to bother with it. Grimacing, he pushed past the pain and grabbed the dagger on the bed as he jumped up. His condition caused slower movements than normal. A large demon lumbered in, connecting a lunging fist on Jarrett's injured side before he could move out of the way.

While half-demons were common enough, full greater-demons such as the one he currently faced must be summoned with magic

~ 51 ~

and often proved difficult to defeat. They possessed impossible strength, and there were limited methods to destroy them.

Pain lanced through him, and he doubled over, missing the blow coming for his head. Coarse, clammy hands wrapped around his neck and lifted him from the ground. The skin felt like wet sandpaper scraping against him. The creature pulled him toward its lumpy, bald head and pock-marked face. Looking at Jarrett with sickly jaundiced eyes, it bellowed loudly. The pungent smell, much like decayed meat, poured over Jarrett. He choked on the acrid scent and coughed out, "What the hell do you eat?"

In reply to the caustic question, the demon thrust Jarrett upward. He felt the jarring impact of the low ceiling as it connected with his head. As his head made contact, the cheaply made ceiling gave way. Drywall and insulation fell to the floor.

For Jarrett, tested and seasoned in battle, thought ceased to exist. Instead, his mind fell silent and his fighting instincts took hold of his every action. Each automatic movement focused only on survival.

Bringing up his legs and walking up the demon's chest, he used the monster's face as a springboard and pushed off with his feet so forcefully the monster relinquished its painful hold. Jarrett fell clumsily to the ground by the bed, barely missing the softer landing it would have offered. The breath in his lungs was forced from him. New pain exploded in his torn side, and his ears began to ring.

Clearing his head, the Hunter in him knew he needed to deal with this thing quickly and then move on. The demon likely had a puppet master. A person, unknown, summoned it and gave it orders, and whoever did the summoning was his real concern. He rolled to a crouch while forcing the change to come. Despite hating his demon half, he knew it was the only way to match this beast.

His body reformed into a half-man, half-wolf. It was the form many called hybrid, and in this body, he was a deadly weapon. The demon bent down and reached for him again, but this time Jarrett was waiting for him. Staying low, he charged, using all his strength

~ 52 ~

and wrapping his thick muscled arms around the hefty stumps the demon used as legs. His biceps and shoulders bulged as he growled viciously, toppling the overbalanced creature.

Hitting the ground together, the demon grunted and snarled, and they rolled once until the wall stopped the momentum. Jarrett, with a slight advantage, ignored the club-like fists beating his fur covered back with bruising force. He was past pain, as his thoughts were focused solely on the death of the demon. The raw viciousness of the monster inside him took over.

Using teeth and claws, Jarrett tore into the creature, ripping the rough skin and flesh. The ichor in his mouth was foul, but it didn't stop him. He kept biting and clawing fiercely until, with predatory instincts, he managed to lock his jaws onto the neck of the beast.

The greater-demon understood its impending death, and its struggling became even more desperate. Rolling over again, it tried to use its heavy weight to crush the enraged hybrid, but by then it was no use. Jarrett had locked on, and his jaw clamped down with unbreakable force. He pulled and shook his head violently; tearing flesh, crushing bone, and cutting off air.

The demon made a sound between a gurgle and a growl as the ichor pulsed from its torn neck. It kept pounding and rolling back and forth while fighting for its life. The strikes began to lessen, the struggle dissipated, and the sickly gurgles and grunts fell silent. By then, Jarrett didn't notice any of it. He continued to fall deeper into the monster he hated, yet heavily relied upon to survive, wanting only to kill.

After a few more minutes, Jarrett tore through the last vestiges of bone, muscle, and clammy flesh. The demon body stiffened and went limp with a grotesque finality, as its head came free. The carcass that was left disintegrated into an ash-like substance, leaving the enraged werewolf with nothing left to fight against.

As the adrenaline began to subside, Jarrett's arms lost their strength, and he flopped to the ground on his back for a while, working to regain his control. He huffed and panted for air. Every breath he took hurt. His large wolfish ribcage expanded and contracted with the effort.

After a few minutes his anger was spent, and realizing how his body hurt, Jarrett considered changing, but decided it would be too much for his already drained body. He forced himself to get up, knowing he couldn't stay here too long. As if on cue, he heard the sirens in the distance.

Though his back was bruised and beaten, and his side was once again an open bleeding wound, he knew time was short. Changing would be too painful just then, and running would be much easier in his hybrid form. He grabbed his duffel in his clawed hand, slung it over his sore back and took off into the night at a run, regretfully leaving his bike behind.

Cade paced anxiously around the room while Collett related all she had "dreamed" to everyone present. Rederrick and Nate were there and listened calmly, but Cade could not do the same. His worry overwhelmed him.

He was stirred up inside for more than one reason. His immediate concern was the very real possibility that his twin brother—though estranged and more often his enemy—may be dead or dying at that precise moment. After Collett explained her vision of Jarrett's peril and pain, his gut turned with guilt. He'd known that Jarrett was likely in trouble, and he yet hadn't gone looking for him.

Slightly less urgent, but just as worrisome was Collett's pain. When she cried and grabbed onto her side right before waking, his heart almost stopped beating from fear. He would do anything to protect his new bride. The very real pain she felt on behalf of his brother tore at him. Even worse, there was little he could do about it. Despite the fact that she had no visible wound, he understood from her retelling, that whatever pain Jarrett had initially suffered was projected to her somehow. It was a frightening change, and watching as she still rubbed occasionally at the ghost wound haunted him.

His gut pinched and knotted over the fact that his wife was "dreaming" or "connecting" to his brother, while she lay cuddled up to him. Logically, he knew it was petty jealousy, not worth another thought. But he couldn't let go. He was bothered by this sudden connection his new wife shared with a person he'd spent so many years ignoring. When she grabbed Cade's face with a soft intimate touch of familiarity, thinking she was seeing Jarrett, he felt betrayed in a way. It hurt, a point he was loath to admit even to himself. He felt sick, wondering what they could have been to each other. Maybe that's what kept Jarrett from killing her. Maybe he knew her better than she knew herself.

Ever since Jarrett kidnapped her, Collett had become more guarded and vague about her few snapshot memories, especially her shared memories of him. When she told Cade it was to protect Jarrett's privacy and dignity, he thought nothing more of it, but now. . . Deep in the darkest part of his mind, he wondered a little if there wasn't more to it. For a minute it was all he could think about and felt an unknown jealousy swelling within.

Discouraged, he looked over at her once again while she answered Rederrick's questions to narrow down possible locations where Jarrett could be hiding. Their eyes met, and seeing the innocence and love in her eyes, he berated himself for even thinking about such things. This was Collett, she was the most kind and compassionate person he knew. She embodied a kind of virtue and integrity that practically made her incapable of deception. That was one of many things he loved about her, and he needed to get over these ridiculous thoughts. There was no room for it here. Shaking his head, Cade put the horrid thoughts out of his mind. It simply wasn't possible, and he was ashamed for even thinking it.

Two hours had passed since Collett woke from the vision of Jarrett being attacked. She told them every detail, making sure to include how badly she believed him to be injured. The injured part was hard not to believe because of the way she had cried out. Her pain was obviously real—too real for him—implying that Jarrett's pain was real as well.

The truth was, they really knew very little about Collett's capabilities when it came to her newly discovered powers. Less than a month ago, they had discovered that Collett wielded four Powers of Influence: precognition, empathy, projection, and telepathy.

At first it was a surprising discovery. That day they understood how powerful she could be, given enough time. The ability to use four Powers of Influence was simply unheard of. A rare witch or gifted individual would possibly have two of these powers, and most struggled with fully controlling them. The miniscule few that had two often went insane or became reclusive because of the burden these powers often created.

The more Collett practiced, the easier it became, especially projection—one the rarest powers. She also surprised them with other talents regularly.

She could tap into some magic, but she couldn't use it the same ways Cynda did. So far, most spells attempted had been a bust, but Collett could light a flame and stir a light wind with her will. This required control of elemental magic. However, her use of it was more like the way Jeffery controlled magic. He did not speak words or incantations, nor could he brew potions like Cynda. As a sorcerer, he was physically connected to magic, and it seemed Collett, in a minor way, was much the same.

She was a quick healer too. She could have a bruise one day, and wake up the next morning with no sign of it.

They were discovering that this incredibly gifted woman he was devoted to had a weird and inconvenient connection to people who could be hundreds of miles away.

It was beginning to overwhelm him. He hated the uncertainty plaguing them. He'd once told her he didn't care if she ever got her memory back, and he'd meant it. However, he did believe that things would be a lot easier for her if she could remember.

~ 56 ~

The Price of Knowing

It was as if all of these influential talents had been seeking release ever since she'd forgotten them, and since meeting this group, the power somehow figured out exactly how to slip free. Except it all wanted to be released at once. Because of her lack of memory she hadn't knowingly used the gifts. Upon finding herself alone on a destroyed beach with no memory two and a half years ago, Collett knew precious little about her abilities. She never would have fathomed she wielded any power at all. Back then, she only thought it was merely instinct, or sensitivity to evil. Now, with all of her powers jumping out so easily, even she could barely keep up. Part of Cade wondered, if she hadn't met them, would she have ever understood; would she have ever struggled as she does now? He knew though, he wouldn't wish her away even if it was true. If she hadn't met them, he wouldn't have her as his wife, and that was something he couldn't wish away, even if it was selfish.

With her the surprises seemed to be never ending. The real concern was—why *Jarrett?* Of all the people in the world, why did she connect to him? She wasn't linked to anyone else the way she was with him, and Cade could admit, at least to himself, that was what really bothered him. It was a lot for anyone to take in, even for Cade, a werewolf by birth, who regularly saw a great deal of the incredible. Her involvement in Jarrett's past and her new confusing link to him were difficult to comprehend, and even more difficult to like.

With the help of everyone here, he had to hold faith that she would conquer this connection and control it. For right now, as much as he hated it, her new ability to connect with Jarrett was something they would have to use as a necessary tool to find him. She was their only connection to his brother, even if he hated it. She was seeing what he was seeing, and worse: feeling what he was feeling.

Cade was pulled from his inner thoughts when he heard Collett telling Rederrick once again, with frustration, that she didn't have any idea where Jarrett could've been. Her voice was laden with

~ 57 ~

guilt. Her expression also spoke volumes. She was beginning to blame herself for Jarrett's current dilemma, and not figuring out his location based on her vague vision only made it worse.

"There has to be a way for us to find him," he heard her insisting.

"We will, Collett," Rederrick assured. "If it happens again, try to look at his surroundings so we can nail it down. We'll find him, but it might take time."

She looked at Cade with soft, sad eyes. "I don't think he has much time to spare."

All day, she tried to convince Cade to go find him. She was sure there was no time to waste. Cade wanted to argue, but he couldn't anymore. He couldn't refute how Collett acted during her dream. So, he, Nate, and Rederrick kept working on the computer, entering the information Collett could remember into various systems, trying to find possible matches for a starting point. But the information was too vague. Ultimately, they all knew it was like searching for a needle in a haystack, with hundreds of stacks to choose from. The odds weren't in their favor, and nobody knew what to do about it.

The evening after Jarrett was attacked, he knew the pain was definitely worse. Every breath racked him. The throbbing, a sensation he was unaccustomed to, pulsed through him with an unforgiving rhythm. Normally, his wounds would have healed themselves already. Instead, movement of any kind caused him to want to cringe outwardly, including the movement required to breathe.

He pushed past it and kept moving with a perseverance unsurpassed. He knew he needed a new strategy. He tried his best to blend with the people of New York, until he could find a safe place to get a little rest, but he needed a plan of some kind too.

His head pounded viciously, as if someone had struck his skull with a sledge hammer. He darted into the next alley, and leaning against the concrete wall of the building, he faced the street. Carefully reaching back and probing with his fingers, Jarrett sought out the wound on his head, a result of his impromptu examination of the ceiling last night. He found the injury by the matted hair, and felt the puckered skin of the slowly healing wound.

Despite the ache in his head, he found himself satisfied with its healing progress. He reached down, lightly lifted his shirt to examine his burning side next, and found himself not so satisfied.

The deep hole in his side was infected, oozing, and healed much too slowly—if at all. The silver dagger did its job well, and Jarrett wasn't certain how bad it really was. There was no way he could know how many organs might be affected at this point. He felt as if the whole of his insides were on fire—not a good sign by his accounting. Cursing, he gingerly pressed the towel he acquired from the motel back to the wound, and eased his shirt down to hold it in place.

He cautiously poked his head out of the darkened alleyway to assess the street and verify he wasn't being followed. All seemed quiet enough for this area. He watched as a couple walking together passed by arm in arm and full of optimism. Old resentment stirred in him, as it often did. If they only knew the truth of the world, it's likely they wouldn't be so optimistic. They wouldn't walk so freely in the dark either.

He took a minute to decide which direction to go. There was one place where he could get a bit of help, but he hated the mere thought of it. He pushed the idea away before it even fully formed. He knew going to see her would be too dangerous. He couldn't do it. No matter how bad he felt. They would follow, and he wasn't willing to risk that. *No*, he thought, shaking his head defying the weak thought. He wasn't that far gone in the game yet.

He would have to bide his time for a little longer and come up with a plan. He wouldn't bring this mess to her doorstep, even if it meant dying. Straightening to his full height, and grinding his teeth as he did, Jarrett moved back out onto the street. Resolved once again, he figured he needed to find a dark, crowded bar where he could get some whiskey. In a place like that he would be in his element, giving him a slight advantage. As he walked he determined that tomorrow he would need to figure out his next move, and then...well, he'd have to see if he even made it that far.

He wasn't afraid to die. In fact, there were times when he would've almost welcomed the end. The problem was his sheer stubbornness. It wasn't in him to give up, and he hated losing at anything. He thought back on his life as he traveled down the streets of New York, and considered how it would have been easier to give up long ago, but he'd let anger fuel him all these years.

More than once during his long life, Jarrett found himself surprised that he still drew breath. If not for the vengeance he sought for Rowena all those years ago, he may have ended it all on that horrific night. He'd wanted to.

He went to take his revenge and thought he would likely be killed as he zipped through the area, killing as many as he could before they ended him. He went to the preacher first, as he promised himself that he would. Another unwanted memory invaded his mind as he thought on the past.

"Don't," he vaguely heard.

In his wolf's body, he stared down at the preacher with hate in his heart, anger in his soul, and sadness in his twelve-year-old eyes. The man before him was huddling and whimpering in fear. He had come here looking for revenge and satisfaction. Rowena was dead and someone should pay. He started to move in for the kill and heard the soft, familiar voice again.

"Don't. It won't bring her back."

He snarled through his canine muzzle.

The priest began to pray, asking for mercy. Conflict and confusion entered his heart. His anger though, was stronger than his confusion. He jumped at the priest, and encountered a barrier of sorts. An electric wall he couldn't see shocked him just before he reached the preacher. The man started crying, babbling about Satan's monsters. Jarrett growled again, but when he moved to try once more, he heard a small child's voice.

"Papa?"

He snapped around to a find a little girl, no more than five maybe, standing confused and afraid a few feet away. He barked and snarled in frustration. He heard the woman speaking to him despite his anger and frustration. "Will you take from her what they took from you? Will you be like them?" asked the angelic voice in his head.

He howled loud and long, scaring the child even more, and she began to sob, much as he had the day before.

As he came out of the unwanted memory he cursed, as he realized somehow Collett had been with him at that moment of his life too.

CHAPTER 6

A little after four in the morning, Cade sat up in the room Collett and he shared, watching her sleep. She seemed peaceful, but heaven only knew if it would last. For the last two days, Collett kept having nightmares and flashes of strange things. Among them was Jarrett. She had dreamed of Jarrett three times more since her first dream of him being attacked by a demon. It was difficult for him to watch, because each time she awoke horrified and in pain. He hated watching her suffer on behalf of his brother.

The problem was they still didn't have any idea where Jarrett would be. Collett insisted he was injured badly and getting weaker, but she couldn't cue in to where he might be. If her constant dreams were real, then Jarrett was practically under constant assault. They were indeed running out of time.

Rederrick called his eldest daughter, Tracy, and asked her to investigate a bar in New York that they discovered was owned by a Jarrett Hunter. When she went there and asked for the owner, she was informed that he had gone out of town, and they were unsure when he would return. That sent them right back to square one.

~ 62 ~

The Price of Knowing

As it was, Cade felt certain that neither of them had managed more than a couple hours of sleep at a time these last few days. He unconsciously brought a hand to his forehead and rubbed it as he thought over his options. He didn't want to leave her, but he knew it was coming down to that. He dropped his hand, leaned back in his chair, and tried to relax. He was afraid to climb into the bed and risk disturbing her fragile sleep.

They should be on a honeymoon. He wanted to take her away to a tropical beach and spend the days, and nights, enjoying one another. Instead, they were dealing with this situation, and he knew he alone was powerless to fix it.

Unfortunately, Jarrett's presence in her dreams was only number one on a whole list of problems they faced. Collett kept having random dreams. Even awake, feelings and impressions would wash over her, and she wasn't sure if it was past, present, or future. It was wearing her down, and there was really nothing they could do to stop it. Cynda even tried giving her a homemade concoction to help her sleep last night, but it only made it worse. Instead of easing her dreams, the tea trapped her within them with no way to wake, making it the worst of the nights yet. He had held her and watched helplessly as she reacted to painful injuries, mostly favoring her ghostly side wound, all night long.

Despite all she was experiencing, her strength and fortitude amazed him. She brushed his worry aside, optimistically telling him it would all come together when it was supposed to. She also insisted that as her abilities surfaced, she only needed time to get accustomed to them. She was confident they would get easier to control. She also voiced her hopes that she would remember everything soon.

He wasn't convinced. Cade's fear for his wife continued to grow. To him, it looked as if her powers were not only coming back, but that they were taking over. He couldn't keep himself from thinking that before long there wouldn't be much of her left.

With their problems compounding, Cade knew they were all running out of time here in Colorado. He could feel it. He and Rederrick had been hesitant to give up the security they had access to here at Rederrick's home, and he didn't know where to go from here. However, The Faction would soon resume their attempts to get to Collett, and he had a bad feeling in his gut that she was no longer the only target. Unfortunately, he hadn't been able to convince Rederrick or Cynda that they should all relocate.

Eventually, Cade decided there was nothing more to be done tonight, and he tried to empty his mind so he could rest for a little while. His eyes felt heavy, and he started drifting into the oblivion of sleep. It didn't last long though. A slight whimper came from Collett.

Releasing an exhausted breath and rising from the chair, he went to her. "Shhh," he whispered gently. He laid down, eased her into his arms, and breathed in the citrus scent that always clung to her.

He kissed her neck tenderly as she settled back into sleep, and her long hair tickled his cheek as he lay down. Cade gently moved the locks aside, and in the dim moonlit room, he saw a mark that struck him as odd. Carefully, so he didn't wake her, Cade rubbed it with his thumb.

Collett's skin was puckered, but not by a tattoo. It felt like a scar or birthmark of some kind, but the mark was too precise for either. His brows drew together as he peered down in the dim light. It looked like a strange pattern with a line at the bottom. A smaller mark lay in the center of the circle. He pondered the oddity, rubbing it gently, considering its origins.

She stirred again, but not because of a nightmare. She sensed him there. She rolled over to look at him, smiling. "Hi," she murmured sleepily.

His insides warmed, and his thoughts about the strange symbol flitted away. "Hi," he answered back, leaning in to kiss the tip of her nose. He pulled back to look into her eyes. Smiling, he leaned in

The Price of Knowing

again and pressed his lips to hers, softly at first, but as his lips began the dance against hers, he gradually sought more.

Collett felt desire spread through her. Bringing up her hand, she twined her fingers in his thick, black hair. He moved his hand tenderly over her arm, tickling the skin, and continued down to her hip. The warmth was replaced by tingling chills and eager anticipation.

Everything else melted away. For Collett and Cade, little else mattered than what was between them right now. They both let go of any distractions as they embraced each other, finding comfort and security in being together.

Later, Cade woke to bright rays of sunlight shining in his eyes. He tried hard to ignore it, but it was no use. He was too sensitive to the change in light. He groggily rolled over and eased out of bed to close the curtains before it woke Collett. After that, he looked at the clock with dry, scratchy eyes and realized it was about 7:20. He shrugged and reminded himself that a little sleep was better than none, even though he didn't really believe it just then. His focus moved back to his wife who still slept peacefully in the tangled sheets, and he was grateful the sun hadn't wakened her as it had him.

He quietly strode to the adjoining bathroom and turned on the shower. After washing off, he stayed under the spray for a long time and let the warm water soothe his tired body. When he was finished, he quickly shaved and made his way quietly to the bedroom with a blue towel around his waist. Upon opening the door, he realized Collett was awake. She was sitting up with her arms wrapped around her legs, facing away from him. Her cheek rested on her knees as she stared at the curtain-covered window.

"Hey, I'd hoped you'd sleep longer."

She didn't respond, and he knew.

"Another dream?" he asked as he moved to sit next to her.

She nodded and looked up at him. Her eyes held so much sadness. "Cade, we have to do something. If my dreams are real,

~ 65 ~

then…" She didn't have to finish. They both knew what it meant. His mouth pinched together. He hated that she kept going through this—hated what it was doing to her. He also felt growing resentment for Jarrett.

"Can we find him?" he asked in a calm tone he didn't quite feel.

She shook her head. "I'm not sure, but we have to try."

With a tight nod, Cade said, "Get dressed. We'll go talk to the others. Maybe we'll get an idea this time."

A half hour later, they all sat in the hidden room that housed the security systems. It also served as the control center for the Brotherhood. Rederrick called it the "Extra Room." Cynda, Rederrick, Nate, and even Jeffery sat in the comfortable chrome and black office chairs surrounding a glass and steel conference table. Cade stood behind Collett in support, and they all listened while she relayed her latest dream.

She told them Jarrett was badly wounded and that it wasn't healing. She also explained the latest attack against him and how it was getting harder and harder for him to beat them each time. Collett expressed her fear and worry. Then she explained how his thoughts gave her the impression he was going west, but west from where, she couldn't say.

When she finished, nobody said anything for a time. Collett nervously sat there, wringing her hands together. "There's something else," she confessed. "I keep having this weird dream that I'm with someone in the dark, and there is no way out. I feel hunger and pain. I don't know who it is for sure. The presence feels different than Jarrett, but I can't see anything. If it is Jarrett, he might have already been captured. Though, as I said, this feels different, so I can't tell if I am seeing the present or the past."

Cade squeezed her shoulder.

Rederrick spoke first, "Maybe we should start at the beginning. Cade, go to New York and see if you can pick up a trail—"

"I've been doing a little reading and think that maybe there is a better way," interrupted Cynda. "I think that instead of waiting for

Collett to accidentally get dreams or visions from Jarrett, she should try to reach out to him on purpose with meditation or something like it."

"I don't know. The dreams are hard enough," Cade countered skeptically.

"Is it even possible to do something like that?" Collett asked.

Cynda shrugged. "I'm not really sure. But since I haven't been able to find him by scrying, and you're having no luck with the dreams, I think maybe we should do something together. It would be tricky, but it's better than blindly chasing him all over the country."

Jeffery cleared his throat as if looking for permission to speak. Since arriving with Jarrett's note, Jeffery had been timid and reserved. Recent events had humbled him, and he knew he hadn't yet earned their trust. Another reason he behaved this way, Collett suspected, was because working with a team was so new to him, and he wasn't sure what his role was. They all looked to him, and Collet watched as he shrank back before their scrutiny. His head tipped down, and his long black hair, colored with purple and blue streaks, hung over his narrow face.

"Go ahead, Jeffery," she coaxed.

Without even looking up, he said, "You can probably do it given enough concentration and energy, but it would take a lot of magical energy. Too much I think. You can't just use a simple scrying spell either, or it would have worked by now. Somehow, he blocks magic, and you would need a big punch of it just to get through. I think it's why the scrying is failing.

"Even together, you would have the same result—nothing. Not to mention, your visions are all over the place. Instead, we could try a sort of location magic I am familiar with, but it's difficult and requires…extra components."

"What kind of components?" inquired Cade skeptically.

"Well…" he hesitated.

"Blood. We would need his blood," guessed Cynda.

"To start with," Jeffery agreed with a nod.

For a moment, no one dared to speak. Rederrick shook his head emphatically, and Cade glowered. Blood magic was considered the darkest magic because it often proved uncontrollable. In fact, few even tried it.

"Well, we just should have thought of that while Cade was beating the crap out of him in the woods last month," Nate quipped. He tilted his head mockingly. "Excuse me, could you boys settle down a minute? I need a vile of blood please. You know, just in case."

Cade glared at him.

"Blood is not the biggest problem," Jeffery said quietly.

"What's the biggest problem?" Cade asked gruffly.

"I mentioned that he is blocking magic. Somehow, your brother is immune to, or protected from, most magic. I've run into him twice. Well, he really ran into me," he added, remembering the painful second encounter. "Both times, he could not only see through my spells, he blasted past my shields too. I couldn't figure it out. He's blocking the magic effects is my only guess. Even using blood magic, it may not work depending on what he is using. Really, it's a shot in the dark."

Cade looked to Cynda. "What do you think?"

She shook her head. "I'm not sure. I've heard of items that can mute the effects of magic, but who knows if it could block a spell, like Jeffery is suggesting. Blood magic is pretty strong,"

Nate spoke up next, "Well, I don't see how it matters. We don't have his blood. Anything left in the woods after your fight would have been washed away by the storms we've had."

"Yes, we do," Collett said quietly. "Well—kind of."

Cynda's eyes brightened, and she looked at Cade. "I didn't even think of that."

"I think Jeffery did," Collett replied.

"What?" Nate and Rederrick asked together.

"My blood. Because we are twins, we share blood, or at least we did once," Cade answered.

~ 68 ~

The Price of Knowing

"I want to make it clear. This kind of magic is unpredictable. I've used it—well, before—before I came here, and my results have been—varied," Jeffery said awkwardly. "It may not even work. Collett's lack of control over the connection and twisting the magic to use Cade's blood instead of Jarrett's are challenging factors."

"We have to try, don't we?" Collett practically pleaded.

"What else will it take, besides blood?" Cade questioned, still not convinced. He recognized this may be the best possible chance, but the idea of blood magic bothered him. In his lifetime, very few good people would even mess with it.

Jeffery looked to Cade, a little nervous. "It takes a lot of energy, so it will take more than one person to do it. Cynda and I would have to do it together, but even that won't be easy and…"

"And, what?"

"We need a connection to circumvent his block. Collett's connection would be the easiest, but she can't just be an observer. She would need to be connected to him when we do it."

Collett looked up at Cade, who was clenching his jaw, and considered all that Jeffery was saying. "I don't know how to connect to him on purpose. It just happens," she told him.

Jeffery nodded. "When you're sleeping, I know. We can do it one of two ways. First, you can try to figure out how to connect to him on your own, which may take a lot of time and practice on your part. Or we—I mean I—can help you sleep. Using magic."

"No way!" Cade snapped. "You may have won her over, and even Cynda, but I don't trust you enough to use your magic on her. Especially this kind of magic."

Jeffery sighed dejectedly and conceded, "I get it. It was just an idea."

"Cade, we are running out of time! I think we have to," prodded Collett.

"NO! Not a chance. Let Cynda do the spell instead. He can supervise."

~ 69 ~

C.B. Haight

Cynda gave him a pensive look. "Cade, I can't do it. I have no idea how. I've never done that kind of magic. You heard Jeffery. Blood magic is touchy. Besides, you saw what happened when I tried to help Collett sleep. My spells and herbs only made her worse because she couldn't get out of it."

"How do we know his magic would be different?" Rederrick asked.

"Because I can wake her easily by discontinuing the spell," Jeffery answered.

Cade raked his fingers through his hair in frustration. "I'm telling you, this is a bad idea."

Collett stood to face him and put her hand on his arm, softly pleading, "Cade, I won't do this without you. We're a team, all of us, and we have to agree. We're running out of time though. I know it, and I think you do too. Cynda and I can't learn what he already knows fast enough. We have to let him try. Please! I can't stand doing nothing when there is a chance to help Jarrett right here. We have to try."

Seeing the desperation in Collett's eyes undid Cade. He released a breath and looked over to Rederrick and Nate for support. Nate shrugged easily, indicating he was in either way, and Rederrick said, "It's your wife and brother. We'll do what you want. Make the call."

Cade peered over Collett's head and eyed Jeffery. He looked past the eyebrow piercing, the strange black clothes, and the color-streaked hair. He met his brown eyes and saw the young man Jeffery was becoming. Looking deeper, Cade saw what he needed. There was a level of fear and humility that he'd never witnessed in Jeffery in the past. "You really think you can do this?"

"Huh? Yes, um… well, I can't. Not by myself, but *we* can," Jeffery stammered as he gestured to Cynda, Collett, and himself. He was clearly surprised to hear they were going to trust him. It was a new experience for him.

~ 70 ~

Cade gazed into Collett's eyes and relented, "All right. Do it then, but you better know that—"

"I will not do anything intentionally to hurt them. I don't want to piss you off. I like living too much," Jeffery interrupted, knowing where Cade was going with his threat and not really wanting to hear the gory details.

Cade glared at him.

"How long do you need to get ready?" Cynda asked.

Jeffery considered the logistics mentally, then answered. "With your help, we could probably try it tonight."

"Tonight then," said Rederrick.

"Let's go, Jeffery," Cynda said, rising to leave the room, and Jeffery followed.

"I'll keep an eye on him," offered Nate, as he followed them.

Rederrick made his way back to the computers and monitors along the wall, and Cade turned back to Collett to whisper, "Are you sure you want to do this?"

She smiled sadly, "Yes, Cade. I have to do something," she replied. "I know you really don't trust Jeffery, but I do. Remember, everyone can be great with the right help, and Cynda is the right kind of help."

He released a sigh. "I hope you're right. I would sure hate to kill him."

Smiling, she replied, "I'm sure he wouldn't like it either."

That night, the temperature in the field where they gathered was warmer than the day before, but it was still bitter cold. Everyone bundled up in gloves, hats, and heavy winter-wear except Jeffery and Cade.

Jeffery wore his traditional t-shirt, black Levi's, and heavy biker boots that sported silver skulls on the ties. He completed the ensemble with his usual long, black coat that made him look like a punk kid who should be hanging out at a high school goth party. He came complete with facial piercings, a neck tattoo, and purple and blue streaks in his black hair. However, everyone present understood he was so much more than he appeared, and they could only hope it was enough.

Cynda worried over him, exclaiming he would get cold, and Jeffery brushed it off, insisting he needed to have free movement. Cade, on the other hand, looked at home in the woodlands of Colorado. He wore a simple leather jacket. The cold temperature was not something that bothered him as much as it bothered humans.

Despite the cold, they had hiked up to this clearing because Jeffery suggested that they not use this kind of magic indoors. He explained it could be volatile, which did nothing to ease Cade's concern.

Cynda's feet crunched in the snow as she finished the circle. Inside the circle was a triangle with crystals on each point. Cynda had insisted they would help. In the circle's center lay a sleeping bag for Collett to lie on. Shadowed trees surrounded them since the evening light had already dissipated a couple hours before.

Cade, Rederrick, and Nate watched stoically as Collett, Jeffery, and Cynda finished the preparations. Cade was sure that Rederrick felt as uncomfortable as he did with this situation. Only a short time ago, Jeffery was working for The Faction in an effort to capture Collett. He had almost killed both of these women by pushing their SUV into the river. Cade fought his way to them, but it had been a close call. Now, in this time of desperation, they were willingly letting him use his magic on those same women.

"Okay, I think we can get started," Jeffery called. "Cade, we'll need you over here at this point of the triangle, and Cynda, you stand over there opposite me."

Cade strode over to take his place, and Collett met him there. Letting out a nervous breath, she held a shiny dagger out to him. He recognized the silver metal right away and arched a brow.

~ 72 ~

"Jeffery says that it's not only the blood. It helps if there is sacrifice made, so that's why it's silver. You won't heal right away, making it more meaningful."

He took the dagger from her, but held on to her hand. He leaned down until their foreheads touched. "It's not too late."

"It may be for him," she said with sad eyes.

"I love you."

"I love you," she replied, and projected her feelings into him.

Cade closed his eyes and savored the sensations.

"Are you ready, Collett?" Jeffery called.

Collett rose to the tips of her toes and kissed him tenderly, then she pulled back and met Cade's eyes so he would know her words were truth, "I'm ready."

Cade reluctantly released her hand, and she moved to the sleeping bag. Cade called out to Rederrick and Nate, "Watch our backs."

Collett laid down, and Jeffery said a few things to reassure her. She nodded, and out of respect, he looked back to Cade for his final consent. "Once we start, we can't stop. It's too risky."

Cade was slightly impressed that Jeffery met his eyes, for the first time, with confidence while seeking permission to begin. He nodded in reply. Jeffery turned and began gesturing over Collett.

They all watched as he moved his hands carefully. Cade continually found the difference between sorcerers and witches interesting. A witch generally received power passed down through bloodlines and must diligently study and practice to hone those skills. If they didn't learn, they often lost touch with the magic over time. Witches cast spells with words that are cautiously planned in order to avoid misfired magic with poor word choices. They were also generally herbalists to some degree, and used that know-how to amplify their magic.

Sorcerers, on the other hand, could tap directly into the unseen lines of magic, even sometimes by accident. They had a natural affinity for it and needed no words. Instead, a sorcerer would feel for the magic, reach deep within, and then learn gestures to bring it out from its source. An average person could mistake a sorcerer's movements and gestures for Thai-chi or something like it. Even untrained, they could still tap into the source without realizing it. In fact, many discovered their powers by using accidental gestures coupled with strong desires.

Rarely did sorcerers obtain skills from inheritance or bloodlines. Few of the sorcerers he knew in his life could find a link to any relative with similar skills, and it would only happen randomly. That lack of support was the reason many of them strayed to groups like The Faction. These days, in a world where most didn't believe in magic, sorcerers had no way to find teachers. And unlike witches, their untapped powers didn't dissipate if they weren't used. As a result, they usually accepted help anywhere they could find it.

He continued to watch as Collett quit moving, relaxing under Jeffery's spell. After she was still, Jeffery moved to his point in the triangle. As planned, Cynda would support Jeffery. Cynda needed words to tap the magic within her, so she would use a few. Her main purpose was to add magical energy to Jeffery and strengthen the spell.

Cade was there to give his blood, and he would be Collett's connection here to anchor her while Jarrett would be her connection there, wherever *there* was. Cade was also supposed to focus on Collett to see any signs of distress.

Jeffery was the control. His skills of channeling energy and controlling the power would complete the task.

Cynda began first. She started chanting, asking the four elements and the four corners, North, South, East, and West, for strength and sight. Jeffery started when she was done with her first chant. As she repeated it, he moved his body in slow, rhythmic motions. To Cade, it seemed like he was moving in time with her words. The wind stirred, and he felt a tingling on his skin. In a hot rush, flames burst up from the salt-outlined circle surrounding them, but they quickly settled down to a light, steady burn.

The Price of Knowing

Rederrick and Nate watched helplessly from outside the flaming ring. The next thing they knew, Collett's form, still relaxed, lifted from the ground. Cade instinctively started to step forward, but Jeffery guessed his intent and snapped with authority, "Don't!"

When Cade looked to him, he noted Jeffery's eyes were no longer brown. Instead, they were pitch black. Even the whites of his eyes were consumed by an eerie, opaque shadow. "Focus on her. Make sure she is calm, but stay there until I tell you," he said while he continued to move in a rhythmic dance.

Closing his eyes, Cade reached for calm focus. Opening them again, he watched only her, thought of only her. Collett levitated above the earth, but she remained still. Jeffery called to him again, "The blood, Cade. Cut your hand, then go to her."

Cade lifted the silver dagger to his palm and sliced it, feeling the sting as it carved a line in his skin. He squeezed his hand into a fist to let the blood drip on the ground as he moved to Collett. He looked at Jeffery one more time to make sure. "Yes, now," Jeffery replied, and Cade gently removed her glove and grabbed Collett's icy hand with his bleeding one. Suddenly, before he could even take his next breath, he was jolted into her thoughts, and he found himself sitting across from Jarrett.

Though everything seemed blurry and disconnected, Cade realized immediately that Collett was right. Jarrett was not in good shape. His brother was gaunt and pale, and his hair was damp from sweat. He leaned against the wall of an old building with his eyes closed. To anybody else, he would look drunk, but Cade knew better. Alcohol didn't really work on them. Their metabolism and healing capabilities made it nearly impossible to get drunk.

"Jarrett?" Cade heard Collett say. The sound of her voice echoed strangely, sounding in his mind. He jerked his head and found that he could not see her at all.

"Ah, hell. Not you again," he heard his brother growl in annoyance, confirming that Jarrett could hear her too. "You're a little late," he accused. "They've already been here, so thanks anyway."

She ignored his bitter comments. "Where are you?" she asked softly.

"I wonder if it is normal to dream about your brother's woman all the time," he continued, ignoring her in turn. "Wanting what you can't have and all that, I suppose." He laughed cynically and winced as a result.

"Please Jarrett, where are you?" she begged patiently.

"I suppose I shouldn't mind. There are worse things—I would know. And you are quite a package. Cade can sure pick them. Really though, I wish you'd get out of my head, or at least come dressed in clothes of *my* choice," he continued to himself, as if she must be part of his imagination. Cade bristled at his words and wanted to slug his brother.

"Jarrett, there's not much time," she pleaded urgently.

His head jerked up, body straightened, and his eyes became alert. His reaction was so quick, Cade understood Jarrett must be hearing her dream warnings, and Collett was like an alarm. Her simple words put Jarrett on full alert. Collett must have realized it too, because she responded quickly, "They're not here yet, but you need help."

"Yeah? And I suppose you're gonna help me?" he scoffed, but didn't let his guard down. He continued to peer through the darkness.

"I will," she answered with sincerity.

Now he did look at her, and there was pure hate reflected in his eyes. "You tried that once, remember? It didn't turn out so good." Jarrett shifted, and his facial expression pinched slightly from the pain. Somehow Cade felt Collett wince too. "Go away! You can't help me. Besides, I'm pretty sure you're not really here. Don't you have a honeymoon to get to?"

Impatience and annoyance surged through Cade. He started to curse at his brother, but his voice wouldn't carry any sound here. He realized he was just seeing the whole thing through her point of view. He also noticed everything was getting even more blurry.

"You think that we would abandon you to this fate?" she snapped. "I am almost out of time. Tell me, where are you?" Her words were firm, sounding much like a mother reprimanding her child.

Jarrett shook his head. "He did, and *you* are the reason I'm in this mess to begin with." Jarrett began moving away. "Where I am doesn't matter because, as you can see, I am leaving."

"Where will you go?" she questioned.

To Cade's surprise, Jarrett looked over his shoulder and answered quietly, "To her."

"Who—?" he heard Collett begin, but didn't hear anything more. He was ripped through a cloudy tunnel and found himself back in the glen in Colorado. His mind disconnected from Collett, and he felt like himself again, except completely exhausted. The flames around them sputtered out, leaving behind a steamy mist rising from the heated, moist earth.

He looked down to where Collett lay and saw she rested on the ground once more. Her eyes were still closed, and her breathing was still slow. Worried, Cade called angrily, "Jeffery, why isn't she awake?" Turning, he glared at the sorcerer, ready to let blood, but his anger dissipated at the sight of Jeffery.

The sorcerer was bent over on hands and knees. His face lifted at Cade's question, and even in the meager night's light, Cade could see the pallor on his face, as well as the blood dripping from his nose. Nate moved to help him before he fell over. Cade looked over to check on Cynda and found Rederrick steadying her too, but she didn't look as weak and drained as Jeffery.

"She still sleeps," Jeffery forced out between breaths, drawing Cade's attention back to him, "because," another breath, "I haven't cast the spell to wake her." Even with Nate's help, Jeffery stumbled as he moved to her. "Give me a minute to gather my strength and I'll take care of it."

~ 77 ~

C.B. Haight

"How long will she sleep?" Cade questioned, considering Jeffery's condition.

"As long as you want."

He looked at Collett lying peacefully before him. "Let her sleep. She needs the rest, and I'd guess so do you," Cade told him. "If her dreams get bad again, I'll have you wake her up."

Jeffery could only nod in reply, but he felt relief at the respite offered. His head felt as if a madman had cleaved it in half with an ax, and the bones in his legs felt gelatinous.

"Let's get out of the cold and talk about what happened," Rederrick said grimly.

CHAPTER 7

"Will you be like them?" The question from Jarrett's lost childhood memories echoed in his head as he walked down the dark streets. Her expression, so full of compassion, haunted him from the vision he'd had earlier. *Hallucination more likely,* he thought.

Until he voiced it to her, Jarrett hadn't realized where he was going. What better place to finish it then back at the beginning?

He thought back to the night Rowena died and the home he knew—or what had been left of it. He hadn't been able to stay away. He could still remember the desperate need he felt to return and see. There had even been a part of him that hoped for a miracle, but the fire did its job. It was a home no more, only the charred remnants of one.

There was no miracle—at least not the kind he had hoped for. Very little of the small wooden cabin was left standing, and his life was reduced to blackened ashes of nothingness. Still, he searched for anything he could hold on to from that life.

Shortly after he started, he found an item that made his heart break. The single connection he retained from that night still hung at his neck. Unconsciously, Jarrett fingered the green amulet. Rowena's amulet. He remembered how she always wore it, and how he found it where she should have been. There was nothing left of her, save the amulet. Seeing it lying there among the charred and blackened ashes sent him into a rage, and he renewed his promise to kill the preacher.

He felt the emotions stir again as his past forced its way through the barriers he'd erected long ago. It annoyed him that images and memories kept popping in and out of his head. They brought back feelings he didn't want—feelings best left alone. What's more, he couldn't figure out how these recent images of his brother's mysterious wife fit into his complicated life. Who was she to him? Why had she been there? Why the hell did her sympathetic looks and sweet melodic voice have to keep torturing him?

"Will you be like them?" He could still hear the question ring in his ears as if he still stood frozen in that moment in his mind. *I am like them*, he thought.

Shaking it aside, he forced himself to focus. No longer in his favored home state, Jarrett found himself in a town so small he hadn't even bothered to note the name. It felt like the middle of nowhere to a man accustomed to "The City That Never Sleeps." He reached a dark, seedy building that boasted neon signs promising patrons a variety of beer and other spirits. Wanting to quell the vague memories with a distraction, he decided here was just as good as anywhere else, but he soon found that wasn't the case.

Entering, he found a dark, dingy room and a small, lifeless circle of men. Mostly empty, it was a far cry from his establishment in downtown New York where a person would hardly be noticed, unless they wanted to be.

This bar was more the kind that catered to regular patrons. The old wooden counter filled one side of the room and was accompanied by several tattered stools lining the front of it. Cheap Christmas garland hung above the liquor bottles, and a small

Christmas tree sat next to the cash register. The T.V. was mostly turned down, but it was on and tuned to the local news channel.

Two haggard men sat together about three-fourths of the way down from where Jarrett stood. On the other side of the room, there were several empty tables for patrons who wanted to be together, instead of seeking the solitude found when staring at the rows of liquor bottles behind the scarred bar top.

Upon seeing Jarrett enter, the middle-aged barkeeper straightened from where he bent over the counter to visit with two patrons. The three old men stared at Jarrett as if he was the newest novelty in a circus act.

Okay, not just as good as anywhere else, he thought. He wanted to get lost in a crowd somewhere, not stand out like a sore thumb. Here, he would draw too much attention.

"Can I get ya somethin', son?" the graying bartender asked before he could back out.

Figuring he may as well deal with a few important things, Jarrett replied gruffly, "Bathroom?"

The bartender indicated the location, pointing behind where Jarrett stood.

Jarrett nodded tersely and entered the tiny bathroom. It was a small, rundown room for either male or female customers. He flicked the lock, dropped his pack on the floor, and eased off his jacket. He hissed in pain as he gingerly removed it. He carefully lifted his black t-shirt and saw blood was starting to leak through the towel. Removing the towel, he clearly saw that the angry, red, and swollen injury was infected.

His supernatural ability to heal was barely present at this point. Not to mention, the continuous attacks against him kept it from sealing properly. Even if he'd stitched it up, his constant exploits against Faction bounty hunters would have torn it open again, as it had several times now. Unless he could get at least a little rest and give the wound proper time to heal, the infection would keep spreading, and he knew it.

C.B. Haight

Resigned, he set to cleaning and dressing it anyway. Voices from outside stirred his curiosity. His superior hearing allowed him to eavesdrop on the conversation.

"Did ya see that boy? I think the baddest biker in hell just walked into your bar."

"C'mon Bill."

"Don't you, 'C'mon Bill,' me. Are you tellin' me, Jim, that you're not the least bit worried? He's got trouble written all over him. Good grief, he's got to be at least seven feet tall and looks strong enough to tear this place apart. What's a boy like that doin' here?"

"Well you're here, ain't ya?" the bartender replied.

"Well yeah," answered a new voice, "but Bill and I ain't wearin' all black and walkin' around like death, with sunglasses on to boot. What'cha wear glasses like that at night for anyway? Other than hidin' your eyes as so people can't ID ya. If ya ask me, he looked meaner than a rabid dog."

"Well it's good that I'm not askin' then," snapped Jim. "Cut it out. I'm sure there ain't nothin' wrong with him. The man needed a bathroom."

"I'm just sayin'," Bill said with his hands held up in surrender.

"Yeah, sayin' you best get your gun ready cuz you're gonna need it," the other man mumbled then added, "He's probably in there right now getting his guns out to come out an' rob ya."

The bartender grunted, brushing them off. "You're nuts, the pair of ya. 'Sides, if he was gonna rob me, why didn't he just come in and do it? Ya big dolt."

There was a pause in the conversation, and Jarrett began replacing the towel because no alternative bandage was available. He eased his jacket back on, covering the blood on his shirt before bending to pick up his pack. Just as he reached for the door, he heard the man, Bill, talking again. Curious, he waited.

"No kiddin' you take a good look when he comes back out. Mark my words, if you slap some flames on that boy's head and put a chain in his hand, you just might have the makings of the devil's bounty hunter. What's his name?"

"Ghost Rider?" his friend replied.

"Yeah, that's him! That boy looks like bad news."

Jarrett couldn't help but smirk at the irony of the aging man's comment. He was, after all, a bounty hunter of sorts, and the leader of The Faction was certainly devilish.

He turned the knob and exited the bathroom to see all three men staring at him once again. Jarrett could almost see the two blustering men picturing him with a flaming head. Bothered by the attention, but not showing it, he approached them. He laid a hundred on the scarred wood. "A bottle of whiskey," he ordered gruffly.

Without a word, the bartender moved to grab a bottle of Jack from the shelf and a cup for drinking. He set both down, the glass clattering as he did. He moved to get change, but Jarrett stopped him, "For two of your cleanest towels, and you can keep the rest." Puzzled, the bartender drew his eyes together, scrutinizing him. "No questions." Jarrett said sharply.

Skeptical, but willing to take the extra fifty, he popped the money in the till and leaned down to grab the requested towels. While his back was turned, Bill and his friend watched the exchange with avid interest and speculation.

Jarrett looked at the pair of men. He couldn't resist the urge to give these boys something to really gossip about. He tipped his sunglasses down and let the wolf come out just enough to turn his eyes a glowing crimson. The maneuver was quick, and they barely saw it, but the jaws of both men practically hit the floor. Disbelief and fear covered their faces, and they simultaneously leaned back in their chairs away from Jarrett.

The bartender straightened and set the two towels down on the counter next to the whiskey. Jarrett snatched up the bottle and towels, leaving the glass behind. He gave a curt nod to the three men and exited, knowing he gave them a story to talk about long after tonight. As he left, he heard both men scrambling to tell the bartender what they saw, in disjointed words, talking over one another. He also heard the bartender bark out, "That's it boys. I think you've had enough. No more drinks tonight."

Jarrett slunk to yet another alley behind the bar and sought shelter in the shadows. Last night, hiding in an alley hadn't worked. He'd been attacked by a nasty little half-demon leech that trailed him. The little monster was barely 20. It was ridiculous really. They were sending anyone they could after him, and Jarrett knew it was to wear him down. Given enough attacks, even he couldn't fight forever. They would succeed eventually.

Sighing, he leaned against the aged brick wall and lifted the bottle of whiskey to look at it longingly. Jarrett twisted the cap and smelled the rich amber liquid, bitter that such things didn't work on him. He would have welcomed any relief from his troubles.

Steeling himself, he lifted his shirt and pulled off the used towel. He poured whiskey over his stab wound and grunted through his teeth as he felt the painful sting of alcohol bite into the infection. The liquid ran down his side and soaked his clothing, leaving the scent of whiskey in his head as he repeated the process. After he finished, Jarrett gently pressed one of the new towels to his side. Grimacing, he held it there, breathing through clenched teeth.

He cursed, not for the first time, and lamented how exhausted he was. He knew it must be close to midnight at this point. The infection was taking a huge toll on him. Coupled with the tiny snippets of sleep he had, his body was heavy and worn. At the moment, he felt every decade of his long life. Jarrett gave into the weariness and slid down the wall to the cold, filthy ground behind a dumpster.

With his knees bent, he leaned forward to rest his head on one arm while the other still held the towel in place. "Just a few minutes," he whispered. It took less than one minute for him to pass out completely.

The Price of Knowing

Jim McFarland finished counting the till and began cleaning up as his nightly routine demanded. He had been running his little, nondescript bar for almost twenty years, and like every other night, he cleaned mugs, wiped counters, and emptied the trash. It was a pattern that was as simple and natural as breathing. In recent years, his routine included thinking, *I'm too old for this,* and he considered retiring for the hundredth time that year. Ultimately though, he knew he would be too bored and lonely if he retired. This was home, and the work gave him comfort.

He finished collecting the trash and headed out into the alley to toss the two bags. As he stepped out toward the dumpster, he unexpectedly found himself tripping and almost falling over a huge heap of a man lying at his feet. He stumbled and danced with an agility that defied his years until he regained his balance. Then he turned to see what homeless twit had camped out in his alley this time.

The sight before Jim left him stunned, and he dropped the bulging trash bags. For almost a full minute, Jim could do nothing but stare, dumbstruck, at the big biker that graced his bar earlier and left his two best friends stuttering about red demon eyes.

He moved cautiously toward the prone figure. "Hey there, boy. You all right?" he asked, but there was no response. Jim tried kicking the toe of a heavy boot next, but he still received no response. Thinking the stranger may possibly be dead, for he certainly looked pale enough to be, Jim crouched down to shake the man. When he got closer, something drew his attention to the man's middle. The open leather jacket revealed a dark stain covering the black shirt, and a bulge lay underneath. Jim had been in enough bar fights to recognize blood when he saw it, even if it was dark.

He carefully reached over to where the wound must be and eased the t-shirt up. Jim immediately understood why the man had

C.B. Haight

paid so much for the towels. One towel had been tucked into the waistband of his jeans, and the once bleached-white towel displayed a dark, brownish-red stain from blood that soaked into its fibers.

As he peeled back the towel to inspect the wound, a hand gripped his wrist with brutal force. Startled, Jim looked up with wide eyes and found unnatural golden orbs staring back at him. Despite the obvious pain in them, Jim saw a cold, lethal glint as well, and didn't doubt that the young wanderer could easily kill a man—even in his current pitiful state. "Easy there," Jim reassured.

"What are you doing?" Jarrett demanded between his teeth.

"Just tryin' to help ya, son. Come on inside and let me have a look at that wound."

Shaking off the haze in his head, recognition slowly came back to Jarrett. He released the old bartender's hand and began moving to stand up. He barely managed it. The bartender tried to steady him, but Jarrett pushed him aside. He stumbled forward like a slobbering baby taking his first step. Again, the old man caught him. "Come on, son. Let's go. I have a cot in the back you can lie on."

"Can't..." Jarrett mumbled, shaking his pounding head as he tried to straighten once more.

"You can barely stand. Let's get ya inside, and ya can rest a bit. You'll feel better for it."

Jarrett looked down into Jim's kind, brown eyes and knew he really had no choice. Despite the fact that staying in one place too long was risky, he couldn't keep going like this. The wounded werewolf could barely move. His tongue felt thick and heavy, and his head continued throbbing relentlessly.

Finally conceding, Jarrett inclined his head toward the bar. They moved forward together with slow, staggering steps. Jarrett leaned on the old man more than he would have liked to. They stumbled in, making their way through the back room to a little office that held the meager cot, as promised, against one wall. Jim kept it here for those extra late nights, times when the storms kept him from getting home, or for the occasional over-indulger in the bar.

The Price of Knowing

Jim helped ease Jarrett down onto the cot and heard him groan in pain as his body bent. Once his guest was lying down, Jim left, and Jarrett closed his eyes. He heard movement in the other room but ignored it. He must have drifted out again for a few minutes, because the next thing Jarrett knew, he felt his shirt being lifted once more. Instinctively, his hand shot out to grab the person touching him. "Leave it," he snarled.

"Not likely, boy," Jim retorted unafraid. "It needs to be tended. Let me have a look and clean ya up," he finished in a fatherly tone.

Jarrett stared at him for a moment before releasing his grip on the old man's hand, relaxing again. He closed his eyes and tried to ignore the pain of having the inflamed gash examined. He felt the towel being pulled from tender skin and heard the bartender suck in a breath when he saw the damage.

"You need a doctor, or better yet, a hospital!" Jim exclaimed.

Opening his eyes, Jarrett replied firmly, "No doctor."

"Are you mad, boy? This is gonna kill you before too much longer. This cut is deep."

"It will heal," Jarrett insisted.

"Boy, you must be nine kinds of stupid. This stinks of infection," he replied as he pressed a warm, wet cloth to puckered skin. When Jarrett didn't wince or flinch, he looked at it more closely. "Whoever did this to you wanted ya dead, and it seems to me, they might get their wish if ya don't get help."

With his eyes closed, Jarrett couldn't help but acknowledge the accurate assessment with a grunt. He began drifting again and tried to force himself to pay attention.

"Ya need stitches."

"No hospital," Jarrett mumbled weakly.

Jim sighed. Resigned, he continued cleaning the angry slash in the stranger's side. "It's your life then," Jim relented. "You can stay here tonight, and then we'll see what's what in the mornin'." When he didn't hear a reply, Jim looked at Jarrett's face and realized he

~ 87 ~

had passed out again. Shaking his head in disbelief, Jim shifted from cleaning to bandaging the wound as best he could.

It went against his own way of thinking, but Jim respected the wish to avoid any doctors. Jim always figured a man's business was his own. He just hoped the boy would rethink it in the morning.

After he finished dressing the injury, Jim moved to his desk and began to balance his books. His eyes became heavy, and he propped his legs up on the desk to prepare for an uncomfortable night in the chair.

Sleep overtook him, and when his bobbing head and aching back eventually forced him awake, it was 5:38 a.m. He looked over to check on his surprise patient, half expecting to find him dead, and realized that the cot was empty. The biker was gone, and in his place, the blanket lay folded with one of his own envelopes resting on top. He swung his legs down from his desk, ambled over, and snatched up the envelope. Upon looking inside, he found $200 cash and "Thanks" written on a post-it.

"Well I'll be," he muttered to himself and went about his daily chores, wondering who the mysterious man was.

Niall tried to focus on what the pathetic man before him was saying, but he got caught up noticing the underling's weaknesses. His face was pockmarked from scarring caused by acne long ago, and his balding head often glistened with sweat. He wore small wire frames on his sharp-angled nose, and he spoke in a whiny, nasal tone instead of commanding the authority of the position he held. It was almost sickening to look at a creature such as the one standing in front of him, knowing his origins.

Niall often had to tolerate these things with mild disgust, but today, in his current mood, it was almost unbearable. As his influence grew over the years, so did his impatience with mortal imperfections. Now that he knew what true power was, he found dealing with humans repulsive—especially when they looked like this.

His aide was a weak, needy kind of man who repeatedly looked for someone else to save him. There was a time in Niall's life when he would have helped the man, but he had learned since then. He had learned the value of real power. Niall smirked, *Stupid humans, always seeking a hero to save them from problems of their own making. Pathetic!*

Currently, this man served Niall's purposes, and while filling a specific need, he remained ever obedient and eager to please. He would outlive his usefulness, as they all did, but Niall would put up with his shortcomings until then.

"Sir, did you hear what I said?" the pitiful human, Victor, dared question.

Niall tipped his head at a curious angle but said nothing.

"Three of the five have not reported for two days, and any attempts to reach them have been unsuccessful," he repeated.

Already knowing this, Niall nodded and answered coldly, "That is unfortunate."

"You're not upset?" Victor asked, clearly bothered by Niall's indifference to the death of those sent to hunt Jarrett.

Niall gave him a sinister smile. "I hardly believed killing him would be so simple," he assured. "It is a matter of wearing him down. Anyone who does not succeed is merely fodder and of no value to me."

Realizing the weight of his own accountability, Victor turned to leave, but Niall stopped him, "Wait." The pasty man twisted. "It is past time we dealt with the woman. This should be enough to get you started." Niall waved his hand, and a file appeared on the desk. "Find her, and deal with it. Send whomever you wish." Victor picked up the file and went to leave once more. As he opened the

C.B. Haight

door, Niall commanded in a tone full of dark promises, "Quickly, this time. I tire of waiting."

"Yes, sir," his assistant replied somberly, and ducked out to do his master's bidding.

CHAPTER 8

As the group returned to the house, they went to the comfortable parlor to discuss what happened. Cade laid the sleeping Collett on the couch, and Jeffery and Cynda rested in a chair. By unspoken agreement, they patiently waited for Jeffery to regain his strength. While they waited, Jenny bustled in with coffee, herbal tea, and a tray of fresh baked muffins. Cade watched from his perch on the edge of the couch by Collett as Jeffery practically inhaled three of the muffins.

More than twenty minutes later, and still slightly pale, Jeffery stood. "I can wake her now so we can talk," he said.

Nodding his assent, Cade stood and moved only as far as necessary for Jeffery to work. Releasing a calming breath to center himself, Jeffery bent over Collett. He waved his hands over her face, snapped his fingers, and her eyes fluttered open. He moved out of the way so Cade could help her sit up, and a worried Jenny bustled over to put a cup of warm tea in her hands.

Returning to his seat, Jeffery began the conversation, "I know that Cynda, Cade, and I saw most of what Collett saw, but I think we should go over it for Nate and Rederrick."

"I thought I was the only one there with her," Cade stated.

"No, it kinda works like electricity. We were a conduit. Her thoughts passed through us via you because we were magically linked, but we get a muted version. That's why it's blurry," Jeffery explained.

"All right then, who wants to give Nate and me the whole story?" Rederrick asked.

"I think Collett should, since it was the clearest for her," suggested Cynda.

Collett nodded, and brushing her hair away from her face, began to recount the events for everyone. She told them how she thought he must be in a city of some type because of the surroundings, and that Jarrett still believed she was a dream.

When they discussed his physical condition, she informed them he was fighting a fever and his side was burning. She explained that no matter how he moved it hurt him. Cade looked away as she described his injuries in detail, and she sensed his frustration. She understood it bothered him that she also felt the pain.

Collett changed the subject by reciting her conversation with him and finishing with his intentions to go be with *her*, whomever that may be.

"That's a bit of a letdown then. We're no better off now than we were before that whole light show, are we?" Nate observed.

Jeffery held up a hand as he finished off a fourth muffin. "We know where he is going, or at least one of us does."

Cade drew his brows together quizzically, so Jeffery went on as he brushed his hands together to get rid of any crumbs clinging to them. "It was a spell cast to determine his location, and the magic I evoked wouldn't have ended until we got that information. Blood magic is dangerous because it lacks the control most other magic's have. You can't just start and stop it with will alone. The caster must set and meet certain parameters."

"And if we didn't meet them?" Cade asked darkly.

"It would have drained all my strength until there was none left," he replied easily, as if it was obvious.

Nobody said anything for a long time. His revelation was too unexpected, and they didn't know how to respond. Jeffery acted as if he evoked such magic often, and it was no big deal that he placed his life in danger when he did so.

"Collett and Cynda too?" Cade inquired, irritated that Jeffery hadn't told them sooner.

"No, Collett and Cynda were connected through me. If my heart stopped, the spell would have released them. I told you I would not hurt them, and I meant it," Jeffery declared with conviction as he met Cade's accusing eyes.

Cynda felt the need to refocus the conversation before anyone thought too much on Jeffery's proclamation. She made a mental note to discuss it with him later. "So, we should know about where he is, but how do we figure out who knows what he meant? I would think it is one of you three, because you've had personal contact with him in the past," Cynda finished, indicating Collett, Jeffery, and Cade.

Jeffery nodded, "It's Collett."

"Why Collett?" Rederrick asked.

"Because Collett was the connection, and his words were a reference to someone she knew. Jarrett didn't know the rest of us could see him, or that we were even there. He was speaking only to her."

Everyone looked to her, and she looked down at her hands to avoid their attention. "Only one thing comes to mind," she paused, "I don't have my memories back clearly, but I told you all about his memory of me being with him when he was a boy. The details were too personal to share with you, but it seems in light of his current situation, privacy takes a place in the background."

~ 93 ~

Cade felt a weight of apprehension settle on his chest.

"I should tell you first, that my memories have mixed with his, so it is hard for me to distinguish them. I don't like thinking about it because the emotions are mixed together as well. The emotions are, for me, the strongest part of it.

"The flashes I had the night Jarrett took me started with him trapped in a burning house. I had dreams about it before, but I never understood them until I connected to Jarrett. Sometimes in the dreams I didn't save him, and everything kept changing as I tried. With Jarrett though, when I touched him, I could see myself through his eyes. I saw myself helping him from that burning cottage in Pennsylvania. He couldn't have been any older than thirteen, maybe fourteen.

"Since connecting to him that night, I've had more dreams. I understand that he was in the house because people in the village nearby thought he was a demon." Collett steeled herself for what would come next. "The villagers also accused a woman named Rowena of being a witch. She was with him. Jarrett was struggling with his new change to a werewolf. His temper was short, and the people in the village witnessed some of his changes first hand."

She paused and met Cade's eyes. "It was horrid what they did to them. I cannot even begin to describe it, and though he was still a boy, he suffered more than anyone should ever have to." She purposely left out the details of Rowena's and his torture and how Rowena's death broke the small, confused boy that was once Jarrett.

Cynda sucked in a breath. "How horrible." The mother in her cried out for the little boy who saw the worst side of mankind, and Collett felt the strength of her compassion.

"He was twelve. We were big for our age, but he was twelve," Cade uttered solemnly. They all drew their eyes from Collett to focus on him. "That's when I changed for the first time, so it's likely he did too. Our werewolf lineage caused us to be much taller and stronger than other boys our age."

Collett nodded. "I can't always sort it out clearly. It's still very vague. I believe Rowena to be his mother, but he never called her that. He always called her by name."

"That's because she wasn't," replied Cade. "Our real mother died to protect us. Her name was Lyndell, or so I was told by Merilynn, the woman who raised me. She wouldn't allow me to call her Mom either. She told me she couldn't replace my mother and never wanted to, so I called her Aunt Merilynn. She told me a lot about the day I was born and how the village wanted to kill us because they thought our mother was a witch.

"She was—a witch I mean—and Merilynn too. Later, after my first change, she explained that being werewolves was the true reason they sought to kill me that day. The village had seen werewolves roaming in the woods around that time, most likely my father's pack. That's how they used to do it then. Werewolves stayed in packs, some still do for protection and control purposes. They do it to keep each other in check, and it is natural to the animal in them.

"Merilynn explained my birthmark and how rumors about my mother being a witch were spreading even before my birth. Then when I was born, the frightened midwife saw my mark and strange eyes and ran screaming for help. Merilynn told me they saw it as a curse from Satan.

"She didn't tell me of Jarrett. I never knew about him until much later, and it is likely Rowena told him similar things. Merilynn was fiercely loyal to our mother and her memory. I suspect the same of Rowena."

"She would have to be to take a werewolf baby from a self-proclaimed witch back in those days," Cynda agreed.

Something pricked at the back of Collett's mind, but it was gone before she could grasp it. She looked to Cade. "In any case, I don't understand how or why, but I was there that day. I saved him from the fire. I would only save him though, and she died that night.

~ 95 ~

He hated me for that his whole life. He still does in a way. He blames himself too."

"Would only save him?" Cynda questioned.

"I don't know the reason, but I didn't, or wouldn't, go back for her. He begged me to, and I refused."

"So, you think he's going to where she died?" Nate interjected.

"It's the only *her* I can think of."

"It makes sense," Rederrick added. "To him, that's home, and where does a person go when things are at their worst?"

"Home," Cade confirmed.

Collett pronounced sadly, "I think it's more than that. Jarrett thinks he is going to die. That's where he wants to be when he does. We're out of time, Cade. He's giving up."

CHAPTER 9

Early the next morning, Cade was on the phone in the office trying to make the necessary arrangements for Nate and himself to go to Pennsylvania to find Jarrett. When Collett walked in, Cade was distracted momentarily as his heart skipped a beat. Smiling to his wife, he continued talking, and Collett picked up on his end of the conversation.

"Yeah, well I'm not really sure how long."

He paused, listened, and then replied, "I know, but I'd really owe you." His smile spread to a grin, and he laughed, "All right then, we'll call it even."

This time, his pause was longer, and as he listened, he watched Collett walk over to him. He grabbed her hand and pulled her into his lap. "I swear I'll do my best to have you home by Mardi Gras. I wouldn't want to face your wrath if you missed that," he said.

Now that she was closer, Collett heard a quick, feminine laugh come from the other end. "I'm counting on it *Mon'Ami*. If not, I'll be dragging that new wife of yours down here to The Big Easy and show her how to really party."

~ 97

"I'll bet," he dryly replied.

"I'll see you tomorrow," she told him.

"I'll pick you up at the airport then. See you soon." Cade hung up the phone.

Curious, Collett asked, "Who was that?"

"That was Delphene, a friend of mine in New Orleans. She's going to break tradition to come and help out here while I'm gone looking for Jarrett."

"Delphene?"

"She's…well, she's like me."

"Like you?"

In reply, he raised his brows and smiled wickedly.

"Oh, like you, so she's…"

"Yes, like me," he repeated, confirming Delphene's animal side.

"Do we really need more help? I don't want to keep putting more people in the middle of this mess. Rederrick and Nate seem to have it under control, plus we have Jeffery."

Cade sighed and stood with her. "I'm taking Nate with me, and Rederrick can't be at it 24 hours a day. Even with Jeffery, it makes me nervous. I need to be sure you're all safe here."

"And Delphene—she can do that? Reassure you that we're safe?"

"I still hate leaving, but yes, this helps. Even though we haven't been under attack, I need to know you have protection. Deep in my gut, I know this is far from over. In fact, I think we are just getting started. Rederrick agrees with me, and when I get back, I think it would be best if we go somewhere else."

"Jarrett too?"

He hesitated a second but nodded. "If he'll come."

"Cynda and Rederrick?"

Cade shrugged. "We'll see, but I don't know. They would like to stay, especially with Christmas coming."

"Where will we go?"

~ 98 ~

The Price of Knowing

"I'm thinking about getting out of the country."

"I don't have a passport."

He shrugged. "We'll work it out."

Collett smiled at him. "You're the boss."

Cade looked down into her eyes and felt a stirring inside. She was everything to him. It didn't matter that their time together had been so short. He moved his hand to her neck and pulled her to him for a kiss. Nipping playfully at her lip, he felt her grin against his lips. They pressed closer together, their lips in sync. Cade savored the sweet flavor of her. Feeling a powerful, consuming need, he gripped her tighter as the kiss became more fevered. Collett's slender, warm fingers gripped his elbows, erasing any space between them.

"Ahem."

Reluctantly, Cade broke away from the kiss, but refused to break the connection and held her hypnotized in his intensely heated gaze. "You need something, Nate, or do you simply like tormenting me?"

Collett turned her head to see Nate in the doorway. He smiled, and her flushed cheeks turned an even brighter shade as she blushed.

"Actually, I need a minute, but torturing you a bit is an added bonus," he said lightly.

Collett turned around completely, and still craving the contact with her, Cade rested his hand on her shoulder.

"Nate," Collett greeted.

"Hello, Mrs. Werren," he teased. "That's still going to take a little getting used to. I'll have to keep saying it so I can adjust. Cade, married?" He shook his head in mock disbelief.

"What is it you need?" Cade asked.

"I set up everything for tomorrow night like you wanted," he said, smiling.

Collett released a breath. Whether it was melancholy because he was leaving or relief that he was finally going for Jarrett, Cade was unsure, but he remained focused. "Are you still going with me?"

~ 99 ~

"Yeah, you think I'm going to let you fly that plane?" he quipped.

"You're a pilot?" Collett asked.

"Yes ma'am. What you see before you is a born and bred Air Force brat," he replied with a mock salute. He shrugged and turned serious. "My dad was anyway. He died about a year before my mom, and then, after my mom was killed, Cade took me to a family that was also in the Air Force, thinking it would be easier for me. When I was old enough, I picked up where my dad left off—for a few years anyway."

"All right then," Cade interjected, "We'll head out tomorrow and hope we can find him before any more of The Faction's flunkies do."

Collett looked back to him. "You will," she said confidently, as the alternative was unacceptable. Cade squeezed her shoulder, and she placed her hand on his. The separation would be hard for both of them, but they knew doing nothing would be worse.

That night, Collett sat on the edge of the bed in her silk robe and rubbed lotion into her freshly showered legs, when Cade came in. He stopped and could do nothing more than stare at the sight of her. Still massaging, she looked up at him. "When will you leave?"

"Huh?" He shifted his gaze from her long legs to her eyes, and her question registered. "Oh, tomorrow afternoon. I'll pick Delphene up around nine and show her the ropes. We're scheduled to head out about four." Moving closer to her with a grin, he took the lotion from her hand and placed it on the bedside table. "Let's not talk about that right now."

"Okay. What exactly would you like to discuss instead?" she asked playfully.

He pushed her backward on the bed and leaned over her. "I really would like to not discuss anything." Her leg came up and her robe opened, exposing her supple skin. "I think it's time for you to get out of this robe." He softly ran his hand over her leg, sending shivers through her.

"Okay, I'll get dressed then," she teased, while nudging his chest and moving to rise halfheartedly.

Holding her down with one hand, he used the other to move further up the soft skin of her leg. "Maybe in a bit," he mumbled and kissed her knee. "Or maybe not," he taunted and grinned with a sexy gleam in his eyes. His hand sent chills through her as it progressed until it reached her hip, and he heard her sigh. Cade grinned in satisfaction. "For now, let me help you with this." He reached for the sash that held the robe closed and tugged on the tie, watching as it slipped free.

Upon loosening the robe, he saw a sliver of skin on her belly and gently skimmed his fingers over her warm flesh, further widening the opening. Enjoying the rare intimate moment together, they lay back on the bed and indulged in the sensation of shared love and sensual touch.

Later, feeling satisfied and warm after their time together, Cade rolled to Collet's side. He pulled her close so she could lay on his chest and basked in the feel of her skin against his. He gently caressed her back for a time until he noted the abandoned bottle of lotion on the table. Reaching across her, he picked up the cream and sniffed near its top. He grinned and said happily, "So this is where it comes from."

"What?"

"Your scent."

"Oh," she replied quietly.

"Have I ever told you it's what first drew me in?" He pulled her wrist up to his nose and inhaled a deep breath.

Her lips twitched. "No, you never have."

"You were standing by your apartment building, waiting for the limo that would bring you here. You looked so nervous then. I wondered what could be wrong, and I watched you for a while.

Then, I couldn't look away. That dress—You—" He shook his head. "No man alive could have looked away. When the wind blew and carried your scent over to me, I was lost."

She lifted her head and propped it up to look curiously at him.

"It's true. You have the most intoxicating scent I've ever come across, and you are the most captivating woman I have ever seen. I thank God that Rederrick brought you here that day and told me to look out for you."

"You believe in God?" she asked genuinely.

His lips tilted up in a crooked grin. "Yes, I do. Why are you so surprised?"

"I… I don't know. It's just something I didn't really consider. You're a…"

"Because I'm a demon?" he finished for her.

"You're not a demon."

"Legend and myths say otherwise, but Merilynn wouldn't have me believe it. It didn't matter that she was a witch—she believed wholeheartedly in God, Heaven, and Hell. She taught me that consequences, whether good or bad, are our own design." He grinned fondly.

"She would say, 'We are what we make ourselves, and even the most normal of men can be a demon if they choose to behave as one.' Then she'd remind me that we are all a part of the Divine Creator's design, and that He does not make mistakes. Judgment is for him alone.

"She taught me all of that and more. Experience has shown me she was right. Though, sometimes, I had to learn the hard way.

"Plus, I've witnessed all kinds of events and miracles to reinforce those beliefs, incidents like you coming here, to us, when you could have ended up in a million other places. To me, that was not mere luck. It was meant to be."

Collett lay back down and pondered his words. She trailed her finger over his chest with a smooth, soft touch. "What was she like?"

"Merilynn?"

She nodded in reply.

"She was kind and loving, though she had a nasty temper," he chuckled softly. "You didn't cross her without feeling her wrath, but she was also quick to forgive at the same time." His smile widened as memories came to him. "She believed in justice, balance, and that education was the key to all of it. Even back then, in a time where many didn't bother to learn to read or write, she insisted we knew how. Even more, she taught us to stand for what's right."

"Us?"

"She got married when I was two and bore six other children," he answered as he absently twined his fingers in her hair.

Collett smiled and curled into him tightly. She listened as he talked about Merilynn and his long-deceased family.

He spoke for a long time, telling her all about them. They helped him to blend in, and Merilynn trained him to control his animalistic instincts. He described Merilynn's patient husband, Conner. He was an Irishman who believed in magic, fairies, and the like, making him the perfect match for Merilynn.

Every memory Cade shared warmed her. He spoke as if it all happened yesterday, instead of more than two centuries before. She closed her eyes and pictured the strong, confidant woman with compassionate, dark-brown eyes and a little boy sitting with her—learning to read by candlelight.

"If she didn't tell you about Jarrett, how did you find him?" Collett asked drowsily.

An unbidden memory flashed through Cade's mind...

The man on the rock kept his back turned, but Cade could smell the scent of wild beast within him. It was a scent he would never forget. Despite being in the form of a man with long black hair, Cade knew this was the werewolf he was hunting.

The man spoke with a deep voice, "I knew you would come eventually."

Surprised, Cade asked, "You did?"

"Yes. I have been waiting a long time to meet you,"

Cade was not sure what to say, so he kept silent.

Then the man on the rock stood. With his keen eyesight, Cade could see he was about his same height, same build. He looked a little leaner, but his muscles were sharp. Cade knew if this came to blows, it would not be an easy fight to win.

The man turned to face Cade. "Yes, I have been waiting a long time to meet you, brother."

Before he could answer, Collett sat up. "He found you. He was looking for you!" she exclaimed.

He sat up with her, intrigued. "You saw my memories." It was a statement, not a question.

"Did I? I wasn't even trying, and it was so clear—much clearer than it has been for others. It was almost like…"

Cade waited, and when she didn't continue, he prompted, "like…"

Her brows pinched together in thought. "It was like with Jarrett but not as strong or as painful. It almost felt like my memory too."

"It couldn't have been. Jarrett and I were the only ones there. You said that when you remembered saving Jarrett, you saw yourself there."

"I suppose," she hesitated. "It felt different somehow."

"It's simply coming easier to you, that's all," he assured.

She nodded absently.

Tired of the serious conversation, and knowing this was their last night together before he went hunting for Jarrett, Cade pulled on her arm. "Come here," he growled playfully and maneuvered her beneath him once more. She laughed lightly as he pressed down on

The Price of Knowing

her and nuzzled her neck. She ran her hands up his back to lace her fingers into his thick hair.

He began teasing her with his lips and teeth, and she giggled. He raised his head to look at her and caressed her cheek. Then he watched in horror as her eyes suddenly rolled back and she stiffened unnaturally.

Collett cried out in terrible pain, and her body convulsed.

CHAPTER 10

Cade yanked his hand back as if it was burning. Shocked and with fear coursing through him, he knew she couldn't see him anymore. Her pretty, iridescent eyes twitched back and forth.

She convulsed a second time. Cade's heart rate increased. She moaned, pulled away from him into the fetal position, and pressed a hand to her shoulder.

"Run," she pleaded in a painful, choked gasp. "You have to run!"

In the recesses of his mind, Cade heard pounding on his door and voices in the hall, but he ignored them and wrapped his arms around Collett, pulling the covers up around them when she shivered. "Shhh, I've got you. Come back to me. Come on baby, come back." He noted the color in her cheeks was gone, leaving her ghostly pale, and felt panic creeping in.

Cynda used magic to open the lock, bursting through the door with Rederrick on her heels. "Cade, what is going on? What happened?"

"I don't know," he answered fearfully.

~ 106 ~

The Price of Knowing

"Is she dreaming again?" asked Rederrick as Cynda reached down and placed a hand over Collett's brow.

"No, she was awake. We were…she was wide awake, and she…" he muttered. Unwilling to look away from the sight of his wife in such a state, he laid his forehead to hers and whispered again, "I've got you." His worry was so consuming that Cynda felt a pang in her chest for him.

"Run, Jarrett! There're too many," Collett called weakly, crying now. "Run you idiot!" Then she went completely limp, her eyes fluttered closed, and her breath left her.

Cade cursed his brother and shook her slightly. "Collett! Come on, come back."

Nothing happened. He rolled her onto her back again, praying he would find a pulse while Cynda checked her pupils. He was getting ready for resuscitation when she sucked in a deep, gasping breath, as if rising from deep water. Her heavy lids slowly opened.

"She's coming back," Cynda voiced with hopeful relief.

It took some time to focus. When she did, she turned and clung to Cade sobbing, "Cade! You have to go! You have to go! You have to help him. He won't make it this time!"

Cynda took control while he held her, "Rederrick, go and get Jeffery. Tell him to meet us downstairs! Cade, I'll go find Nate. You two get dressed." Cade finally looked up, and she met his worried eyes. "Hurry! I have an idea, and I am guessing we don't have much time." Then she darted from the room.

Before Cade could move to help her, Collett began scrambling out of his arms to dress. He stood and watched her as she pulled out clothes. Her face was sheet white, and he could see she was favoring her shoulder as another ghostly wound plagued her. He hated seeing this, seeing her hurt. His worry morphed into frustration.

"Why him? Why now?" he couldn't help but ask as he reached for his own clothing.

She turned to him, wiping at her wet cheek. "What?"

~ 107 ~

C.B. Haight

"Why Jarrett? Why is this happening? Did you ever dream of him before? I mean, he must be pretty important to you to have this connection to him."

"Cade."

"Did you?"

Even though his words sounded like an accusation, she knew they weren't. He only wanted to understand, but she didn't have any explanations. In truth, she shared his concerns. "No, not that I can remember, but you know things are different now. I didn't know about my powers either."

He sighed heavily and began to dress. "I know, but I don't like this. This link or whatever you call it. It's getting worse." He paused and noted she hesitated mid-movement as she readied to put her shirt on. Then, when she pulled the sweater over her head and tried to hide a wince as she did, he felt the anger surface again. "Do you know how hard it is to see you go through this? I know he needs help, but what he's doing to you...pulling you in. Dammit, Collett, we were—" he gestured to the bed, "You were wide awake this time!"

She turned back to him, and he turned away while pulling his own shirt on. "Hold on a minute, Cade. He's not doing this on purpose. In fact, he's not doing it at all. It's me. I don't know how, but I understand that much. I'm the reason this is happening."

He shook his head.

"Cade?" she questioned desperately.

"Is that supposed to make me feel better?"

"We have to do this later," Collett insisted.

"Yeah," he said coldly as he grabbed his shoes and sat on the bed to put them on.

She moved to sit with him and laid a hand on his back. "There is no time to argue right now. Remember what you said about God and balance earlier. I must have the link for a reason, and eventually it will all make sense.

~ 108 ~

The Price of Knowing

"We should just be glad that this makes it possible to help him. I know you're worried about me, but Jarrett needs a miracle." He angled his head in her direction, listening. "You and I are going to find a way to give him one. Maybe, if we find him, it'll stop. I may even get more of my memories back."

Sighing, he looked at her fully, then took her hand and stared at her shoulder with a scowl, knowing it still hurt. "I can't stand to watch you suffer like this."

She forced a smile. "I promise I'm okay, but he's hurt and maybe even dying. We're out of time. Help him, and it will help me."

Seeing the fear in her eyes and knowing she was right whether he liked it or not, he nodded grimly. "Let's go." He pulled the door open and, looking to her, confessed, "I couldn't handle it if anything happened to you."

"I'm stronger than I look," she assured him with a half-smile, then pulled him out the door and down the stairs.

As they neared the den, Cade and Collett overheard Cynda questioning Jeffery. "Can it be done?" she asked firmly.

Jeffery looked over to them and answered hesitantly, "Possible but risky."

"What's possible?" Cade asked as Nate entered with Rederrick.

"Jeffery can blink. I have been thinking about a way to use it since he told me," Cynda explained.

"Blink?" Collett didn't understand.

"Jeffery can use magic to jump from one place to another, even over long distances. Cade could reach Jarrett instantaneously," Cynda told her.

"What are we waiting for? Send them now!" Collett insisted.

"I need to have been there before. I can't jump to a place I haven't seen. Do we even know where he is?" Jeffery supplied skeptically.

~ 109 ~

C.B. Haight

They all looked at Collett. She shook her head. "I can't be exact, and he may have left. I hope he did. He was severely outnumbered, and he's been shot."

Cade clenched his jaw to hold back his curse. He suddenly understood why she favored her shoulder. He couldn't help but wonder: if she kept feeling all of his brother's injuries, what would happen if his brother died?

Cynda stepped toward her. "Can you see it though? Do you remember what it looks like—the place, I mean?"

"Yes, I see it all very clearly," she replied softly.

Cade put his arm around her and lightly rubbed her back to comfort her. "What are you working up to Cynda?"

"If she can project what she sees to Jeffery, it would be as if it was his memory too, like in the glen when we all saw what she saw. Then Jeffery could blink there. Even if Jarrett isn't there anymore you'd be close enough to track him."

"How?" Cade questioned. "Jeffery can't track him and may pop right into a war zone. He may be good, but if it's as bad as Collett thinks… What then?"

"If it works, and I am not sure it will, I can take you with me. One extra traveler per trip. Like I said, it's risky. I may jump into the wrong place, or worse—into a wall," he muttered.

"Can't you go to him and bring him here instead? Then nobody gets hurt," Collett asked.

Jeffery looked apologetic. "It won't work. First, because I can't force him to come, and you can bet he won't trust me enough to do what I tell him. Plus, it takes a fair amount of concentration and energy to blink. If he's engaged in a fight, I won't be able to blink him out of it easily."

"How many times can you do it? How many trips before you lose too much energy?" Cade asked.

"Three, maybe four if I push it."

Cade nodded. "One for me, once back, and one to bring Nate if we need him."

~ 110 ~

The Price of Knowing

"Time's wasting," Nate replied.

"Can you do it, Collett?" Cynda asked, "Can you project it to him?"

"There is only one way to find out." She stepped toward Jeffery and held out her hands. Jeffery grabbed them, and she closed her eyes. Focusing on Jarrett and her newest vision, Collett tried to share what she saw. Instead, she projected emotions and physical pain.

Jeffery gasped and let go. "That's intense."

"I'm so sorry. I don't really have full control yet, and I've never projected images."

He waved it away and steadied himself. "Try again, but don't focus on the pain. Don't even focus on him. I don't need to see him. Think only about the place, not on who's there. I don't know if it helps, but when I use magic, I know what I want and focus only on that. You have to block everything else out. Know what you want to do, then do it. Don't hesitate."

"Okay, let's try again."

She did as Jeffery suggested and blocked everything but the place from her mind. She first focused on the dismal exterior of the dark warehouse she'd seen Jarrett escape into. Incomplete lettering stood out near the roofline where a business name once existed. She saw the crumbling, paint-chipped walls. Then she pictured the interior with everything in it. She saw the rusted metal staircase leading to the second floor, dirty and broken windows, and long beams and cross beams. She shared it all as quickly as she could, knowing how dire Jarrett's situation was. When she finished, she opened her eyes. "Did it work?"

He nodded, "I can see it. It might work." He took a few minutes to process it all carefully and then stepped back, brushed his hands together, and said to Cade, "All right then, let's take a ride and hope we land."

Determined to leave her on positive terms, Cade turned to Collett and kissed her cheek. "Keep the light on. We'll be back before you know it."

"Be careful."

"I'm stronger than I look," he said, copying her own words and winking at her. He then turned to Rederrick and Nate and advised, "Be ready, Nate, in case we need you, and don't forget Delphene, old man. Tomorrow, at the airport."

"Got it," Rederrick replied, and Nate gave him a mock salute.

"Ready?" Jeffery asked.

Cade lifted a single brow and joked, "Do we hold hands?" Jeffery gave Cade a genuine smile for the first time.

"No hand holding," he chuckled and placed one hand on Cade's shoulder. He waved his other hand, and right before they blinked out, they heard Cade tease, "No parties while I'm gone."

They all stared at the empty space. All they could do now is wait.

The trip took a single second, but in that minute span of time, Cade felt a sharp tingling pain pull him inside and out. The transfer was quick, but terribly uncomfortable. Unfortunately, there was no time to adjust because, a few feet in front of them, a very large man stood with his back to them. The man turned and grinned, displaying his sharp, pointed demon teeth. There was a loud crash from somewhere in the distance, and Jeffery jumped, startled by the noise.

Cade growled low, claws began to form, and his eyes glowed. "Go! Get out of here!" he commanded Jeffery as he rushed the half-demon.

The sorcerer was transfixed for a short time as he watched Cade transform and engage the demon. His clothes ripped from his body, and he became a deadly monster of legend right before his very eyes. He'd seen Cade as a werewolf before, but he had never before witnessed the change from man to beast. In the past, he'd been busy defending against Cade, and Jeffery couldn't help but feel grateful that he wasn't the target of those sharp teeth any longer.

While Cade attacked the demon, Jeffery saw another figure emerge above them on the second floor. The stranger lifted his hand with a 45mm Glock aimed right at Jeffery's new ally.

Acting fast, Jeffery angled his hands up and cast his magic to force the man back, disrupting his aim. The gun discharged, and the bullet flew wide, right past Jeffery, pinging against the metal railing on the other side of the expansive space. With a deft movement, Jeffery gestured once more, pulling the man forward and knocking him back again, as if he was a puppet on a string. Slamming the assailant into the wall again, the sorcerer watched the gun fly from his grip and clatter on the stairs.

A sense of satisfaction filled Jeffery. He had never fought for anyone but himself, and he was surprised by the amount of loyalty he felt toward Cade. He prepared to jump back and retrieve Nate when another crash echoed in the distance. Reluctant to leave Cade alone, Jeffery hesitated.

The werewolf looked at him with blood-red eyes and snarled with a guttural, beastly voice, "GO!" Jeffery jerked his head in assent and forced himself to concentrate. In no time, he found himself back in Colorado with several wide eyes locked anxiously on him.

Putting a hand to the bridge of his nose, Jeffery squeezed his eyes tight to steady himself. He snapped, "Nate, hurry! We gotta go!" His body hummed and tingled as pinpricks of pain from the successive blinks faded. He'd expended a lot of energy already, and he was far from done. Tonight would push his limits, but he knew he would do whatever it took to help his new friends.

Nate stepped forward holding a heavy backpack. Jeffery finally opened his eyes and noticed that Nate had added a few things to his attire in the brief time he was gone. The warrior before him was sporting a black bulletproof vest and carried two deadly daggers within scabbards strapped to his waist.

Jeffery looked at the bag, curious about what it held. Nate, understanding his puzzled expression, responded, "Some essentials." He then looked to Collett, who stood watching with fear and worry in her eyes. "We'll be back before you know it," he reassured with a wink.

She nodded, but Jeffery felt a knot twist in his stomach. He wasn't so confident after seeing what awaited them. He took Nate's arm. "Get yourself ready. They already started without you," he warned. Jeffery then drew on the supernatural energy within him a third time, hoping it wouldn't be his last.

Collett stared at the empty space once more before saying, "He was afraid. I could feel it. It must be as bad as it felt in my vision."

"Don't worry. They're all good at what they do," Cynda said, as much to herself as to Collett. The worried women clasped hands, and Rederrick began to pace.

Jeffery and Nate appeared amongst complete chaos. Because Jeffery had been here once already, blinking in was easier to direct, so he chose to appear on the second floor this time. He hoped to be out of any direct combat upon materializing.

No such luck. Only two feet away from where they appeared was yet another armed man. If things were less tense, Jeffery might have laughed at him. It was the second man he'd seen with a gun, and the weapon still seemed out of place here, surrounded by demons and magic. Luckily, the sudden appearance of the two men shocked the gunman, and Nate easily disarmed and incapacitated him.

"You didn't say it was going to hurt," Nate accused while he zip-tied the unconscious man's hands.

Jeffery shrugged, looked over the railing for Cade, and replied, "Magic has a price."

"Maybe a little warning next time, huh?" Nate rose and followed Jeffery's line of sight.

Cade was flanked by two men. From several feet away a woman with thick, black hair shouted commands to them. "Finish the traitor!" she shrieked and began to moving her lips in a chant.

Nate acted on instinct developed from years of training. Vaulting over the railing, he fell the significant distance to the floor and rolled to absorb the impact. In a crouch, he swept out one leg, dropping the surprised woman on her rear.

Jeffery searched carefully for any sign of Jarrett. He noticed the half-demon Cade had attacked when they appeared together was lying bloody and still against the far wall. *Well, one down*, he thought, and moved to the stairs. Jeffery practically slid down them in his rush to search the warehouse. At the bottom, he darted toward a hallway on the other side of the massive space.

He stopped short when he saw a squat, balding man step through a side entrance that led outside. Four more burly men, whom Jeffery recognized as leech demons, followed the man, Victor. His eyes widened at the group, and fear churned in his gut.

These powerful demons were the source of vampire legends. They looked like men, except for their long, canine-like fangs, and they relished stealing and drinking blood from whomever they could in vicious and calculating ways. However, they were unable to turn others into leech demons. They also weren't the source of Jeffery's dread.

The bespectacled man possessed no special traits. He didn't command magic, wasn't part demon, and couldn't hold his own in a fight. He was however, as Jeffery knew, an important part of The Faction's upper management and one of the few who actually knew the leader's identity. Victor reported directly to the master himself, and even the newest Faction members knew to fear this portly man by association.

"Jeffery?" the bald man questioned. "This is a surprise. We thought you were lost to us." Jeffery glanced at his new friends, then back to the hostile party. "I see," Victor said, following his gaze. "Kill him as well," he commanded lazily.

The four vampire demons brushed past Victor, grinning. He knew they hated being directed by someone so weak, but would follow his orders as long as Niall continued to favor him.

Jeffery didn't hesitate any longer, as his will to survive took over. He threw out a burst of bright light to blind the men and sprinted across the room to warn Nate and Cade.

As Jeffery made his way back to his newfound friends, Nate was thrown into him. They clattered to the ground, grunting as air was forced from their lungs upon impact. Nate rolled off Jeffery and muttered, "Stupid, half-breed demons."

"That's not our only problem." Jeffery jerked his head toward the vampires.

Nate yanked his bag off his shoulders and looked back to Cade, and noted his situation was under control for now. "I guess it's time for the essentials then," he replied conspiratorially, and a grin spread across his face.

CHAPTER 11

Jarrett's breath left him as he was thrown against the wall. Sharp, burning pain stabbed his shoulder where the previous idiot shot him. His body was on fire, and every inch of him hurt. *Well, maybe not his toes,* he thought. As soon as that thought crossed his mind, the ugly, mindless demon he was battling stepped on his foot. Now every inch of his body hurt. He was in so much pain that he couldn't even force the change to fight back. He thought he heard a gunshot in another room, but before he could dwell on it, he was lifted and bashed against the wall so hard he felt tissue tear and bone break.

The demon pulled him forward, intending to repeat the action, but halted when his Russian leader interfered, "Cease!" He walked over to Jarrett and looked upon him with disdain. "Do you know, Hunter, it is said you killed my brother?" he asked with a thick heavy tongue from his native language. He drove his fist into Jarrett's wounded side as he hung in the demon's grasp. Jarrett's snarl rapidly turned to a groan as the fist ground deeper into his tender flesh.

C.B. Haight

"I wonder if it is true?" the Russian sorcerer continued casually, emphasizing the consonants like a man unused to speaking them in English.

A loud crash echoed from somewhere in the warehouse, but the man was unconcerned. This was, after all, a competition of sorts, and the prize was in his possession.

Jarrett's sensitive hearing picked out a familiar voice, but he wasn't sure if he imagined it. After all, imagining things kept happening to him a lot lately.

He couldn't focus as his eyes rolled back from the crippling pain in his side. He could barely breathe. Even Jarrett had limits, and he was beginning to think he had reached his.

Hanging there limply, understanding he was minutes from death, Jarrett considered keeping quiet to avoid added torment, but his stubborn nature wouldn't allow it. He forced his eyes open, glared at the Russian defiantly, and spat out, "Yven was weak and stupid. He deserved everything I gave him and more."

His enemy's expression turned cold, and Jarrett felt a shadow of a magic shock course through him. He groaned to keep up the façade and buy more time to think.

"Well, it is no matter. I was happy to hear you were…what is it, ah yes, game open," he sneered. Upon mixing up the idiom, Jarrett couldn't help but think that apparently stupidity ran in the family. "I waited years for this. You should have not upset Him. Now you will finally die, and I will get my revenge," he vowed.

When the Russian released his spell and his fist, Jarrett released a heavy breath of relief that wasn't feigned. Jarrett saw the owner of the familiar voice outside, past the doorway in the other room. While surprised, he now knew the voice he heard earlier wasn't imagined, and he may yet live another day after all. Relieved, he gathered what reserves he had left and tried to speak, but his voice was quiet, sounding so weak even he was surprised by it. "Mistake," he managed to murmur.

"What?"

"You made a mistake," he rasped.

"And what was that?" the sorcerer asked annoyed.

"You stopped the demon from killing me."

He laughed, "What will you do about it? You are practically dead already, and I will finish you now."

Jarrett lifted his head with a sinister grin covering his features. "You won't have time," he replied wickedly, and a renewed energy coursed through him.

Cade barreled into the room at full speed. The Russian's eyes widened with shock, and he back-peddled away from Jarrett. The black werewolf plowed full force into the demon holding Jarrett, knocking them all to the floor. An explosion rattled the walls of the building. Concussive sound waves rocked them, and smoke leaked its way in from the entrance.

For several minutes, Jarrett could do nothing more than lie still as he listened to Cade rip and tear into the demon. He half wondered why the sorcerer didn't finish him off. Wincing, he rolled slowly to get up, and a strong hand pulled on his arm. He instinctively jerked back with violent intent, but he stumbled into the wall and cursed instead.

"Not the bad guy here—I'm with *Rescues 'R' Us,*" the man stated as if it should make complete sense.

Jarrett looked up and scrutinized the man in front of him. He was young, by Jarrett's standards, but looked capable. Instead of fear, his eyes held an excited gleam, indicating experience and guts.

"I'm Nate, let's be friends. How 'bout we get the hell outta here?" he quipped rapidly and moved again to help Jarrett stand. This time, Jarrett actually let him.

They assessed the melee in the darkened room. Cade was still viciously locked in battle with the large, gray demon, and Jeffery gestured wildly as light arched from the Russian into him.

Nate carefully helped Jarrett to lean against the wall. "Hang tight a minute. I'll be right back," he said as he put a hard object in Jarrett's hand. Jarrett looked down and arched a single brow at the grenade. "In case we have any survivors from the other room," Nate replied with a smirk, and then he ran full speed to flank the Russian sorcerer.

Jarrett looked back to his brother, feeling an unexpected gratitude. Cade battled fiercely against the full-blooded greater-demon with a viciousness Jarrett could appreciate. Claws and teeth tore into the rubbery flesh, leaving gruesome, leaking wounds in their wake.

The demon smashed him against a brick wall hard enough to crack and split the framing and drywall. Before Cade could react, the behemoth repeated the action.

Cade's breath was forced from him, and he gasped in pain. His clawed animal hands dug into the demon's back as he clung to it in an attempt to reach its neck. He felt the crushing impact of each blow against his spine.

To make matters worse, the demon did not relent. It planted its feet and pushed with all the force it had, trying to crush the life out of Cade. The old, weakened wall began to give from the weight, and considering the condition of the long-abandoned structure, Cade began struggling to free himself, inflicting as much damage as possible as he did. He knew that if the wall gave, at least part of the ceiling would also collapse. He managed to clamp down his sharpened teeth on the demon's shoulder, near its neck. Satisfaction coursed through him when the thing opened its unnatural jaws and yowled in pain. It was short-lived though, as he felt the behemoth press against him harder.

A burst of light flooded the room from the battle between the sorcerers. In that blinding moment, Cade thought he saw a new enemy racing toward him. When things cleared, Cade realized the figure was a ragged and bloody Jarrett. He clamored up the opposite side of the demon and shoved something past the demon's serrated teeth into the wide hole created by the demon's painful bellowing.

"Get out of there!" Jarrett snapped urgently at Cade.

Cade wasted no time and worked himself free as the beast leaned forward, gagging on whatever was lodged in its throat. It swung its arms wildly at Jarrett as he made an attempt to escape the beast. The fleshy fists connected, and he was thrown to the floor.

Cade forgotten, the ugly creature stepped toward Jarrett as it continued to choke on the obstruction. Before it could reach him, there was a sickening, popping sound originating from the creature's throat. The beast's head exploded, leaving only a gruesome body behind. A split-second later, what was left of the creature dissipated into dust and scattered over the two brothers.

Cade scanned the room, seeking Jeffery and Nate. He found them easily, as they had finished with the Russian and hurried toward them. Cade then went to Jarrett, who tried rising from the floor, but completely drained of his waning strength, fell down to his knees. Cade bent down, offered Jarrett his fur covered hand, and pulled him up. "You look like hell," he growled grimly.

"Well, you're not so pretty either," his twin shot back before he passed out, leaving Cade to deal with his battered body.

"What next?" Nate questioned seriously.

Cade could only stare at him, not quite sure himself.

Minutes moved slowly and turned into an hour. For those left behind at the house, each minute felt eternally long as they waited to hear from Cade. With frayed nerves, Collett and Cynda passed time by practicing magic.

They heard Rederrick from time to time, pacing and grumbling. Both knew it bothered him to be here, out of the action, when Cade, Nate, and Jeffery might need him. He kept going from room to room in an unconscious routine. Jenny was the only one who slept, and only after she extracted promises from everyone to wake her the minute they knew anything.

C.B. Haight

With her eyes closed, Collett focused to control the fire she was manipulating. She increased the flame and pulled it back, using the practice to stretch her mental muscles. Over the last month, Cynda taught her the importance of repetition. Much like running gave a person more endurance, the more a person used the arcane arts, the stronger their will could become. This basic exercise with the flame helped Collett use her mind and stretch her limits, plus it kept her thoughts from wandering and worrying.

She heard Rederrick check his cell phone once again for missed calls and felt her own worry rise despite her distraction. Biting her lip, she concentrated and forced her flame to spread out in a wider circle and then contracted it into a tall, slim flame.

"Good. Collett, you're getting very good at this," Cynda encouraged. Her praise felt empty though, and Collett knew she was hardly looking at her. Rather, Cynda's attention kept drifting back to the phone in Rederrick's hand, hoping it would ring.

As if by some sort of telepathic command, the little black cell phone began to hum a standard tune. Jumping, Collett lost focus on her fire, and it flared wildly. She released the magic and rushed to follow Cynda to Rederrick's side.

He had already answered by then and put it on speaker so all could hear. "Go ahead, Nate," he stated firmly.

"We've got him," came Nate's clipped response from the other end of the line.

Collett felt relief rush through her and let out the breath she didn't realize she'd been holding. Cynda, equally relieved, placed a hand on her shoulder and squeezed.

"How bad?" Rederrick questioned.

"It's not good. We even had a visit from a man Jeffery calls Victor. Know him?"

Rederrick considered it. "Heard of him once. Don't know much."

~ 122 ~

The Price of Knowing

"Got out by the skin of our teeth. We've got a few bumps and bruises, but all of us made it out. That's what counts," Nate reported.

"And Jarrett?" asked Rederrick as he glanced at the two anxious women.

There was a slight pause. "He's in bad shape, not even conscious right now." Nate let go of a heavy breath. "He took a beating, that's for sure, but I'll know more after we find a safe place to hole up. We'll let you know. Cade says get some sleep, as we're likely safe enough for tonight."

"Nate—" Collett began.

"Don't worry, I'll tell him," Nate said, guessing her desire to tell Cade she loved him.

"Watch your backs then, and stay in contact," Rederrick warned.

"Same goes," replied Nate, and disconnecting the call, he followed his friends away from the warehouse.

The four men eventually made their way from the dilapidated building and out of the industrial district. As they did, Jeffery explained the significance of Victor's appearance. They knew Victor had escaped the blast because he was not among the wreckage. Which, unfortunately ensured that more of The Faction's glory-seekers would be on their heels, per his orders. They all understood they were not as safe as they proclaimed on the phone, and they had little time to figure out what to do next.

In the early hours of the morning, Cade sat on the edge of a bed in a substandard motel looking at his still unconscious brother, trying to figure out what to do with him. He was in bad shape and had barely stirred in the hours since they rescued him. Cade, on the other hand, didn't sleep at all.

Jeffery and Nate still slept in the adjoining room, but the sun had begun its ascent in the sky. Cade knew they had to get moving. He also knew they all needed more sleep, but they couldn't afford any more than the few hours they'd already taken. Somehow, The

~ 123 ~

Faction kept tracking Jarrett, or so he mumbled during his one and only semi-lucid moment, as they practically carried him here.

Resigned, Cade heaved himself from the bed and moved to the door that connected the two rooms. They left it open in case of attack, so he easily moved into the room and gently kicked the bed Nate occupied. "Time to go," he said simply.

To his credit, Nate, who slept fully dressed on top of the covers, jumped-up, dagger in hand, ready to fight. Seeing only Cade before him, he groaned and relaxed.

"Time to go," repeated Cade, to make sure Nate understood. He moved to the other bed and tried to similarly rouse Jeffery, whose reaction was the exact opposite of Nate. He barely moved. Cade had to physically shake him to get him moving.

"He's a little slow in the morning," Nate smirked as Jeffery rolled wearily out of the bed. "Needs his beauty sleep. Though, it doesn't seem to be working."

Jeffery didn't even reply. He was too tired to bother, but Cade grinned slightly, knowing well that Nate's teasing was his way of lightening the mood in the early hours of what was likely to be a long day. That was Nate's way.

"Well, let's go, Sleeping Beauty. We've got to make plans and get moving," Cade replied, playing along.

Jeffery rubbed his hands over his face and mumbled, "Coffee."

In response, as he left the room, Cade tossed one of the coffee packets offered by the motel to Jeffery. He still held his eyes closed, and it smacked right into the side of his head.

"Let's go, pretty boy," chuckled Nate as he followed Cade into the next room. His smile died when he walked in and watched Cade inspect the worst of Jarrett's injuries. "He's not healing," Nate observed.

"No," Cade confirmed.

"Silver?"

"Must be."

"What about the rest?" Nate asked.

The Price of Knowing

Cade glanced back at him and saw Jeffery finally stagger in. "His body can't keep up. We heal fast, but he has too many injuries. He hasn't had time to rest or deal with them. Some of these are days old, and this wound looks badly infected. That would slow things down." He replaced the bandage and stood. "At least that's my guess. I've never seen one of our kind in this bad of shape. At least, not still breathing."

"The shoulder?" Nate asked, already suspecting the answer.

"Silver, but new, probably last night. It went straight through. Doesn't look too bad yet."

"Not a good sign—that they know how to take you two down."

Cade shrugged.

"They make it their business to know someone's weakness," Jeffery added solemnly. He knew better than most how good they were at exactly that. After all, Finnawick had kidnapped his mother to keep him in check. Shaking off his regret, he questioned, "What do we do now?"

"Can you blink again?" Cade asked.

Jeffery reached for the magical energy in his body then replied, "Yeah, after I get something to eat, probably."

"Jarrett needs medical attention. These wounds aren't likely to heal without it."

"We can't just take him to a hospital, Cade," Nate pointed out.

"I know, and we can't go back to Rederrick's if they're tracking him—at least not yet."

"Then where—" Realization dawned, and he replied firmly, "No!"

"What?" Jeffery asked confused.

"We don't have a choice," Cade responded.

"If we go there, we're bringing this mess with us. You can't really think that's a good idea."

"Where?" Jeffery questioned, but they continued to ignore him.

Cade shook his head. "I don't, but there's no real choice here."

"She can't come with us," Nate expressed with determination.

~ 125 ~

C.B. Haight

"No, she can't. That's why you'll have to help her, and I'll help him."

"What are you two talking about?" Jeffery demanded.

"Jeffery, have you ever been to Michigan?" Cade replied.

Nate scowled and left the room.

CHAPTER 12

As Cade, Jeffery, and a reluctant Nate made and executed their plans, Rederrick sat with a newspaper in hand and skimmed over the day's latest stories while waiting for Delphene to arrive. Her flight ran late due to weather. Rederrick couldn't help feeling nervous by the delay. He tipped the paper down for the third time to check his watch, to see only three minutes had passed.

His frustration built. Rederrick had a strange feeling in the pit of his stomach that he couldn't shake, no matter how much he tried. He adjusted his paper again, only this time he reached for his cell. He called Cynda to check in, and she picked up on the first ring. "We are all still accounted for, and nothing interesting has happened—if you don't count Jenny's amazing lunch. And it was amazing," she exaggerated.

Rederrick smiled, "All right, just making sure."

"We are fine. We have the best security system available, and if anything happens we all know what to do. Quit worrying."

C.B. Haight

"I hate being so far away, and these delays are killing me."

"Anything from Cade?" she asked.

"No," he replied uneasily, "It's not like him to not check in."

"He must have a reason. Though, Collett is pretty nervous."

"Keep her distracted if you can. He'll call," he reassured, but his words sounded flat, even to him.

"He'll call," Cynda insisted more forcefully.

"Yeah," he muttered. He looked up at the monitors again and realized Delphene's flight was finally arriving. "Her plane is landing. I'll call you back when we're on our way."

"All right, be safe."

"I love you too," he replied as he stood to watch for Delphene.

A little later, as the winter afternoon sun began to set, Rederrick pulled into his garage and helped Delphene gather her belongings. As they entered the house, Cynda and Collett met them at the door. "I saw you pull up," she explained and kissed him on the cheek.

Upon seeing Cynda, Delphene dropped her bags with a loud thunk and pulled Cynda up with a girly squeal. "*Mon'Amie ont manqué vous*—my friend, I have missed you. What you been up to *Chèrie?*" she drawled with a thick, French-southern accent.

Collett watched in fascination when Delphene lifted Cynda in a move she could only describe as pure delight. She wondered if she'd ever had a friendship like this one.

Collett took a moment to observe the excited woman. Delphene looked like an Amazon queen from Greek mythology. A woman with an African-American heritage, her smooth, dark-chocolate skin held a flawless, soft appearance. Her long hair, the color of ebony, was held together in a thick braid. She was tall, fit, and heavily muscled. Collett could easily picture her in elaborate warrior's armor exacting lethal damage upon any who dared to stand before her. Though, her powerful build did not detract from her beauty at all. Really, the opposite was true. Her appearance was striking in an impressive way.

The Price of Knowing

As if feeling Collett's scrutiny, Delphene turned to her, and Collett saw eyes similar to Cade's. Her's were slightly darker and sparkled with a girlish animation that Collett doubted she would ever see in her husband's. They were the eyes of a strong, happy woman.

"*C'est qui ce remue-ménage est tout propos*!—So, this is who the fuss is all about," Delphene exclaimed in a smooth, richly accented tone, and winked to Cynda.

"Delphene, I would like you to meet Cade's wife, Collett."

"Nice to meet you," Collett offered.

Delphene tipped her head, evaluating her. "And you are a pretty one, aren't you?"

"Thank you," replied Collett, slightly embarrassed.

"She blushes, *Jolie one I comme celui-ci, où avez-vous trouvé son?*"

"Actually, she found us," Cynda said in response to Delphene's question.

Collett suddenly realized two things. First, Cynda understood French, and second, so did she. It struck Collett that she could understand too. She bit her lip and considered the startling revelation carefully.

"Collett, is everything all right?" Cynda asked.

Collett looked up and stared at the three of them. "*Je pense que je parle Français.*" Her eyes lit up. "I do, I can speak French!"

"Congratulations, I am excited for you. Though, I am confused that you didn't know before," Delphene added.

"It's a long story," said Cynda, "One I'm sure Cade intended to tell, but since he's gone, come in and get something to eat. We'll fill you in a bit more." Together, Cynda and Delphene made their way into the house while Rederrick followed with Collett.

"French, huh?" Rederrick asked.

She shrugged. "French. I never knew that before, but I heard her and realized I understood."

"That's one more puzzle piece, and that's a good thing."

~ 129 ~

"That is a good thing," she agreed with a smile. As they reached the kitchen, her smile wavered. "Has he called?" she asked him.

Shaking his head, he answered, "Not yet, but he will."

Cynda's delighted laughter at something Delphene said pulled Collett's attention away from Rederrick. "Rederrick, honey, you can just put those things in the room Collett stayed in across from Cade's room. We're going to have some girl time."

"Well then, I will leave you ladies to it. I'll be hiding from all of your estrogen in the extra room if you need me."

"So noted," replied Cynda playfully.

"Ah *Chèrie*, girl's night. It has been so long," chimed Delphene with a mischievous light in her eyes.

After studying for almost a week straight and enduring the agony of taking the final exam, Ashley came home that afternoon to take a long, hot bath to relieve the stress in her shoulders, not to mention, warm her frozen toes. The winter temperatures in Michigan were downright brutal, and she felt frozen from head to toe.

All the study and sacrifice paid off though. While she thought the test had been awful and difficult, she was sure she aced it. She was well on her way to being a veterinarian. *If only I could do it without the degree,* she wished regretfully.

In reality, because of her empathic abilities, she could, but the government tended to be particular on technicalities. Her future customers would also care if she had that little paper showing she was formerly trained. So, for now, she would deal with the torture of school.

Ashley Williamson, daughter of Cynda and Rederrick Williamson, inherited her empathic and healing talents from her maternal grandmother. However, unlike Grandma Essie, Ashley's gifts were stronger with animals than humans, something she was

The Price of Knowing

extremely grateful for. Feeling and understanding the pain of animals was hard enough. If her empathic abilities were any stronger with people, she would likely be insane.

Her siblings inherited different traits. James, her younger brother, inherited all the brains and could create or manipulate almost any electronic device. He had a knack for technology and could retain facts without all the study she required. Currently, he was stationed at Fort Carson, Colorado, putting that brain to good use for the government and for The Brotherhood.

Ashley's older sister, Tracy, was far more skilled with spells and magic than she would ever be. Tracy was great with elemental magic and a natural with any spell. She inherited her talent for such witchcraft directly from their mother. Ashley could perform small spells. After all, she was Cynda's daughter as well. She just couldn't manage magic at the same level as her mother or sister. It never bothered her though. She knew what she needed to be and loved what she did.

She entered her quiet, little townhome, hung her coat, and threw her keys on the small table by the front door. Thinking about her family and how much she missed them, she gently kicked off her shoes and reached up to pull the band from her shiny, brown hair. Ashley made her way to the bathroom to indulge in the anticipated bath. She started the water, added colored salts, and began to undress.

Because her family was on her mind, she made a mental note to call and check in on them when she was done. The recent overnight trip for Uncle Cade's wedding had been too short for her liking. Since her Thanksgiving trip had been cut short as well because of The Faction's pursuit of Collett, Ashley realized she was pining for family a little more than usual.

As she dipped a foot into the steaming water, Ashley heard a knock at the door. She debated ignoring it, thinking it was most likely Lisa from next door, but another, more urgent knock sounded.

C.B. Haight

Ashley wrapped herself in a green silk robe, grabbed a kitchen knife, and made her way to the door. With everything going on in her family lately, she felt it best to err on the side of caution. Her dad and Cade had trained her to be paranoid, and she was skilled in self-defense.

"Who is it?" she called.

"Nate."

Now that was interesting. Ashley scowled. *Why would Nate be here in Michigan?* She peeked through the peep-hole to confirm it really was him and hurried to unlock the door. Happily, she swung it open for him.

He cleared his throat at the sight of her robe. "Ash," he greeted.

"What brings you—" her words died mid-sentence as she saw the three other men standing at her door. Well two, since one man was unconscious and slung over Cade's shoulder. Without waiting for an invitation, Cade moved right past her to her couch.

"I need your help, Ash."

"Come on in," she gestured to Nate and a dark young man with purple and blue in his hair. She couldn't remember his name.

Pulling her attention away from the newcomer, she turned to Cade. She started to ask how she could help, but upon seeing the man he laid on the couch, she rushed over to them. "What's wrong with Jarrett? What happened?"

Cade's brows drew together. It sounded like she recognized Jarrett. Of course, she knew he had a twin brother, but to his knowledge, she had never met him. Figuring he was reading too much into it, he let it go for now and answered her question as best he could. "I'm not completely sure. That's why we need you. The wound on his side is infected, and it looks really bad. If I had to guess, I'd say a silver weapon caused it. It doesn't smell like poison, and it's not magic. The bullet hole in his shoulder went straight through, but tore things up on its way out. He's got some bruises too, but there's nothing else major that I can see."

~ 132 ~

The Price of Knowing

Without hesitation, she pushed past Cade and yanked up Jarrett's shirt, where she noticed the dried blood. She winced as she saw the angry, festering wound that had been reopened. She immediately began barking out orders, "Nate, go and get some towels from my bathroom closet and a pillow from my bed. Cade, take him into the kitchen and put him on the table. You—"

"Jeffery," the stranger injected.

"Jeffery, over there by the door is my bag of supplies—go and get it then follow Cade." She went to her room and quickly dressed.

"Cade, how long has he been out?" she asked as she rushed over to the kitchen sink to wash her hands. When she turned to examine Jarrett, he started panting, and he mumbled something not even Cade understood.

He shrugged. "In and out since last night. About forty minutes maybe since the last time he sounded coherent."

She took out scissors and cut his shirt off. She then turned and began cutting his pants as well, because the wound was so low. "Good grief, Jarrett! What have you done this time?" she mumbled.

Cade and Nate both looked at her with surprise. "This time?" Cade questioned, realizing that she did know him.

Ashley could feel his reaction, but she did not let it sway her from her task. "We can get to all that later. Right now, I need to focus on him. Cade, let go of your emotions. I can't have you in my head too. Hold him, will you? I'm going to have to open him up a bit."

"You're not going to give him anything first?" Jeffery asked.

"Most sedatives don't work on these two. Their natural healing ability easily absorbs any I have available to give him."

Channeling her empathy and healing skills, Ashely focused on the most painful sensations and went back to work. Cade held Jarrett down as instructed, but it turned out to be unnecessary. He didn't even stir the whole time she worked on him. His lack of lucidity confirmed how serious the wound was.

~ 133 ~

C.B. Haight

In her experience, Cade and Jarrett usually healed pretty fast, in a matter of hours really, but this slash in his side was days old. It was jagged and deep, and she knew it would push the limits of her training. She was going to have to clean it, repair the damage to any organs, and sew it up in layers in order for it to heal.

The bullet wound was a clean through and through, but it wasn't healing as it should either. His skin was mottled with bruises and very pale. Resigned to the task, she feverishly attended to her patient.

CHAPTER 13

Not feeling needed at the moment, Jeffery wandered from the kitchen. Completely exhausted from using so much magical energy and too tired to stay on his feet, he made his way to the couch in the living room. He plopped down, expelled a breath, rubbed his hands over his face, and blinked hard trying to erase the sleepiness dragging at him. Surveying the little room, Jeffery noticed several family pictures in various places.

He reached over to the end table next to him and picked up a photo in a small silver frame. It displayed Ashley and Cynda with their faces cheek to cheek, both of them flaunting bright and happy smiles.

He tried to remember the last time he saw his own mother smiling in such a way. He'd made her so unhappy over the years. He rebelled against her constantly and ultimately endangered her life. Instead of a smile, all he could think of was the sadness in her eyes the last time they were together. It had been right after Jarrett, of all people, saved her from Finnawick's sadistic imprisonment.

Laying his head back and closing his eyes, Jeffery recalled the night that changed everything for him. Jarrett came to him in the bar where he'd gone to forget how he failed to save his mother. It was there that Jarrett offered Jeffery a deal. A deal that saved his mother's life. Jeffery hadn't known at the time that it would give him a new life as well.

Still slurring slightly but beginning to think more clearly, he asked, "W-What's the cost?"

The Hunter knew what was coming for him, so he answered with resignation, "You have to pass on a message."

"To who?" Jeffery asked.

"To Cade Werren." The Hunter then slipped out a small envelope and handed it to Jeffery.

"I must be really drunk. You just want me to give this to him?" he slurred.

"Something like that," Jarrett answered with irritation. "Tomorrow. Give it to him tomorrow."

Jarrett stood from the stool casually. "What 'bout my mom, man?" he asked desperately.

"She is already at your motel waiting for you."

Jeffery could only stare after the dark, confusing the man as he walked out of the dimly lit bar into the cold winter night. He looked down at the sealed white envelope that had the word, "Cade," scrawled across the center, standing out with black ink.

Jeffery stumbled from his seat and walked out the door to follow. When he got outside into the freezing cold air, The Hunter was already long gone.

He staggered into the alley, drunk but sobering, and prayed what Jarrett told him was true. He blinked back to his hotel room, and there she was. His mother sat at the scarred table in the corner

The Price of Knowing

of the meager room. With her head in her arms, not knowing he was there, she remained in that mournful pose.

"Mom?" he croaked, disbelieving what was right before him. She lifted her head and looked at him with tear-filled eyes. She smiled sadly and rose.

Almost completely sobered by the night's extraordinary events, Jeffery looked at the envelope in his hand. He placed it on top of the outdated TV and rushed to embrace his mother. It had been two years since he had last seen her.

"I'm sorry," he muttered against her.

"Shh. It's all right. It's all right," she soothed, holding him as if her life depended on it.

After he clung to her for a time, Jeffery eased back and looked to the mysterious message given to him by an even more mysterious man. Then, Jeffery did something even he did not expect. He looked to his mother and said, "Mom, there is something I have to do. It might take me some time to get back to you."

Untangling from her embrace, he walked over to the dresser and opened the top drawer. Jeffery pulled out a little cash box, handed it to his mother, and said, "You have to go. Get out of the country. Go to the Bahamas, like you've always wanted. I'll find you there when I can. Don't use your real name. There is a fake passport I had made for you...before I thought..."

He couldn't even say it. For a time, he really thought her dead, killed by Finnawick. Seeing her standing here still felt surreal—dream like. He choked down his emotion and continued, "The passport is in there. Use that name, and don't trust anyone."

"What?" she asked, confused and sniffling.

He looked at her regretfully. "I've made some mistakes, Mom, some really big mistakes. You know that better than anyone. I've rarely done the right thing, but there is this one thing I can do now that's right. It's important.

"Maybe there is hope for me to come back from it all and fix some of what I've done." He shrugged. "I don't know, but I have to try. I have to pay this one debt, then I'll come find you if I can."

"I just got you back," she insisted with a mother's desperation, her voice cracking.

"I have to do this. I need to do this," he declared with fierce conviction.

His mother didn't speak, but she nodded her head at him while choking on her sobs.

He looked at her sad, broken expression and deeply regretted all the pain he had caused her. He'd gone against everything she tried to do for him, everything she tried to teach him. It was time to make her proud of him. No matter what, he would give her a reason to believe in him again.

To start with, he would deliver the small message, and from there he would find a way to make it without The Faction.

He hugged her again. "I am so sorry...sorry for all that I've done to you, sorry for the pain I caused you. I swear I'll make it right somehow. Then we can have a normal life.

"I do love you. No matter what I've done in the past, I think I always knew you would be there for me. I was just too stupid to appreciate it." His words were filled with sincerity and even a level of maturity that didn't exist in him before.

"Oh, my baby boy, I've always loved you. I always will." Pulling away from him, she tried to wipe away her tears. He could have sworn he saw hope in her eyes. "Do what you have to do, and if you can, come find me when you're done. God be with you, Baby. Go and finish this. I'll be waiting for you."

Jeffery looked into her deep brown eyes one last time, grabbed the envelope, and blinked from the room, leaving his mother alone with her fears and grief.

He'd wanted to call her so many times, but didn't have any idea where she was, which was for the best. If he contacted her, it was likely someone with The Faction would find and use her to get him to give up Jarrett or Collett.

Jarrett's words to him in the forest near Rederrick's home echoed in his head. *"You know the problem with young idiots like you casting your lot in with demons, Jeffery? They will always find a way to control you. By using men like me or using what you care for. Either way, they own you."* Hunter or not, Jarrett had been the first person, besides his mom, to help him—even if he did almost break his arm in the process.

It was surprising how much he changed in the last couple weeks. Not long ago he'd been an angry kid with too much power, no self-control, and way too much attitude to boot. He'd once been trying to capture Collet for The Faction. That haunted him now, and he wanted to make up for it. What was worse, he'd never thought of his mom the whole time he worked for them.

Now, working with The Brotherhood, Jeffery thought of her every day and wondered how she was doing. He even enjoyed being part of a team and was loyal to their cause.

He'd been liberated from The Faction's dominion thanks to the man lying unconscious and bleeding on the kitchen table. *If only I had met Jarrett sooner,* Jeffery thought as he drifted to sleep.

Three hours later, Ashley finally tightened the last stitch and straitened to stretch her stiff muscles. Jeffery had left some time ago to rest, but Cade and Nate remained vigilant in case she needed them. Pulling the surgical gloves from her hands and removing her mask, she instructed, "Go ahead and take him into my other room, but be gentle. Don't open those stitches."

Cade nodded, and lifting him together, the men carried Jarrett into her bedroom while Ashley cleaned things up. There was blood

C.B. Haight

all over. She realized the rug under the table was ruined and would need to be replaced. She lamented the loss, but berated herself for such petty thoughts. Shaking her head, she grabbed a trash bag and began tossing away the remnants of her impromptu surgery.

Nate returned and moved to take the bag from her hands. "Go sit down, Ashley. I'll take care of this."

"I've got it," she insisted as she arched her back in an effort to loosen the cramped muscles.

He gently pried the bag from her fingers, and she offered little resistance. He set the bag down, laid his hands on her shoulders, and could feel the tension beneath his fingers. "You've done all you can do, and you look beat."

Shaking her head, she placed a hand on his. "I need to clean things up to stay busy." She stepped away from him, and he let her go. Over at the sink, she placed bloody instruments in the basin for later sterilization. "So what are you all doing in my neck of the woods anyway?"

He came up behind her and began to knead the tight muscles in her neck. "Well, isn't it obvious? We missed you."

With her eyes closed, a little smile pulled at her lips. "Some girls get flowers when they're missed. Me, I get bloody men to clean up. Be still my heart," she retorted with exaggeration.

Nate smiled at her quick comeback. "Only the best for you, Baby."

She snorted.

"Ash?"

The pair turned at the sound of Cade's deep, but quiet voice interrupting their banter. Ashley sobered and moved from Nate's reach.

"He'll be fine," she said hurriedly. "The wound was very deep and hit some organs. He was still slowly bleeding internally, not to mention the infection spreading through him. If he had been human he'd be dead instead of unconscious in the next room."

~ 140 ~

"And the rest?" he asked, referring to the other lingering wounds.

"I can't be sure, but even though he didn't fully heal, I could sense his body was trying. A few of the wounds had started to, but they were the oldest ones. I suspect the infection and constant injuries made it too hard to keep up."

He nodded because he suspected much the same.

"He'll be okay now that it is stitched up and cared for properly. If we get rid of the infection, his body will do the rest. Though, his side will take a while to completely heal."

Nobody said anything else for a long time. The silence stretched out too long and created an uncomfortable awkwardness. Cade ran his fingers through his hair, knowing what he wanted to ask, but reluctant to breach the subject. He could tell she knew what was coming, so he blurted out, "Ash, you know Jarrett." It was accusation, rather than a question.

"Yes, Cade. I know Jarrett." Ashley lowered her head, not wanting to see Cade's disappointment after the confession. She held her breath and waited for what would come next. Despite Cade's tone and Nate's grim expression, she did feel relief from finally saying the words.

"How…why didn't you—"

"Why didn't I tell you? Tell you what?" she interrupted. "Hey Cade, I ran into your twin brother the other day. You know, the one you never wanted to talk about, not to mention your general reaction to his name.

"Oh yeah, and let's not forget how my over-protective dad would have reacted. You know him, Rederrick, the same man who wanted to hire bodyguards for me when I started high school. Hmm, I wonder why I couldn't tell you." Her last words were laced with a bitter longing, as if she had wanted to tell him.

"You should have told me. He's not—he could have…"

"Hurt me?" she finished for him. "No, in fact, our first meeting was quite the opposite. He saved me, from a dog of all things." She

C.B. Haight

laughed nervously. "Ironic, huh? Something was wrong with the boxer, and I tried to help. It attacked like it was rabid, but it wasn't. Some idiot infected it with demon blood. I assume he did it to make it a better fighter." She shrugged. "When it happened—when he stepped in—well, I thought it was you, and after—it didn't really matter to me."

"How long ago?" Cade asked, feeling slightly betrayed.

She answered his tone with resolve, "A little over a year."

He cursed, "Ashley, a year?"

"It's not that I didn't trust you, Cade. I just didn't want to hurt you." She kept her tone placating, "Plus, there was also that whole over-protective father to consider. Can you imagine what Dad would have done if he found out? Jarrett said it would bother you, and I knew it was the truth."

"Why would you listen to him?"

"Because he's my friend," she defended sharply.

"Ash, you don't know what he can be like. He kidnapped Collett. Does that sound rational?"

"I think it's you that doesn't understand what he can be like," she shot back. She couldn't have shocked him more if she'd slapped him. His eyes went wide, and Nate reacted similarly. "Why are you here, Cade? Why help him and bring him to me?"

"Collett said he needed help, and I didn't have anywhere else to take him." He raked his fingers through his hair again in frustration.

"That's it? You're here because you had no choice?" He said nothing, so she continued, "I don't buy it. Not entirely anyway. Collett may have got you moving, but if you didn't care, you wouldn't be here. Deep down, you hope he's not all he pretends to be. You're here because he's your brother like he's my friend. We both want to save him, right?"

"Of course I want to!" he snapped.

She nodded knowingly. "I can't figure out why he didn't come to me sooner on his own. He's come here before."

~ 142 ~

"He couldn't come here without endangering you," Nate offered, understanding Jarrett must have wanted to avoid bringing this to her as much as he did.

"He knew I could help though, and we're friends." She looked to Cade with sympathy and apologized, "I'm sorry if that hurts you. It was never my intention."

"How good of friends?" Nate questioned.

Tired, his innuendo annoyed her, and Ashley glared at him.

He didn't relent, and Cade acted surprised because that line of thought never occurred to him.

"Give me a break! I've only helped him out a couple of times with people that needed medical attention, and he stops in to check on me from time to time when he's around. That's all," she said, waving away their concern.

"You do know he works for The Faction?" said Nate.

"Of course I knew that. How could I have grown up with my parents and Mr. Protective here and not known that?" she said incredulously, gesturing at Cade. She was frustrated that all the men in her life thought she was still a silly child with no common sense. "I have to wonder though, do either of you know what he does for them, or rather, what he doesn't do?"

"What are you getting at, Ashley?" Cade asked, tired of being in the dark and feeling defensive.

"You really think he was just a mindless killer doing as he was told, don't you?" Saddened and exasperated by the session of twenty questions, Ashley decided to tell them all she knew. "He deals with the worst of the worst, Cade. The greediest and most power-hungry members of The Faction that step out of line get a special one-on-one meeting with Jarrett. They don't even call him by name. To them, he's known as The Hunter.

"Essentially, he kills the killers, Cade. He takes care of the worst kind of selfish, vicious killers. Really, he's somewhat of a legend to them, but you likely didn't know that."

C.B. Haight

Cade just stared at her, and she didn't stop. Knowing she had his full attention, she prepped him for the rest, "You might want to sit down for this next part.

"What do you think he does when he goes after someone who isn't the scum of the earth? I'll tell you. If Jarrett believes that person is simply caught up in the wrong mess, he takes care of them too. Only, he doesn't kill them. He fakes their deaths, at his own risk, then moves them somewhere else at his own cost. He makes it so no one else will come looking. In short, the brother that you think so little of has essentially become the only way out of The Faction— one way or another."

Cade didn't know how to reply, but Nate, being the more cynical of the two, shot back, "Is that what he told you?"

Keeping her soft grey eyes on Cade, she replied, "No, he didn't have to. The people he's brought to me have told me enough. I've put the rest together, not that he would admit to any of it. As hard and stubborn as he is, he would rather I believe him to be the monster you think he is.

"So chew on that for a bit. Be careful though, you might choke when you realize your brother isn't so bad after all." She pushed past Cade and mumbled, "Excuse me," as she left to check on Jarrett.

~ 144 ~

CHAPTER 14

Cade looked down at the floor pondering Ashley's revelation and knew it made sense. Jeffery's story about his mother and the event with Collett were evidence of Jarrett's good intentions. He thought his brother's change of heart was a recent event, but having Ashley explain that Jarrett may have always been this way made him re-examine their history.

Blowing out a breath and rubbing a hand over his face, Cade looked up to Nate who, stood with his back toward the counter and his hands resting upon it. "Where's Jeffery?"

"His head was spinning a bit from the jumps, so he's on the couch." Nate said as he gestured with his head toward the living room. "Oh, come on, Cade, don't act so shocked. You always knew something was different, or you would have ended it instead of only ignoring it."

"I tried, remember?" he said, rubbing the scar on his chin.

C.B. Haight

"Bull! You never wanted to kill him, otherwise you would have, and vice versa. You knew that if Jarrett wanted you dead, he would have seen to it a long time ago. You even stopped me from shooting him two years ago. You knew then. Hell, maybe I knew too."

"You don't seem too happy today either," Cade accused.

"I have different reasons for my reaction." Nate paused and, shaking his head, finished, "It doesn't really matter. We came to find him, and we did. There's old memories and bad blood between you, but we have to put it aside. What's next for us?"

Cade's thoughts jumped to Jarrett's connection to Collett for a second, but as Nate suggested, he brushed it aside. "I have to get him to stay with me until he heals and we can make a plan. He won't survive long on his own in this condition."

Knowing that would be no easy task, Nate groaned. "Well on that note, I think I'll go make the arrangements to get Ashley and me out of here. I'll let you tell her the good news."

With a nod, Cade turned and went into the bedroom. Entering, he found Ashley listening to Jarrett's chest with her stethoscope. "His heart rate and rhythm are, well, as normal as you guys get anyway. He isn't panting so much anymore. He's a bit more relaxed too," she said with her back to him. She lifted the blanket and probed the skin around the wound.

"Look Ash, I didn't mean to upset you. It's complicated, things between us, I mean. You don't know everything, and his past behaviors make me nervous."

"So tell me then." His jaw clenched, and he said nothing even though she could see he wanted to.

"You're right, Cade. I don't know everything, but what I do know is enough. His badass, super scary, 'I'm the villain' persona is just a front. He really isn't what you think. What he was like before doesn't matter. I won't judge him for life choices I know nothing about. Who he is today is what matters to me."

The Price of Knowing

"Why didn't you tell me at the wedding? You knew about Collett, and you knew about the letter. Why not tell me then?" he asked.

She sighed, "I don't know. All I can say is, it just didn't feel right. Besides, what good would come from telling you? Like I said before, I didn't want to hurt you, and to be honest, I wasn't really sure what to say." She paused, and the room remained silent except the sound of the ticking clock that hung on the far wall. "I thought about telling you so many other times," she admitted, "but it kind of felt like I was betraying you both. So, it was really hard for me to know how to handle it."

"Okay."

"Okay?" she questioned.

"I get it, and I'm sorry." He did too. He fully understood her dilemma, and somewhere buried deep inside, he was even relieved that Jarrett had somebody who was looking out for him.

"Thank you, Cade," she said, relieved that everything was out in the open and back to normal between them. She turned her attention back to Jarrett. "He needs rest, and I'll get some antibiotics from the clinic I work at. I'm not sure it'll work great, but his body needs something."

"We can't stay. It's not safe."

"He shouldn't be moved yet. Stay tonight at least, then you can get back out tomorrow. Are you going home?"

He was already shaking his head. "We can't. They've been tracking him. When I say we can't stay, it includes you."

"Oh," she replied softly.

"I'm sorry, Ash. I wouldn't have come here if there was anyone else, but I needed your help," he said with regret and compassion in his eyes. "You're going to need to take some time off and get out of here. Nate will go with you to keep you safe."

"Um, all right. I just finished my exams today, so I guess I can do that." Her voice sounded unsteady, even to herself. "I'll go home for Christmas then."

~ 147 ~

C.B. Haight

"You can't go there either."

"Oh," she repeated. Ashley was disappointed, but understood the situation must be very bad for Cade to refuse sending her home. Home was the safest place she knew of. "Where then?"

"I want you to go with Nate and listen to him. Got it?" She nodded. "Head to New York, and get Tracy. I'm not sure how long she'll be safe if they trace us to you and you to her. Nate will take care of the rest."

"What about you?"

"I'm not really sure yet, but don't worry. I'll figure it out."

Nate popped his head in and asked, "Did you tell her yet?" Ashley looked over to him, nodding in reply. "Good. The hotel is arranged. We need to leave. Get your stuff together."

"I can't leave that quick. What about Jarrett? You can't just drag him all over. He needs rest, antibiotics, and you might open his stitches."

"Tell me what he needs. I'll take care of it," Cade replied and watched her eyes dart back to Jarrett.

"I'll get what you need, and then I'll go with Nate," she replied with grim determination.

"Ash—"

"No. You want me to go, I get it. But you came here so I could help him. Let me do that. I can easily get what you need. Nate can tag along if it will make you feel better."

Cade looked at Nate and considered the risks. Finally, he nodded. "Get what we need, then get back here. I'll put your stuff together."

"It's too dangerous. That'll take too much time," Nate insisted. His expression made it clear that he was only concerned about Ashley's safety and getting her out of harm's way.

"Really, it's better this way. She'll be gone if they come looking. I'll get her stuff together while you two get the meds. Pick up a TracFone and call the house before you bring her back to make sure it's safe."

~ 148 ~

The Price of Knowing

Pressing his lips together in a tight line, Nate jerked his head in assent. Ashley moved to him, and together they left. Cade went to her closet and began to pull clothes from hangers to throw into a bag.

"You should've made her leave," came a deep, groggy voice Cade barely recognized.

Cade emerged from the closet holding a suitcase. "Not dead after all."

Jarrett only grunted, not even bothering to open his eyes. He wasn't even sure he could.

Cade moved to Ashley's drawer and began pulling jeans out.

"She's wrong. I am exactly what you think," Jarrett rasped.

"Well, I'm not sure what I think," he paused, "at least not anymore. Get some rest. We'll be leaving soon."

Jarrett remained silent as anger and gratitude battled within him. He was furious that Ashley was in danger now. It was an outcome he'd tried to avoid, but he was grateful they had rescued him. He didn't expect that Cade would be the one to save him from death's door.

He couldn't go with them of course, but for now, he needed rest. When the chance presented itself, he would be gone. This was his problem, and he didn't need his brother tagging along trying to fix him.

He felt a small pang of regret but pushed it aside. It hardly mattered that a small part of him wanted Cade to stick around. *Attachments only make things worse,* he reminded himself. He'd learned that lesson more than once in his life.

As he lay in Ashley's bed, surrounded by her scent, he knew he was right. He'd been attached to Rowena, and it got her killed. Then, at the age of twenty-two, he fell in love with a girl named Sara. After courting her, he decided to divulge his secret so he could ask for her hand. He could still envision the look of horror on her face as she ran screaming from him that night. He couldn't help but smirk at his own stupidity for that one.

~ 149 ~

Jarrett accepted that it was human nature to form attachments, and the human part of him was no different than anyone else. Unfortunately, experience taught him how easily those attachments turned on you or ended up becoming a weapon against you.

Meeting Ashley wasn't the fluke she thought it to be. He'd sought her out in hopes of finding Cade. During that time, Jarrett heard that Cade was in Michigan. He assumed Cade would have been here with her. He wasn't, but Jarrett hoped he would turn up.

He knew Cade helped people escape The Faction, and of course, he knew all about Rederrick and his Brotherhood. He found it laughable that a human lawyer would involve himself in such things, but then, humans rarely made sense to him.

Jarrett was confident he could fabricate a situation where Cade would take a Faction member off his hands, and he stayed close for over a week. Despite his original intention, he ended up charmed by the compassionate Ashley.

When the demon boxer attacked her, Jarrett couldn't stand by and watch as she was maimed or killed. He reluctantly intervened and was extremely ticked she'd put herself in that situation in the first place. The rest, as they say, is history.

He tried to keep his distance, but her kind, outgoing nature kept him from staying away. After being alone for so long, Ashley drew him in like a moth to a flame. Stopping on the street late at night to help a feral Boxer instead of leaving it to die was no less dangerous than taking him on as a friend, or so she told him.

The whole thing was selfish on his part. He knew better, but he couldn't deny how good it felt to have someone know his secret and not care about the demon inside of him. She never mentioned The Faction, even though she knew he worked for them. Now, because of his and Cade's selfish bond to the young woman, she would likely end up dead like the others.

Will I ever learn? Jarrett berated himself.

Resigned, he shifted to get up. He couldn't hold back the low groan or push aside his annoyance at his weak limbs. His abused body rebelled against his movements. Everything ached, but he realized, though still stiff and sore, the burning in his side had lessened. He could feel the tug of the stitches as he made it to a half-sitting position.

"What are you doing?" Cade snapped, dropping the clothes and rushing to Jarrett. His twin only glared as he carefully moved his legs over the edge of the bed. "We've got time yet. Stay down as long as you can."

"I gotta piss, and I'm sure Ashley would appreciate it if I did it in the bathroom."

"Fine. At least let me help you," Cade said resignedly, bending to assist him.

"No thanks. I got it," Jarrett replied while shaking his head. "I'm still alive, and I'm not sure our relationship covers that."

"Barely," Cade mumbled and still reached to pull him up.

"Barely what?" Jarrett snapped, standing—or as close to it as he could get.

"Barely alive," Cade stated flatly.

Jarrett couldn't disagree, so he remained silent as he shrugged off Cade's hands and lumbered to the bathroom.

Collett sat on the couch in the theater room with her legs tucked beneath her and laughed as Delphene animatedly finished her latest story about Cade.

"There he was, in all his glory and couldn't change, else the humans would see," she explained in her rich southern-French accent that she adopted over the extended time of living in The Big Easy. "I told him he did not have time, but did he listen? Never does, I suppose." She laughed. "Two large wolves in the city would scare 'em he told me, but what does he think his naked butt did?" Finished with her tale, Delphene plopped down heavily on the couch and sighed happily. "That boy is always one to find trouble."

Throughout the evening, Collett had learned that Delphene was originally from France, and she moved to New Orleans shortly after it was settled. She also came to understand that Delphene was older than Cade by quite a few years—exactly how many, Delphene would never tell. "I am still a woman after all. My age is my secret," she had said.

At this point, Collett figured Delphene was likely the most enthusiastic person she ever met. She was vibrant and energetic, and Collett enjoyed every minute of their time together. She wasn't sure she had ever laughed this hard in her life.

"Thank you, Delphene," she said. When the other woman looked over to her, perplexed by Collett's gratitude, she explained, "I needed this. I needed some laughter and excitement tonight."

"Oh *Chèrie*, you're welcome. We all need a little laughter once in a while, no? It's even more fun because it is at Cade's expense, *oui*?" she said with a wink.

Collett smiled, "Oui."

"Well ladies, this old woman has had enough," Jenny announced, standing. "I'm off to bed."

"Oh well, *fè bon rèv*," Delphene offered.

Collett and Cynda each said their goodnights, and Jenny replied in kind then left. Things quieted a bit after that. The three women settled in to watch a movie, talking here and there, but Collett, feeling content and relaxed for the first time in days, began to drift off.

Cade dozed in the kitchen chair, or at least he tried to. He sat in the most uncomfortable position he'd ever been in. The chair was small and had such a low back that it offered no support. He stayed in Jarrett's room that night. He suspected that Jarrett intended to make a run for it, and Cade refused to let him. It was hard enough to track him down once, twice would likely be impossible. It was a little after midnight, and he was worn out from the last few days. He was plagued with worry for Collett, but he didn't dare call. He suspected someone may be tracking his phone, so he'd ditched it at the motel earlier that day.

Nate and Ashley had long since returned with antibiotics and new clothes for all of them. However, instead of leaving right away, they decided, after much protest from Nate, that it would be worth the risk to stay until Jeffery could blink again. He could then take Ashley and Nate farther, faster.

Ultimately, they planned to go to Tracy's place in New York and convince her to go with them. If The Faction connected Jarrett to Ashley, then they would have another motive to attack Rederrick, his family, or anyone close to him. Cade knew Rederrick's home was becoming more vulnerable with each hour that passed.

Frustrated and tired, Cade leaned his head back against the wall, unsuccessfully seeking a restful position. Giving up, he stood and looked out the window as he continued to mull over the many dangers and insufficient assets.

Collett fell into a deep sleep after only a few minutes. The visions returned, but this time was much worse. Her mind flashed to a series of locations: in front of a white door, Cynda's kitchen, then she was in a bedroom with—who was that? Jarrett?

Oh no, she thought, as a horrible sense of foreboding rushed through her. She knew she only dreamed of him when he was in trouble.

Collett began to call out, but before her warning could escape her lips, she came back to the kitchen. She could see Jenny getting a drink from the sink. *Why am I seeing this?* She felt so confused.

Once again, before she could grab hold, the images changed. It was as if someone held a remote to her mind and kept flipping back and forth between channels. She was outside the door again, and there was something there. A shadow moved. She forced herself to focus, and without understanding how she drifted inside the house. Once inside, she saw Jeffery on the couch and Nate in a recliner.

Still confused, she moved further into the house toward a room with an open door. She sensed it was the room Jarrett occupied. However, she saw Cade standing by the window with his back to her. "Cade!" she called. He turned slightly but didn't look at her. Instead, he looked at Jarrett, who bolted up with a muffled growl and looked straight at her with a hate filled glare.

Before she could say any more, Collett felt a sharp, burning pain rip through her. It originated at the back of her head and filled her entire body. Turning, she found herself in the kitchen with Jenny, who lay lifeless on the floor.

A tall, dark man stood over her with something in his hand. Collett realized it was a Taser as she felt the shock run through her when the man happily used it on Jenny a second time. He viciously kicked Jenny and laughed gleefully. Both women cried out in pain.

Collett pulled herself together, and forgetting this was a sort of dream, she rushed forward in anger intent on attacking the man. She wanted to turn the horrid weapon back on him, and she sensed angry energy build within her. She didn't make contact with the man. Instead, she ran right through him. The growing energy spiked, demanding release. She instinctively reached out, and it poured out of her. A misty light flowed from her hands, and the man cringed. His body stiffened and vibrated as if he had been shocked, and then he crumpled to the ground.

Sickness ran through Collett as she realized she had done exactly as she wanted. She had managed to project Jenny's pain to him, and he felt an electric shock similar to the Taser.

Collett's focus shifted immediately to Jenny. She called out to her and began reaching for her, but before she could reach her, she heard Cynda's voice pulling her out of the vision.

In the extra room, Rederrick was also having a difficult night. He was on surveillance duty, but he was struggling to keep his eyes open. It had been a long couple of nights, and the worry and stress were wearing on him. He wasn't the young man he used to be, and his years were catching up to him whether he liked it or not.

He turned to check the monitors once more, and seeing nothing, looked back to his paperwork. He hated reviewing depositions. It was a tedious part of his day job, but he knew it was necessary.

Wondering why they had not heard from Cade since last night, he checked his watch for the tenth time. He was concerned and considered the possibility that something had gone terribly wrong. Cade was no slouch in a fight, but even a lycan could find himself in an impossible situation.

Rederrick leaned back, vigorously scrubbed his face, and let out a heavy breath. Trying to relax, he allowed himself to close his eyes. It lasted no more than a minute. His cell phone rang. Startled, he scrambled to grab it and saw it was his daughter, Ashley, calling. Wasting no time, he answered, "Ashley, is something wrong? Why are you calling so late?" Distracted by the call, he neglected to look back at the security cameras where he would have seen Jenny and her attacker lying on the kitchen floor.

CHAPTER 15

Cade thought he heard something, but his attention shifted as Jarrett bolted upright with a low, painful growl caused from moving too fast.

"What's wrong, what do you need?" he asked as he went to him.

"Clothes. We're out of time," was Jarrett's clipped reply.

"Out of time for what?"

Jarrett grunted as he moved to stand. "Your lady just stopped by to make an appearance. Time to go."

"What?"

"Just throw me those clothes, and get Ashley out of here!"

Complying, Cade threw the clothes and ran down the hall to wake Ashley. He couldn't help wondering why he hadn't seen Collett. She should have come to him, he was her husband.

Before he had any more time to consider it, Cade heard a thump come from the office where Ashley slept on the smaller extra bed she kept for guests. He rushed through the door to find a man in her

~ 156 ~

bed with his hand over her mouth and Ashley's eyes wide with fear. The man turned and smiled, revealing the sharp fangs of a leech demon. Blood was the only thing that could sustain them, and they would usually drain their victims dry rather quickly. Their venom was poisonous and made humans rather sick if they somehow managed to survive the attack. The sickly state the victim is what started the myths about vampires turning people.

Seeing Ashley in trouble, Cade saw red as rage ripped through him. He rushed forward, wrapped his arms around the attacker, and plowed it into the wall on the other side of her bed. "Get out of here, Ash!" he barked inhumanly as his body shifted.

Ashley wasted no time complying, and she practically leaped the distance to the door. She dashed from the room, knowing the small space would soon be a violent mess. She was right too. Cade and the vampire leech crashed about the room in furious combat, tearing at each other with enthusiastic vigor.

Her escape didn't do her much good though. Ashley ran directly from one combat to another as Jarrett and Nate battled with something else entirely in the living room. Jarrett locked his arms around a creature she'd never seen the like of before.

"Your stitches!" she admonished.

"Jeffery, get her out of here!" Jarrett snapped.

Quick as a snake, Jeffery grabbed her from behind, scaring the life from her. Before she could even react, the sorcerer blinked her from the room. Darkness enveloped her, but not for long. There was light, and she felt a crawling burn rush over her entire body followed by a sharp sting running throughout her nerves. She bent over to cope with it.

"Stay here, where it's safe!" Jeffery ordered her.

Ashley stood, fully intending to confront him for his commanding tone, but he was already gone. She looked around to figure out where she was, only to discover she was right in front of a Wal-Mart Supercenter. Then she glanced down at her hands to the cell phone she'd grabbed from her bedside table before fleeing her bedroom. Stunned, cold, barefoot, and still in her pajamas, Ashley lifted her phone and did the only thing she could think of. She called home.

"Ashley, is something wrong? Why are you calling so late?"

"Um well, it's kind of a long story. I'll try to shorten it as best I can."

"Okay," he answered suspiciously.

"Uncle Cade brought Jarrett to my house because he was in bad shape. I fixed him up, took care of a few things, and was going to head to Tracy's with Nate in the morning because Uncle Cade thinks we all might be in danger. We went to bed, and we were attacked. Then Jeffery grabbed me, and now I'm standing in front of a Wal-Mart in heaven only knows where!" she finished in one strained breath.

The words tumbled out so rapidly, Rederrick had a hard time keeping up. What he heard sent chills racing through him. "Where's Cade?" he snapped.

"Back at my house!" she replied desperately.

The bad feeling he had was getting worse, and he turned to scan the monitors. "Ashl—" the chill in his blood turned to ice when he saw Jenny and a stranger laying on the floor in the kitchen and Cynda and Delphene shaking Collett in the other room.

"Dad?"

"Ashley, I want you to go inside and stay there until someone comes for you! Do you understand?"

"Um, yeah, okay."

"Call your sister, and tell her to get out of her apartment! Tell her to find a public place with lots of light and stay there!" Rederrick ordered while he armed himself. "I'm not sure when I can call you again, but if no one comes by morning, find a way to meet up with your sister and stay out of sight."

"What about James?"

"James will be fine. He's on a military base! Just do what I'm telling you, and you'll be fine." He made his way to the heavy, leaded door leading into the house. "I love you, baby. Be careful, okay?"

"I love you too, Dad."

"Now go inside!" he ordered again. He hung up the phone and carefully opened the door, intending to make his way to the kitchen.

"Collett!" Cynda called for the third time.

Collett's eyes fluttered open, and the fear and frustration followed her into consciousness.

"Jarrett and Cade, are they all right?" Cynda questioned, understanding Collett had experienced another vision.

Still a little out of it, Collett stared at Cynda, then her fear turned to horror. "Jenny!" she gasped and tried to rise.

"Take it easy, *ma petite*," Delphene said kindly.

"No! It's Jenny, we have to get to Jenny! She's hurt."

All of the color in Cynda's pretty face drained as if someone had sucked it right out of her. "Jenny?" she questioned desperately.

Standing, Collett moved past Delphene who grabbed her arm. "*Non, je ne pense pas, petite fille*. I am here to keep you safe. I made a promise. There'll be no running toward the trouble for you."

"Jenny's hurt! We have to go to her!" Collett insisted.

"Don't fret, I will get her."

"No, I'll go," Cynda injected tersely.

"*Non!* Stay here with her. I'll get Jenny," Delphene commanded in a tone that left no room for argument. "Do you know where she is?"

"The kitchen, hurry! There was a man with her. He had a stun gun!"

With a clipped nod, Delphene left the room to move silently down the hallway.

"It's okay. Jenny will be okay," Cynda murmured, as much to herself as to Collett.

Collett refrained from revealing that Cade may also be in trouble. She knew that their immediate safety was the priority here, and such news would only worry Cynda more. It surely worried Collett. Besides that, she was still confused by everything she saw as she jumped from place to place. She needed time to sort it out.

They heard a crash and then splintering glass falling to the floor. Resolved, Collett grabbed Cynda's hand.

"Come on," Collett insisted.

"Let's go," Cynda said in unison.

Their concern for Delphene and Jenny had them sprinting toward the noise. As they ran down the hallway, they saw broken glass scattered on the floor beneath a picture hanging oddly on the wall. It was clear where the glass originated from.

Cynda slowed and pointed to the floor where grayish ash dusted the ground, and Collett nodded. Neither one of them spoke in case there were more intruders. Cautiously, the two women made their way toward the stairs that led to the main living area of the home.

Loud, popping gunshots echoed from downstairs. Terror gripped both women, and they rushed the final distance to the stairs together.

At the bottom, it was clear that the danger was in the den. Cynda ran into the room, and Collett was overwhelmed by the emotion emanating from her friend. Cynda's fear for Rederrick and Jenny invaded Collett, and she stopped for a moment to cope with it. Cynda, however, did not stop. She charged to help Rederrick with a spell on her tongue.

Collett opened her senses and allowed emotions to wash over her. She felt the rush of adrenaline that accompanied battle and a vicious, angry need for vengeance from Rederrick. She also still felt Jenny's injuries and fear more acutely. All of these compounded within her. Collett's stomach churned, and her skin prickled.

Horror gripped Collett as she looked into the room to find Rederrick in fierce combat and completely surrounded. There were at least seven opponents, and despite giving them a good fight, he was clearly losing ground.

Doubt assailed her. What could she do against such an enemy? She shoved her doubt aside and reminded herself that any help would be better than none at all. She rushed over to the corner and snatched the standing lamp. She used it like a staff and slammed it across the nearest enemy's back with as much force as she could.

Her attack succeeded. Well, sort of. He did turn to stare at her.

He looked confused briefly, then he grinned at her wickedly. Collett took in his small, sharp teeth and his grayish, blotchy skin and realized he wasn't an ordinary man.

With a gleam of excitement in his black eyes, he advanced on her rasping, "Ah, there you are. We've been waiting for you."

Collett thrust out with the lamp, trying to keep him at bay, but he sidestepped it easily and continued to advance. Instinctively, she backed away from him. She could hear the chaos around her, and her eyes darted to her friends. Rederrick grunted and fought with the dagger he had in hand, while Cynda chanted her spells. A man screamed and crumpled to the ground before the witch and another intruder hissed inhumanly as Rederrick connected the blade with demon flesh.

Collett knew there would be no help from them. Resolve began to course through her. She silently reminded herself that she had trained for this very scenario for months. Determined to put that training to good use, Collett stood proud, refused to cower, and she attacked with a fierce yell.

Cade fared better than his friends in Colorado. He fought with deadly purpose, and it wasn't long before he overcame the leech that dared enter Ashley's office. Once finished, he glared down at the dust coating her floor. Violent energy still coursed through him.

C.B. Haight

Turning his head, Cade pricked his ears at the noise coming from the living room. Still in his hybrid form, he charged toward the melee, crashing through the hallway as he went. He didn't even notice the hole he created in the wall as he made contact with it at the turn.

When he entered the room, things were almost under control. Jarrett remained engaged with his opponent, but the fight clearly favored his injured brother. Nate was pulling a nasty looking knife free from the man stupid enough to attack him.

Jeffery though, was locked in a strange sort of magical battle of his own. The sight would have been comical if Cade didn't have first-hand knowledge of how deadly their magic was.

Jeffery's features were pinched, and his posture was rigid. Sweat beaded on his brow. His muscles were rigid, his arms out wide, and bent slightly at the elbow. His hands, pointed in towards his waist. It looked as if he was trying to mimic a bear. He glared at his much older opponent who grimaced, and tightened his fists, showing his own intense struggle to ward off Jeffery.

Cade moved to assist him, but before he could cover the short distance, Jeffery released a determined shout, and stepping forward moved to bring his hands together. Veins bulged in his neck, his face reddened, but when his hands finally met, a thunderous clap reverberated in the small room. The walls shook. Cade cringed and yelped, and Jarrett, still in his human body, winced and covered his ears as the violent sound wave pulsed in their sensitive ears. An orange-colored light filled the same spot where the dark man battling Jeffery stood. It dissipated almost instantaneously, taking the other sorcerer with it. Jeffery crumpled to his knees, and Nate moved to help him.

"WHAT the hell was that?" Jarrett snapped darkly with angry fever in his eyes.

Jeffery shrugged, not fully understanding the complexities of the spell himself. Mostly mentorless, Jeffery often followed his

~ 162 ~

instincts or obeyed the pull of magic. This often created varying results.

"A better question is how they found us?" Nate chimed in, taking Jarrett and Cade's focus away from the young mage.

"Niall," Jarrett replied tiredly. "If he wants you, he'll find you. He has ways to find anybody." Looking around at the carnage of Ashley's home, he shook his head in defeat.

Cade saw the emptiness in Jarrett's eyes an instant before he turned and left the house. Nate and Jeffery diverted to Cade with puzzled expressions, wondering who Niall is and what to do next.

Cade shifted back into a man then asked, "Jeffery, where's Ashley?"

"Wal-Mart in Bedford, Virginia."

"Wal-Mart?" Cade questioned with surprise. He was confounded by Jeffery's choice of location.

"It's the only place I could think of that would be open with people around, at least it's the only place I could think of on short notice," he explained.

Cade couldn't help but smile at the quick-thinking sorcerer. "It's fine," he assured. "Take Nate to her, and then stay with them. I'll call you when I can."

Jeffery began shaking his head in his first small act of defiance.

Cade's expression turned grim, "Do It! Stay with them."

"You'll need me if they are tracking him," Jeffery argued.

"What I need, is for you and Nate to make sure Ashley and Tracy are safe. Jarrett and I can handle ourselves."

"I'm not even sure I can. I've used too much magic the last couple days."

"You'll do it because you have to!" Cade snapped uncharacteristically.

Jeffery assented with a quick, silent nod, but his eyes conveyed his mixed emotions. He grabbed Nate's jacket, and they disappeared before Cade could say anything else.

Cade cursed as guilt began to fester in his gut. He glanced to the door Jarrett had exited and knew he didn't have time for guilt. He went to the bedroom and quickly put on his pants from earlier that day. *So much for the new clothes,* he thought. He grabbed his shirt, boots, and backpack and rushed to follow his brother.

Taken completely by surprise, the gray-skinned man stood dumbfounded while Collett cried out and rushed him. She used the lamp as a barrier of sorts and lashed out with it, connecting several times with flesh. On the last strike, a bright light flashed between them and the half-demon crumpled at her feet.

Before she could shift her focus to the next opponent, Delphene, or the animal she assumed was Delphene, rushed past her in a blur of violence. She began tearing and biting into demon and human flesh with equal vigor, laying out the remaining enemy ranks in no time at all.

Collett took that short respite to study the female lycanthrope. Unlike Cade, her coloring was a dark brown with reddish tints, and oddly enough, her tail sported a white tip. Seeing the chocolate colored wolf with black ichor covering her lips, Collett found it difficult to associate the startling creature with the Amazon-like woman she laughed with a few hours before.

As if sensing her scrutiny, Delphene pinned her with her golden gaze, and Collett could see the woman within the animal. She immediately recognized the compassion and fire in her eyes.

She had a similar experience with Cade. When she met Cade for the first time, his eyes drew her in even before she knew he was her werewolf rescuer. Later, when she discovered his secret, Collett understood his very identity could be seen within the depths of his gaze. Delphene was no different. Collett felt she could connect to her, even in this form, through her eyes.

The Price of Knowing

The lycan flicked her eyes away and, with an inhuman, gravelly voice that somehow still sounded like the woman herself, ordered, "Time to go!"

Rederrick nodded and bent to pick up his discarded gun. Without a word, he turned back to the door leading to the security room.

"Jenny?" Cynda questioned hopefully.

Collett felt a shiver run through her. She knew the answer before Delphene's expression turned sad, and she looked back to the doorway where Delphene had laid the beloved woman.

"Is she..." Cynda inquired with choked words and tears in her eyes.

Shaking her head, Delphene bent to gently scoop up the limp form with the same clawed hands that, only minutes before, ripped through their enemies with cruel efficiency. "*Non*, but it's not good, *Chèrie*." Her sympathy rang through her animal-like voice.

A small light of hope sparked in Cynda's tear-filled eyes. "Collett, you have to help her."

Dumbfounded, Collett looked back to Cynda. "What can I do?"

"Whatever it is, it has to wait!" Rederrick barked from the other room. "We're at risk here. We have to go!" All of them obeyed and hurried into the extra room. Rederrick secured the door behind them. "Cynda, get the rifles. Collett, get the extra phones and the packet from the safe." He moved to the other side of the room and opened what looked like an electrical panel. He flipped the breakers in a seemingly random order, and there was an audible click that came from the closet.

Rederrick looked back at the women to verify they had gathered up the items he instructed them to. As they made their way to him, he opened the closet and then pushed open a false wall, easily accessible behind the few items stored there.

Delphene moved to go through. "You remember the way?" he asked. She nodded her canine head in reply.

~ 165 ~

He jerked his head, motioning for her to go through first with Jenny in her arms. Cynda was next, handing him one of three loaded rifles as she passed by. Collett wasn't far behind.

"I'm sor—" she began.

He stopped her with a shake his head. "Don't. It is not your fault. Go on now. I'll be right behind you."

She gave him a sad look but obeyed.

Rederrick looked back into the room with a pang in his chest. He had known the chances of something like this happening increased when he invited Collett into his home, but to walk away from everything he had built here grated against his pride and his will to fight.

He watched the monitors, resigned, as more demons and men rushed through the house ransacking it as they moved toward the den. It was as if they knew exactly where his security room would be found.

In response to the pre-programmed code he had entered in the breakers, the computers began to crash and electricity sparked in various places. All his files were being destroyed, and he watched as the last TV went black, no longer affording him a view of the monsters destroying his home.

He'd meant it when he'd told Collett it wasn't her fault. He'd been opposing The Faction and everything they stood for since they tried to take his beloved Cynda from him decades ago. He and Cade organized The Brotherhood to protect others who couldn't do it for themselves. This room was created as a base of operations, and it was only a matter time before The Faction brought the fight to his door.

He heaved a sigh and moved into the escape tunnel. The closet door would shut on its own. Rederrick slid the secret panel back in place and didn't look back again. He wiped the regret from his mind and began to focus on the present. They were at a point of no return. It was time to take down The Faction once and for all. Otherwise, their enemy would stop at nothing to destroy The Brotherhood, and Rederrick refused to even consider that.

He knew the best way to kill a serpent was to cut off its ugly head. That is exactly what they intended to do, but some sacrifices would have to be made to do it. Dismissing thoughts about the home he was leaving, Rederrick moved to catch up with the others.

CHAPTER 16

He sat in the still quiet of the cold evening leaning back, his arms supporting him, with his long legs stretched out before him. A light breeze stirred the chilly air around him, making it feel even colder. Not that he noticed such things. He could see the lights of the nearby town flicker on as darkness set over the landscape.

That is how Cade found him, sitting in solitude, on the frozen hillside in Pennsylvania. Cade knew Jarrett heard his approach. He also knew Jarrett would have caught his scent and allowed Cade to follow him through the night and into that day on the long journey to this place. The fact that Jarrett made no attempt to conceal his actions or stop Cade was a good sign.

Jarrett remained silent as Cade walked up carefully and sat down next to his brother on the cold, frozen earth. They sat together, the silence between them stretching out, as the sun finished its descent and long after the moon took its place above them. The night was as quiet as they were. Only the bitter wind stirred, making the trees rustle softly. In a way,-the night felt subdued and peaceful.

~ 168 ~

The Price of Knowing

Finally, Jarrett showed his annoyance with a clipped, "What are you doing here?"

Cade didn't let Jarrett's crisp words bother him. He simply shrugged. "Helping."

"I'm long past the age of needing a babysitter," Jarrett replied tersely.

"Oh I don't know, you're still prone to temper tantrums," he retorted with a smile—inciting a fierce glare from his twin. Cade remained unfazed by his brother's attempt to provoke him. He simply waited for Jarrett to do the talking.

After a few more minutes passed, Jarrett asked, "Do you sense it?"

"What?"

"The shift in the balance—the darkness."

Cade offered no reply.

"Things are changing," Jarrett continued.

"They always do," Cade supplied, scrutinizing his brother. "Sometimes things have to go wrong in order to go right."

Jarrett snorted. "I'm tired," he admitted. "I'm not sure if I want to see any more changes. I hate change," he finished and looked at Cade with empty eyes.

"Change isn't all bad," Cade began, and Jarrett scoffed. "There's indoor plumbing." Shaking his head in disbelief, Jarrett couldn't help the slight grin that pulled at his lips. Though, he didn't allow Cade to see his reaction. After another long pause, Cade asked, "Why fight so hard to live then? I've seen you in action. You don't fight like a person who's too tired to go on."

"Habit," he replied with a shrug.

"I don't buy it. You fought like a demon, like someone who wants to live. In fact, I forgot how fierce you can be. I'm not sure I've ever seen your equal."

Jarrett ignored the compliment, letting Cade know he didn't care much what his brother thought.

~ 169 ~

C.B. Haight

"The demon part isn't far off," he finally mumbled as the breeze picked up.

"Why are we here, Jarrett?" No reply was forthcoming as Jarrett turned his attention back to the town below. Cade tried again, "Why this place?"

"Didn't she already tell you? Don't you two talk, or are you too busy doing other things?"

Cade felt his temper rise at the crude reference to his relationship with Collett, but he carefully held it in check. He knew it would only satisfy Jarrett if he lost it. He decided to let Jarrett tell him what he wanted, and keep what Collett had revealed to himself. "She doesn't really understand it all herself," he explained instead, "Plus, she's determined to protect you, something I'm unsure about. She only told me to find you, so here I am." He waited a beat then asked again, "Why *am* I here?"

"Ever the obedient lap dog," Jarrett sneered, but Cade could tell it was forced. There was no anger in his tone. Jarrett was as worn down as he claimed. Cade knew patience would be needed here.

The night fell quiet again for a long time. Right when Cade felt his patience thinning, Jarrett finally spoke. "This is where it all changed," he paused, "where I changed." His willingness to share that revelation surprised them both. Jarrett wasn't even sure why he said it. The memories were so hard for him to think about, let alone talk about.

Jarrett hated the monster inside. He hated himself every time he lost his fragile control. Deep down, even so long after those horrific days of his childhood, he still believed the preacher's words. He was a damned soul, a monster without hope of salvation. There was nothing left for him but death. He'd pondered it often these past weeks and believed he was nothing more than the bastard son of a demon. Frustrated by where his thoughts were taking him, he stood abruptly and started to walk away.

"It's not your fault you know. It is what it is," Cade said to his back.

The Price of Knowing

Jarrett's shoulders slumped, and he looked back with an expression that could only be described as pure agony. "You'd be wrong about that. It was my fault. She died because I wasn't strong enough."

Cade understood with sudden clarity why Jarrett had fought so hard against everything throughout his life. It was a rebellion against weakness. He refused to bend to another's will because of ancient events that were out of his control as a child. Anger helped mask the pain and guilt that were his constant companions. Cade recognized from the look in his brother's eyes that the life-shaping events from childhood were not the only ones haunting him—merely the first.

No wonder Jarrett had clung to Ashley, despite the obvious risk in doing so. Ashley was bright, loving, and most of all, forgiving. After all these years, Jarrett still yearned for forgiveness, but was unwilling to accept it. Cade was finally beginning to see the truth, and he was placated toward his brother for his relationship with Ashley. He almost felt grateful to Ashley for it.

Though their relationship was tenuous at best, Cade risked asking for more information, "And Niall? Your allegiance to him?"

Jarrett was silent for a full minute before answering, "Allegiance? It's not so simple." *More like imprisonment*, he thought to himself.

Cade did not miss the pure sound of resentment filling Jarrett's tone. Jarrett's words gave him some of the relief he wanted. No, that he *needed*. "Who is he?"

"A sorcerer, most believe. The Devil's general, others say."

"And you? What do you think?"

"Does it matter? He's Niall, the one in charge of The Faction, and the man holding the power behind it. Beyond that, nothing matters," he replied with a shrug.

"What does he want with Collett?" Cade asked.

"Her life, one way or another," Jarrett answered. "I don't know why. Rarely do."

"And you?"

"My death, one way or another."

"How do we stop him?" Cade prodded.

Jarrett huffed out a defeated laugh, "I'm not sure we can."

Maybe, thought Cade. Raising his head he looked to the sky and thought about it. Despite Jarrett's opinion, he knew they had to try. They needed to take down The Faction's leader if they ever wanted to be safe again. Cade and his brother had one thing in common, neither of them gave up easily.

Turning, Jarrett moved to leave again, and Cade moved to follow. He didn't make it far before he heard the dark protest. "You're not coming with me."

"Yes I am, for a while anyway. At least until your wound is healed up, and you can protect yourself."

With his back to Cade, Jarrett closed his eyes in exasperation. "Go back to your wife."

"I will if you come with me."

Jarrett scoffed and shook his head.

"Well, then I guess I get to keep following you."

Jarrett clenched his jaw. He didn't want to hear those words. He wanted to push them aside, push Cade aside. He couldn't deny the mixture of relief and frustration he felt knowing that Cade would be with him.

It would be easier if Cade didn't matter. The truth was though, that his brother had always mattered. It was why Jarrett had separated himself from Cade all these years. Cade just never knew it was to protect him.

Neither man moved. Jarrett heard Cade fold his arms over his chest in defiance and knew he would not relent. Opening his eyes, Jarrett conceded by changing the subject, "Do you remember the first time?"

His words were quiet, yet Cade heard them. He was surprised by the question, but he answered honestly, "It's not an event you easily forget."

The Price of Knowing

Jarrett's lips twitched, but it was quickly controlled. "No, I suppose not."

After that, they walked for a long time, silently making their way to the town below. They were in this together for now, but neither man felt comfortable with the situation. Their relationship was far too complicated. As they walked together, neither of them believed they would likely stay together for long, because neither man thought they could be friends.

Cade was idealistic, hopeful, and generally happy by nature. He sought out and protected innocence and goodness in people. Jarrett, the opposite, embodied cynicism, hate, and anger. He believed innocence and goodness were as rare as blue diamonds, and the sooner a person understood that the better off they were.

Walking through the small town, they both took notice of the festive wreaths hanging on the lampposts and the decorations the small shops used to boast their wares. The decorations reminded Cade of how close Christmas was, and he even thought about stopping in one of the little shops to find Collett a gift. It was proof that life does go on and hope still existed. For Jarrett, the decorations meant little. They were merely a thing he had to endure every year. He hated the holidays.

"What's your plan?" asked Jarrett.

"I call back home, check in, and make sure Ashley made it to a safe place with Tracy. They should have checked in with their parents by now. Then we can decide what to do."

Cade promptly found the nearest phone. He convinced a gas station attendant to allow him to use their phone, claiming a lost cell phone and wooing her with his crooked grin. He proceeded to call Collett first. He frowned as the voicemail came on. He hung up and tried Rederrick's cell only to hear the familiar chime signaling no answer once again. He tried Cynda next, his worry increasing. No answer. He hung up the phone and scowled before he picked it up once more, trying to reach Delphene. Still nothing. He carefully replaced the phone on the receiver and looked up. Jarrett stood close

~ 173 ~

by with a hand tucked in his jacket, holding his wounded side. He quirked a brow at Cade.

Shaking his head, Cade moved to his brother. "I'm sure they're fine," he said as they went outside. Jarrett said nothing. "They must think the phones are unsafe," Cade muttered more to himself than Jarrett. "Or maybe they're just out," he continued, knowing the statement didn't make sense.

"They have *mobile* phones, right?" Jarrett replied cynically.

"I meant out of a service area," Cade retorted, pulling at his hair, as he often did when frustrated. He looked around the street as if seeking an explanation.

"Where would they go?"

"Huh?" he replied when Jarrett's deep voice pulled him from his thoughts.

"If they had to cut and run, where would they go?"

Cade's brows drew together. "It depends."

"Depends on what?"

"On who is still alive?"

"*Non*, I will not go to a place with no one I know to watch our back," argued Delphene.

"I'm telling you it's the best option we have."

"Stop!" snapped Cynda, tired of listening to Rederrick and Delphene argue in the front seat of the Tahoe. She sat in the middle row while Collett crouched over Jenny in the back. "Delphene, I understand why you want to go home, and Rederrick, I know why you want to go to the house in Utah, but right now, we can't do either. Jenny needs a hospital. Until we take care of that, there is nothing to discuss. So knock it off so Collett can concentrate. Can't you see how you're affecting her?"

The Price of Knowing

Both of them had the decency to look slightly sheepish before complying with her order. "How is she doing?" Cynda asked Collett.

"Not good. She's in bad shape, and I can't get past the pain. Even unconscious, she feels it. I keep trying to focus my thoughts on hers like you want, but her thoughts are so disconnected. When I try to reach her, she recoils. Her arm is definitely broken, as you suspected, and I think maybe a few of her ribs are broken as well. She has a concussion to go with it all. I just can't grab ahold when I reach for her thoughts."

"I can't believe they did this to her."

"Demons have no feelings, *Chèrie*. I curse whatever black magician conjured them."

"Actually, the first arch-demon was a human king named Nehemiah," Collett said absently.

With her back turned and her focus on Jenny, Collett did not take note of everyone else's reaction. Cynda's eyes went wide as she looked from her to Delphene, who reacted similarly. Rederrick sat up in the driver's seat, leaned over, and put a finger to his lips, warning them both not to say a word. He recognized this as a rare moment when Collett unconsciously accessed her lost memories, and any interruption of those natural thoughts could dam the flow of recollection. He had seen her do this before.

"Nehemiah?" he questioned with casual interest.

"Yes, he was a simple man once, but a leader among his people. He was smart, strong, and everyone trusted him. His subjects lifted him up as king after he defeated a great enemy. He fought the most fiercely of all the warriors and was the strongest among them. The people revered him, almost worshipped him. Then, as years passed, the power drew him in.

"He became wicked and cruel after a time. Tired of his greed, the people revolted and rose against him in an effort to kill him. He escaped, but his wounds were grievous. As he lay there, bleeding to death, he called out to whomever would listen for help.

~ 175 ~

C.B. Haight

"Because his heart was black, it was The Great Opposer that heeded his call and appeared before him. Nehemiah pleaded for his life, offering his soul in return for a chance to exact vengeance. The dark one is crafty and has corrupted many because of it. He made the bargain quickly— Nehemiah's soul in exchange for a chance at revenge.

"Not fully understanding the cost of the bargain, Nehemiah died and the Opposer took the soul as promised. The Great Opposer, not having the power to create man and unable to bring back what was, then breathed his wicked breath over the shell that was once Nehemiah and brought forth the first soulless demon enslaved to the most vile master of all."

Collett brushed her hand over Jenny's hair as she continued, "The Great Opposer's black power allowed the demon Nehemiah to exact his revenge, helping him and gifting him with unnatural magic, poison in his bite, and the strength of ten men. Afterwards, he let the creature roam the earth for a time. In his viciousness, the creature spawned several half demons and helped recruit more vengeful souls for his lord, who sadistically created other variations of demon lines.

"Ironically though, Nehemiah's demon subjects, much like the human ones a lifetime before, rose up against Nehemiah and his cruel acts. As he was being attacked this time, his wicked lord and keeper of his soul appeared, and the arch-demon pleaded for his life once again. The Great Opposer simply laughed, *'I already have your soul, and there is nothing greater you can offer me.'* And because he had no soul and no humanity left, Nehemiah fell apart into dust at the killers' feet. Banished, his soul remained forever imprisoned by The Great Opposer.

"Ultimately, The Great Opposer was satisfied. He possessed an army of demons roaming the earth, wreaking havoc wherever they went. All because Nehemiah selfishly made a bargain with the devil."

No one said a word. They were partially captured by the story and partially surprised at the source of the tale. Rederrick was almost afraid to break the silence and wondered if Collett even realized what she'd done. Recalling such an involved series of events may offer a clue to who she was, but how she knew the tale remained a mystery.

"*Merde*, if that is where the *démons* came from, how twisted is my family tree?" Delphene asked, trying to mimic Rederrick's easy tone.

"Well, that history is a little more complicated," she answered.

"Collett, do you realize what you're doing?" asked Cynda.

Turning to face them, she shook her head.

"You're remembering, *ma petite*," Delphene explained.

Collett's brows drew in as if in disbelief, and then she suddenly realized they were right. "I remembered something."

Cynda smiled at her.

The excitement of the revelation was cut short, however, when Jenny drew in a breath, whimpered, and her breathing turned shallow and gasping.

"No!" Cynda cried out.

Collett had already redirected her focus and checked Jenny's vitals. Her heart was weak, and Collett could feel the pain again as it peaked. The seconds were ticking. Somehow, Collett knew Jenny was leaving them. Desperate, she reached for Jenny's lingering thoughts and began focusing as best she could. She recognized right away that, on top of Jenny's injuries, she was now having a heart attack.

Unsure of what to do, Collett focused on the heart itself and tried her best to send comfort and calm feelings to Jenny as she had practiced doing over the last couple of months. She became enveloped by sensations. She felt the tightness in her own chest while still focusing on Jenny's. Her head swam, and she tasted a coppery tang in her mouth. Putting every effort into staying conscious, she kept trying to remove it all and keep Jenny with

C.B. Haight

them. Collett didn't even hear Cynda telling her to stop. She felt a tug on her arm, and the last thing she heard was, "Please, don't let Jenny be dead." Then there was only blackness.

CHAPTER 17

Cade struggled to keep his worry under control. The truth was, he felt a panic rising within. He knew that Collett was in danger, and regretted leaving her. He kept silently reminding himself his friends were capable and experienced enough to handle almost anything, but deep down, he knew something was terribly wrong. The inability to make contact with her tore at him. They last spoke four days ago, just before he abandoned his cell at the motel.

He knew that Rederrick would have the backup burner phones, but he didn't have the numbers because Rederrick couldn't get them until they were activated. Cade was left with no way to make contact, and he hated it.

As a leader for The Brotherhood, he was used to knowing everyone's status. Now alone with his twin, he was in the dark, a place that made him very anxious.

He and Jarrett spoke little of their concerns during their journey south toward Louisiana. In fact, communication between them was practically non-existent. Despite the recent openness, neither fully trusted the other. Too many years of being on opposing sides did

~ 179 ~

that to them. They had agreed to stay together for now, but their relationship remained tense. Cade wondered if it always would be.

When Cade found he couldn't reach anyone by phone, he considered where they might go. He knew Delphene and Rederrick well enough to know where they may go, and he was betting that Delphene would win the debate. She had a knack for arguing. So New Orleans it was, and Jarrett, in a rare moment of cooperation, offered no argument.

They were currently leaving Tennessee behind and making their way to Alabama on I-24. They had rented a car back in Pennsylvania, using one of many false identifications Cade kept. Despite Cade's protests, Jarrett sat behind the wheel for the first time since they rented the car, and Cade spent the last hour brooding over one more thing he no longer had control of.

While he sat watching the rhythmic passing of interstate lights in the dark night, Cade felt Jarrett's attention drift to him several times. "What?" he asked gruffly, inviting a distraction from his dire thoughts.

Jarrett only shrugged.

A few more silent minutes past, and Cade reevaluated the series of events of the attack at Ashley's. "You saw her at Ashley's house?"

Taking his eyes from the road, Jarrett looked at Cade slightly confused.

"Collett. You saw her at Ashley's before the demons attacked us."

He moved his eyes forward again. "Yeah," he said simply.

A tick started in Cade's jaw. He still wondered why she didn't come to him. He knew she was somehow connected to Jarrett, but her last appearance bothered him. It stung on a deeper level. "Do you see her often?"

"Don't."

"Don't what?"

"Don't over analyze it. It's nothing," Jarrett said annoyed.

"It has to mean something," Cade replied with equal annoyance.

"What do you want here, Cade?"

"I want—" he started to snap, but he changed his tone and muttered, "Never mind." Not only was talking to Jarrett difficult, he wasn't exactly sure what he wanted. Cade longed to understand why his wife kept showing up in Jarrett's dreams and why she felt his injuries. Most of all, he worried what about what it meant when his wife reached out to Jarrett the other night instead of himself. Unfortunately, Jarrett wouldn't be able to answer any of his questions.

As if reading his brother's mind, Jarret broke the silence, "It's not like I asked for this. In fact, I'd be happier if she'd leave me alone."

Cade looked at him sharply, "She saved your life."

"Yeah well, who asked her to?"

"You ungrateful—"

"Look, I never asked her to save me—not even first time! I didn't want to be saved! She shouldn't have come into the cabin that day, but since she did—she should've pulled Rowena out!" Jarrett snapped back.

Cade's brows drew in, and his anger dissipated slightly. A sudden thought came to him. "She saved *you* though."

"Yeah, and what about it?" Jarrett snarled.

"Nothing," Cade mumbled as he thought about it and realized Collett must have had a reason for repeatedly saving his brother, even if she didn't remember why. He knew that she was a kind and generous person, but her interference must mean more. There must be something important he was missing. Cade could only hope she wasn't married to the wrong brother. Selena's cryptic words to Collett haunted him still, "*When you remember who you are, you will only want help from one...*" What if that person wasn't him?

C.B. Haight

Unlike Jarrett and Cade, Rederrick did stop along his route. He managed to pull a few strings and stopped at Fort Carson where James was stationed to get Jenny admitted to the hospital there. Having secret military ties, as well several political ones, had saved his butt more than once. He knew the base would be one of the safer places they could leave their dear friend, though it bothered all of them that they could not risk staying here with her.

After seeing to Jenny's needs, Rederrick and Cynda met up with James to let him know what was going on. Meanwhile, Delphene waited in a motel not far away with an unconscious Collett.

They had all agreed that admitting Collett to the hospital would not be wise considering her healing abilities and, more importantly, her empathy. Unconscious, Collett would have no way to block the pain and emotions from the people there, and Cynda instinctively knew whatever was wrong with her would only get worse in that situation.

After Collett passed out, Jenny's condition seemed to stabilize. None of them understood what Collett did for her, but they all knew it had taken a tremendous amount of energy to do it. The entire event bothered Rederrick more than a little. He knew that Collett had somehow saved Jenny's life, and though he was relieved, he couldn't help but wonder at the cost. He stressed about it and wondered what would happen if Collet used too much energy. Could she kill herself if she wasn't careful? He hated not understanding how the whole thing worked and dreaded that he may still lose them both. He decided he would have a serious talk with Collett on the matter if—no— *when* she woke.

Presently, they were on their way to Lakefront Airport, located close to New Orleans. Rederrick cleverly worked out a military flight from Fort Carson. It wasn't as comfortable a ride as a flight on The Brotherhood's private jet would've been, but that would be too risky. Since The Faction knew everything about his home and found out about Ashley's apartment, the hanger where the jet was kept was no doubt compromised.

The Price of Knowing

Rederrick glanced down at his watch, December 15th 1:15 a.m. It amazed him that 72 hours had passed since the attack. Everything had changed in such a short time.

He turned his attention to Cynda, who held Collett's head in her lap, and watched as she absently stroked her new friend's hair while closing her own eyes to find what little rest she could on the loud, uncomfortable trip. He felt a tug in his heart seeing her so tired, and yet he knew she would not fully rest until she knew Collett would be okay.

At least we know the kids were all safe, he reasoned. It was a small measure of relief in a situation full of turmoil.

For years now, Rederrick, with Cade's help on the front lines, had battled The Faction and its evil leadership on relatively safe terms. Today hit him hard, and he knew that there would be no going back. Rederrick understood that they were close to ending the evil group and the terror they inflicted upon people with extraordinary abilities. He also knew that they would have to finish it this time to get their lives back.

He and Cynda knew personally how vicious they could be in their quest for control. He closed his eyes, and his mind drifted back to those days when he was a young, ambitious law student, meeting the most beautiful woman he'd ever seen. He could still imagine her standing in the autumn light on the college campus. Her long, red hair shone in the late afternoon sunlight, and her bright, full smile was apparent as she laughed at some unknown joke told by one of her friends. His heart had belonged to her from that moment.

He almost lost her when The Faction found out about Cynda's power and kidnapped her right before their wedding. If not for Cade, Rederrick's family, his life, would be very different.

To this very day, Cade still did not think risking his life to save Cynda, to save perfect strangers even, was anything special. Rederrick, on the other hand, understood how rare people like Cade were and would forever be grateful. He only hoped he mimicked Cade's example and that he could keep Collett safe as Cade had

~ 183 ~

once done for Cynda. He lifted his head and looked back to the unconscious Collett. He knew the problem lay not only in protecting her from The Faction, but he also needed to protect her from herself.

His thoughts changed as the aircraft shifted. He understood the altitude change meant they were close. In the headset he wore, the pilot confirmed his assumption as he notified Rederrick they were clear for landing. He reached across to gently shake Cynda and informed her that they made it to Louisiana.

The pilot set down, and they made their way from the craft. Delphene carried Collett, and Cynda followed her to the pre-arranged car that awaited them. Rederrick approached the pilot who began his post-flight maintenance checks.

"Thanks again for the ride."

The pilot looked up at his V-22 Osprey[BT1]. "No problem man. I am always looking for an excuse to get her in the air."

"Just the same, thanks. I hope there's no trouble."

"You heard my CO, I'm running maneuvers today. No problem with that," the pilot implied the reason for the flight that would be recorded on the official records.

Rederrick pulled out a card and passed it to him. "If you ever need help, call this number and mention my name. We'll make sure you get it."

"Same goes," he said, understanding Rederrick already knew how to reach him. "I don't exactly know what is going on, but from what my CO did and all that other stuff you pulled off, that tells me you must be a good man, or fairly connected. Not many could've gotten results that fast."

"It's a little of both, I suppose. I guess it pays to know the right people," answered Rederrick.

"Well, just a heads up, I'm flying back this way in a few days. I have extra room if you need it."

"Thanks," Rederrick replied, smiling.

"Will she be okay?" he asked, tilting his head toward the women.

"I can only hope," he replied. The pilot offered his hand, and after shaking it, Rederrick turned to catch up to the women.

The pilot returned his attention to post flight maintenance. By the time he finished his checklist, Rederrick and company were gone. He climbed inside to grab his pack and was startled to see an empty saline bag. "Where did this come from?" he asked himself. He knew his three passengers were in good health.

The confused pilot had already forgotten all about the unconscious woman who accompanied Rederrick, Cynda, and Delphene. He'd even forgotten that he was the one to give her the IV in the first place.

Collett felt like she swam through a thick, murky soup. Her thoughts were muddled between awareness and a state of the dreams. She fought for some sort of control, but wondered if she would ever find it. There was a place where she sat in a damp, dark room with someone. When she was there, Collett had the sensations of cold, pain, and fear. It was frustrating because she couldn't see anything, only feel. Then she would have periods in which she could feel the weight of her own body and distantly hear people around herself. Though, during those times, she was helpless to speak or move. Nothing about it felt clear, and throughout her ordeal, she had no concept of time. She occasionally wondered if it had been minutes or hours.

Something had changed. Her body was lighter, and the thick soup became a fog that she felt was lifting. Her body was still weak, but she could move again. Opening her eyes, she nearly panicked when she only saw dim shadows and feared she was still lost in the dark hole. Then she realized it must be night, and the room she occupied had no light on.

Her body ached, but the lingering pain was strangely reassuring. *I'm alive*, she thought. She knew she had lost control when she tried

C.B. Haight

to help Jenny. The strange magic had overtaken her. Near the end of it, before she lost all thought, it occurred to her that maybe her power would kill her. "I'm alive," she whispered in relief and closed her eyes to regain her bearings.

"Collett?"

She thought the deep voice from the corner was perhaps imagined. Then she felt warm fingers reach out and grip her hand tightly. She squeezed the familiar hand in return, and in the next breath, Collett was wrapped within Cade's desperate embrace.

"I thought I'd lost you!" he said with his voice muffled against her neck.

"Cade!" she exclaimed, her voice was full of emotion. "You made it! You found us. I thought that maybe—"

"I know," he said, pulling back slightly. He cupped her cheek, and despite the dark, she could see his golden eyes looking at her. "I thought the same things, but we made it. We're all here."

"Jarrett came with you?"

"Jarrett came with me," he confirmed.

"Oh Cade, you did it!" she exclaimed joyfully. Leaning into him, she pressed her lips to his. He returned her kiss gently at first, careful not to hurt her, but she pulled him in deeper and brought the kiss to a more passionate level.

After a long time, he pulled back and looked at her once more. "What happened?"

"We were attacked."

"Rederrick already told me about that," he interrupted. "What happened to you?"

"Oh no, Jenny! Is she. . ."

Collett sensed him shaking his head. "She's alive, for now. She hasn't woken yet, but the doctors told Rederrick that she's resting easily and doesn't seem to be experiencing any pain."

Collett's worry lessened. She had felt Jenny's pain firsthand. She knew it was unbearable and possibly even causing her own heart attack.

~ 186 ~

The Price of Knowing

"She had a heart attack. Cade, do they know she had a heart attack?"

"Collett!" he said with exasperation and rose, leaving her alone on the bed. Surprised by his frustrated outburst, she recoiled slightly. She heard him expel a breath to calm himself. "I know about Jenny. They know about Jenny. I know about the attack and the trip here. I even know what happened the minute Ashley was dropped off at a Wal-Mart somewhere in the middle of Virginia.

"What I don't know—what no one seems to know—is what happened when you touched Jenny, and why you didn't so much as move for two full days." He stopped his rant and inhaled in deeply. He knelt down before the bed, took her hand into his, and tried again, "What happened to *you*?"

To her own surprise, she burst into tears, and the words wouldn't come.

Surprised by her emotional breakdown, Cade couldn't think of how to properly respond. "Shh, it's all right. Don't cry," he soothed as he gathered her up and carefully maneuvered himself into the bed with her. Holding her, he gently rubbed her back, and the physical contact calmed both of them.

Her sobbing eased, and she wiped at tears on his shirt as if she could dry them.

"Okay now?"

She nodded against his chest.

"Talk to me. What made you cry?"

"I thought..."

"Thought?" he coaxed.

"Can we turn on the lights?" she asked on a sniffle.

"No. We don't want anyone to know we're here. For now, we're trying to keep a low profile."

Collett nodded as if she understood. "This is all my fault."

"No, it's not your fault," he reassured softly. "We've been heading this direction for a long time. Even without you, we would have eventually made it to this point."

~ 187 ~

"Jenny was dying. I knew...I felt her giving up," she explained. "The pain was so intense, and her heart...it... She couldn't take it," Collett paused.

"Tell me," he urged gently as he ran his fingers through her soft hair to help her relax.

"The intruder beat her so badly. He kicked at her, and he kept using that stupid stun gun on her."

"You saw this?" he asked.

"I was with her somehow and yet with you and Jarrett at the same time." Collett detangled herself and hugged her knees. Cade, wanting to stay as close as possible, also adjusted by wrapping his arms around her and laying his head on her shoulder. "I couldn't control what happened to her. I wanted to—I tried. I saw the demon's face—his smile. I wanted to hurt him as he had hurt Jenny. The agony he'd dished out still coursed through me." Collett stopped herself. She knew she had killed the half-demon with her projection and felt it had been the right thing to do—the only thing she could do to save Jenny. Still, she couldn't let go of the guilt that churned in her stomach. She'd taken a life, and he'd been at least partially human.

Keeping that part to herself, Collett moved on, "There was this sensation inside me when we were in the car. I can't explain it, but I felt this slipping away, it was an emptiness in Jenny. She was dying. Her chest tightened, and her heart struggled to beat. I could barely breath, barely think, but I couldn't watch her die. I only wanted to help her. I thought I could for some reason, like maybe I could heal her. But when I reached out to her, there was so much. It overwhelmed me, and..."

"And..." he encouraged, gripping her hand.

"We connected. I felt everything she felt. I saw what she saw. Her memories, her life—Then I lost control. Pretty soon, I felt like I *was* Jenny. Her pain went into me. Somehow, I took them from her. My own heart slowed while hers began to even out. I couldn't get enough oxygen. My chest felt so tight. Everything poured from me into her and then from her into me. I couldn't make it stop. I don't even know what happened."

Reality set in, and he understood they really had almost lost her. He held on tighter and closed his eyes, grateful she was still alive. "Collett."

"Before you say it, I know I almost died, but the thing is, I'd do it again if I had to."

"Yeah, I know," he said with a sense of pride and sadness mingled in his voice.

After her confession, they held each other like that for a while. They had come to appreciate the true miracle that had occurred.

"Cade?" Collett asked after the quiet moment passed.

"Yeah?" he said, nuzzling her neck now.

"Wal-Mart?"

He couldn't help it, he laughed lightly. He eased them back down, holding her close, and told her the story.

CHAPTER 18

Collett and Cade woke early and carefully made their way through Delphene's home. They reached the kitchen, and the warm scent of pastries assaulted them. The rich smell made Collett's stomach grumble.

"Mornin' *Cherie*. It's good to see you about finally," Delphene said happily as she sifted powdered sugar over beignets resting on the center island counter.

Cade snatched up one of the sweet pastries, took a generous bite, and hummed with pleasure. "Delphene, you're still amazing," he complimented and then easily finished it off. Picking up another, he passed it to Collett.

Cynda entered the room and squeaked with joy at seeing her friend out of bed. "Collett! I'm so glad you're okay. We've been so worried," she said, embracing her.

Collett watched Rederrick come in while she returned Cynda's hug, and he smiled at her. Then, in all seriousness, he stated, "Try not to do that again—whatever it was—at least until you can control yourself a bit better."

~190~

"I didn't mean to scare you all. I'm sorry I did. You're right, I lost control of it," she replied sheepishly.

He nodded. "You're alive—and so is Jenny for that matter, so I'll thank you for that."

She nodded in kind.

Cynda released her. "You're all right then?"

"Yes, I feel—" Collett began, but when a tremor of fierce emotion passed over her, she faltered.

Footsteps echoed on the tile floor behind her. She didn't need to look to see who it was. She could feel him, and she cringed inwardly from his outward animosity directed mostly toward her. Everyone went quiet, and steeling herself, Collett turned to face him.

He looked upon her, and seeing the tick in his jaw, she held her breath, unsure of what was expected. He was clearly out of his element in such a gathering, and he was extremely uncomfortable being around her. She waited while long, drawn out seconds passed, and no one uttered a sound. The silence was so complete a needle hitting the ground would have been jarring. At last, with uncertainty in his eyes, he simply turned and walked away.

Desperation clawed at her. "Jarrett," Collett called to him pleadingly. He stopped and tilted his head slightly, showing that he thought about answering her, but he didn't look back. Cade placed a hand on her shoulder, whether in support or protection she couldn't tell. When she said nothing more, Jarrett went outside. The front door echoed throughout the house as it closed behind him.

Cade squeezed her shoulder gently. "I'll go after him," he said, moving to follow.

"*Non*. He needs space, *mon ami*," Delphene said, stepping into his intended path. "From all I have been told, it must be hard for him to look upon her and not remember. Allow him the room for now, *oui*?"

Cade clenched his jaw the same way as Jarrett did moments before, indicating he didn't like the suggestion. He felt a light slap on the back as Rederrick came over. "Give him a bit of time, Cade. He'll come back."

Reluctantly, he finally offered a tight nod of agreement.

"Okay then," said Cynda, "while we wait, let's talk about what we know and come up with a new strategy."

"*Oui*, take those into the living room," agreed Delphene, pointing to her beignets. "I'll finish up and join you shortly."

Everyone shuffled into the living room, except Collett. Instead, she scrutinized Delphene carefully, sensing her intent. "Go on, *Une pettit*. I'll be gentle," Delphene assured her. With no solid argument to stop her, Collett left, trying to hide the sad look in her eyes, but Delphene saw it.

Quickly leaving through the back door, Delphene easily leaped over the iron fence that bordered her property and sought her target. Scanning the street and seeing no sign of Jarrett, Delphene considered where to go. She knew this town as well as she knew herself, and she loved every inch of it. She lived within its central hub, the French Quarter, in a beautiful home that was a "family inheritance," or so she made it seem each time she returned.

She lived in various other places of course, changing locations occasionally to protect her secret, but for the most part, this was home. It was easy to live in New Orleans. People here were used to extraordinary things and even reveled in it. You couldn't go far without hearing legends of voodoo, magic, and even vampires and werewolves. Her nature was more easily accepted in this place than anywhere else.

She had basically lived here since the city's birth. Her historic home stood as a testament of endurance by weathering many storms of life, some natural and few that weren't. Yet here it stood, always there for her. Of course, it became necessary to fix things up occasionally, and sometimes major repairs were required, like after Katrina. But for Delphene, the effort was the price paid when something was worth it.

Though she knew very little about her fellow lycan, she saw the pain in his face earlier and considered it something to go on. Discreetly smelling the air around her, she made her way toward what she guessed was his likely destination. After a couple of minutes, she caught his scent and knew she was on the right path. Ignoring the cool morning chill, she wound her way through the busy city streets.

A few blocks later, she spotted him standing in front of the St. Louis Cathedral. He made no move to enter, but looked like any other visitor admiring the historic building. The gate was decorated for the upcoming holidays. She wondered absently if such things meant anything to him. She guessed they likely didn't.

Keeping her distance, she watched him for a long time, trying to understand him. Suddenly, his fierce eyes were on her, and she saw annoyance clearly displayed in his expression. Her heart thudded once under the intensity of his scowl. *There was so much in those eyes,* she thought. She saw so many emotions and thoughts in a single look. It was strange for her to look at him and see so much of her long-time friend, but at the same time, she could also see so much that was nothing like Cade.

Ignoring his displeasure, Delphene sauntered up to him, only stopping a mere step from him. As if she was analyzing it for answers, she looked at the building much the same as he had. "*Il aidera pas,*" she said quietly.

"What?" he groused.

"It will not help."

"What?" he repeated.

"This building," she answered and pointed at it as if he should understand her meaning.

Confusion was evident in his features. He shook his head. "Do you speak English?"

She laughed out loud at the cynical tone. "*Oui,*" she answered with a sweet voice full of sarcasm.

His dark brows drew together, but he said nothing. Instead, he took a minute to look—really look—at Delphene. She was a beautiful woman, so stunning, that any man would notice. She had soft, chocolate colored skin and dark, ebony hair she kept long and tightly bound. He found himself roaming over her figure next. She wasn't small, far from it. She was tall and well-muscled, but not like a bodybuilder. Her eyes held glittering amusement within them and were almost level with his own. Her stature could be attributed to long, shapely legs that drew a man's attention, even when they were covered up by jeans. A lesser man might have drooled.

Her smile stayed bright and full as he scrutinized her, showing him she wasn't shy or bothered by a man's roaming eyes. In fact, she looked purely satisfied by his apparent admiration. She wasn't loose by any standard, but confident and sure of who she was.

"It will not help you—this place I mean," she began again.

He met her eyes once again. "I wasn't looking for help."

"*Oui*, I suspected as much. All the same, you won't find it here."

Confused again, he shook his head and pulled his focus from her to look at the church once more.

Tapping her finger to her lips, she drew her brows in as if thinking about it. "I know what," she said and walked away.

Perplexed, Jarrett actually began to follow her. "What am I doing?" he asked aloud, and stopped himself.

"Come on, *Chère*, I don't have all day," she called over her shoulder without breaking stride.

Nice to look at, he thought, *but strange.*

It wasn't long before Jarrett found himself moving, his curiosity getting the better of him. He caught up to her easily, and they walked for a long time, practically ignoring each other's presence.

Before he could figure out her intentions or where she was going, she stopped. Glancing around, he noticed they stood on Rampart Street in front of the historic Voodoo temple. People milled

The Price of Knowing

around them, paying them no mind as they went about their own business.

"Perhaps here then?" she asked him

"Here what?"

"You might find help here." She paused as he looked at her with a frustrated glance. He obviously thought she must be a little screwed up in the head. Unbothered by his expression, she merely shook her head, "*Non*, not here. It's likely you've already tried something like it in any case. It is no matter. I have another idea." She moved past him, walking onward.

Cocking his head, he puzzled over what she was getting at. He hurried after her to confront her and get to the bottom of her little game. He ran into her when she stopped abruptly, snapped her fingers, and turned to him once more. "This is definitely the place for help, *non*?"

Scowling, he followed her fingers as she pointed to draw his attention to the building before them. He looked up, seething, and clenched his jaw so tightly Delphene wondered how he didn't grind his teeth to nothing.

They were standing in front of a bar, and there was fire in his eyes now. He was beginning to catch on. Despite the rage in his eyes, she remained unbothered. "*Non*, this will not do." She tapped her fingers to her supple lips as if thinking again. "I have tried that too. It doesn't work for us. And between you and me, it stinks in there," she said the last part cupping her mouth as if confiding a secret to him.

As she left him again, Jarrett stood firm and refused to continue playing her silly game. He still couldn't figure out why he followed her the first time. Sensing his intent, she turned. "A thought has struck me. Come, we must hurry though, it may no longer be there." She took off running.

His self-control broke, and a familiar anger took over. He would have no more of this trickery of hers. He took off after her, intending to put her in her place and let her know he'd had enough. She was

~ 195 ~

fast though, faster than he'd expected, and outdistanced him. Refusing to let her win, he pushed himself harder and got within reach of her just as she stopped again.

Despite her sudden stop, he grabbed her, and they both tumbled to the ground. He landed on top of her with a grunt. "I'm done playing your silly game!"

"*Non Chère,* not my game. It's yours."

"What are you talking about? You've been toying with me, thinking you could get into my head," he snapped. "It stops now! Do you understand?"

"*Oui,* I don't want to be in your head, *Mon Ami.* There are already too many voices there, no?"

"Stop it!"

"As you wish."

He scowled. "Leave me alone, and we'll be fine for as long as we're stuck together. Got it?"

"*Oui,* now get off me, *Chère* before I force you off," she said easily, but he understood her intent as her muscles coiled in anticipation. He was curious to see if she could, but eventually he relented and stood up. Jarrett scanned his surroundings to get his bearings, only to find himself standing back where he started. He heard Delphene rise and brush at her clothes, but he ignored her as he stared at her home like a lost boy.

"Ah, at last, this is the place, no? How long has it been since you looked here?"

He swallowed hard as he watched the shapes of people moving behind the light curtains that hung over the window. He couldn't help from asking, "For what? I've never been here before today." The fire in his tone was gone now.

"Ah, maybe not this house, but we were never talking about buildings, were we?"

"What am I supposed to see?" he asked quietly, knowing the answer already.

"What you were seeking?"

The Price of Knowing

"I wasn't seeking help," he retorted.

"We've established that already."

"I don't want help!" he assured her firmly.

"*En déclin et qui ont besoin sont des choses très différentes, Mon ami.*"

Unfortunately, he didn't understand that she was telling him wanting and needing are two very different things. Jarrett never bothered to learn French. "What?"

"I'll see you inside," she said sweetly.

"What did you say?"

"I will tell you someday. For now, I go to my friends." She moved away from him to the front stairs of her colorful historic home.

He stood there for a long time, thinking about the chase she took him on through the streets in the French Quarter. He also thought about what she was trying to tell him.

The hardest part was admitting she was right. He had gone looking for help in the beginning. He tried everything to rid himself of his demon half. He consulted witches, sorcerers, priests, and yes, he even tried voodoo once. He'd endured an allotment of painful and crazy attempts in a desperate need to destroy the monster within. None of it had worked. Not even finding his brother all those years before could fix him.

The only help, if you could call it that, he'd ever found was when Niall taught him how to use his rage as a fuel to sustain him. It kept him alive time and time again, injury after injury. The festering rage forced him to stand when he wanted to quit. Using his anger, he taught himself to fight, and he became a deadly enemy to any and all that evoked his wrath. But he was a tool and nothing more. Only, he'd been too stupid to see that until it was too late.

He'd learned how to survive, and as Niall's killer, that's all he'd been doing ever since. He'd functioned on hate and anger alone, but since Collett, everything changed.

~ 197 ~

The dreams, the recollections of the past, his fights with Cade, and most of all, acknowledging that Collett may be the only reason he still drew breath today—was too much to take in. There was nothing left where the anger once was. He simply felt empty and tired.

Jarrett rubbed his hands over his face and cursed silently. "What's happening to me?"

What good will any of it do at this point anyway? If I do stay, he reasoned, *it's not like they have any chance of succeeding. Even with all of them together. Hell, even with the whole combined force of the ridiculous Brotherhood Cade continues to swear by, we still couldn't win,* he reminded himself.

He couldn't see any alternatives though. He'd considered leaving several times already. On his own, he knew he couldn't be betrayed, or so he told himself. He wouldn't have to worry about anyone else's safety either.

Unfortunately, he hadn't fared so well on his own recently, and if he was going to go anyway, it would be nice to at least take Niall with him. He'd wanted to do that for a very long time, and sticking around Collett may draw the S.O.B. out of his hole.

He paced in front of the house, breaking down every possibility before him. A sudden burst of laughter came from inside the home. Looking back to the window, a slight ache bloomed in his chest. He'd let go of any ties to people so long ago. He didn't realize it was fear keeping him from stepping through the door now. He took a step backward, and then another, intending to walk away while he still could.

Fate intervened. A shriek from inside, and the crash of furniture, carried to his ears. His decision made for him, he rushed to the stairs without a second thought.

He entered the living room with lightning speed and saw a demon choking Collett while Cynda helped Rederrick rise from the floor in the hallway, where he'd obviously been thrown. Delphene pinned another demon to the floor, pounding away at it recklessly,

The Price of Knowing

and Cade crashed around with yet another in furious combat. Jarrett flew into action. Ripping the drapes from the window, he heard a host of hissing monsters as sunlight poured into the room. He kept his focus though, and when the demon holding Collett struggled to cover his eyes with his free arm, Jarrett threw a dagger with deadly precision, embedding it between the creature's jaundiced eyes.

Before that demon could even crumple to dust, Jarrett leaped upon the back of the demon trying to disengage from Cade to escape the painful sunlight. Wrapping one arm around its neck, Jarrett used his other arm and an amazing amount of strength to twist the demon's head almost all the way around to face him. Tendons and bones popped. The demon only smiled. "You are a dead man, Hunter!" it rasped.

"Check again," admonished Jarrett as Cade stabbed the creature through the heart with a broken table leg. Jarrett easily landed on his feet as the demon turned to a gray-white ash that fell to the floor.

He noted the carnage caused by the three demons. Cade went to help Collett stand while Cynda dabbed at a cut on Rederrick's temple. He met Delphene's eyes as she rose from the floor, and he knew she was right. He may not have been looking for help, but here it was regardless. What's more, he accepted that if they worked together, a few of them may even live. The time to leave had passed. It was time to be The Hunter once again, only this time, he would not hunt alone.

"If we're going to make it through this, the first thing we need to do is train," he said. "And I know just the place to do it."

CHAPTER 19

Cade began to set the room back together as best he could, considering the coffee table was destroyed and there was a Rederrick sized hole in the hallway. "I'm sorry, Del."

"Not to worry, *Mon Ami*, there have been far greater storms here," she assured him. "What do you mean train?" she directed to Jarrett.

"I know demons, and you can bet that is the bulk of what will be coming for us. Niall uses them often to do his dirty work. I can teach you all everything you need to survive. It's the only way we stand a chance. Even then, the odds are against us."

"I already know how to fight demons," Cade insisted stubbornly.

Jarrett conceded his point with a nod, "Maybe, but I know how to hunt them. I've spent the better part of my life keeping them in check, and I can tell you all I learned—like how the sunlight affects them. If only one of you had pulled those drapes, things may have been very different in here.

The Price of Knowing

"Niall doesn't care how many of his pawns we kill, he'll send more. There is no shortage of them in the world, and they're always eager to cause problems. He'll keep sending the demons at us to wear us down. He'll start small at first, then work his way up to bigger things, and you can bet that'll work. Unless we *all* know how to fight them, we'll *all* die. Anyone who doesn't know how to fight is a weakness to us."

"You'll teach everyone then?" Collett asked hopefully from the back of the room.

"Yes," he replied, meeting her eyes, "everyone."

"Wait a minute here," said Cynda, "sending these demons out— isn't this *Niall* concerned about the attention it will draw? I mean, I know The Faction is a little crazy, but they're usually more careful."

"Niall is careful, but he's also proud and egotistical. He'll stop at nothing to get his way," Jarrett said darkly.

"Why? Why do we matter to him so much?" asked Collett.

"I know why he wants me dead, but I don't know about you. Likely, the only person who does, is you," he replied grimly.

"Why do you matter?" she asked him hesitantly.

"I don't," he corrected with finality. Collett and Jarrett stared at each other awkwardly before she turned her head away.

Cade moved to her and put a protective arm around his wife. "All right Jarrett, as the demon hunter, it looks like you're in charge—for now anyway. Where are we going?"

"There's a place I know of in New Mexico. We should probably gather up that little punk, Jeffery, and the other annoying guy," he said, referring to Nate. "We need to teach them too."

"I wonder what Christmas is like in the desert?" supplied Cynda, trying to add some positive energy.

"You'll have to find out some other time. We're not going to play, and we won't really be in the desert. At least, not like you're thinking," he replied.

~ 201 ~

The trip required a little strategy on their part, but eventually everything was set up and executed smoothly. They couldn't jump on the next plane to New Mexico, and the brothers agreed that a straight flight there would be too easy to track anyway. Ultimately, using Delphene's contact, they were able to arrange for a couple of small, private aircrafts to take them to Shreveport. From there, they drove to Dallas where they visited another member of the brotherhood, Darrin.

A corporate heavyweight in the oil industry, Darrin also held a strong sense of projection. Because of it, Rederrick insisted they spend at least one night there to see if he could help teach Collett about one of her many abilities. Despite Jarrett's protests and cursing, the opportunity to meet with Darrin along the way was one Rederrick refused to pass on.

It didn't help as much as Rederrick hoped though. Unfortunately, Darrin could only offer a little guidance since Collett's group of abilities seemed too interconnected and time was short. Nevertheless, she spent the entire night working with him, hoping that every little thing learned was something she didn't have before.

Ashley, Jeffery, and Nate flew to Dallas and met up with them while Tracy flew to Colorado to be with Jenny and James. Having faith Jenny would wake, no one wanted her to wake alone. The family planned to meet up again later. For now though, James couldn't get away from his duties, and knowing an empathic Ashley would have a difficult time staying at a hospital, Tracy insisted on being the one to stay with Jenny. She also argued, as strong as she was with elemental magic, she was more capable of defending herself than her sister. Rederrick consented, but he arranged for extra protection on the base for them all, an arrangement that James grumbled about.

The Price of Knowing

The truth was, they all understood that Jarrett and Collett were the real targets here. In fact, despite the attack in New Orleans, James's and his sisters' days had been uneventful since the group separated. Still, they knew the best way to trap something was to use a bit of bait, so they all complied with the precautions.

After Dallas, they flew to Alamogordo-White Sands Regional Airport, rented two separate cars under more false identifications, and drove to a ranch about 30 miles outside of Cloudcroft, New Mexico. Worn out and travel weary, each of them disembarked the vehicles to get his or her first look at where training would begin for the battles they would face against The Faction.

Nate evaluated his surroundings and looked to Jarrett. "Whose land is this?"

"Mine. No one knows about it, though."

Glancing to Cade, Nate quipped, "Well, I would guess not. We can't have people finding out that Mr. I'll-eat-you-alive-and-spit-you-out-just- -for-fun is a bonafide hillbilly."

Rolling his eyes, Cade couldn't help but smile at Nate's taunts. Jarrett didn't see the humor and pinned Nate with a cold stare. Holding his hands up in surrender, Nate tried explaining himself, "Just sayin'—it doesn't really reflect your outgoing personality."

Deciding to ignore the sarcasm, Jarrett addressed everyone, "There are rooms upstairs. Take your pick. There are four if I remember right. I haven't been here in about 35 years, so I can't guarantee their condition. I've had caretakers keep it up for the most part, so it should be livable. There's not much room inside, but plenty outside. No one is close enough to bother us, and that's what we need."

"I'm sure it's fine, Jarrett. Come on ladies, let's get things together inside, and you boys can take care of the luggage," Cynda instructed.

"I'll give you all one hour to get it together—then I expect everyone out here to get started," Jarrett ordered.

~ 203 ~

"Now just a minute. It's been a long trip, and we're all a bit tired," Rederrick replied.

"What's your point?" Jarrett shot back darkly.

"It's cold and getting late. Let's rest a bit today and start tomorrow," Cade said, stepping between the two men.

"Let's get one thing straight," Jarrett stared at Cade but addressed them all. "Those demons don't give two damns if you're tired. They don't care if you're beat down or injured, and they sure as hell aren't the least bit concerned with the weather or time of day."

Cade's expression turned grim as Jarrett lashed out at them, but he said nothing.

"Well, neither do I! One hour.-That's better than you'll get from them," Jarrett finished, and walked away from the group toward the heavy tree line, disappearing within its folds.

"I think he may be as mean as my drill sergeants back in basic," Nate said when Jarrett was out of hearing distance.

"He's right," Cade said reluctantly. Everyone looked to him when he spoke. He knew they often sought his guidance, and he knew they were looking for that now. Jarrett was right. The demons wouldn't care, and they needed to get used to that. "Up until now, we've always been the one to engage The Faction. Things fell on our terms more often than they didn't, but the game has changed. They're coming after us blatantly and in stronger forces. Considering Jarrett's condition last week when we found him," Cade paused as the image of Jarrett fighting for his life despite multiple wounds and broken bones flashed in his mind. "He's right. Things are different now."

"An hour then," Delphene said with determination.

"An hour," Rederrick agreed.

"Man," Nate complained.

"Careful, little boy, or you will be the first one he eats and spits out for fun," Delphene teased.

"Nah, don't you know? I'm spoiled and hard to digest," he said with a grin, and he went to the back of the rented Tahoe to retrieve the first set of luggage. Following his actions, and wondering what they would learn an hour from now, the rest of them went about their appointed tasks.

Arrangements weren't really that hard. The farm house was old and small, but roomy enough for their purposes. It was mostly furnished, though most of the furnishings had seen better days. A functional kitchen had probably been last updated in the 1960's, but Cynda insisted it was extremely charming. The nice living room was clean and would serve as a meeting place. The caretakers of the home had done a fine job, and the dust in the home was at a minimum.

The four bedrooms were divided smoothly. Cade and Collett would have the master because it had the queen bed, and Cade was so tall it made sense. Cynda and Rederrick took the room with a double bed, and Delphene and Ashley would share the room that had two twin beds. While it would be a little bit of a crunch for Delphene, she didn't seem bothered in the least. That left Nate, Jeffery, and Jarrett with the smallest room with bunk beds. Nate eagerly claimed the top, but Jeffery reminded him they would be sharing a room with Jarrett. Nate then suggested Jarrett sleep outside. Luckily, Jarrett hadn't returned and missed the entire exchange.

The bigger problem would be the single bathroom the home offered, but determined to make the best of things, Cynda simply pointed out that showers would need to be quick. She insisted to Cade that tomorrow they would need to make a trip to town to gather up a few supplies, and he assured her he would make it happen.

An hour later, they all filed outside to get started as Jarrett had demanded. Already waiting, he crouched near the ground, and stared at the shining blade of a large sword with an intentional focus, as he slowly turned it. The sword was intimidating. The dark man holding it so carefully made it even more so. The late afternoon sun glinted off the polished, sharpened metal. The hilt looked as if two separate pieces of silver and gold were expertly twisted and tied together. Each twist snaked over the cross piece and knotted at the end in a circular shape. Within the pommel was a strange, scrolling mark. It looked somewhat like a letter or symbol. There was finer etching in the silvery steel of the blade as well, but Cade could not make out the full image from this distance.

Cade experienced an odd sense of familiarity at the sight of the curving marks. Something about them tugged at his memory, but he couldn't quite place it. Collett similarly felt a stirring within upon seeing the weapon, but thinking it was her confused feelings toward the sword's owner rather than the actual weapon, she pushed it back. Forcing herself to focus on the task before her, she steeled herself for the upcoming lessons.

Jarrett rose and firmly gripped the hilt of the sword. "Training starts now," he said and leaped at them with vicious intent. Unknown to the group, his attack held purpose. Jarrett wanted to gage their reactions.

Each person handled Jarrett's advance differently, but it was pretty much the way he expected they would. Pulling Collett away from possible harm, Cade yanked her behind him. Rederrick and Cynda both dived aside together. While Nate bravely tried to bull-rush him at a low angle. Delphene stood her ground, not moving an inch. That one surprised him. Calling his bluff, she simply planted her feet. Jeffery yelped and moved his hands to disappear—or least he tried to.

Jarrett easily out maneuvered Nate, going right over him. Unable to stop his forward momentum, Nate couldn't round on him in time. Then Jarrett easily shifted his direction, avoiding

Delphene's readied stance, and charged Cynda. Rederrick and Cade reacted predictably and went at him from behind. Jarrett heard them coming and ducked, then rolled backwards and gained his feet right in front of Collett. He grabbed her and twisted around. With the shining sword flat against her chest, Jarrett positioned so his back was against the porch with her in front of him.

"Now what?" he questioned. Nobody moved to attack him, but eyeing each other, they all held readied stances. "There's more of you than there is of me, so what are you going to do?" he demanded.

Collett attempted to free herself by stomping on his instep and twisting in his arms, but it did her little good.

"We can't move on you while you use her as a shield, or we risk killing her!" Nate shouted.

"By all rights, she's already dead, and you've hesitated too long. You think the enemy will act any differently than I have? They won't. They'll attack your weakest points, and use them to kill you."

Surprising them all, Ashley, who had stayed on the low porch well away from the exchange, jumped and kicked out at his injured side. Jarrett cringed, let go of Collett, and fell to his knee. His sword point stuck in the ground, but he stubbornly held it.

Collett felt his pain and turned to help him with pinched features. "Are you all right?"

"I'm so sorry. I didn't know what else to do," Ashley explained.

"Stop it!" Jarrett ordered and stood abruptly. "I challenged you, and you responded as you should have! You took advantage of my weakest point."

"We don't want to hurt you," Cynda said.

"Well Niall and his demons do want to hurt you. Pay attention, because I've just shown you where your greatest weaknesses are. You," he said to Cade, "can't run to everybody's rescue. If they can't cut it, they shouldn't be here. And you," he pointed to Jeffery, "can't think that disappearing will always save you. I can see you, and odds are, so can some of them. Use your magic, fine, but learn to fight, dammit!" He pierced Collett with an icy glare, and his tone became deeper and more threatening, "And you better figure out that you're the primary target. Get tougher or die!"

He brushed past her, and she shivered at the contact. Planting his sword in the ground, Jarrett addressed them, "The first thing you should know is demons don't die as you might think. They are banished when you take their shell, their body. Most stay banished, except the select few recalled by extremely rare powers. There's only one man I know that can resummon them, but it requires so much energy that he has only done it on a few occasions that I'm aware of."

"Niall?" Collett questioned, "He can resummon them?"

Jarrett glanced at her, a grim expression covered his features. "Yes, he can but seldom does. It's easier to call up new ones."

Collett looked away from the intensity in his eyes.

"To banish leech, greater, and archdemons, as Cade and I am sure Delphene know to some degree, you must decapitate it or stab it through its black heart. Hence the sword," Jarrett instructed. "A knife between the eyes works as well on lesser demons such as fiends and imps. Bullets, injuries, and amputation slow all of them down, but not for long. Because of their quick regeneration, time is your enemy. They feel pain and can't grow limbs back, but they heal faster than even lycanthropes can. They'll even adapt without an arm given enough time. Half breeds die the same as humans.

"They're never without a weapon. They use their claws and teeth expertly, and they *all* have enough strength to crush a man's head. Some even have poison and innate magic. From arch-demons down to half-fiends like Finnawick, they are a race created for one purpose—chaos.

"I intend to help you stay alive. You'll pair off, learn the sword skills, and work on your deficiencies and strengths every day. I made sticks of varying size for those of you that are novices." He kicked at a pile of sticks no one noticed before. "Cade, teach Collett the basics, and Delphene can pair off with Ashley. Rederrick and Nate together, while Cynda and Jeffery practice. I never bothered to understand such things as magic, so Cynda will be in charge there, but you'll train in swordplay. Make time for both. Everyone grab a stick."

Collett, hurt to her core by Jarrett's sharp words earlier, turned to the pile of fake swords, bent, and snatched up the first one she reached. She moved into position in the middle of the large property, hoping to prove to him she could toughen up.

Cade moved next and the others followed, to choose a training weapon. Passing Jarrett on his way to Collett's position, Cade said in a low tone, "You don't need to be so cruel."

"They'll be far crueler, and you know it."

"But you're not them, and you don't need to act like them," Cade replied and made his way over to train his wife.

I am like them, Jarrett thought to himself. "It's the only way I know to keep you alive," he lamented so quietly that no one, not even Cade, heard. Pushing his self-incriminating thought aside, he swung his sword up to his shoulder and moved from pair to pair to offer instruction as needed.

He found himself impressed for the most part. Nate especially caught Jarrett's attention with his quick, snake-like strikes and his rhythmic, athletic grace. Jarrett watched and understood that Nate must have spent an extensive amount of time studying and practicing fighting techniques. Rederrick, while skilled in his own right, was obviously outmatched by the younger warrior.

Delphene patiently explained sword basics to Ashley, who listened carefully and learned quickly. However, she struggled with being aggressive because of her naturally timid behavior. He hated that it was even necessary for her to learn.

Jarrett noticed that neither Cynda nor Jeffery had any solid skill using a weapon that didn't include magic. They defaulted to it naturally, so he took some extra time to instruct them together. He remained tough and cold, but was careful to not push any of them past their limits. Each person earned a few bruises and more than a few aching muscles to show for it.

C.B. Haight

Lastly, he glanced toward Cade and Collett's direction. Cade was teaching her technique, and she took in each lesson. She kept a stern expression on her face and easily mimicked his every instruction. Jarrett scrutinized her every move and how she angled her body with every strike. She held the "weapon" confidently. Her posture was disciplined, her arms were strong, and her stance balanced. She exhibited definite skill, but Cade seemed to be missing it.

Curious, Jarrett watched them for a while longer. Collett looked pale, and her features pinched as Cade slowly acted out the swordplay. Despite Collett's discomfort, she continued to follow his instructions without complaint. He directed her actions, telling her, "Up, down, good, now block." Collett did as instructed, but Cade didn't see how she began the movements naturally a second before his commands came. Jarrett noticed though, and he knew something was off.

Before he could be certain, Cynda called his name, asked a question and redirected his attention.

CHAPTER 20

Jarrett ran them through their paces that night. He only let up when he was certain of how to further help each individual in the days ahead. Several hours after the sun set, everyone went to bed completely exhausted, and they slept hard, all except Jarrett anyway. Uncomfortable with the idea of sharing a room with anyone, let alone Nate and his smart mouth, he decided to take the living room couch.

Since the small, 30-year-old couch was a less than an ideal bed for his tall frame, he slept little and was the first one awake the next morning. It was barely after five when he finally gave up on sleep and went to the kitchen for some water.

Carefully tip-toeing down the stairs, Collett came in shortly after. When she saw him, her expression changed. He could see the discomfort in her eyes, and he couldn't really blame her for it, because he felt no better around her. The connection between them was difficult to cope with, especially with Collett's lack of memory. It made it hard to really know how to act, and yet they both looked

C.B. Haight

to the other for answers. He knew she feared him, and he'd given her good reason to.

"Um sorry, I thought you'd still be asleep."

"No," he replied.

"Well, I'll...um. I'll come back," she said nervously.

"Sooner or later we're going to be in the same room at the same time. You might as well get used to it now."

"Well I just, I needed..." She couldn't think of what she came for.

"Needed?"

"Water," she finished, finally remembering.

"We have that," Jarrett said and gestured to the sink.

"Sure, yeah, okay," she stammered as she came into the room. With nervous fingers, she picked up a glass from the counter dish rack and moved to the faucet.

Jarrett didn't understand his motives, but he found himself unwilling to give her space. Instead, he stood stoically and leaned against the counter right next to her while she filled her glass.

When she attempted to make her escape, his hand shot out and, gripping her shoulder, halted her retreat. "I could have killed you," he said and felt her muscles tighten underneath his hand. When she offered no reply he confessed, "I wanted to."

"I know," she whispered, closing her eyes to stem the tears she felt for the little boy he once was.

He released his grip on her shoulder. "I hated you," he said firmly enough that it still sounded true.

"I know," she repeated, and despite her best efforts, a tear slipped past her defenses.

"I see you in my head all the time, and I remember things that weren't there before."

"Do you still want to?" she asked sincerely.

"I can't figure any of it out. I can't figure you out!" he said, ignoring her question. "You come to me in my dreams and talk to me. I see you as clearly as if you are real and alive right next to me

~ 212 ~

like now, but you're not. Your blue eyes—they look at me, through me, as if you know something I don't. You're there in my mind, from the past, the present, and I can't—"

"Do you still want to?" Collett repeated.

"What?"

"Kill me," she said carefully over her shoulder. She was still afraid to turn and face him.

As if he sensed that fear, Jarrett lifted his hands again and gently turned her around. He saw the tears and uncharacteristically felt the urge to wipe them away. Annoyed, he ignored the strange need and dropped his hands. "You're the empath. You tell me, because to be honest, I'm not sure of anything anymore."

"I'm not sure of much these days either."

"That's not true," he said, "You're sure of the fear you have for me."

"I'm not afraid of you."

"No?" he said with disbelief evident in his tone.

"I'm frightened of what you represent."

"I see." He assumed she referred to the same thing every other person he encountered hated, including himself. She was frightened of the demon inside him.

"You're mistaken. I don't fear that," she corrected reading his thoughts.

"I'm scared of my past and what it could be. I worry about who I am, the things I may have done," she paused, looking down ashamed. "Or not done," she said so quietly he barely heard her. "You represent my past because you're the only connection I have to it." Jarrett was so startled by her confession he could do no more than stare into her eyes and see the truth. "But mostly, I'm afraid of my connection to *you* and what it means."

"Why…" he scowled, confused, "why send him to get me then?"

"You were dying, and I couldn't bear it."

"I was fi—"

C.B. Haight

"You were dying," she stated firmly, not allowing any lies between them.

Looking away, Jarrett finally conceded that she saved him and had done so more than once.

Saying nothing more, she moved past him. Unwilling to go up and face Cade in her current state, she walked through the living room intent on going outside.

As she reached for the knob, Jarrett admitted, "I don't."

Collett knew right away he was referring to his previous desire to kill her. "But you do still hate me, or at least what I remind you of." She looked down at her hand on the knob. "And so do I," she confessed quietly and went outside. The old house suddenly felt very, very small.

Jarrett stared after her for a long time. His stomach clenched tightly as a result of their exchange. Finally, he turned back to the kitchen only to find Cade standing there with his arms folded tightly over his chest and a cold look in his eyes.

In response, Jarrett shook his head and tightened his jaw, silently warning Cade to let it go.

"You're hurting her," Cade stated flatly.

Unable to stand the accusation in Cade's eyes, Jarrett moved to the sink and gripped the edge of the counter, lending Cade his profile. He knew his brother's words were true and hated it. He hadn't sought her out purposely to punish her. *Hell*, he thought, *I didn't seek her out at all*. She had come to him.

"You have to let go of the past," admonished Cade.

"I should have never come with you," he said more to himself.

"I wouldn't have given you a choice."

"You wouldn't have been able to stop me," he replied with dead certainty, meeting Cade's glare once more.

"For her, I would have." Cade stepped forward with fierce determination in his eyes. It was the same angry determination Jarrett saw the night Cade almost ended him. "What I haven't told you, and what she won't tell you, is that every time you were hurt, so was she."

Jarrett glared at him disbelievingly.

"Since that day at the cabin, she linked to you somehow, and every time she slept, she saw you. Each time you were stabbed, thrown through a wall, or even suffered a bruise, she felt it. Even today when Ashley kicked you, I saw the pain in her eyes." His frustration mounted as he told Jarrett the rest. "I watched all of it, and was helpless to stop it. I was with her each time she shook and shuddered in pain calling out *your* name. I was there every time she woke from her dreams and cried—begging me to save you. While you've been running, her sleep was no more than yours—only a couple hours at a time—and every time she woke in real, physical pain." He stepped forward another step. "During that time, I watched her wither, turning inside herself from her worry over *you*! I even let her convince me that Jeffery's blood magic could find you. *Blood magic*," he spat. "And the last time," he started, but paused as if the next words were difficult for him, "the night I came to you, I watched as my wife stopped breathing, for longer than I care to think about, as result of the horrible agony she felt. *Your* agony, *your* pain."

Jarrett was stunned.

"For her, I would have jumped off a cliff into a burning pit and dragged you back kicking and howling by your snapping, snarling teeth, and that's a promise." Cade moved to follow Collett, and he grabbed her coat from the coat rack as he passed.

"I didn't know."

Looking over his shoulder, Cade retorted sharply, "Now you do," and went outside to comfort his wife.

Jarrett knew that Cade had feelings for her, maybe even loved her, but this devotion for her astounded him. It was a foreign emotion to him. He knew one person in his life willing to make that kind of sacrifice, and she was dead because of him. In his mind, her sacrifice had been a waste, and until this moment, he'd yet to see that same kind of selfless love. In his world, it didn't exist.

The people he hunted often tried to bargain for their own lives, offering him all manner of rewards. Once, a man even proffered his own daughter up as a slave in exchange for his life. The action against his own flesh and blood had disgusted Jarrett and sealed the man's fate.

He pounded his fist against the counter and walked purposefully to the stairs. Feeling guilty and irritated, Jarrett decided there was no better time to start today's training and roused everyone in the house.

The group trained almost non-stop for the next two days. Jarrett pushed them to the brink of their limits, and just as they were ready to quit, he pushed harder. Aside from the lycanthropes, Nate was the most skilled. Although, he refused to use a sword, preferring sticks the length of a dagger or long knife. He still bested his opponents more often than not because he was creative and fast. Nate kept so close to his partner he made wielding a sword nearly impossible.

Cynda did all right, but it was clear, to Jarrett at least, that swordplay would not be her strongest skill. Jeffery was much the same, but Jarrett continued to train them, knowing that magic would not always work.

Rederrick held his own, despite his age, and would surprise them all with wild, unexpected maneuvers every now and then to win the fight. Ashley struggled with all of it. She hated the violence but refused to give up. She often mimicked Rederrick's desperate attempts to outthink and shock her opponent with sudden, exotic moves.

To Jarrett's surprise, Collett rapidly became second best. The only things holding her back were her hesitation and Cade's incessant coddling. Each time she was dropped or bumped, Cade would react, and his focus was always on her instead of his current partners. Jarrett knew it would get them both killed. He couldn't figure out why she kept faltering at random times. Each time she almost beat her sparring partners, she pulled back and wouldn't take the killing strike.

He considered three possibilities. One, she was afraid of taking a life. Some people couldn't stomach it even if they were in mortal peril. Two, maybe her hesitation was due to her faulty memory. She would maneuver beautifully, get distracted or frustrated, and pull back. The third and most likely possibility could be that she was terrified of what would happen if she allowed herself to be her best.

He understood from her confession in the kitchen that she was afraid of what she may be capable of. She also feared her past deeds. She was letting those fears rule her, and he knew it. It dictated her every action, and he thought it was, in a sense, her shield. Jarrett believed her fear kept her from trying harder to remember. Even though she proclaimed a desire to know who she was, Jarrett suspected Collett was her own barrier to her past.

For the most part, the group followed his stern instructions, and Jarrett watched them all improve. He couldn't help but feel slightly satisfied from it, but he kept that to himself. Unconsciously, he began to feel a sense of hope that they might actually have a chance. This shifted his demeanor too. He was still broody and snapped irregularly, but he became more approachable and even offered the occasional compliment during sessions.

Another thing helping everyone's mood was the lack of demon attacks. They were exhausted every day and slept well every night. The weather also cooperated with no storms and bearable temperatures. Warmth from the heavy workouts kept them all almost comfortable.

The third day on the mountain was a different story. The training wore on them, and dark, heavy clouds rolled in. The chilly wind that came with them was biting and miserable. Still, Jarrett wouldn't ease up.

C.B. Haight

Though none complained or argued, they struggled. It was clear to Jarrett that the cold wind and depressing clouds dampened their moods. It didn't help that they were battered and sore from the previous days. Each day, he had paired them up differently to provide opportunities to adapt to different styles and superior opponents. He also did it to keep Cade and Collett apart. Jarrett knew Cade wouldn't challenge her as he should, so today, he put Collett with Nate.

For the first part of the morning, almost everyone danced around each other, neither person wishing to receive a new bruise to add to his or her collection. Pairing Collett with Nate didn't work as well as he hoped either. Nate acted similarly to Cade. In fact, Jarrett realized Rederrick treated Collett differently yesterday than he was Cynda, his own wife, today. It was as if they all viewed her as fragile and incapable, despite her obvious skill. He understood their behavior was a detriment to them all and decided a different course of action was necessary.

After lunch, the group reassembled to start again. "We're going to do something new. I'll give the rest of you a chance to take me down. If you beat me, you can have the remainder of the afternoon off," he challenged.

All at once, a new enthusiasm rippled through the small crowd. Delphene smiled wickedly. Bumping Cade with her elbow, she said, "Ah, is easy, *non*? We will be napping soon."

"Excluding Cade and Delphene—to make it fair," he added.

"How on earth will that be fair? I don't stand a chance against you," Ashley protested.

Shaking his head, Jarrett looked to Ashley and explained, "I'm not all that bad in comparison to the monsters taking orders from Niall. I promise it is far better to practice with me than them."

Nate bounced on his feet and twisted his neck, readying himself for the challenge, and Jarrett didn't miss his eager expression.

"Do we have to use the sticks?" Jeffery asked.

"No," Jarrett answered.

Jeffery gave a tight nod, and Jarrett didn't miss the relief in his eyes.

"Cade, you two take a walk," Jarrett ordered.

Cade glared at him.

"No interference," he answered back firmly.

"We wo—"

"Get some firewood while you're gone. A storm is coming."

"Come on, *Chère*. Let him play his game," Delphene said before Cade could protest further.

Scowling, Cade jumped from the porch and said to Collett, "I won't be far."

Delphene was the only person who saw the tick in Jarrett's jaw. He was clearly bothered by Cade for some reason and wanted him gone, so she pulled him along. "C'mon, *Mon Ami*. We will go do a little practice of our own."

Collett's head came up, and she looked to the two retreating companions.

Before any of them had time to think, Jarrett dropped low, and with a glint in his eye, he taunted, "When you're ready."

Delphene tried to keep Cade distracted. Deep in the forested area of the large property, the two of them were now a good distance away from the rest of the group. Cade didn't pay attention to her. He kept looking back toward where they came from, and she knew he was listening carefully for any clue as to how it was going. She was beginning to comprehend Jarrett's motives in sending him away. She understood that Cade's thoughts these days revolved around a single blue eyed blond. "Cade," she said for the second time.

"Huh?"

She held out her hands wide.

"What?"

"Ready?" she questioned.

"Sure…" He cocked his head as if he heard something.

Rolling her eyes, she leaped at him.

Because each of them enjoyed the challenge the other presented, the engagement between them lasted for a long time. At one point, Cade thought he heard someone cry out. Delphene heard it too, and she would not allow him to disengage. She knew Jarrett had silently charged her with keeping Cade out of the fight for a while.

After Cade finally won their mock conflict, he called it and refused to go a second round. Not tracking the time, but thinking that she had kept him occupied long enough, Delphene agreed, and they started back. As they neared the edge of the clearing, they both heard the clear sounds of the battle to take Jarrett down. Then they heard an angry howl of pure frustration echo through the woods, and both of their sensitive ears knew it had come from Jarrett.

Rushing the remaining distance, Cade and Delphene entered to see a peculiar site. Rederrick was bent over on his knees and holding his side. He grimaced in between gasping breaths. Nate was pulling himself up from the ground a good 30 feet from where Jarrett stood, rubbing the back of his head as he rose. With protective arms around his waist, Jeffery coughed and sputtered as if the wind had been cleanly knocked out of him, and Cynda, moving stiffly, tried to help him by patting at his back. Jarrett held a wide-eyed Ashley captive with one arm around her neck and glared daggers at Collett.

None of that surprised them. The peculiar part was how Collett stood unharmed a mere three feet in front of him with her feet firmly planted. Her features did not waver under his glare. The anger and resentment emanating from the pair filled the entire clearing, and not one of them needed Collett's empathetic skills to feel it.

"So, *Chère*, do we get the afternoon off?" Delphene asked in an attempt to break the tension.

Nate scoffed and rubbed his head some more.

"No," Rederrick replied when Jarrett didn't answer right away.

The Price of Knowing

"We're done here," Jarrett growled, firmly setting Ashley aside.

One single stride put him right in front of Collett. Seeing how Jarrett clenched and unclenched his fists in anger, Cade rushed to her side. "What's going on?" he tried to ask.

"You had me, and you wouldn't do it," Jarrett snapped at her, ignoring Cade. "You bested me, but you were too weak to move on it."

"I—" she began.

"Don't bother making excuses. I don't really care, except it might get me—get all of us—killed! Because you hesitated, Ashley's dead and half your team are injured."

"That's enough!" Cade ordered firmly.

Jarrett looked up from Collett as if seeing Cade for the first time. Nobody moved. All they could do was watch as the brothers with identical golden eyes stared one another down. Finally, Jarrett glared at Collett once more, and unable to stand the accusation in his eyes, she turned her head away. Jarrett stalked past them, bumping Cade's shoulder on the way, and entered the woods.

Cade tried to turn her around to look at her, but Collett pulled away from him and went inside. He began to follow her, but Cynda stopped him.

"Ashley, go see that Collett's all right. Cade, you and Rederrick have to take care of other matters. He knows all about it," she said before he could protest, "and take Nate with you. Delphene—"

"*Pas de problèmes*, leave it to me," she replied and went after Jarrett.

"Good. Jeffery, come with me."

CHAPTER 21

Delphene knew she would have to carefully maneuver Jarrett into coming back to the house. She was beginning to make sense of his moods though, and in the end, she simply waited him out. She knew he would settle on his own, but by stubbornly shadowing him she knew he would do so far quicker in his effort to be rid of her.

He was a paradox to her, a puzzle she wanted to pick at until she figured out how the pieces made the whole picture. Delphene, for the most part, was an easy-going creature. She was relaxed, outgoing, and open to life's experiences. Jarrett was dark, dangerous, and angry. He was everything that she was not, and she found herself curious about him.

In the woods, she sat on a rock nearby and watched while he completed a vigorous series of training exercises. He ignored her throughout his routine. He moved as smoothly as a dancer with fluid motion. Each movement held purpose and easily flowed into the next. It wasn't slow though, in fact, far from it. He jumped and twisted, ducked and turned as if he battled an imaginary opponent. His sword glided with the motion as an extension of his body.

The Price of Knowing

Despite the cold, sweat dotted his brow, and he didn't even pause as he shirked his long, leather coat with impressive agility. At one point, his shirt lifted, and she got a peek at the angry, red scar marring the right side of his torso.

She knew it was there of course. Cade's account of the events before they met up at her home included Jarrett's condition when they found him. Furthermore, Ashley insisted on checking it regularly despite his cursing at her. Delphene observed that it was not fully healed, even after so much time, and would still be sensitive. Yet, he moved as if it wasn't even there.

As a woman, she admired his physique. As a warrior, she admired the smooth rhythm of his dance and the efficient ease of his form. She recognized his masterful skill and knew the discipline to achieve it would have taken years. She couldn't help but wonder how many fell before his blade, meeting their end while looking into his golden eyes.

When Jarrett ended his routine, he sat on the ground and closed his eyes in meditation. She deliberated what to do, wondering if she dared talk to him now. Delphene knew they needed to get to the heart of the matter, and she recognized the change in him as he concentrated on relaxing. He was calmer, more collected, so she took a chance. "Cade will get himself killed, *non*?"

Jarrett didn't respond.

She was fairly certain of his motives now. Jarrett believed Cade was weaker with Collett. "*Oui*, she is untrained," she continued as if he agreed with her. "*Her* actions, not so bad, but *he* knows better." She stood and brushed at her pants.

Jarrett opened his eyes and pinned her with his gaze. She clearly saw annoyance shining within them. Delphene wondered if he realized how often he conveyed a thought with the emotions on his face. She understood why he'd been upset earlier. He thought his way was the only way to survive, but Delphene knew that surviving was not the same as living.

~ 223 ~

C.B. Haight

"*Amour* can be dangerous." she said, knowing he believed it. "He can't help it, you know. Protecting people, it is his nature."

Without a word, Jarrett stood and went for his coat.

Jarrett was not completely wrong. Cade could not continue on like this. Except, it wasn't love that was dangerous, it was a lack of trust. Cade couldn't trust Collett to defend and protect herself. So she said as much, "He doesn't believe her capable, so how can she believe differently?" She paused. Knowing he was listening, she led him along, "If she can't fight, she is a danger to us all."

Turning, Jarrett met her eyes with curiosity. With Collett's empathy she would sense and feel everyone's doubt. It was something he hadn't factored in. If everyone thought her incapable, how could she believe in herself? In a sense, she was trapped by her own power.

His mind fell back to the other day when Cade told him about Collett feeling his pain, and he wondered what else she felt. He considered how difficult that would be to cope with.

As he processed it all, Delphene taunted with a callous tone, "We should throw her to the sharks and be done with her."

He looked up sharply, shocked by her cavalier tone, and when she smiled, he realized he had played into her hands again. His eyes turned flinty and, keeping his own counsel, he walked away. Of course she followed, and resigned, he made no move to stop her as they headed back. As they progressed, Jarrett thought about the best way to handle Collett moving forward.

When they entered the little house, Jarrett scowled as the strong scent of pine assaulted him. He found himself staring at a freshly cut tree standing in the living room. He cursed. "What is that?"

"It's a tree. I assume you've seen one before," Cynda said, ignoring his scowl.

It bothered him how easy and comfortable all of them had become with his moods. "I know what it is. What is it doing here?"

"It's Christmas Eve, and I want it here," she said with equal firmness.

"We don't have time for this," he growled.

"On the contrary, you said we were done for the day, and I have nothing but time for this."

Ashley came into the room, and sensing the tension from the three of them, said nothing.

"You think the demons—or even Niall—take time out of their hunt for us to celebrate ridiculous holidays?"

"No, Jarrett," her tone was soft and her eyes sad, "I don't."

"It is why we are different, *Chère*," Delphene supplied from behind him. "What is the point in fighting if there is nothing to fight for?"

Deciding that he would not win the argument against three women, and not sure he even wanted to try, Jarrett made a quick escape. "I'm going out," he said and grabbed a set of keys.

"You'll be lucky if you can find anywhere open tonight in town," Cynda said to his retreating back.

Delphene stood in his path and met his eyes. "You can't keep running," she said low enough only he could hear.

His eyes darkened, and the pure violence in his eerie, golden orbs told her she would be smart to move. Never one to heed a warning when she saw it, Delphene stood firm, meeting his cold stare with compassion.

"Move!" he snarled.

When she didn't budge, he growled, turned, and left through the back entrance, slamming the door behind him. Ashley startled at the sound, and Cynda merely said, "Well, that actually went better than I expected."

Niall sat alone in a darkened room, staring at the burning fire before him. He'd lost them all. Collett slipped through his fingers in Colorado, and he'd lost his connection to Jarrett. He'd picked it up again for a short time when he sensed the murderous whelp in New

Orleans, but then nothing since. Of course the demons sent to fetch him hadn't returned, and Jarrett simply dropped away again. No matter how much Niall concentrated, he could not feel him.

Fury bubbled and churned within him, but centuries of discipline kept it at bay. He had others working on finding Collett and the meddlers with her. He had to rely on technology and other mortal methods to locate her, and that displeased him immensely.

Jarrett though, was his. Niall knew him—had created him. Niall knew the anger that was within the cursed creature and could perceive him whenever he wanted, but nothing came now. Too many days had passed without feeling anything from the werewolf. He suspected the source of the disconnect, and it only served to infuriate him further.

He wanted Jarrett to pay for defying him, but he knew first hand it would be no easy task to bring him down. He reflected that neglecting Jarrett, giving him too much freedom, had led him here. Then he brushed the self-recrimination aside, reminding himself the lycan had always been a difficult, but valuable, tool. Jarrett had always been brought to heel, but not this time. No, this time the cursed wolf had gone too far. His latest transgression was unforgivable, and it proved he was becoming a danger to Niall's plans.

Collett could ruin everything Niall had built, and letting her live could not go unpunished. He fantasized the tortures he would inflict upon Jarrett if brought back alive, and he wanted to punish his Hunter personally. However, the inability to find Collett and her possible influence on The Brotherhood were bigger concerns to him now. He was needed here to deal with the details of leadership and orchestrate the chaos that might bring her out. She was a risk he could not afford. In this, he did blame himself. If he'd handled her more carefully centuries before, things would be different. He'd underestimated her and was still paying for it.

He'd thought her memory loss would be a greater hindrance as well, and figured Finnawick could finish things up for him. At that time, he thought her powerless without her memory. If she couldn't remember who and what she was, Collett would be no immediate threat to him. He had even hoped he could still convince her to join him or fill her with false memories to bind her to him.

That was then. Now he simply wanted to be rid of her. He realized he should have dealt with her himself originally, and intended to remedy the situation.

Breathing deeply, he focused. He assured himself that neither of them could evade him long. Using his abilities, Niall mentally sorted through connection after connection, hunting the hunter. He sorted through each one, carefully looking for that anger he knew so well. More than an hour later, he saw a brief flash, and though it was short-lived, it was enough. He opened his eyes and grinned in satisfaction.

"Henifedran!" he snapped.

Behind him, a bluish-grey demon with wide, leathery wings appeared. "Yesss, Masster."

Niall sent images to him telepathically. "Deal with the traitor!" he ordered.

The demon nodded.

"Henifedran?"

"Masster?"

"Kill anyone with him."

The demon nodded respectfully while offering Niall an evil smile and showcasing its sharp, shark-like teeth.

Jarrett grumbled to himself almost the whole drive into town. *A Christmas tree,* he thought, *unbelievable. They need to train.*

He didn't believe any of them were ready to face more than a couple of greater-demons at once, let alone a few archdemons and the multitude of sorcerers, witches, and leeches under Niall's thumb. This was never going to work. They were all too soft. They needed a plan. They needed—He didn't know what they needed, but it definitely wasn't a Christmas tree.

Jarrett couldn't understand how they could even think of something so stupid at a time like this. Then he realized it was the idiocy of believing in the whole peace on Earth and good will toward men crap that would give them the idea. In his experience, neither existed, and it wasn't like the ridiculous tree would fix their problems or make everything better. Nothing short of killing Niall would do that, and that scenario was highly unlikely.

He questioned his decision to stay with the others again. A group was easier to find, and people as attached as these could be used against one another. Looking around as he entered the small town of Cloud Croft, his mind flashed back to another haunting memory.

June 1876 Deadwood

"Nooo, please don't hurt her."

"What do you think, Hunter? Should she live?"

The Hunter said nothing. He'd learned long ago that no matter what he said, Niall would twist it to his own design.

Niall approached the young girl, no older than 17, and stroked his hand over her cheek. She cringed and tried to pull back from it.

"I'll do whatever you want. I swear! Just don't hurt her," the man on his knees begged.

Niall looked back to the man he was playing like a master puppeteer. "I know you will," he replied with a wicked grin.

He nodded to The Hunter, who grabbed the young girl by the hair and dragged her from the room while she screamed, "Sam! Sam! Help me!" She began sobbing, "Pleeease."

"If you hurt her—" The Hunter heard from the other room.

"Don't worry, Mr. Bass. Do as you're told and she'll be returned to you."

"Unharmed?" Sam demanded.

"Well, I suppose that depends on how long this takes, doesn't it?"

Disgusted, The Hunter left them, taking the sobbing girl outside to await Niall. He didn't wait long before he heard his master's boots clacking against the wooden planks of the saloon.

Jarrett ground his jaw as Niall approached him.

"Deal with her."

He looked up, surprise covered his features. "You said—"

Niall's strange eyes went cold as ice, stopping the protest. "Is there a problem?"

Jarrett's muscles bulged and his body shook with outrage, but he said nothing.

"Good, I'll find you soon enough then," he said and disappeared.

The Hunter, as Jarrett was so aptly named, clawed and gnashed at him from within. His eyes smoldered, turned bloody red, and a furious growl rumbled in his chest. The woman cowered and shrank away from him. With wide, terrified eyes, she looked to the spot where Niall once stood and back to the monster commanded to kill her. Fear overtook her, and she fainted before his feet.

The memory faded, and Jarrett cursed. Why did this have to keep happening? He didn't want to go back and relive every damn moment of his life. It was better left where it belonged. As he thought about it, he knew the source of these particular haunting images. It was this place—her place. This is where Jarrett had taken the young woman to hide her, and then he tricked Niall into believing she was dead. He sat back in the seat remembering those life changing events.

Sam did as he was told and pulled off several heists for Niall. In fact, he and his gang even managed to rob a Union Pacific train. The take was bigger than even Niall expected, more than $60,000 in gold coins, plus several miscellaneous passenger watches and gems were acquired. Of course, that success only had Niall demanding more. Even magical orders need money to function.

Sam Bass never made it back to Mary Beth. After a year with little success, Sam was betrayed by one of his own gang and killed in a shootout. Jarrett was sure Niall had arranged the death.

Jarrett knew the young girl Mary Beth married, Sam's best friend, Frank. He came to tell her what happened and that Sam was dead. Frank stayed to watch over her as he promised Sam, and the rest is history.

Once he learned of their marriage, Jarrett never came back here during their lives. He had no plans to ever return until two generations later when the family was ready to let go of the homestead. Their grandson sought out any connections to the stories his grandma had told of the man who saved her. He sought out Jarrett's descendant only to find the man himself. That had been an interesting day. In the end, he left Jarrett the land despite multiple protests.

He avoided this place because it represented a life stolen and the reality of his own prison. Yet, he couldn't sell the land either because it also signified an important change in his miserable life. Taking Mary Beth here had been his first true act of defiance against Niall, and even though he hated admitting it, that meant something to him.

For almost as far back as he could remember, he'd been Niall's enforcer, the demon hunter people cowered from. Jarrett's first encounter with Niall had been shortly after the fire that killed Rowena. When Niall first appeared to him, he believed Niall was his saving grace. Using various methods, he taught Jarrett how to use the monster to fight and, more importantly, how to kill. Niall

~ 230 ~

seemed like a hero to the young Jarrett, and for too long, that boy even stupidly looked to Niall like a father.

He'd been too young and stupid to see who the real monster was. Niall was smart too. He carefully manipulated Jarrett to see things from his point of view. For the first several years, he controlled Jarrett with nothing more than fear of punishment and a little praise. Small looks of disappointment had Jarrett trying to please him. He didn't even see the trap closing in around him until it was too late.

Before too long, he began to question Niall's ideals and the assignments he was given. As Jarrett became reluctant, Niall's methods became more sinister. He could still remember how Niall would bring a child forward and insinuate that the child would die if Jarrett failed in his tasks. He would kill people Jarrett crossed paths with to ensure Jarrett stayed in line. The manipulations worked for longer than Jarrett cared to admit.

The day Jarrett heard Niall make promises to Sam Bass and then, in the next breath, order Jarrett to kill Mary Beth, was when the reality of his life struck him. All those times Niall made promises to him, he never once witnessed if they came to fruition. He never found out if the children lived, but rather, he naively believed him when Niall insisted they had been returned safe and sound to their parents.

Each time someone around him died as a result of Niall's cruelty, Jarrett would simply accept it as penance for what he was and his own failures. Those seeds of doubt were carefully planted in him by none other than Niall himself.

After he hid Mary Beth, he tried to find his way out from under Niall's control. For a time, he believed there must be a way to escape, and made several unsuccessful attempts. For years, he searched for a solution, looking for any way out that he could find, but there were none.

He kept coming to the same conclusion, courtesy of his wicked master. If he left, innocent people would die, and he never got far or escaped punishment. Jarrett placed no value on his own life. In fact, there were times when he believed death would be a relief, and Niall knew that. Niall also knew Jarrett couldn't stand to see innocent people, especially children, suffer simply to obtain his own freedom.

He even considered reaching out to Cade for help, but he realized Niall was still unaware of his brother's existence. The brief time spent with his brother in friendship had come to a bitter end. An event that once left him feeling betrayed and angry gave him relief years later. Jarrett understood that if he had stayed with Cade all those years before, Niall would have discovered and destroyed him just to hurt Jarrett. To protect his twin, he never tried to forge a relationship again. In fact, he went out of his way to antagonize Cade to ensure he stayed away.

Stubborn as an ox, Cade still came looking for him sometime around 1910. Jarrett didn't know the exact date because he never kept track of them. Every day was one more he didn't ask for. Cade showed up one night after he discovered Jarrett was tied to The Faction.

During their argument, Jarrett happened to have one of the Faction's lackeys he had been charged to bring in. During Cade's speech about right and wrong, the twit tried to kill Jarrett with magic, but sensing it, The Hunter beat him to the punch. He sliced the half demon's throat right in front of his brother. Something broke in Cade. His eyes held such disappointment.

Angry, Jarrett took it a step further and attacked him. When it was over, Jarrett left Cade with a vicious scar on his chin from a silver knife and a couple broken ribs for his trouble. It was easy to defeat his brother, because Cade was ever the optimist and didn't really want to hurt him. His mercy cost him dearly that day, and Jarrett could still remember the disgust in his twin's eyes. It was the same disgust Jarrett saw in the mirror every day.

"The only reason you're alive is because we share blood. Don't ever come near me again," Jarrett pronounced. *Venom laced every word as he walked away.*

Cade spat blood on the ground. "We can't share blood! You're a monster."

Jarrett had hesitated in the darkened street, thinking, *You have no idea.* Then he'd left his brother for what he thought would be forever.

There were no options for him back then. There was no way out. From there, Jarrett did the only thing he could, the only thing he was good at. He embraced it. He became a true hunter, a predator, and he relished killing those that delighted in being members of The Faction.

He made a point of being especially efficient at hunting down the out of control demons and half-demons that thirsted and craved the blood of innocents. He became so lethal that Niall slowly shifted his assignments, only sending him after the very worst of them. He was challenging Jarrett's skills, testing his loyalty. More than once, Jarrett found his very life hanging in the balance, and knew if he died Niall wouldn't mourn.

To his relief, his successes were rewarded in the best way possible. Niall quit coming to him personally. Whether from fear, disgust, or disinterest, Jarrett never cared. He liked it better that way because it allowed him more freedom. Niall sent his assignments through the demons he controlled instead.

Over time, Jarrett killed three of those lackeys simply because they bothered him. First, he killed Menrock. Then he beheaded Siliana, and most recently, Finnawick. The imp had only been half demon, but he'd been the worst of them all.

Niall dealt with Jarrett harshly each time he killed the messenger. The Hunter was beaten severely when he killed Menrock. After Siliana, Niall killed three innocent people, or so he said they were innocent, and dumped the bodies at Jarrett's feet as a punishment. Still, killing her had brought about more freedom.

Fearing his reputation, Finnawick only used Jarrett as a last resort. And fearing more innocent lives lost, Jarrett tolerated Finnawick for a much longer span. Getting rid of Niall's minions was a nuisance that merited punishment, but it wasn't why Niall wanted him dead. Jarrett guaranteed his own death when he sent Niall a colorful letter basically telling him to shove it after two and a half centuries of servitude.

If he was honest about it, Jarrett could admit rebellion was the main reason he had continued to take assignments. He embraced every chance he could find to oppose Niall, and by some miracle, he managed to do it several times. *Fifty-one,* he thought to himself. Fifty-one people got a chance to live out their lives in relative safety because he refused to be a pawn in a wicked man's game. He knew the exact number because there were so few in comparison to how many he killed.

Each time he was assigned a job, he would go in hoping he could defy Niall one more time. Unfortunately, almost every time he found himself disgusted with how cruel and wicked people could be. As he completed those assignments, he lost a little piece of himself as well as any hope for mankind as a whole.

Sweeping a hand over his face, Jarrett silently berated himself for wallowing and reminded himself that he quit caring a long time ago. *It doesn't matter anymore*, he told himself. He was out now and would likely die soon, which was fine with him. He only wanted Niall to go down with him.

Sitting alone, parked in front of the Burro Street Exchange in the center of town, Jarrett tried to figure out his next step. He looked up at the dark sky. Heavy storm clouds above promised snow, and he thought about how training would be set back if it snowed too much.

The streets were empty, confirming Cynda's prediction that everything was closed for the holiday. He was completely alone.

The Price of Knowing

Really, he wasn't sure why he came here in the first place. He simply didn't want to stay at the house and felt this was his only option.

Jarrett considered leaving and going his own way again. As he thought about it though, he knew that he didn't really have anywhere else to go. He realized that even after stepping away from The Faction, he was still trapped by them.

Deciding to go back to the house, he shifted the car into gear. Checking his rear-view mirror, he stopped cold. Two nasty looking demons stood in the street, carefully dressed in human clothing in an effort to blend in. They stood side by side and grinned devilishly at him.

Jarrett cursed.

CHAPTER 22

"Did he come back yet?" Cade asked as he entered the kitchen after his shower.

"Yes," replied Ashley, "He came back and left again. You missed him by maybe 20 minutes."

"Where did he go?" Collett asked while coming down the stairs.

Cade looked over to her where she stopped in the doorway and searched for any remaining signs of stress. There were dark circles under her eyes that showed her exhaustion. He knew the last few nights she'd started having visions again. She didn't tell him, but he'd heard her. Between training, dreaming, and trying to find comfortable ground with Jarrett, it was no wonder she was so tired. It was hard to watch, and even harder to stay out of.

Cade reflected on the lecture Rederrick gave him while running errands for Cynda. Rederrick insisted Cade needed to give Collett a little more room and let her work things out on her own. Stepping back to let her figure out her place in this simply didn't sit well with him. He wanted to be with her through every step, protecting her. He wanted to see her happy, but it seemed Jarrett kept making her unhappy.

The Price of Knowing

"He was bothered by the tree and took off—said he was going to town," Ashley explained, interrupting his thoughts.

A foreboding entered Collett's chest, and her features pinched in consideration. "He shouldn't have gone alone."

"He was pretty upset. I think he needed some space from all of this," Ashley said while gesturing to the Christmas tree and smells from the kitchen.

"He's too vulnerable," Collett stated, and her worry was evident.

"You're right," Cade agreed, silently wishing he didn't. "None of us should be going out alone."

"I'm not sure we could have stopped him, *Chère*. The decorations really put him on edge, more so than he already was."

Cade moved passed Collett and into the kitchen to grab keys to the other vehicle.

"What are you doing?" Collett asked.

"I'm going after him."

"I'll come with you."

"No, you stay here. It won't take long to track him down," Cade said, shaking his head.

"I'm going with you," she said firmly.

"Collett—"

"None of us should be alone," she retorted with a pointed look.

Cade looked to Delphene.

With wide eyes, she shot back, "Don't look to me, *Mon Ami*. I have enough to do with the dinner here."

Cade's eyes went back to his wife. He immediately recognized the determination in them, but he tried to talk her out of it anyway. "Collett, you don't need to come. I can get him and be back in no time. Stay here where you're safe."

"No place is safer than another at this point, and you know it. I am coming with you."

He said nothing.

"I'm going, Cade."

C.B. Haight

With an exasperated breath of defeat, he relented, "Fine, let's go then."

"I'll meet you outside. I need to grab something first," she replied and rushed up the stairs.

Cade could only look up at the ceiling in frustration. He considered leaving while she was out of the room. He could be in the Tahoe and gone before she even made it back downstairs. He wouldn't though. Not only would she be furious with him, but knowing her as he did, she would likely talk Jeffery into blinking her to wherever she wanted.

No, if she was going, it was better to go with him. At least that way he could keep an eye on her, and he could keep her safer than anyone else. So he waited. She came rushing down the steps holding something in her hand. He looked closer to see a poorly concealed dagger. He quirked a brow at her.

"What?" she asked.

He pointed to the dagger.

"Just in case," she replied. "Jarrett said we should always be ready for an attack."

"You're just going to walk around a small, friendly town on Christmas Eve carrying that nasty looking blade in your hand like it's a purse?" he asked.

She looked down at it. "You're right. Maybe I should put it in a handbag." She pursed her lips and examined the size of the blade. "I'll get Cynda's bag. It's bigger."

Cade shook his head and smiled at her innocence. He took the blade and scabbard from her hand, bent down, and tucked it into her tall, winter boot.

Twisting her foot, Collett examined the hiding place and thought it felt a little strange. She could only see the tip of the hilt when she looked directly down at it. "I suppose that works too," she said, satisfied.

Grabbing her hand, Cade pulled her along. "Come on *She-Ra*, let's go."

"What's *She-Ra*?" she asked as they left.

"Not what, who," he replied as they got into the car.

"Who?"

"Who, what?" he asked, teasing her now.

She gave him an annoyed look but smiled all the same.

"That's better then," he said and leaned over to kiss her cheek.

"What's better?"

"It's good to see you smile. You don't do it often enough."

Tipping her head away from him, Collett couldn't help but feel embarrassed.

"No, no, none of that. We're going to enjoy the rest of the day and stop thinking about everything else. You should be happy. We have a lot going on, I agree, but let's focus on the good stuff right now. Let's see, what's good then? Oh, I know," he said, starting the engine and putting it into gear, "how about being married to an amazing, smart, and perfect man?"

She smiled at his light sarcastic tone. "I suppose I'll have to ask Cynda about that," she quipped.

"Ah," he said, placing his hand to his heart, "you wound me."

She laughed quietly, and Cade basked in the sound of it.

"Now back to *She-Ra*," she said, participating in the frivolity.

They kept things light and fun as they drove toward town. The easy tone of their conversation was an element they'd had far too little of in their brief time together. They almost felt normal. Cade distracted her from thinking about anything other than trivial topics to keep her mood easy. He was very tired of seeing a frown on her face and worry in her eyes.

It didn't last long though. By now, it was early evening, and the winter darkness settled in. Collett and Cade were only about 7 miles from town when her face changed. She visibly paled and a fearful expression covered her features. "Oh no."

"What? What's wrong?"

"Hurry! It's Jarrett."

Jarrett immediately reversed, swerved the SUV around, and aimed for the demons. It was too much to hope that he would actually hit them. They both jumped out of the way of the vehicle, one of them landing easily atop the Tahoe.

The slightly smaller of the two creatures began attacking the luggage rack in hopes of gaining access through the vehicle's roof. Jarrett hit the brakes as hard as he could, and he felt satisfied when the grey skinned demon rolled over the windshield and hit the pavement hard, landing right in front of the SUV's tires. Intending to run him over, Jarrett switched gears, but before he could accelerate, the other demon threw his fist through the side window.

Glass shattered everywhere. The demon that broke the window pulled back to strike again, intent on shattering Jarrett's skull while his companion began rising from the ground.

For Jarrett, everything slowed and his focus cleared. His instincts took over, and his reactions were the automatic maneuvers of a seasoned warrior. No, not a warrior—he was more than that. Jarrett was a predator conditioned to survive. His heart pumped rhythmically as he fell into himself, embracing the monster. Blood flowed through him, warming him inside and out. His skin tingled. His mouth salivated. His body wanted to change. His mind refused.

He knew he didn't have to be a wolf to defeat the demons. His superior strength and skill would be enough to accomplish the task. He welcomed the adrenaline that rushed over him.

As the demon's fist came at him, he shifted his body and reached out, moving swiftly. Grabbing the moving arm with long practiced martial proficiency, he jerked the demon forward and smashed its face into the top of the of the vehicle's door frame.

It roared in pain.

Jarrett hooked the demon's arm around the steering wheel, twisted hard on the wheel, and pressed on the gas simultaneously.

The Price of Knowing

The demon in front jerked oddly when he was rammed by the SUV. Jarrett didn't see any more as the airbag smacked into him. He felt the impact against the windshield, but he couldn't take the time to feel gratified by it.

The demon caught in the steering wheel bellowed as the force of the airbag hit his awkwardly angled arm.

Jarrett didn't relent. He jerked the wheel around again with violent ferocity and kept his foot on the gas, aiming for what he hoped would be the alley behind the buildings. When he'd gone as far as he dared, he slammed on the brakes a second time.

He jabbed his elbow into the beast's face. Razor sharp teeth scraped his skin as it tried to bite him. Reaching down past the deflated airbag, Jarrett retrieved the dagger he kept strapped to his leg.

Receiving enough punishment, the putrid creature reached for Jarrett with its other hand and scored his neck with razor-like claws as it sought purchase.

Jarrett allowed the demon to pull him up by his jacket. Swinging his right arm around as he came up, he plunged the wicked blade deep into the demon's chest. Its mouth fell open in shock just before it disintegrated. Jarrett held tight to the dagger and watched it crumble away.

The other demon attacked the other side of the car, and Jarrett wasted no time escaping the confines of the SUV.

He leaped onto the hood, lunged toward the remaining enemy, and tackled it to the ground. His dagger dug deep into its heart and struck pavement as the ash-like dust replaced the banished creature's body.

Rising, Jarrett brushed the dust from himself and flipped the dagger up to look at it. It was the same silver dagger that had almost killed him. Since acquiring it from the witch who stabbed him, it had been a lethal asset. Not for the first time, he admired the craftsmanship.

C.B. Haight

A shiver traveled up his spine, and Jarrett knew he wasn't alone even before he heard the slow clapping behind him. Keeping his back turned, he waited.

"I liked that. It'ss fun to watch," something hissed.

Jarrett knew without looking that it was no more than 30 feet away. He sniffed the air and detected three more demons standing there. Worse, he knew one of them by name. "Henifedran."

"Hunter," Henifedran acknowledged. "I missssed you."

Turning, Jarrett assessed his enemies carefully. He cursed as he got a good look at the three winged greater-demons. The two on either side of Henifedran were huge, easily twice his own size, and Henifedran, an archdemon, was no slouch either. Plus, Jarrett knew personally how vicious he was. Shrugging it off, he trusted his instincts and waited for his opening.

"I'm surprised you're here," Jarrett said casually. "Haven't we done this before?"

"What can I sssay? You're not the only favorite."

The two beside Henifedran stared at Jarrett with hateful malice reflected in their bloodshot eyes, but they remained slightly hesitant. They knew The Hunter's reputation.

Henifedran, on the other hand, stood tall, completely confident, and eager. "I have been sssent to collect," he explained as the vapor of his warm breath swirled around him.

"Well, you can join the rest of those who've tried," Jarrett replied.

"Kill him," Henifedran ordered.

Opening their wide mouths and gleefully baring their sharp teeth, the two demons advanced.

Jarrett didn't move. Instead, he closed his eyes.

He heard them moving; one step closer, now two, he counted.

Eyes closed, Jarrett inhaled the cool air, centered himself, and listened to his pumping heart, following the rhythm of it in his mind. *One and two*. He listened to everything around him, setting its rhythm to his own. *One and two,* he thought.

~ 242 ~

The two demons didn't quite know what to expect from him. His calm reaction was something they'd never seen. They looked at each other and back to him. Then, all at once, they rushed him. Attacking viciously, they barreled in, hoping to topple him easily.

Jarrett acted instantly. Ducking, he rolled away from the speeding demon train heading for him, gained his footing, and struck out with his weapon. He scored a solid hit across one of the creature's arms as its momentum carried it past where he once stood. The grayish beast roared, but Jarrett took no pleasure in the strike. He was not stupid or arrogant enough to believe for one second that the odds were in his favor.

This time, all three approached more carefully. "Don't give him room," Henifedran ordered.

Jarrett was considering the pros and cons of throwing his dagger at the demon on the left when the sound of screeching tires echoed around them.

Everyone turned their heads to see another black Tahoe turn the corner leading to where they stood behind the buildings on Burrow Street—everyone except Jarrett. The bright headlights had the three demons hissing and blocking their eyes, and Jarrett seized the opportunity.

Rushing forward, he threw his dagger at the demon on the left and without waiting to see if his strike was true, tackled the demon on the right. Shouldering the behemoth like an expert linebacker, he drove his enemy back.

Once the initial shock abated, the demon began to fight back, punishing Jarrett with bruising fists to his ribs and serrated teeth in his shoulder. Jarrett stubbornly held on, using all of his strength. As each strike landed, Jarrett felt his control slip. His eyes burned as they shifted to red, and his skin tingled as black hair began to grow. Jarrett felt his jaw crack as long sharp teeth extended from his mouth, and his face elongated to that of a wolf's. Still, he tried to hold the change back.

"Stay in the car!" Cade shouted as he exited.

"Are you kidding me?" Collett asked.

"Stay here!" he snapped and ran toward the melee.

She watched as a particularly wicked looking demon tackled Cade, then she looked over to see Jarrett locked in combat with another while yet a third grabbed at a blade protruding from its neck. She considered Cade's instruction and hesitated, unsure of what to do.

Snowflakes fluttered down, landing on the windshield as Collett mentally reviewed all that Jarrett taught them over the last few days. She knew the demon with the knife in its neck wasn't finished. Surely one that big had to be beheaded or stabbed in the heart. Two against three would be harder than three to three, she concluded. She also remembered the demons were at a disadvantage in the beam of the headlights. Their black eyes were made for seeing in the dark. They hated sunlight, any bright light for that matter.

Deciding, she leaned over to the driver's seat and pulled the lever that would engage the brights. She pulled her dagger from her boot where Cade tucked it, and she followed him out of the car.

By this time, Cade was completely engaged in combat. He heard the car door close, and the audible distraction cost him. The demon Henifedran threw him against the brick wall of the building. Mortar and brick cracked under the force.

"Collett!" he warned as the demon turned toward the new, weaker victim.

Jarrett heard Cade yell out for her. Even knowing he shouldn't, Jarrett couldn't keep himself from looking up from his current predicament. He saw Henifedran advancing on Collett. Cade rushed to stop him, unaware of the other demon, dagger now gone, at his back. All of Jarrett's predictions were playing out before his eyes.

The worst of it was, it had distracted him too, and he lost his own advantage over the demon he'd been on the verge of killing. The demon beneath him rolled and landed a solid blow to Jarrett's muzzle. Blood formed in his mouth as he watched the sneak attack against his brother play out. It was the final straw, and Jarrett lost

The Price of Knowing

control. The monster he kept buried within burst forth with frightening speed. Muscles bunched, bones cracked, and the blood in his mouth was replaced by black demon ichor as a wolfish jaw clamped down on the arm holding him in place.

Collett ducked Henifedran's first swiping hand and swung around him, seeking the best place to strike. He was huge, and she knew she couldn't comfortably, or easily, angle to reach his heart with her small frame, never mind reaching his neck.

"Get out of here Collett!" Cade ordered from beneath his attacker.

She ignored him, concentrating on the one before her. *Think!* she told herself. With surprising speed, the demon rounded on her and grabbed her arm. He yanked her off her feet to meet his cruel gaze. She shivered as his taint entered her heart.

"I like thisssss one," Henifedran hissed with depraved intent.

Collett quit thinking and reacted in order to survive. She lifted her dangling feet and kicked out at his face as hard as she could. Her feet connected. Bone crunched as she broke his nose. He growled, covering his nose with his free hand. She swung her free arm up to grab the dagger from her right hand that was incapacitated by the demon's bruising grip. Even in his grasp, she wasn't close enough to reach his heart, and she didn't trust her aim enough to throw it. Instead, she used the weapon to gain her freedom by stabbing him through the wrist, but in reaction, he bashed her into the Tahoe. Her body slammed painfully against the idling vehicle. Crying out, she lost her grip on the hilt of the blade.

Warm fluids dripped down her arm, and she could see ichor steadily flow from the wound where the dagger remained. A strange sound drew her attention back to his ugly face, and she realized he was laughing at her.

He brought her in close enough to smell his wretched breath. "I think I will take you back inssstead."

She gagged, but when she looked into his grayish, bloodshot eyes, she couldn't help but channel the evil pouring from him in

~ 245 ~

C.B. Haight

sickening waves. Chills shot down her spine, and her stomach twisted and roiled against the onslaught of disparaging images and vile intent she read in his thoughts.

"Collett!" she heard from somewhere distant.

She felt a sudden despair and desperation for all of the victims those images showed her. She saw sadness, fear, horror, and heard pleas for mercy. Righteous anger bubbled from deep within her. In her mind, his destruction became the only thing that mattered.

He yanked her hair and brought her even closer, sniffing at her like an animal. "Sssomethingss different 'bout you."

She wasn't listening. She closed her eyes and focused, forcing her thoughts back to the memory of Jenny in the kitchen. She couldn't explain why or how, but power stirred within her. It was frightening. Something shifted inside her. Channeling all of the pain she could remember, Collett welcomed it as the power built and spread throughout her body.

Ignoring the combat around him, and Collett's sudden stillness, Henifedran sniffed again. His jaundiced eyes widened. "You smell like—" He didn't get the chance to finish.

Her muscles twitched as she remembered the shocking sensations of the Taser and passed it, through her, to him. She tasted blood in her mouth as she bit down on her tongue. She forced herself to experience the beating Jenny endured once again. Realizing the demon hadn't moved or spoken in more than a minute, Collett carefully opened her eyes and saw terror in his.

Before she could even consider what it meant, a streak of black fury attacked. The jarring force of Jarrett's attack had her flying from the demon's grasp and slamming against the pavement. Suddenly, Cade was there frantically checking her for wounds as his hands moved over her.

"Collett, talk to me."

She looked at him with confusion in her eyes and realized he must have said it more than once. Her head felt heavy, and her ears were ringing.

~ 246 ~

The Price of Knowing

"Are you hurt?"

She could see a gash in his head and couldn't help thinking about the irony of his question. She tried to get up.

"No. Stay down for a minute. It's over. Where are you hurt?"

"I'm okay. At least, I think I am," she assured him.

He used the pad of his thumb to wipe at the blood on her lip and lifted it to show her.

A strange, gurgling shriek from Henifedran drew their attention as Jarrett clawed and tore at his neck with unequaled animalistic savagery until his body disintegrated.

"Let's get you out of here," Cade insisted.

Collett shook the image away and tried to settle herself. She gently grabbed his hand and squeezed. "I'm fine. I bit my tongue, and I'm sure I have a few bruises, but I'm okay."

Helping her rise, he examined her wrist. Then kissing her forehead, he replied, "You scared the life out of me. You should have stayed in the car."

Approaching, Jarrett watched the exchange. Anger still seethed in him, but he bit back his comments. After days of watching how Cade and the others trained with Collett, and realizing how even he reacted in battle around her, Jarrett found himself losing patience with all of it. At this rate, the pair of them would accomplish nothing more than getting the whole group killed. Cade enabled her, and worse, Collett let him.

Being blind to everything other than Collett's safety, Cade couldn't see Collett was hiding. Jarrett saw it though, and he saw it clearly. She didn't fear for her safety, or for her life even. Collett was afraid of what she could do rather than what she couldn't. After this last encounter, Jarrett knew it had to change and decided he would fix the problem himself before they all ended up dead, or worse.

Bearing his canine teeth, Jarrett growled low in his throat. Cade looked up sharply. "I heard something," Jarrett uttered in a guttural snarl. He sniffed the air around them as if searching for an assailant.

~ 247 ~

Cade mimicked his behavior. "Up there, above us," Jarrett said, carefully moving closer as if the assailant would hear.

Cade glared up at the rooftop and stepped in front of Collett. Jarrett struck like a coiled snake. Grabbing a fist full of her hair and wrapping his arm around her, he yanked her against himself. She yelped.

Cade snapped around. His eyes glowed red at the sight before him. "What are you doing?!" he demanded.

"I'm curing us of a problem."

"Let her go!" Cade ordered.

"I'm sick to death of watching you with her."

"Let her go!" Cade repeated with deadly intent filling every syllable.

Jarrett knew this had to be done, but he didn't look forward to the fallout. Cade tensed as if he was going to attack, but before he could move, Jarrett pressed the wicked dagger against the white skin of her neck.

"Jarrett, you don't need to do this. You don't want to do this," Collett pleaded.

"Oh, but I do. I've wanted to do this for a long time," he growled in her ear.

"Jarrett, please," Collett tried again.

"You hurt her and you're dead," Cade spat. His measured control was slipping, and his voice revealed signs that the wolf was surfacing to protect his mate.

Jarrett shrugged. "There are worse things." He pricked her skin, wanting Collett to feel the cold bite of silver. He wanted her to be afraid. If he was a better man, he might cringe at what would come next, but he didn't—it had to be done. Without hesitation, he pulled at the blade.

The consequences of that single action were everything he expected it would be. Well, almost. He didn't really expect it to hurt so much.

The Price of Knowing

Cade rushed him, but he never made it. Collett reacted to her supposed imminent death.

There was a bright flash, and Jarrett felt a burning sensation travel throughout his body. The green gem of his magic ward flared bright, but it did little to protect him from the blow. His body slammed into the wall three feet behind him. He slid down, fell to his knees, and involuntarily shuddered. He crumpled to the wet pavement, lying in the fetal position as snowflakes fell from the sky. He felt like his entire nervous system was fried, and had to fight to keep his current form. He figured the only thing more humiliating than his current state would be lying naked while he shuddered and spasmed. Finally rolling to his knees, he found Cade standing over him.

His brother cocked his head to the side and looked at Jarrett with a combination of shocked confusion and distrust. The twins glanced back to Collett simultaneously.

She stood there with tears glistening in her wide eyes and a hand pressed against her neck. "I felt the blade. It cut me. How is it I'm not dead?"

"Be...cause...I used...the dull side of the blade," Jarrett forced out as his body quaked again.

"Why?" asked Cade. The simple word asked so many things at once.

"You're holding her...back," he replied, and focusing on the convulsions, thought to himself, *At least it's getting easier to breathe.*

Confused but no longer angry, Cade bent down and helped Jarrett to his feet. To both of their surprise, he couldn't stand on his own for several minutes. Finally, he pushed Cade away and leaned his back against the wall. He didn't feel like he was on fire any more. He only felt like a hundred or so bees were attacking his organs instead.

"You're going to get her killed, Cade. You're going to get us all killed."

~ 249 ~

C.B. Haight

"I won't let that happen. I won't let anything get close enough to try!"

"That's the problem. Collett isn't helpless. She's far from it, but you won't see it. Look at me. I can barely stand. *She did that*!" he replied as he pointed at her. "You're so blind with worry you can't even see her potential. You can't protect her all the time. She has to be able to protect herself."

Collett stood there with a guilt-ridden expression, "I'm so sorry. I just—"

"Don't!" he snarled and forced himself to stand. He stared straight at her. "Don't. You better learn to use what you got." He looked to Cade and ordered, "and you better learn to let her."

"You would do the same if it were someone you loved."

Jarrett scoffed, "Well it's lucky then that I don't know what that's like, because it's made you vulnerable. Look around, Brother, it isn't the eighteenth century anymore, and even then, women—especially that one right there—shouldn't be underestimated. I've seen and felt what she is capable of."

Cade had no reply. He looked back and forth between his wife and Jarrett.

Turning his back on them, Jarrett started to walk toward the front of the buildings. "Either you teach her how to survive without you, or I'll do it my way. Otherwise, that wretched hope you're always preaching about won't make a damn bit of difference, and we'll all be dead before the next full moon." As he reached the end of the alley, he turned. "If you get yourself killed, who will protect her then?" He spun on his heel and left them to contemplate his last words. When he was out of sight, Jarrett stopped and closed his eyes. Leaning against the building again, he cursed and wondered how much longer it would hurt. He released another pain filled breath.

CHAPTER 23

After a quick assessment and cleanup of the area, the small group made it back to the old house in short order; albeit they were all in the same vehicle this time. The SUV Jarrett drove would likely never drive again. Deciding it would be best to hide the car until they could figure out what to do with it, Jarrett and Cade pushed it behind the shopping center and concealed it as best they could. Cade thankfully kept clothes in any vehicle he traveled in, so Jarrett was able to get dressed. They then drove the 30 miles back to the cabin together.

For Collett, the trip felt at least twice as long. No one said a word the entire way back, and she couldn't help but soak in the tense emotions surrounding her in the confines of the Tahoe. Upon arriving at the house, Collett felt extreme relief as she exited the car and deeply inhaled the chilled air.

Taking a step, she felt a new tightness in her hip from her encounter with the archdemon, Henifedran. Cade and Jarrett awaited her on the other side, so she limped forward. The snow was coming down steadily, and she looked down at her footprint. She stopped and took in her surroundings. Behind her, Cade and Jarrett stopped too. *A white Christmas,* she thought and knew it would be a beautiful sight to behold in the morning.

"Collett?" Cade questioned with concern.

She turned to see the brothers both looking at her oddly. She almost laughed at the site. In almost every way, they were identical. Though neither would ever admit it. She noticed new similarities in them every day. Their expressions, their mannerisms, their incessant need to be in charge were evidence of their inherent traits. Even the incident that morning, when Jarrett blew up about her not taking the strike against him, reminded her of the day Cade called her out on not accepting help. Now here she was, a little more than a month later, relying on them all too much. *I need to find a balance,* she thought, *There must always be balance.*

"It's going to be beautiful tomorrow," she observed aloud, looking up at the sky and watching the flakes fall.

Jarrett huffed disbelievingly.

"Come on, Collett, let's go inside," urged Cade.

"We have to leave again, don't we?" she asked Jarrett.

He shrugged.

"I like it here. There's this feeling...almost familiar," she said sadly.

"Come on, they're all waiting for us," Cade said again.

She looked down at her hands, wondering how so much could happen in a single day. "Will you teach me?" she asked Jarrett.

"What?" the brothers said together; Cade's tone was surprised, Jarrett's confused.

She smiled. There it was again. It was amazing that twins who had been so far apart for so long could still be so much alike. "I've been either hiding or running for too long. I thought if I kept running, the problem would go away. It didn't. I thought if I could hide, I could be normal. I'm not though. I guess I never will be."

The two men remained quiet.

"I want my life back," she said with desperation. She saw the tick in Cade's jaw and amended, "Not my old life, just my life. I want to enjoy Christmas without being afraid. I want to have happiness without an enemy at my back. I want...I want to quit running. I'm want to stand and fight." She paused and looked back to Jarrett. "I can't do that yet, but I think, with both of you at my side, I could."

"The only way to end this is to take down Niall," Jarrett told her.

"I know that now," she replied.

"I can't teach you how to remember, and I don't know magic," Jarrett said irritably.

"But you do know how to push me."

"I'll teach you, Collett," Cade offered.

Jarrett shook his head.

She nodded. "You will, and you have, but you won't be hard enough."

"I will," he insisted.

"No, Cade, you won't. You want too badly to protect me. What Jarrett said earlier? He's right. You can't always be there to save me, and I can't keep expecting you to. I couldn't stand to lose you because of my own weakness."

He moved to her and, putting his hands on her arms, said firmly, "I don't want you hurt."

"You can't protect them all, Cade," Jarrett groused.

As he spoke, Collett vaguely remembered the taunting voice from her dreams, *"You can't save them all."*

Collett took Cade's hand. "I know you'll be there if I need you, but I won't see you hurt when I could have prevented it. Neither one of us should be handicapped because of how we feel about each other. We'll do this together and protect each other." She looked to Jarrett. "All of us." Cade looked over to his brother then back to her. "If you love me, trust me. I would never do anything to hurt you, but I have to do this."

~ 253 ~

Cade thought back to when Selena had told him to trust her over a month before. Collett's words mimicked the Native American seer's words, *"Cade, when the time comes, trust in her to know what's right. No matter what, no matter the cost—believe in her. She is not willing to cause anyone undue pain, especially you. Some things simply must be done with fierce courage and resolve."*

Cade searched her eyes and saw Collett's determination in the depths of them. "If anything happens to you..."

"I can't guarantee everything will work out, but if anything bad happens, it won't be because I didn't fight back," she answered.

Cade turned his attention to his estranged brother and knew, whether he liked it or not, there was no one better to teach her to stay alive. Jarrett was a fierce fighter, and Cade also knew they were right. His love and instinct to protect Collett kept him from stretching her limits.

"We'll try it your way," he relented, still watching his brother.

Jarrett looked at them both and realized that not only was Cade trusting Collett, they were gifting him with a certain level of trust. He felt a sudden, unfamiliar twinge in his chest, but he pushed it aside.

Finally, he inclined his head in agreement. "It won't be easy."

"Nothing worth it ever is," replied Collett.

"All right then," Cade replied.

Collett smiled up at her husband but then stepped from his reach to pin them both with a serious expression. "We're in this together now. To the end, whatever it may be."

Jarrett said nothing. He knew she wanted a promise from him. She wanted the promise that he would stick around. The odd part was, looking into her hopeful blue eyes, he found himself wanting to give it.

"Together, to the end then," Cade offered first.

"To the end," Jarrett reluctantly vowed, hoping it wouldn't be a mistake.

They entered the house together, which Delphene took as a good sign. She'd known they were outside for a while now. She'd heard them pull in, but she kept herself from peeking or butting in, which was hard for her.

She recognized Jarrett was wearing new clothes and evaluated the group's entire appearance more carefully. Smelling the demons on them, Delphene could guess what had held them up. Cade and Jarrett met her scrutiny with expressions of confirmation.

"What happened?" asked Cynda.

"We had some trouble," Cade answered. "A few friends came to visit for the holidays."

"Oh no! Are you all right?" asked Ashley, putting her book down and rising from the couch.

"Fine. We're all okay. There's nothing that won't heal by tomorrow anyway," Collett reassured.

Nate came in, munching on a piece of bread. "Whoa, you three have a fight?"

"They encountered some demons," Cynda explained knowingly.

"Oh. Can we eat yet?" he replied, unconcerned. Cynda stared at him sternly. "What? They're alive, aren't they?"

Jeffery entered next, crowding the kitchen doorway even more. "Did someone say demons?"

Jarrett rolled his eyes. "I'll be outside."

"No, wait," said Cynda. "Stay. We have dinner ready, and I thought—for tonight anyway—we should have a little peace."

Delphene grabbed him by the arm, ignored the scowl on his face, and pulled him toward the kitchen. "*C'mon, Mon Ami*, and have a taste of my *Civet de Cerf*. I promise you've never had the like of it before, and likely never will again." Looking over her shoulder, she winked to Cynda as she passed by.

C.B. Haight

Jeffery and Nate stepped from the doorway to allow room for the pair to pass.

"So, we can eat now?" asked Nate again.

"Yes, Nate," replied Cynda in her motherly tone. "We can eat."

Dinner passed by easily for most of the group. The conversation was off and on, and even Jeffery added to it, something he rarely did.

Jarrett said nothing the entire time. The whole thing felt extremely awkward to him. He'd never eaten with this many people before in this kind of a situation. It was much easier to concentrate on his food, which was everything Delphene promised. He learned that *Civet de Cerf* was braised venison. He was amazed at how tender and delicious it was, especially given the fact that she obviously had little time to marinade the meat. He still couldn't figure out how she managed to get all the stuff for this dinner, but he guessed Cynda must have had this in mind all along when she purchased supplies on the first day. Either that or she used magic to get ingredients. Still, it was a good meal, so he didn't bother to ask.

They couldn't all fit at the little, retro table in the kitchen, so they got their food and crowded into the living room instead. Jarrett opted to stand near the door. Ashley began gathering plates when Collett asked, "Have you heard from James?"

Cynda nodded sadly. "There's been no change. She seems peaceful enough, but Jenny still hasn't woken. The doctors are a little baffled, but hopeful. She's not brain dead and breathes on her own. That's good, I suppose."

"I suppose," answered Collett. "How are Tracy and James?"

"Good," replied Rederrick. "Tracy is chomping at the bit to get back to New York, but for now, she's staying around. Anyways, Ashley here has decided to join them after Christmas."

"You have?" asked Nate, surprised.

"I can't stay here for too much longer. With Tracy being so edgy, she needs me there, and I need to see Jenny."

"What about the attacks?" Nate asked.

The Price of Knowing

She smiled at his concern. "There haven't been any. In fact, they've been safer than we have if you count what happened in town today. Plus, I'll be on the base. James has already arranged it," she replied softly.

"You can't fly commercially," Jarrett said, "They'll be tracking that." He shrugged when the room of people looked at him. "I would be."

"Actually, we considered that. The pilot Dad arranged is the same one that brought them to New Orleans," responded Ashley. "He's coming this way in two more days, so I'll fly back with him. I'll need a ride to the airport though."

"We'll take care of it, Ash," assured Cade. "I suppose this is as good a time as any to tell you all that we can't stay here anymore. What happened in town proves it. We'll hold out here until Ash leaves if we can, but after that, we need a new place to go."

Cynda stood, "I don't want to talk about this right now. We can discuss travel plans later. Right now, there is another matter I want to deal with. Give me a minute, I need to get something."

Everyone watched as she left and then looked to Rederrick curiously. Everyone except Jeffery, Jarrett noted.

"Don't look at me. I rarely know what she's up to. I only follow along and hope I can keep up," replied Rederrick under the intense scrutiny.

Jarrett kept quiet about how he suspected Jeffery knew exactly what was going on.

Cynda came back downstairs a few minutes later holding a paper bag. "I'm a little traditional, and I would have liked to give you each a pretty present wrapped in festive paper today. That being said, under the circumstances, this is the best I could manage," she explained and held up the small bag.

"It's nice that you thought of anything," Cade supplied.

"This isn't only from me. Jeffery had his hand in it too."

Everyone looked at the young sorcerer with surprise. "It's nothing," he mumbled uncomfortably.

~ 257 ~

C.B. Haight

"He's wrong. It's more than nothing, but first, because it is Christmas Eve, we need to set the mood. Jarrett, could you get the lights for me?"

With his customary look of annoyance, Jarrett flicked off the switch near the door, leaving the small fireplace stove as the only light in the room.

"Jeffery," Cynda coaxed, "could you?"

There was a shuffling as he stood from the floor and deftly moved his hands. The group suddenly found themselves bathed in the soft glow created by glittering lights dancing around the tree.

There were several sounds of approval, and Rederrick said, "Well done, boy, well done!"

Even Jarrett couldn't deny the sight was…shaking his head, he tried to think of a word to describe the magnitude of what he was seeing, but there wasn't one. The magical lights Jeffery conjured were like little stars plucked right from the sky. They moved and twinkled brightly in contrast with the evergreen branches. Jarrett was impressed. Never in his life had he seen magic used in such a way. In his experience, people cursed with magic abilities used them to hurt or destroy.

"Beautiful, Jeffery. It's better than I'd hoped," Cynda exclaimed. "Now," she said with a deep breath, "I have a gift for each of us. It's nothing as impressive as that," she said pointing to the tree. "All the same though, it's needed."

Cynda reached into the bag and pulled out a thin, copper colored chain. On the end of it hung a strange, circular patterned charm. Within a large circle, there were several smaller circles; all of them were interconnected.

"You got me jewelry. That's just what I asked for," Nate joked.

"No, Nate. I didn't get you jewelry," she replied with a smile. "What I made, what *we* made, Jeffery and I, is a symbol." She twisted the chain, and the charm on the end twirled in response. "Collett, in a way, you are the beginning, and each of us have become pieces around you. But now, we are whole together."

~ 258 ~

The Price of Knowing

Jeffery cleared his throat.

"Go ahead, Jeffery."

"We're a team. We have to be. I...well, I've never been a part of something like this, but..."

"This is a team," Ashley finished.

He nodded.

"If we're going to remain that way, we have to stand as one," Cynda explained further. "I thought that, maybe, this would be a symbol for us all, a reminder that we are each a smaller portion of a whole. Without one of these smaller circles, the rest would be compromised. Each circle connects to the others like each person here connects to the group. It's small, but so are the links in armor. Together, we strengthen those around us. Jeffery helped conjure a charm for me, and I believe the protection magic in it will help us. More importantly, the meaning behind it will bond us. Both of us already wear one. The question I have for all of you is——will you wear one? Can we be different parts of a whole?"

Collett stood first. "I've been told that victory can create hope, but a little hope will ensure victory. I'm not sure where or when I heard that, or how I remember, but I believe it's true. I'll wear it, because to me, it is a symbol of the hope we need."

Cynda slipped it over Collet's head then reached into the bag and moved to Cade, holding up another charm before him. "Cade?"

"I'll wear one," he replied respectfully and held out his hand. Instead, Collett took the chain from Cynda and slipped it over Cade's head. He kissed her hands as she finished.

Cynda turned. "Nate, Rederrick?"

"You know I'm in," replied Rederrick.

"I told you I asked for jewelry," quipped Nate, and with a smile and a wink, he snatched his before Rederrick could.

Rederrick took an extra one, offering it to Ashley. "Will you?" he asked.

Nodding, she took it from her father's hand.

~ 259 ~

C.B. Haight

"I will wear one, and I will wear it proudly, *Mon Chèrie*," Delphene proclaimed.

Jarrett watched the whole exchange uneasily. He said nothing as Cynda walked over to him, holding up another chain. She met his doubtful expression with her sea green eyes, and he could see the power behind them.

He also saw something he hadn't seen for hundreds of years. He saw emotions he'd only seen in Rowena, emotions he could not fully understand anymore. He understood hate. He understood anger, jealousy, and greed. He even understood pity. But love, kindness—these were foreign to him. Unsure what to say, his brows drew in, and he bit the inside of his cheek.

Cynda smiled, and his memory flashed to Rowena's face. "Where Collett is the beginning, in a way, you are at the end. I know that you have been mostly alone throughout your life and this whole thing must be difficult for you, but I've realized something else these past few days. Our circle wasn't whole until you arrived."

He said nothing, but inside there was so much turmoil and confusion. And, he noted, there was fear. He was as afraid to be a part of this group and rely on these people as Collett was of her abilities. He glanced to her with sudden insight into how she must feel. She was afraid of hurting them, letting them down, or making matters worse, and in his own way, so was he.

He suddenly felt like a twelve-year-old boy again and saw the fire-lit green eyes of his surrogate mother staring at him with compassion, as his body betrayed him for the first time. He could see the same motherly compassion in Cynda as she offered him the gift of unity and family. All of it, coupled with Collett's pure trust a few hours before, broke something long ago frozen inside of him.

Jarrett gently took the charm from her and admired the intricate design of the medallion for more than a minute. He knew that it was meant as a symbol of their team's unity. But for him, her gift signified change. A change he feared, but deep down, it was a change he'd been looking for his whole life. Without a single word,

~ 260 ~

he placed it over his head, feeling the charmed metal against his chest as it slipped beneath his shirt. He silently swore to himself that he wouldn't let her down. He wouldn't let any of them down. Jarrett would do everything in his power to see this to the end.

"Merry Christmas, Jarrett," she said softly, smiling.

Humbled, Jarrett could only nod in reply.

CHAPTER 24

The door to his room opened. Niall knew it was Victor who entered before he opened his eyes. He didn't look up. He already knew what Victor was here to report. Henifedran had fallen. Niall's link to him had severed the instant it happened.

"Sir?"

"What?"

"Henifedran hasn't returned yet," Victor explained.

"Do you think I'm unaware of that?" he asked darkly.

"Of course not, sir. Should I send more bounty hunters to that area?"

Niall glared at him. "This is not like it has ever been before. He is The Hunter, and the sooner you realize that the better. He will have left already, but I'll find him."

Neither man spoke while Niall closed his eyes once more. Sweat dotted his brow, and his temples throbbed from the level of concentration he continued to invoke.

"Is there something else, Victor?" he said without opening his eyes.

The Price of Knowing

"We have nothing on the woman. She and the people she is with have disappeared. We've tracked one of the children down to a military base in Colorado, but his records indicate he's overseas for another six months."

"If you wouldn't have let them get away the other night, this wouldn't be a problem, would it?" Niall replied, implying a clear threat behind the words.

Victor kept silent, not daring to irritate his master any further.

"I don't care how you do it, find a way to draw out that family," he ordered.

"Yes sir," said Victor, and he moved to the exit. As he reached the door, he turned back. "What about the other boy, the one called Cody?"

"I promised he could live. I never said where or how. Let him stay where he is for now."

"I understand, sir."

Niall said nothing more and heard the door close quietly. He knew Victor wanted to slam it in outrage. It was one of the reasons he kept the sniveling twit around. That and one other reason no one knew of.

It helped that Victor was nothing if not obedient. He showed no emotion and never questioned his master. Victor would do exactly as he was told for the rest of his life, and Niall knew it.

The fact was, Victor was nothing without Niall, and years of brainwashing and control had ensured Victor would be unable to envision his life any other way. It was ironic that for as smart and capable as he was, Victor was one of the most easily manipulated of his followers.

Stupid, weak-willed mortals, he thought. He knew exactly how to control the worst of them and how to turn them to his side. Power and fear. Almost everyone craved power, and those that didn't could be controlled with fear.

Niall was worshipped, feared, respected, and revered all at the same time. He'd bent many to his will, and he gathered strength and

~ 263 ~

power from it each time. He'd learned over the centuries he'd existed that life was not about hope, love, and courage. Those ideals made a man weak and vulnerable. They were a trap. It wasn't how the world worked anymore. It hadn't been for a long time—maybe longer than even he realized.

No, life—*his* life—was about power, fear, and vengeance. To get power, you needed respect. To get respect you commanded or demanded it. To demand respect, he instilled fear, and fear could cripple a man, bending him whichever way Niall desired. He'd been shown how to feed on fear, anger, and chaos, and he needed to do so to retain and strengthen his abilities. This kind of power had made him far stronger than ever before.

Collett threatened all that he built, and that he could not allow.

Taking a deep breath, he began to concentrate again. When he exacted his revenge on the betrayer, Jarrett, she would see the truth. She would understand how powerless she was. There was no way to save those who wouldn't follow the rules. Once she learned that, she would beg for his mercy. Niall suspected she was protecting him. Somehow, despite no memory of who she was, Collett had blocked his connection to the traitor, but he resolved it wouldn't take long to feel The Hunter's rage again. "I am Strength, and you cannot save them all," he said to the dark.

Christmas came and went. Time for celebrating had ended, and Jarrett had them all back outside training, despite the foot of snow that covered the ground. The day after Christmas, they spent a good part of the morning making arrangements to move on to a place in Park City, Utah, at Rederrick's insistence.

They called the rental agency about the totaled SUV, explaining the damage away as a result of winter weather. Luckily, Rederrick had opted for the extra insurance on it. Of course, all of this was done using false names. The soonest they could arrange to transport

The Price of Knowing

them all out would be two days from now, so they continued to cross their fingers that their location would be safe enough for now.

Having said their goodbyes, Ashley was on her way with Nate, Rederrick, and Cade to the airport to hitch a ride with the Black Hawk pilot. Jarrett felt it would be a good time to get a little one-on-one training done with Collett, so she stayed behind. In fact, it was one of the reason's Cade went along; Jarrett had insisted.

Delphene stayed with them and watched, as per Cade's instructions, while Cynda and Jeffery meddled with more magic.

Instead of using sticks, Jarrett padded his sword and supplied Collett with a smaller sword that was likewise protected. After running through the basic routines for twenty minutes to loosen her up, Jarrett began to pick up his pace. More than an hour later, he felt his old frustration coming back. She kept falling back into bad habits of defensiveness and hesitation, and she wouldn't take an offensive position.

"Are you playing with me or trying to kill me?" he ground out.

"Oh, I'm sorry, did I hurt you?" she answered automatically.

He roared in frustration, and striking hard, disarmed her. Getting in her face, he snapped, "You're supposed to hurt me. You're supposed to kill me. I'm a demon, remember?"

"I'm sorry," she said again.

"And stop saying that!" He picked up her sword. Seeking calm, he tried a different tactic. Handing her the sword, he asked, "What did you do to me in the alley?"

"I…don't really know. I was scared you'd kill me."

"All right, how did you do it?"

"I don't know."

"Yes, you do. Think about it," he ordered.

"I can't, because I didn't think—I—I just did it."

"Exactly!" he exclaimed.

Collett looked at him with confusion in her eyes.

~ 265 ~

"You didn't think. You followed your instincts. Quit thinking and act. Quit trying to time your every move, instead, feel them. Wait for them. There's a rhythm to it."

She nodded.

"Again," he ordered.

Collett lifted her sword and readied herself for his attack. It didn't come. He didn't even lift his sword. He waited for her to move against him.

Cautiously, she advanced, lifted her weapon to strike, and found herself stopped by his own blade. Looking into his eyes, she saw the challenge in them. She hesitated. *A rhythm,* she thought. *Just feel it.* She struck out again and again. He expertly blocked her, but she kept coming, pressing in and engaging him fully.

The speed of the melee picked up, and she thrust, cut, and countered. He met her blade every time, twisting and turning with his massive sword to deflect and parry her every action. Before long, he turned the tide of the battle and advanced on her. Breathing deeply, she tried to fall into the rhythm of combat as he instructed. She blocked several strikes and began to build her confidence. Until she felt a heavy thump on her back shoulder. It hurt too. If he pulled back the hit, she couldn't tell. She let her sword fall, point down, and rubbed the new bruise.

"Again," he ordered.

He forced her back into combat, and again he landed another stinging blow. He pushed at her again and again, forcing her to engage. She took several hits, but he refused to give her quarter.

Tripping over a rock, she fell to the ground, but even then he didn't relent. He attacked her, so Collett tucked her weapon against herself and rolled away from the strike. Her breaths were coming in short gasps, and despite the fact she was covered in snow, she was sweating and warm. She dodged again, moving fast as he lowered his sword once more. Doing a backward somersault, she made it to her knees and managed to get her sword up in time to lock the two weapons together.

He held his weapon against hers, and their eyes met. Her breathing was labored and heavy. His breaths were slightly quickened, but each one remained smooth and steady. Quirking his brow, he gave her a cocky grin, and she noticed his mouth tilted up higher on the right side, the same as Cade's.

"Now we're getting somewhere," he said grinning. "Again."

A few hours later, Cade came back with Nate and Rederrick. Feeling better because they'd encountered no trouble in dropping Ashley off, he was eager to see Collett. He wanted to see how her first training alone with Jarrett went. Even more important, he needed to tell her the pilot that brought her to New Orleans when she'd been unconscious couldn't even remember her being aboard.

Entering the living room, he found Delphene looking at a travel map on the floor.

"Where's Collett?"

"Upstairs, nursing her aches." She looked up with bright excitement in her eyes. "You would not believe it, *Mon Ami*. She is…" Her words trailed off as she realized Cade had already left. "*Etonnant*," she finished on a breath for Nate and Rederrick's benefit.

Cade went into their room and immediately saw a purplish bruise on Collett's upper thigh. Startled by his entrance, she stopped rubbing on the healing cream Cynda insisted she use. She watched his expression change from eager to anger in less than a split second. As his eyes traveled over her, he saw the purpling marks between her shoulder and her neck. Cade's jaw clenched so tightly that Collett figured any minute his teeth would begin to crack. Turning, he started from the room.

"Cade?" she called.

He ignored her.

~ 267 ~

C.B. Haight

She scrambled to stop him and was able to shimmy past him just as he reached the stairs. "Cade, stop!"

"He went too far," he accused. His expression darkened when Jarrett appeared at the bottom of the stairs as if he expected the encounter.

Cade tried to step forward, but Collett put her hands on his chest. "Stop! He did exactly what you couldn't do—what we agreed on."

"What's that—beat the crap out of you? I don't recall that part of the agreement."

"I challenged her," Jarrett replied with venom.

Cade pointed out the dark bruise on her neck. "You call this a challenge? It looks more like you punished her!"

Jarrett took two stairs in one stride. "Better me than them. She has to learn. She has to remember."

"This is your way of reminding her? You're going to beat the memories out of her?"

By this time, the whole house had gathered at both ends of the stairway to witness the verbal battle. Nate, Delphene, and Rederrick stood at the bottom, and Jeffery and Cynda lingered behind Cade.

"It's the only way!" insisted Jarrett, coming up further.

Seeing the look in Cade's eyes and feeling both of their anger, Collett knew where this was heading. "Enough!" she shouted. Putting her hands up, she turned on Cade first. Her eyes, usually soft and kind, were now fierce and hard. "Stop using me as an excuse to pick a fight with him. I'm going to get bruised a bit while I'm doing this, and that's all there is to it! And you—" she rounded on Jarrett, "stop being so surly and egging him on. You came here knowing he would be upset!" She huffed out a tired breath. "I'm fine, Cade, and what aches today will likely be gone tomorrow, or close to it anyway. Jarrett, you're not telling the whole story either.

"After a time, he let me off the hook, but I wanted to keep going. So if you want someone to blame, then blame me. It's time for you two to get along. I don't have the energy for your

~ 268 ~

testosterone tantrums anymore, and I'm tired of absorbing all of the anger. So both of you go outside, trade fists, smack each other around, or do whatever it takes to put this idiocy behind us, but do it away from me. I'm going to take a nap."

She brushed by Cade on her way to their room at the end of the hallway.

Cade turned to go after her, but Cynda stood in his way. "Oh no you don't. You heard what she said. You two, outside." She pointed her finger down the stairs.

"Let me go talk to her," he insisted.

"I will." He stepped forward only to be stopped when she held up her hands. "*After* you go cool off for a bit." She was using the same motherly tone he'd heard her use many times on her children. "Both of you," she added, looking past Cade to a grim Jarrett halfway up the stairs.

Turning, Jarrett complied with the order and leaped the distance to the bottom landing. Everyone parted to give him room, and he left the house, slamming the door behind him. Cade hesitated. He wanted to go and talk with Collett.

"Think of it from her point of view, *Chère*. She's a sponge for everything you're feeling right now. Give her time. Go and talk to him," Delphene encouraged.

Fortifying himself, Cade walked down the stairs and followed Jarrett outside. He found his brother sitting on the edge of the porch with his legs buried in the deep snow that had accumulated. Cade moved to the other end of the porch and looked out at the landscape surrounding them for a few minutes. Then, feeling a bit like a petulant child, he moved back to sit down near his brother.

He'd overreacted. He knew it, but it was so hard to admit. His relationship with Jarrett was new, and he didn't always know how to deal with him. The connection his twin shared with his wife made it worse. He could admit that it was partly jealousy that made it so difficult to trust him with Collett. Instead of apologizing, something

~ 269 ~

he knew Jarrett wouldn't appreciate, he tried to bridge the gap between them by talking about Collett.

"How did she do?"

Jarrett looked at him for a minute, as if trying to decide if Cade really wanted to know. "Better than I thought," he said finally. "She has a long way to go though."

"It's hard for me to see her hurt," Cade admitted.

"I would have never guessed," Jarrett replied sarcastically.

The silence stretched between them again. Sometimes, for them, no words were better than any words, but today Cade felt the need to talk. "I don't know what to do around you."

Jarrett ignored his comment and asked, "Why did you marry her?"

"I love her."

"I get that she's nice to look a—"

Appalled and confused, Cade shook his head, "It's not about that."

"You think you had to marry her to protect her then?"

"I love her. I *wanted* to be with her."

"I see the way she looks at you. You could have been with her anyway. You didn't need to marry her for that," Jarrett replied.

Jumping from the porch, Cade moved to stand in front of Jarrett. "See it's stuff like that, that makes this hard," Cade said frustrated. "It's not just physical. I love her, and she loves me. I don't know how else to explain it."

"Love's a myth. How would you even know anyway? It's not like you can really understand who she is. She doesn't even know," Jarrett countered with a level tone.

"It doesn't matter," Cade insisted, feeling agitated again.

"Why? How can you believe she'll still love you when she finds out who she is?"

"Because I believe in her," Cade retorted.

Jarrett lifted a single brow and adopted a smug expression. "Do you?"

~ 270 ~

The Price of Knowing

Cade recognized the trap Jarrett created too late. He brushed at his hair with his fingers, pushing it away from his face and turned his back to his twin. He couldn't answer. He thought he believed in her. He knew she loved him, but he suddenly realized part of him worried her feelings might change when she found out who she was.

"There's really only one way to find out, you know," said Jarrett from behind him.

Cade cocked his head to the side in response, still keeping his back to Jarrett but listening all the same.

"Quit trying to hold her back. She has to remember."

"And when she does?" Cade asked.

"You'll know one way or another at least. Besides, you'll have your hands full of more demons than you'll know what to do with when Niall finds us. She'll have to fight. Don't doubt that for a minute. It's better for you if she knows how. When the time comes, really comes, Niall will stop at nothing to see her dead," Jarrett reminded him.

"She's not the only one he wants dead," Cade said and turned back toward the sunset. He watched the reddened sky shift to purple. "Why? Why does he want her so badly? It can't only be her power."

Jarrett shrugged. "I quit trying to figure out Niall a long time ago, but don't doubt that power is something he always craves more of."

Cade pondered about it for a bit longer and turned with a curious expression on his face. "Why isn't he here yet? They already found us the other day."

"Maybe he can't pin it down to an exact location yet, and it's not like Henifedran made it back to tell him."

"But he found you more than once. When I came for you, they were hot on our heels for days. In fact, we barely made it to Ashley's."

"So?"

"How long after you saved Jeffery's mom did they find you?" he asked excitedly.

~ 271 ~

"A couple days," Jarrett replied.

"Not Collett though. After you kidnapped her, nothing happened at Rederrick's for almost a week. The Faction only attacked after we ended up at Ashley's."

"I burned the records, and Finnawick was too worried about self-preservation to let Niall know he found her until he had her in hand. They would've needed to track her down again," Jarrett admitted.

"Exactly. When she was running, Collett would go months in between attacks, but they came after you daily," Cade said, and Jarrett began to catch on. "How did Niall contact you in the past?" Cade questioned. His idea was progressing.

"He appeared. Even his demons appeared no matter where I went."

"But when the half-demon—"

"Finnawick," Jarrett supplied.

"When he sent you for Collett, he gave you records, a paper trail. Niall isn't here yet because he can't find her the way he finds you." He paused, remembering his conversation with the pilot earlier. "The pilot didn't remember her. When I thanked him, he couldn't figure out what I was talking about. Rederrick mentioned something about this to me when he first called me about Collett. He told me people forget her. That would make it even harder to find her."

"Why don't we?"

"I'm not sure; perhaps because she's allowing us to remember somehow."

Jarrett thought about it. "I didn't know who she was when I took her. She was a stranger at first. I didn't realize she was the women that took me from the fire until she touched me and I saw her in that moment again."

Cade scowled as he formed the series of events together.

"When I went to town, I went alone," Jarrett added, following his brother's train of thought.

~ 272 ~

"In New Orleans, the demons didn't come until after you'd left us. They must have tracked you back to the house."

"She's blocking him. By some means, Collett is blocking him from finding us," Jarrett concluded Cade's theory aloud.

Urgency coursed through Cade. He ran into the house. Jarrett followed, completely surprised, not only because Cade figured that out, but also because it actually made sense to him.

He'd expected Niall to show up with a demon hoard and a few magic users by now. The scarcity of attacks since joining the group and the small number of demons per attack made more sense. Sending a few demons after him was no big deal. This way, Niall could wear him down and concentrate his energy on finding Collett instead of wasting it on him.

When he thought about it, he understood Jeffery's report of Victor's appearance at the warehouse. Victor would have been charged with keeping the demons under control and tracking down Collett by way of technological means. He was a wizard at such things, and if he managed to find out about Cade and Jarrett being brothers, as Finnawick did, he would have pursued that lead in hopes of finding Collett—or at least a link to her.

The demons sent to the house in Colorado botched it because they hadn't realized who she was. Niall would have reserved that information for Victor alone. With no Victor or Niall to keep them in check, they gleefully went after the housekeeper, Jenny. Collett's vision of Jenny inadvertently alerted the house they were there all too soon.

The two men burst through the front door and ran through the kitchen. Rederrick, Nate, Cynda, and Delphene looked up with shock from the table where they finalized plans for their relocation. Cade rushed up the stairs, taking them two at a time, with Jarrett on his heels.

"Trouble?" questioned Delphene.

C.B. Haight

Without a second thought, they all followed, making it in time to see Cade surge through his bedroom door and wake Collett with a start.

"We're not leaving!" he proclaimed. "I think I figured out a way to stick it to Niall and buy us some time." A superior smile spread across his face. Behind him, Jarrett also had an excited, battle-hungry gleam in his eyes. For the first time, Cade was sure the two brothers were thinking very much alike.

CHAPTER 25

"You want to do what?" Collett exclaimed.

"It's not as bad as it sounds, really," Cade countered.

Everyone gathered in the living room and tried to digest the outrageous plan Cade laid out before them.

"No? Because it sounds insane!" she retorted.

Jarrett stepped forward. "Look. It's as good a chance as we're going to get to throw him off our trail, and if it gives me a chance to piss him off, I'm in," he said with a determined look in his eye as if it made perfect sense.

Pinching the bridge of her nose in frustration, Collett said, "So you two would like to take a little trip to Mexico—alone mind you—and stay there until Niall comes after you?"

"Then, when we're sure he thinks that's where we are, we'll have Jeffery bring us back safe and sound," Cade finished.

"Why Mexico?" asked Cynda.

"Jeffery's been there before," answered Cade.

"How'd you know that?" Jeffery asked.

~ 275 ~

C.B. Haight

"Because, you idiot, when we first got here, you whined about the cold and quoted the temperatures in Mexico this time of year," Nate said with a smile. "Several times, in fact."

"Oh, sorry," he replied sheepishly.

"Hey, don't worry about it. I was in your corner on that one. In fact, is it too late to change our minds and relocate anyway?" Nate joked.

Cade shook his head in exasperation while Jarrett glared at him.

Nate didn't relent, "What? Not all of us are immune to the cold like you two."

Collett drew them back to the present issue, "This is crazy! I can't believe you're considering this. You don't even know if it'll work."

"But if it does, we'll have an edge, and it will give us more time to be ready for when we actually do have to face him," Cade insisted.

"What if you're plan backfires and he comes after both groups at the same time?" Rederrick asked. "Or worse, only us? We'd be hard pressed to keep Collett safe without you."

"I'm telling you, she's the key. I feel it in my bones," Cade said with confidence. "But just in case, I'll have Jeffery come back. Then if there is a problem, you'll have him and Delphene to help."

Rederrick nodded, satisfied.

"Collett, we have to face him sooner or later, but let's give him a thing or two to think about until that time comes."

Meeting his gaze, she asked him softly, "What if something bad happens?"

"Then it won't be because I didn't know what I was doing," he answered with a smile, throwing her words back at her.

She looked down at the floor. "You would say that."

"Look, you can sense when Jarrett's in trouble, so if you do, send Jeffery to us." He tilted her head up to force her to look at him. "But only if you're all safe at the time," he finished firmly. "Otherwise, we'll use the burner phone and call when we're done."

"Your whole plan hinges on Jeffery, who may not have enough energy to blink you both back at once. He's never done more than one person at a time."

"Actually," Cynda interrupted, "I think he can. Sorry, Collett, but I do. Jeffery has far more magical energy than I do, and he managed the three blinks in succession with Nate and Cade. He then used even more energy in combat by Nate's accounting. I think the only reason he's never tried two at once is inexperience. I'll be sure to make him an energy tea before just in case, and I'll have one ready when he returns."

"It's our best chance," Cade said.

With a heavy breath, she looked past him to Jarrett. "You think so too?"

"It doesn't matter what I think. Either way, we're going to be in a fight, but I'd sure like it to be on my terms."

"Fine. I don't like it, but I do see the logic in it." She met Cade's eyes. "Take your trip, and while you're there, spit in his eye if you get the chance. But you get back here quick."

"Yes ma'am," Cade teased and kissed her.

"When did you want to go?" Cynda asked.

"Tonight," Jarrett replied from where he stood in the corner with a wicked gleam in his eyes. "The night is our time, and I intend to make sure he knows it."

Delphene came into the living room as Jarrett stripped his shirt from his body. Licking her lips, she admired the view before her.

Not bad, she thought. She noticed a fading scar on his shoulder and knew what it was from. At some point, he'd cut the moon birthmark from his skin. For some unknown reason, all lycanthropes were born marked with a crescent moon. There was a weird irony to it since they didn't experience their first change until the first full moon around the time they hit puberty. She couldn't fathom how much he must have hated his other half to do that to himself.

Scanning Jarrett, she noted that his green amulet was absent tonight. She also observed that the newest scar on his side looked far better than it had a few days before. Then she couldn't help but notice the other faded lines and marks in various places, proving him to be a true warrior. Each wound would've had to come from a silver weapon or magic to leave permanent marks upon their kind.

"Wolf, you ought to stay away from sharp pointy things. It seems they don't agree with you," she said to his back.

"Everyone has scars," he said and shrugged as if it didn't really matter. "Anyway, are you telling me you don't have scars? If so, you must still be young. Sooner or later someone will figure out your weakness is silver."

She laughed, a rich, hearty laugh, at his intended advice. "Oh *Chère*, a woman never tells her age. But this much I will tell you— to me—you're only a puppy."

He turned to face her, surprised.

"Only, I don't go looking for a fight. I'd much rather enjoy life instead of bashing my way through it."

"When you're a demon, the fights come to you," he replied.

"You're not, you know," Collett said, entering the room. And, like Delphene, she couldn't help but look at the old wounds on Jarrett's body. She knew his more painful scars couldn't be seen.

"Not what?" he asked.

"A demon. I know that. I may not have my memories, but I know that."

Jarrett tipped his head, curious at the conviction in her words. Delphene looked at Collett, her interest also peaked.

"I remember the story. I don't know how, but I do."

"What story?" Delphene questioned, knowing Jarrett wouldn't.

"About the first of your kind," Collett replied. She moved to the front window and looked out as if the story played out before her very eyes. "I remembered it after I told the story of Nehemiah to

The Price of Knowing

Delphene the other day, but it slipped away from me again until you said that."

Jarrett saw Delphene silently gesture to Cade who entered then.

Lowering her voice, Collett explained, "About 200 years after Nehemiah passed, there was a man—a slave, who fell in love. He had no name, as was often the case, and was merely called slave. He was sold to a cruel master when he reached manhood. The woman he fell in love with was, in fact, his new master's wife. She was a small, but beautiful, noblewoman of superior birth. There would be no chance for him to ever act upon his love. It was a bitter torment that he endured every day.

"The slave learned that his master was vicious not only to him and other slaves, but to his wife as well. Regardless of her nobility, she was only a woman after all, and her servitude was no less than his. Many times he witnessed or heard his master's wicked treatment against his wife, and many times the slave wished he could do something to stop it. He was powerless to intervene.

"One night, the Great Opposer came to him and offered him phenomenal strength as well as a chance to kill his master to gain his freedom. Of course, this would come at the standard price—his soul. The slave didn't know that this would condemn him to life as a demon, but it didn't matter; he refused anyway, angering the Great Opposer.

"The Opposer did not give up and came to the tortured slave several more times. Each time, he refused, knowing that his soul was the only thing he owned. Instead, he accepted the fate handed to him and went on unhappily.

"More than a year passed this way with the slave obediently serving his master. Several times, he even accepted the blame for things that upset his master just to protect the woman he loved, and he received the biting punishments. He never regretted his choice, even when his drunken master's whip slipped and hit his eye, forever crippling his vision.

~ 279 ~

"Everything changed one night when, while nursing such wounds, the slave heard a scream come from his master's house. Bravely running to investigate, he saw the woman lying dead in a pool of her own blood. He was too late to save her. Looking up, he saw his master holding the knife that killed her. His owner had cut her throat in a drunken rage.

"Powerful anger surged in him, and when he cried out for justice, the Great Opposer, being wise and crafty, whispered in his ear once more.

"'I will make a deal with you,' the slave growled.

"Satisfied, and believing another soul his for the taking, the Opposer infused the slave with the strength of a great animal. Using his newfound power, the slave viciously and easily defeated his drunken master.

"After it was over, the Great Opposer appeared before him and demanded the slave's soul. To his shock, the slave refused. 'I never agreed you could have my soul. I only said I would make a deal with you, and I will,' he insisted. 'My life you may have. Take it from me now, for I have nothing to live for any longer. My soul is mine to keep.'

The Great Opposer was enraged because the man was right. He never had agreed to relinquish his soul, so the Great Opposer lashed out at the slave, cursing him. Inspired by the animalistic strength he'd lent him before, the Opposer turned the slave into an immortal beast that he would struggle to control for the rest of his life.

"'Your life is mine then. Because you wish to die, I curse you to live forever. Death is not a punishment. It is a release—one you will never experience until I deem it to be so.'

"Thus, the first lycanthrope was created—he was a cursed man who wisely refused the Opposer's design for him. The Great Opposer miscalculated though. Having never relinquished his soul, the slave was able to retain his humanity, and he learned to control what was inside him."

The Price of Knowing

Collett turned to face the three of them. "So, you see, you're not demons or monsters, but creatures born from desperation, the belief in justice, a strong will, and utter defiance of the Great Opposer."

Nobody spoke right away, then Jarrett said cynically, "It's a story, nothing more."

"Maybe, but it is a good one," Delphene countered proudly.

Jeffery and Nate entered through the door but stopped almost right away. "Whoa," said Nate, noting the somber expressions, "did something happen?"

Cade shook his head. "Did you see anything that could be a problem?" He had asked them to go out to sweep a wide perimeter of the grounds to make sure they would be clear to leave soon.

"Nothing. It looks good. Well, except that I think we're in for another storm before too long. Pretty heavy sky right now, could snow tonight," Nate replied.

"Snow won't kill you."

"Speak for yourself, you're going to Mexico."

Cade smiled. "All right, looks like we're about ready. Del, you wanna get Cynda and Rederrick from upstairs?"

"*Oui*, I'll get them." Before leaving, Delphene smiled at Collett and spoke to her in French, "True or not, it is a good story, and you remembered it, which is more important, *non*?"

Returning Dephene's smile with one of her own, Collett replied, "*Oui*."

Jarrett scowled but didn't ask. Cade approached Collett, having understood Delphene's French. "It is a good story."

Butterflies entered her stomach as Collett realized the time for them to leave drew near. "You'll be careful?" she questioned.

"*Oui*," he replied with a cocky grin and a wink, "we'll be back before you know it."

"After-we've done what we need to do," Jarrett insisted in his familiar brooding tone.

"Please don't do anything stupid to prove a point. Lead him there, then come back. We'll have to face him soon enough," she said mainly for Jarrett's benefit.

"It's time then?" Rederrick questioned upon entering.

"It's time," Cade replied. Leaning down, he kissed Collett softly. It was a kiss full of promises. As his lips met and gently moved against hers, she felt the warmth of his love spread through her. Pulling away, he rubbed his thumb over her lips. "Before you know it," he promised again.

"You'd better be. And make sure to bring him back with you," she told him, pointedly looking at Jarrett.

He scrutinized his brother and found her worry for Jarrett did not bother him. He wondered if it meant the three of them were beginning to understand each other. Or maybe he was just becoming more secure. Either way, it was a relief.

He stepped back and looked at his brother and his state of undress. He wore no shirt and no shoes or socks. Lifting a brow, he asked, "You gonna get dressed?"

Shaking his head, The Hunter stoically replied, "I don't plan on staying this way for long."

Cade's grin spread, "Jeffery."

As previously decided, Jeffery would try and make the jump to Mexico with both of them in tow at once.

Heeding Cade's call, Jeffery moved forward, but hesitated when he approached Jarrett. He was uncomfortable directing him and wondered if it was safe to touch him without getting his head bitten off. Rolling his eyes, Jarrett put a hand on Jeffery's shoulder. Then Jeffery put his hand on Cade's arm.

"I love you Cade," Collett declared.

"I love you too," he replied softly.

Collett addressed Jarrett with apprehension, "Please be careful."

He gave her a short, quick nod of his head in reply.

"Here we go," Jeffery said, motioning with his free arm. In the next instant, they were gone.

We made it! Jeffery could hardly believe it. His insides felt like they were on fire, and his vision took a minute to clear, but looking around, he confirmed that he had managed to take all three of them safely to their destination. "I did it," Jeffery said aloud.

Dropping his arm, Jarrett said, "Well, we're not dead."

Smiling at the sorcerer, Cade agreed, "Yes, you did." Slapping him on the back, Cade surveyed the surrounding area. There were big, sweeping, leafless trees on either side of a small stream. The trees would likely be nice shade trees in Mexico's summer heat, but even here, signs of the season changed the landscape. Bare of leaves, the trees gave the area a much more ominous feeling.

Darkness was complete as it was nearing 7 p.m. Not that the lack of light or chilly night temperature affected either brother. It was not nearly as cold as where they'd been, and they rarely were bothered by such things. Jeffery, on the other hand, felt the desert chill and had a difficult time seeing anything. The only light offered was that of the moon which, by a minor stroke of irony, was full tonight.

"It won't be long before they come knocking. Jeffery, you need to get going while you can," Cade told him.

"What should I do if you don't call?" Jeffery asked.

"Find a safe place to hide and stay there," Jarrett answered.

Cade agreed and said, "If we don't call, don't come looking, no matter what Collett tells you."

"That won't be easy."

"There's something else," Cade added. "If they attack the cabin, get Collett out of there. I need you to promise me you'll take her away from any danger."

Jeffery looked at him, saying nothing.

"I know you think this is about protecting her, and in a way, it is. But it's also more than that. I know she's the key to this. Now, more than ever I know it! If things turn on us, you have to get her to a safe place so she can keep running until she remembers. I don't know what Niall wants with her, but I am not willing to play this by his rules and hand her to him," he paused, "Even if that means we die protecting her."

"He's right. Don't give Niall anything he wants. If she was ready, it would be different, but keep her away from him for now," Jarrett added, surprising the other two men with his agreement. Then he added, "Even if you have to leave everyone else there to die, get her out of there."

Jeffery nodded. "I'll figure out a way to get her to a safe place, then I'll help the rest of them."

"I'm trusting you to protect my wife, Jeffery, the woman I love. Do so with your life," Cade commanded.

He could only nod again, surprised by the level of Cade's trust.

"Now, get back to the others."

"There's a town not far from here called Nacori Chico. If you get into trouble and need a place to go, you can go there. Juan at the cantina is a good man. He may help you," Jeffery told them, pointing behind himself to indicate the direction to town.

"Got it," Cade assured him.

"I'm outta here then."

Jarrett tilted his head back to take in the bright and full moon in the cloudless sky, and Cade too was drawn to look up, thinking Jeffery was leaving.

"Hey—" Jeffery said before blinking back to the cabin.

Twin pairs of golden animal eyes looked to him and glinted strangely in the natural moonlight. The sight sent a chill down Jeffery's spine.

"Give 'em hell," he said and waved his hand to invoke his magic. A second later, he appeared back at the old house in New Mexico, thinking that he almost felt sorry for the demons that would be sent after the two brothers.

Niall's eyes popped open. He looked into the fire as satisfaction coursed through him. He'd come to his sanctuary to meditate tonight on a whim after spending the entire day in the desert dealing with greater matters. He'd even resigned himself that he may not find the traitor until he found Collett, but he finally sensed his creation. He felt the full force of Jarrett's anger run through him and reveled in the sensation. It wasn't like the quick glimpse he'd had a few days before. This time, Niall was sure. He knew exactly where he'd find his hunter. He rose and manifested himself before Victor, who sat at a computer, no doubt tracing the Williams family members.

Victor glanced up and stood immediately upon seeing his master. "Sir," he said calmly.

"I found the traitor. You are to take whatever and whomever you deem necessary to deal with him."

"Yes sir," he answered as he always did.

"Do not fail me, Victor!" he ordered.

"Consider it done."

CHAPTER 26

Cade moved to the tree line, splashed through shallow water, and surveyed his surroundings while stripping his own shirt and removing his heavy boots. "What're you thinking?" he asked Jarrett, who moved up close and rested against a particularly large tree.

"He'll send in heavy hitters. He's frustrated by now. One thing I've learned—Niall can be impatient. He portrays himself as calm, but when his superiority is in question, he often acts rashly. He's too arrogant not to."

"Impatient enough to come himself?"

Jarrett shook his head. "He likely wants Collett dealt with even more. There's something about her that bothers him. Finnawick's behavior indicated that. The price for her was high, and that filthy imp kept all the files to himself until she was dealt with. He also sent in both Jeffery and me at the same time. No, Niall won't come until he finds her first. He made a mistake in not going after her personally, and he knows it by now. I'm beneath him, but she's a threat to him."

~286~

Cade agreed. They didn't fully understand everything going on, but they did understand the fierce pursuit of Collett to be a sign of desperation by Niall.

"Not to mention, he's still running The Faction. Babysitting demons and recruiting forces requires his attention. Not even Niall can be everywhere at once. It's how I was able to get a few people out," Jarrett added as they scoured the area, looking for a solid place to make their stand.

Cade stopped, "I never suspected—"

"Don't. I'm not the saint Ashley thinks I am."

"Perhaps not, but you're not the monster I thought you were either."

Jarrett shook his head. "You're not gonna get all soft now, are you?"

Cade laughed, "Nah, I still think you're a jerk."

Jarrett felt his lip twitch and raised an eyebrow. They relaxed a bit, sitting in easy silence to wait out their enemy. They didn't wait long. Within two hours, a familiar scent wafted through the trees to them.

Standing, Cade sniffed the air. "You smell it?"

"Leeches," Jarrett growled, "They're coming."

The two men moved with slow, deliberate ease. By unspoken agreement they'd left their swords behind for this trip. Maybe it was the full moon. Maybe they wanted to send a message. Or maybe it was simply the predator inside, but on this night, each man left New Mexico craving the violence of their natural weapons for this fight.

The first vampiric demon emerged on the left. It came in cautiously toward the them. Another dropped from a tree on the right. Both of the leeches likely saw the golden animal eyes shift to a burning red, and yet the brothers did not advance.

Having seen and sensed the figures moving forward in various places, Jarrett said, "Ten at least, maybe more coming."

"Not very fair then," Cade said with a smirk.

"I take the left; you take the right," Jarrett offered. His blood pumped and body tingled.

"Meet you in the middle," Cade agreed, feeling identical sensations crawling over him. During the discussion, neither of them diverted their direct attention to the coming force. They didn't need to. "To the end then," he declared, referring to their recent pact.

Jarrett, feeling his mouth salivating and his muscles twitching, inclined his head in reply. Quicker than a person could blink, the brothers surged forward in unison, transforming into dark creatures born of night and moon.

Truly, it was a sight to behold. The two lycanthropes easily jumped fifteen feet in the air. Tanned skin turned to long, black fur as muscles bulged and each brother shifted. The shackled werewolves burst free of their human bodies.

Landing in tandem, each bore down on their intended victim with fang and claw. The leech demons were surprised by the viciousness they faced and fought furiously. Moments later, there were only eight.

Four more leeches and two greater-demons shot through the dark to attack and poured over the wolves in hopes of overwhelming them. They met with disappointment as they turned to ash.

Meditating with Cynda in an effort to stay relaxed and try to have an open link to the two men, Collett found it very difficult to do either. Her worry for Cade and Jarrett superseded any effort she made to focus. Frustrated, she stood. Cynda opened her eyes and looked up to Collett. "I'm sorry, I can't sit still right now," Collett told her.

Cynda rose. "I'll make some tea to help you relax."

"I should have felt something by now."

"Not necessarily," replied Cynda from the kitchen. "Take it as a good sign that you haven't sensed anything. In the past, your connections haven't activated until someone was in dire need of help."

A few minutes later, Cynda returned with the tea in hand. "I added a few herbs to help ease your tension. You likely won't be open to sense them if you don't take it easy. Most of the time, you've been asleep when you connected to Jarrett, and according to Cade, you haven't slept as well as the rest of us. He says you're having dreams still."

"I didn't realize he knew," she admitted.

"Husbands notice more than we give them credit for. At any rate, sleep deprivation will only make it harder for you to focus. You have to relax in case they do need you. So don't argue, as I can tell you want to. Just drink."

Collett looked at the cup of tea. She knew Cynda was right, and she reluctantly accepted the drink.

An hour later, feeling effects of the hot drink, Collett began drifting off on the couch with the cell phone clutched tightly in her hand. Her head bobbed. She jerked it upright again and blinked several times to revive herself. Even though she had sworn there was no way for her to rest while Cade and Jarrett were out playing bait and hook with Niall, she felt the heavy weight pull at her.

"*Dormir une petite.* I will wait," she heard Delphene say in a soothing tone.

"I'll wait too. I want to know the minute they get back," she mumbled.

Delphene only smiled as she watched Collett's eyes drift closed once more. She winked at Cynda and waited a few heartbeats before retrieving the blanket on the end of the couch to cover her new friend. "*Dormir une petite,*" she repeated.

For a little while, Collett thought of nothing. Before too long, she felt a familiar icy cold crawl over her skin. She'd felt this before in her dreams the last few nights, and even back in Colorado a couple of times. This time was different. Her wrists hurt terribly, and an achy heaviness fell over her. An unimaginable thirst welled up in her throat as well.

A shuffling noise startled her, and Collett realized, like the other times, she still couldn't see. Wherever she was offered no light of any kind. "Who's there?" she called, determined to understand the recurring dream.

A strange sound reached her. It sounded like someone sobbing. "C-c-collett?" The voice was familiar to her. "I'm sorry, I didn't know. I'm s-s-s-sorry," came the muffled words. In her previous dreams, there'd been no sound, no voice. Her mind processed the vague dreams she'd had the last couple weeks of being in the dark and in pain.

As she focused on the voice coming at her through the blackness, her mind flashed back to the young boy who sat across from her on Thanksgiving Day in Rederrick's home. "Cody?" she asked with disbelief.

"I didn't know," he answered with a cracked voice from the dark recesses.

Desperate, she began moving around the room to find him. She found herself surprised that she could feel the walls. She figured her powers to connect must be growing. With Jarrett and Jenny, even when she tried to reach out, she never made contact before.

"I didn't want to," he insisted.

"It's okay, Cody," she said and suddenly felt skin beneath her fingers. She pulled away as the brief contact surprised her. "Cody?" She reached out again.

"He knows. I tried—I tried—not to tell him. I swear I did."

When she touched him again, the physical connection pulsed through her. The full extent of his condition assaulted her. She felt a sudden need to vomit, but held it back. It was even more vivid than it had been with Jarrett. Collett's legs almost buckled under the weight of it. "Cody..." she panted, bracing her other hand on the wall. "Cody, who knows?"

The Price of Knowing

"Finnawick told him about me. I tried to lie, but he knew. It doesn't work on him."

Miraculously, through the pain, she understood his thoughts. She felt more in control of her power than ever before. Her mind searched through his and she saw a big brute of a man beating him as he hung from chains like a human punching bag. She tried to block the horrible images but couldn't do it fast enough. She saw the large fists coming toward her as if she was Cody.

Her breath left her, and this time, her knees did falter. She pulled herself back up as the horror of what she saw ebbed. Her tears for him flowed freely. She struggled to find her center again. It was somewhere in that effort for control that she realized Cody wasn't really talking to her. He was sure she was a figment of his imagination or a ghost.

"Cody, where are you? Where is this place?" she asked between her teeth, still absorbing his pain.

"Are you dead then?" he moaned. "D-did, did he kill you? I'm sorry, I tried not to tell him. He knew—about you. About...what you do. But I didn't tell him. He doesn't know it all—"

"All what?" she asked him.

"You remembered...d-doesn't know that." He shivered suddenly, whether from pain or cold she couldn't tell. It felt all mixed together within her.

Collett reached into herself for any feelings of warmth and comfort she could find in an effort to lend peace to the battered boy and calm him. "I'm not dead, Cody. I'm here to help," she assured him with a smooth voice.

"I tried," he repeated more softly, as if he was drifting off. Her effort to ease his discomfort was working.

Desperate to keep him awake, she moved her hand, looking for his face. Finding it, she was overwhelmed with shock and anger.

The emotions tore through her as she felt his disfigured features. She didn't need light to know how bad it was. Gently, she probed his face. His eyes were swollen shut, and the strange bump between

~ 291 ~

C.B. Haight

them let her know his nose was clearly broken. He moaned as her hand touched its bridge.

"Oh, Cody," she whispered, feeling the cracks in his lips and then a scab on his cheek where his skin had split. She forced the tears back to focus on him and his immense needs. She considered unchaining him, but since she had no way to get him out of this place, she knew it could make matters worse. If his captors came back, they would likely punish him for it. "Cody? Cody, where are you? We'll get you out of here, but I need to know where you are."

He didn't reply.

"Cody, please! You have to tell me," she begged.

"I...d-d..." he muttered.

Collett suddenly felt herself being pulled from the dream—a dream she'd managed to hold onto longer than any before it. Focusing, she tried to stay with him. She couldn't leave him this way. She could still feel every injury and knew how severe they were. Though she eased a significant amount of it for him, she knew it wouldn't be enough.

This was worse than anything she'd experienced with Jarrett. She hardly knew this boy, but her heart cried out for him. It was simply too much pain for anyone to endure. It was too much for her. She tried to pour more comfort into him, but weakened by pain, the more she gave the more she lost clarity of the vision. She could no longer feel his skin beneath her fingers, and the darkness slowly became muted light through her closed eyelids. The lost connection tore at her, and she began to cry.

"Collett, come on. Wake up. There'll be none of that while Cade's not here, you hear me?" she heard Rederrick order.

Someone shook her, and the residual throbbing pain from Cody came back to her. "Ahhh" she groaned. Her ribs still felt broken. The pain in her face was even worse, and on instinct, she slowly reached up to feel for the expected swelling. She only found salty tears.

"She's coming back," Nate said, but he sounded far away.

The tears she felt while in the dream continued to leak from her closed lids.

"Is it Jarrett? Cade?" Rederrick asked urgently.

Collett shook her head and immediately regretted the action. She pressed her hand to her pounding head.

"What is it then? What did you see? Jenny?" he questioned incessantly.

"Please, not Jenny," Cynda pleaded hopefully.

"Not—Jenny. It's Cody," she croaked past the lump in her throat. "I can feel Cody."

Her revelation startled everyone in the room. Ever since his disappearance around Thanksgiving, many of them had begun to think Cody was dead. It was the only explanation of why they couldn't find him. Even Delphene had been told of his sudden disappearance and suspected the boy's demise.

"Well then, where is he?" Rederrick demanded, helping her to sit up after the shock wore off. His worry for the boy was evident in his tone.

Collett bit her lip, but her features pinched and a whimper managed to escape her. Extreme pain became evident in her tear-filled eyes.

"What is it? What did you see?" questioned Nate.

"Something's wrong," pronounced Cynda, being the first to see that Collett's pain wasn't fading as it had with Jarrett. She pushed Rederrick out of the way and took his place next to Collett on the couch. "Collett?" she questioned quietly.

"It's too much," she cried, laid back down, and sobbed.

Cade and Jarrett were both satisfied with the outcome. Their golden, predatory eyes locked, and they both realized, for the first time, how powerful they really were together.

C.B. Haight

In essence, they'd obliterated their enemy. Only one escaped, Victor, and that had been deliberate on their part. They knew he'd been watching from a distance and wanted to lay him low as well, but they wanted Niall to get the message, loud and clear, even more.

Jarrett thought, for the first time in his life, that being alone no longer looked so appealing. Being with Cade—facing the battle together, and succeeding—felt far more satisfying than simply surviving any battle he'd engaged in alone. He never before realized how supremely gratifying it could be to share in a victory such as this one with a person who had his back.

He knew then that he trusted Cade as he'd never trusted anyone before. Despite their problems over the last century, their combined faith in one another this night set a new precedent that he hoped would last long after this. The revelation was difficult to process. It even left him slightly remiss that they hadn't had that before tonight. Though he didn't voice it, Jarrett wondered how different his life would have been if the little, angry boy he'd been all those years before had searched for the brother Rowena told him about shortly before she died.

For too long, he let Niall manipulate him by using his own fear and anger of what he was. Lately, the anger was almost all he had left, and he clung to it. Except on this night, there was something else. Tonight, he didn't feel the anger so much as he felt...pride. Jarrett felt pride in his brother, pride in himself, and proud of what they'd accomplished together.

"How long do you think it will take—Victor,-is it—to give him the message?" Cade asked with a smug grin.

Jarrett couldn't help it, his lips twitched. "Longer than he'd like. Victor can't use magic. He'll have to call someone who can or find other transportation. Either way, I wouldn't want to be him when he tells Niall the news."

"If he can't use magic, what makes him so important?" Cade asked, reaching into his jeans for his own phone.

The Price of Knowing

Sitting on a rock but keeping his eyes alert, Jarrett answered, "Victor's a genius, technologically and logistically speaking. He can outthink just about anyone, and predict exactly what they'll do in any given situation."

"I suppose it's good we're not just anyone," Cade replied with a little arrogance, which Jarrett appreciated.

"It's likely he's the one who found the others in Colorado," Jarrett added as Cade began to dial. Before he even pressed the last button on the phone, Jeffery appeared not more than 20 feet away from them.

At first, Cade didn't think the appearance strange. He assumed Collett knew they were ready by keeping linked with Jarrett. In the dark, he didn't notice the worry in Jeffery's eyes right away.

It was, in fact, Jarrett that noticed the strange expression on Jeffery's face. He became alert, and a sense of foreboding washed away his earlier satisfaction.

Jeffery looked around, checking to make sure it was safe to be there. "What's wrong?" Jarrett questioned darkly.

By then, Cade also noticed the strained expression. "Collett?" he asked urgently, striding forward. "What happened?"

Clearly uncomfortable, Jeffery gestured to Jarrett. "Come on, you've got to come back with me."

Gripping his arm tightly, Cade jerked Jeffery. "What! What happened?"

"She saw Cody."

Shock covered Cade's expression, but he gathered his wits enough to ask, "Is he alive?"

"Saw?" Jarrett asked at the same time.

"Like she saw you, only this was worse. Much worse," he explained. "Cynda told me to get you back there no matter what. Luckily, that won't be as hard as I thought," he finished and looked around again.

C.B. Haight

More concerned than he cared to admit, Jarrett hurried over to join them, put his hand on Jeffery's shoulder, and together the three of them left.

Unfortunately, as a result of their worry for Collet and Cody, they didn't notice Victor. Filled with indecision, he had come back. If he returned to Niall after the complete defeat the brothers dealt him, he would be as good as dead. Or worse, he could end up like Cody. He had returned, wondering if he wouldn't be better off in the enemy's hands rather than Niall's. Hearing the last of their conversation, he knew his defeat would be a small thing compared to this new insight. Instead of ending up dead for his failure at Niall's cruel hands, it was more likely he was going to be rewarded greatly.

CHAPTER 27

"How is she?" Cynda asked upon meeting Cade in the hall with a tray of food for Collett the next morning.

"Better. She's sleeping now."

"Is she still in pain?"

"No, it seems to have faded finally," he replied. "I'll take the tray back to the kitchen. She can eat when she wakes up. Can you stay with her for a minute? Just in case."

"I'll come and get you if she has another dream," she promised.

He tipped his head in appreciation and took the tray from her. After she went in to sit with Collett, Cade briskly made his way downstairs. Upon entering the kitchen, Jarrett rose from the table where he'd been sitting, and the rest of the group entered from the living room with expectant expressions.

"She's sleeping. Most of the pain seems to have receded," he informed them, and saw some of their worry subside.

"Good. That's good," said Rederrick.

"I need a minute," Cade said, looking pointedly to Jarrett.

~ 297 ~

Understanding that Cade wanted to talk to him alone, Jarrett made his way to the front of the house with Cade behind him.

"Come and get me if..." Cade began, handing the tray he held to Delphene.

"Don't fret, *Chère*. She's in good hands."

Upon stepping onto the porch, Cade took a deep, cleansing breath of the cold winter air.

Jarrett eyed him curiously. He noted the lines of worry creasing his brother's brow, his pale features, and the thick shadow of whiskers on his face. "You know he was working with them from the beginning."

It was obvious that Cade didn't understand, so Jarrett explained, "The night I took her, I happened across the kid you call Cody first. He was just outside the grounds on the phone."

"What are you telling me, Jarrett?"

"He was talking to Finnawick. I heard him. I didn't tell you before because I figured he was dead, as you did, and thought—why destroy your illusion of him?"

It was clear that Cade was caught off guard by this revelation. "Why—why would he do that?"

"Who knows? Look at Jeffery's reason for coming after Collett. They all have reasons, some selfish, some not. It does explain one thing. That's how the demons knew exactly where to go in Colorado, and I'm not only talking about the house. According to Rederrick, they tried to cut him off in his security room, and when he figured out what was happening, he saw the bulk of them in Collett's guest room and your room. They knew where they were going that night. Only luck prevented them from accomplishing their goal.

"It hardly matters now. He may not be dead yet, but he will be soon according to her. If Collett's accounting is correct, he messed up, and Niall is only toying with him now."

~ 298 ~

Cade scowled. "What happens to Collett if he kills him? This is the same thing that bothered me with your connection to her, and this time it's even more severe."

"I don't have the answer," Jarrett said, looking out at the snow-covered ground.

"I can't do this anymore," Cade confessed to him. "I can't keep seeing her go through this kind of pain, worrying which time it will kill her, and do nothing about it."

Jarrett offered no reply. He still wasn't sure where Cade was going with this. "She's like a filter for everyone's pain, and it seems to be getting worse. I need..." he hesitated and paced to the end of the porch and back. "I need your help."

Surprised and confused, Jarrett couldn't even reply.

"She has to get some control. She can't keep going through this kind of extreme torment," he paused. "I can't keep watching her go through it."

"What else can you do?" Jarrett finally said.

"When you're training her, you have to teach her to block the emotions."

"I kill demons, Cade. I don't know magic, or empathy, or whatever it is she does."

"But you do know pain," Cade stated flatly. "I know about Rowena, and I understand now. I also know life in The Faction is not easy." Before Jarrett could even reply, Cade continued, "I watched you when you were bleeding all over the place and wounded well past the point of consciousness. You climbed on the back of the biggest demon I've ever seen and shoved a grenade down his throat."

"It was a fight, Cade. It was either that or die."

"I know, and so is this—a fight, I mean. If Collett can't learn to deal with her connections to people around her, it will be the same for her."

His brother's words struck Jarrett more than he would have expected. He felt the truth behind them, and surprisingly, he didn't like the possibilities any more than Cade did.

"Think about it. How can she handle facing Niall if all he has to do is hurt one of us to hurt her? She said she was tired of our anger. That means she's been absorbing all of our emotions this whole time, and yet she's said nothing. It might even be part of the reason she hesitates in our combat sessions. She has to figure out a way to block it, or..." Cade trailed off, implying his fear.

"He'll use it to kill her," Jarrett finished.

"Cynda's been trying to help her learn over the last few weeks, but she doesn't have the same abilities. The more they work together, the more Collett's power and reach grows, except she still can't control them. When we first met her, she could only get vague impressions—good or bad, sad or mad. Now she feels everything." He cursed. "Last night she told me how many broken ribs Cody had. Jarrett, she knew exactly how many and which ones!"

This time, Jarrett cursed. He watched as his brother pulled his hand through his hair, showing his frustration. He looked out at the landscape and thought about what Cade was asking of him. "It never really goes away, you know," he started to explain. "The pain, I mean."

Cade dropped his hand and listened.

"I suppose I do block it. I push it aside to survive, but it's still there afterward." Jarrett looked at him seriously. "The physical pain, that's the easy part, but the rest... I'll do what I can. I'll teach her all I know, but you have to understand, the emotional pain will still be there. I can't remove scars from life events like Rowena or Collett's knowledge of how many ribs are broken on a kid terrified out of his mind. That's much worse, and I can't promise she won't feel it anymore. I can only show how to use it as fuel."

"We'll have to do this one step at a time. Either way, we have to do something," Cade declared.

"It will be hard, and those bruises you saw will look like scratches compared to this. You'll have to be there too, to be the conduit."

"Why me? She connected to you more closely."

Jarrett scoffed, "She's linked to me by some mysterious magical event, but she loves you. It'll work."

Cade nodded. "Tell me what we have to do, and I swear I'll follow it through."

His words were so full of conviction that, for the first time, Jarrett wondered if love wasn't a farce after all. His brother would do anything to protect her, even if it meant pain and punishment for himself.

When was the last time they gave me a drink? Cody wondered. He knew they stopped feeding him three days ago, or maybe four. His stomach kept reminding him with sharp stabbing pains, but the days were beginning to run together. For some reason, he couldn't remember when the last time they gave him a drink was, and oddly enough, sitting here alone it seemed so important.

The darkness surrounding him was complete. He couldn't see anything at all, and at first, it was a blessing when he heard the scurrying creatures that shared his cell. But after several days he ached to see light again, even if it meant seeing the rats that occasionally nipped at him. He licked his cracked lips and tasted blood.

His shoulder ached from when it had been dislocated and then set right, and his wrists burned where the shackles chafed and cut at them. His every breath wheezed in and out painfully as a result of his broken ribs, not to mention the pain from his broken fingers.

Even with all of that, and hurting almost everywhere else in ways he would have never imagined, none of it seemed nearly as important to him as the indescribable thirst that he felt. Running his

C.B. Haight

tongue over his lips again, he tried hard to remember. His mouth felt like cotton, and his tongue was thick and heavy. He was so thirsty that he was beginning to believe that if they hurt him anymore he wouldn't bleed because there were no fluids left in him.

In an effort to take his mind away from the thirst, Cody tried to think about the dream he'd had of Collett. She came to him and assured him she would come for him, but he knew better. He knew that Niall would have found her by now. He'd been here for weeks—*or was it months?* He didn't even know. Here in the dark, there was no way to keep track of time. Really, it felt more like years.

He must be healing though, because today was the first day since he arrived that he could think past the crippling pain.

Suddenly, he heard shuffling outside his door, a scraping sound, then an audible click as the lock was disengaged and the door opened. The light that poured in from the hallway stung his eyes. He squinted and then cursed in reaction to the pain from his swollen eyes and broken nose pinching together. Cody heard footsteps, but because of his obscured vision, he couldn't determine who it was.

"Well Cody, it seems I have use for you still."

The voice was Niall's. Cody felt his skin crawl at the sound of it, but he became hopeful at Niall's proclamation. Maybe they would finally let him out.

"Of course, we'll need to fix you up a bit so you'll be presentable. We wouldn't want your friends to be disappointed when they see you again."

Cody heard heavier footsteps lumber into the room, and suddenly he was being lifted up by his hair. His feet came off the floor for a second as his arms were pulled over the hook that held his chains. The manacles on his wrists rattled and cut at raw skin and new scabs as he was pulled free, and his head felt as if his scalp would be torn off. He couldn't help it, he cried out.

Desperation consumed him. "P-p-please, water," he managed to croak out from his dry throat.

Niall chuckled, "Water is it?"

Cody tried pitifully to nod, but the grip on his hair prevented any forward movement.

"Give Cody some water," Niall ordered.

The man holding him dragged Cody down the corridor into the big room where they conducted his previous interrogations and threw him to the floor. The impact of hitting the concrete jarred his knees painfully, and he fell to his stomach. Cody tried to roll over, but before he made it the whole way, a sharp, painful kick to his side completed the movement for him. Cody groaned and felt his mending ribs crack again.

He started to beg for a drink, and frigid water was poured on his face, practically drowning him without quenching his thirst. Frustration rushed through him. Cody desperately tried to lick the moisture from around his lips, but he received little of it.

"What's wrong?" Niall asked, "Did you not get enough?"

Cody could only lay there defeated. With sudden realization, he knew no matter what he said or did, Niall would find a way to get twisted enjoyment from it. He was tired of begging and decided he would give Niall nothing more—even if it meant his death—which would be preferable at this point.

He thought about his dream of Collett. Strangely, it fortified him. In the back of his mind, he hoped she really was still alive. If she was, he would give Niall nothing more to help him kill her—no matter what.

Reading his thoughts, Niall replied, "Cody, I'm not going to kill you. And you don't have to tell me anything, not anymore. I am going to use you to rid myself of them. She is alive you know. I should thank you. By having you within my grasp, it looks like I'll finally be able to draw her out, along with all your ridiculous Brotherhood comrades. It seems they actually do care about you, and because of it, they'll die. Pitiful, isn't it?"

Cody closed his eyes in despair and guilt, wondering how anybody could care about him.

"Again!" Jarrett snapped above the chaos around them.

Collett's features were pinched, and her hair was dampened with sweat. He could see the signs of the emotions from the surrounding melee and the effects it had on her displayed clearly on her face. She stood up anyway and picked up her sword from the snow. She nodded to him, and he mimicked the gesture.

She attacked him, and he could see her improvement with every swing. Using the sword was becoming more natural to her with every session. The last two weeks had been full of similar exercises. Jarrett figured the best way to teach her to block emotions surrounding her while building her battle skills would be to keep her engaged in combat with him while everyone else battled around her. This way, they all benefited from the training at the same time. It was working too.

Right away, Jarrett laid clear ground rules to help Collett. First and foremost, the battles were against Cade, and Cade alone. Everyone else, including Delphene, fought against him. Despite what Cade believed, Jarrett knew she was connected to him as much as himself and others. He explained to everyone how Collett had come for Cade that night at Ashley's home, but he hadn't been able to hear or see her for some reason.

Jarrett recognized the relief in Cade's eyes when he'd divulged that information to them. He wasn't sure why Collett hadn't told him herself, but reasoned there simply hadn't been time. Jarrett realized that Cade had worried she couldn't have a connection with him the way she did with others.

Regardless, Jarrett chose Cade as the victim for assault because his body would heal from day to day, and he was, in fact, the closest to a demon they could get in strength and skill. It was merely a bonus that Collett loved him as she did. It would make it harder for her to push past his distress or pain.

Jarrett knew from personal experience that the best way to block something was to be forced into it. Cade was outnumbered, and the group had an advantage over him. They were instructed to hurt him, whereas he was simply trying to counter them and make them work as a team.

The exercise was more than a simple sparring match. Jarrett wanted to ensure Collett felt the pain, and Cade had to restrain himself from taking them all down. He could easily defeat each group member. Except maybe Delphene. Jarrett noticed the she-wolf had skills.

Whenever he felt Collett waver because of Cade or any of the others, Jarrett would increase the pace. The first few days were the most difficult. Every time Cade took a hit, she felt it too, and then the thump of Jarrett's blade would come in on the heels of that pain. He forced her to focus on only him. He made her fight for every inch of ground, and then he pushed her back to do it again.

Both Cade and Collett went to bed every night hurt and aching, only to wake the next morning and do it again. It was wearing on them, and Jarrett knew it. He hated what he had to do each day and loathed getting up as much as they did. But it was working.

Today, Jarrett could clearly see a difference in Collett. He saw proof of that when Cade roared out in pain as Delphene raked him with her claws. Collett managed to ignore it and charge forward viciously, surprising even Jarrett. Even so, he still managed to displace her and land a hit against her ribs. He pulled back the blow this time, knowing she already carried more than a few bruises from today.

There was another thing he'd noticed over the last week. Collett struggled with her current sword as if it was wrong for her. He'd started her with a lighter Japanese sword he owned, but later had her trade Cynda for the short sword she was using now. Still, it wasn't right. Rederrick's and Cade's swords were too long for her, and Nate used a long dagger. They'd gone into the small town once in an effort to find one that would fit her style, but they'd come up empty.

Collett was proficient enough in swordplay, even more so than the others despite her empathetic handicap. Jarrett suspected that, with the right sword and a little more confidence, she could be far better, perhaps even rival him.

She picked herself up again, and he could see the loathing in her eyes as she probed her ribs. He heard Cade roar again as Nate struck a hit with his dagger against his arm. Jarrett could even smell the coppery tang of blood, but for the first time, Collett didn't even blink an eye. Her anger and frustration with him far surpassed her concern for Cade. He could see fire in her eyes as she looked at him and mimicked his words. "Again," she snarled through her teeth.

Jarrett cocked his head and lifted his sword in invitation. She rushed him, using her weapon to cut at him with quick, efficient strikes and parries. Using her smaller frame, she ducked beneath him before Jarrett even realized what she was doing.

Dancing behind him as gracefully as a prima ballerina and crying out with determination, her sword landed at his neck before he even managed to twist his body to block her strike. Pride flared in Jarrett as she skillfully accomplished this feat.

Breathing hard, Collett stared down the length of her blade with wide eyes. "I did it," she mumbled, unaware of the fact that the chaos around them had ceased.

She'd landed blows against him from time to time in the last week, but this was the first time she achieved a killing strike against the battle-hardened warrior. "You did it," Jarrett congratulated, moving the padded weapon away from his neck. Turning to face her, he tilted his head toward the others.

She turned as well and saw Cade standing nearby with the same pride Jarrett felt showing brightly on his face. "I did it," she said to him.

"Yes, you did," he replied, opening his arms.

Squealing with excitement, she dropped her sword and jumped at him. "I really did it!" Cade lifted her off the ground and spun her while everyone else congratulated her.

The Price of Knowing

Rederrick walked to Jarrett, pat his shoulder companionably, and said, "Well done."

"It's her victory," Jarrett insisted, watching the group.

"A victory she wouldn't have without you," he answered back. "The thing about a team is: a win for one is a win for us all. Enjoy it. The moment here will be brief in the big scheme of things."

"She still needs work. It was only once," Jarrett tried to say, uncomfortable with the praise.

Rederrick only smiled. "I imagine once against you is equal to ten demons. Life is really about small victories and a few joyful moments. The rest of it is often trials. It's the small things that help us overcome the big ones, so live in the moment, boy, and remember it. Those trials will come soon enough as you well know."

Jarrett lifted his brow. "*Boy?*" he questioned indignantly. He was more than two centuries older than this father figure.

Rederrick laughed out loud and walked to Collett, offering her congratulations and a tight hug.

Delphene met Jarrett's gaze with a sly smile, and unable to help it any longer, he smiled back. *Small victories,* he thought.

CHAPTER 28

A few days later, Cade lay in bed next to Collett, holding her as she excitedly recounted her newest triumph to him. Ever since that first strike against Jarrett, she'd been a ball of excitement and energy. The long training sessions were paying off, and not only for her. Everyone in their little group was displaying improvement.

Following Jarrett's instruction for a little over two weeks in an effort to help her learn to block empathetic powers had cost them both. Every night after training, the pain and exhaustion claimed them practically before their heads even hit the pillows, but tonight was a different story entirely. Her improvements were evident in more ways than one.

The newlyweds had retired early and spent that time enjoying a rare moment of time alone together. While she finished recounting her newest success, he kissed her bare neck and shoulder. "I'm proud of you," he murmured against her, tickling her skin with his warm breath.

~ 308 ~

The Price of Knowing

She rolled, putting herself above him. Smiling down, she whispered, "I know it's been painful for you to do this. I'm sorry for that."

"It's nothing compared to what I'd go through to see you safe," he declared, pulling her to him and pressing his lips to hers. When the kiss ended, he pulled away and she relaxed onto his chest with her hair fanning over his skin. He began combing through the soft, shiny locks with his fingers.

Laying against him and basking in the tranquil sensation of him playing with her hair, she closed her eyes and reflected on all that had happened in the last two and a half months. Her life had changed so much, though, all of it was for the better. Collett reflected on the reasons it changed, and that thought process led her to one very important detail she couldn't forget.

"I told him we would come for him," she whispered to Cade, bringing up Cody once again.

"I know," he sympathized softly.

"Do you think we'll be able to? Find him I mean," she asked, lazily tracing circles on his chest.

"We found Jarrett."

"This is different. Somehow I know it. I felt him every day for weeks without even realizing it, but since the other night, nothing. Do you think he's…" She couldn't say the word.

"I don't know," Cade answered honestly.

"We have to find out. I'm not sure I could forgive myself if he died. He was there the whole time I was connected to Jarrett. Maybe we could've found a way to save him but didn't because I didn't figure it out. We have to find out, Cade."

He knew she was right, and he felt the same way despite what Jarrett recently told him about Cody's alliances. He'd kept that to himself. Like Jarrett, he saw no reason to upset everyone before they knew the facts.

"We'll keep trying," he promised her.

~ 309 ~

"I'm supposed to help him. I don't think I would have seen him otherwise. Only, I don't know how to."

He drew her in tighter and tugged the covers around them. "I'll talk to Jeffery again in the morning and see if he's come up with a new idea, but for now, let's get some sleep."

"You're right. It's been such a good day, and I'm spoiling it. I'm sorry."

"You didn't ruin anything. You're worried; so am I, but we can't do any more than we already are. We can't help him if we go in before we're ready. We'll only get ourselves killed. In the meantime, we will keep looking for a way to reach him," he insisted.

She nodded against his chest.

Cade reached over to flick off the old lamp on the table, bathing the room in darkness. Closing his eyes, he continued to play with her hair until he felt her relax against him. Plagued by thoughts of Cody, worry for Collett, and puzzling out The Faction's leader, Niall, Cade eventually drifted off to sleep.

Collett smelled the salty sea and heard the waves below her. She felt wind against her cheeks, and she heard rumbling thunder in the sky.

Turning, she looked up at the sky and searched for lightning. Instead, she saw a familiar image. Horror gripped her upon seeing it again. Above her, a man screamed in ear-splitting agony as he writhed about in midair against whatever was causing his pain. Then she watched, helpless, as he fell to the earth.

Panic gripped her even though she knew it was a dream. It was one she'd had before, a dream in which she watched Cade die. Only this time, as she rushed over to the man on the ground, she knew it wasn't Cade. Even before she looked at the man lying amid the tall grasses, staring unblinking up at her with accusation in his eyes, Collett understood the tortured man was Jarrett.

Collett realized that the dream had not changed since the first time this premonition haunted her. She simply knew Jarrett now, and she recognized the differences between the two brothers. Her vision of Cade dying this horrible death was, in fact, a vision of his twin, and a sense of utter failure gripped her.

She heard a comforting, accented voice in her head, *"They are the answer to your question."*

Heart pounding and gasping for breath, Collett jerked awake. Normally a very light sleeper, Cade didn't even stir. Brushing her hair aside, Collett rose. She took Cade's shirt from the chair by the bed and, putting it on, padded over to the window. She folded her arms tightly and stared into the night sky, trying to understand why the vision came back.

If Cynda and the others were right and she had precognition along with her other abilities, there had to be a reason she saw this a second time. She felt a strong sense that she was somehow supposed to prevent it, but how? Jarrett was far more capable than her. If an unknown force caused him that much agony, then how could she possibly stop it?

Grabbing the throw at the bottom of the bed, she curled up in the window seat, spending the better part of the night trying to force herself to remember. *What question?* she thought.

What only felt like minutes later, a warm hand rested on her cheek. Opening her tired eyes, she blinked against the sunlight that streamed through the window where she must have fallen asleep.

She looked at Cade, who wore a worried expression on his face and asked, "Bad dream?"

"No," she answered, unwilling to tell him what she had seen.

He gave her a skeptical look as if he didn't believe her.

"I couldn't sleep is all. I spent the night trying to remember," she explained, offering him part of the truth at least.

He kissed her brow lightly. "Don't force it. You'll remember when you're meant to."

"What if I can't? I know I've said it doesn't matter, but I can't help thinking that none of this would be happening if I had my memories."

"I fought against members of The Faction long before I met you. The way I see it, they would have eventually come after me anyway."

He sat down next to her. "Because I met you, I have Jarrett back in my life, we have a chance to end The Faction once and for all, and more importantly, I have you as my wife. Really, there are more good things than bad."

"And what about Tracy, James, and Ashley? What about Jenny? What about Cody?" she asked.

"Tracy, James, and Ashley are fine. So what if their lives are a little disrupted. They're alive and well, and together. That's more than a lot of people can say. What happened to Jenny and what's happening to Cody is wrong, no doubt about it, but that's why this is important. There are so many other Cody's and Jenny's that we can help if we end Niall's reign over them. You know that. It's just hard because it's personal."

"I can't help thinking about it. What they did to him, what they're doing still—"

"We'll figure out a way to get to him," he promised, not knowing if it was even possible.

Resigned, she stood. "I guess we better get downstairs. Jarrett's likely already waiting."

He scooped her up and made his way to the bed. "I think we have some time yet."

Collett read his thoughts and knew his motives were not all selfish. Cade wanted to delay training to distract her from her worry and protect her from unnecessary pain. She smiled and loved him more for the effort. "He's not going to be happy with us if we aren't downstairs on time."

~ 312 ~

"He'll have to get over it. I have something much better to do right now," Cade replied, grinning wickedly.

Niall examined his handy work. Cody was barely recognizable. They'd drugged him to keep the pain down so she couldn't sense or find him until Niall wanted her to. It was easy enough to cut off her connection when he was around, but he couldn't be here constantly. He had pressing obligations. Niall had an organization to run, people to kill, and plans to finish.

Nonetheless, he'd been instructing them on how to inflict the most possible pain without killing the boy. For this event, he wanted Cody coherent. A thousand years of experience offered him knowledge of exactly how to hurt him while still making him usable. He also knew exactly how contact her now that he knew she'd been visiting Cody. Victor stood with him today, and Niall noticed he couldn't even look at the prisoner. Niall was pleased with his response.

When Victor first returned without that traitor, Jarrett, in tow, Niall became furious. Then Victor confirmed through choking gasps that The Hunter, his Hunter, had teamed up with his twin and Collett. Niall was still considered killing Victor purely for the satisfaction—until he told him about Collett's visit to Cody. In that instant, everything changed. Niall finally had a way to bring her to him, and when he did, he would end her once and for all. The traitor would be an added bonus.

"Everything's ready, sir."

"Wake him then," Niall ordered.

Training started much later than Jarrett would have liked, and after a quick lunch, the group took too long to regroup. A call from

Cynda and Rederrick's children during lunch had created quite a buzz. Jenny began talking in her sleep today. From what he gathered, the housekeeper was asking for Sam, her deceased husband. The doctor's felt any change was a good sign. Plus, she was moving more instead of simply lying still. She would jerk slightly or twitch her fingers.

Jarrett found it hard to care. His concerns were here, and he knew nothing of this woman besides what they kept telling him. It wasn't that he was callus, but they were running out of time. That, coupled with the fact that Collett was making strong progress, made him anxious to get back to work. His annoyance showed through, even though he tried hard to hide it.

He snapped at the group twice already, and he knew he was being more ruthless against Collett. So when she fell to her knees after he struck her lightly on her ribs, he let go of a low growl. "Get up!" She didn't move. Even though he'd become more tempered over the last month, today was pushing him to his limits. He strode around to face her. "Get—" the demanding words died in his throat. "Cade!"

Collett's eyes were open, but she stared unblinking at nothing. Cade and the others came running, and seeing her that way sent panic coursing through his brother. He rushed to her, but Jarrett pulled him back. "Don't touch her!"

Looking at him incredulously and trying to push him aside, Cade snapped, "We should get her inside!"

"Look!" Jarrett snarled and pushed back. "Look at her. She's breathing like we taught her. She's concentrating and in control, for now. If you touch her, you'll break her concentration. She'll absorb your emotions."

"I have a better idea," Jeffery stated. "Let's try to find out if we can see what she sees."

Jarrett scowled. "How?"

"Nate, go get the salt. Cynda—"

~ 314 ~

The Price of Knowing

"Got it. I'll take the left," she said while using her feet to cut a line in the snow.

"Cade," Jeffery called, "you make a line on the right, like the triangle we used to find Jarrett. Rederrick?"

"Already there, I'll make the bottom."

"We have to hurry," Jeffery insisted.

Jarrett watched in fascination as they worked in sync to draw a triangle in the snow around Collett. Nate came out right away and began dumping salt in the lines. Jeffery took a place at the top point and began moving his body in a sort of Tai Chi like dance.

"We don't have any of his blood," Cade expressed with concern.

"We won't need it. She's already connected," Jeffery told him, not breaking his rhythm.

Cynda stood at another point, and Cade knelt beside Collett.

"There are enough of you to lend us strength and still stay balanced," Jeffery said. "Pair up and take a point."

Delphene stood on the remaining spot near Jarrett, and he took an uneasy step toward her while Nate took a spot near Jeffery, and Rederrick joined Cynda.

"Jarrett, take it off," Jeffery ordered.

"Excuse me?" he snapped back.

"Take off whatever it is you have that blocks magic. It won't work if you don't."

Jarrett hesitated.

"C'mon, *Chère*, trust goes two ways," Delphene taunted.

Jarrett reluctantly reached under his shirt and pulled out the green amulet that hung at his neck. He stared at it. Then in an act of trust greater than any he'd displayed in over a hundred years, Jarrett pulled the chain over his head, giving away his final secret. He dropped it on the ground behind the line of salt. Immediately, he found himself in a cloudy, misty place where he could hardly make out the people around him.

~ 315 ~

He could see a surgical table and a battered, broken boy that lay atop it. A big, burly half demon stood nearby with a sharp instrument in his hand. Looking at the horrid condition of the young man on the table made Jarrett marvelled that he was still alive, much less awake.

Then, without seeing her, he heard Collett speak, "It's okay, Cody. Tell me what they want from you."

"I don't want to help him," he said in stuttering, pain-filled words.

"I know, but you can tell me. I'll be careful," she cajoled in a soothing tone.

The burly man standing near him began to lower the tool again. Fear erupted in the swollen, disfigured expression of the young boy, and he began weakly struggling against his bonds.

"Please! Cody, you can tell me. Don't let them hurt you anymore!"

"I...don't—" he began to say, but it changed to a grunt and a moan as the man cut him.

For a minute, everything went black and Jarrett thought they lost the image, but then it came back. Unable to watch Cody's torment, Collett had shut her eyes.

"Cody, tell me. I won't get hurt. I'm stronger now. Please, tell me," she begged him.

"He'll kill you all..." Cody ground out through his teeth.

"It's all right, tell me what he wants."

"To—talk."

"To talk?"

"He—he says he can tell you—who you are," Cody managed to say.

Unsure of how to respond, Collett said nothing.

"He says," Cody paused to pant through the pain, "if you'll come talk...come talk to...to him. Then he'll...let me...go with you."

The Price of Knowing

"Okay, Cody, that's good. We'll go together. What else does he say?"

Cody rolled his head. "If—if you don't…"

"If I don't what?" she encouraged gently.

"Come…he'll keep hurting me, and—" Cody gasped and coughed, and the pain the movement caused him was evident to anyone watching. "If I—if I die…he'll find someone else…"

"All right, Cody, we'll come; I'll come. Where, where should I go?" Collett urged.

"Don't—don't go. Please," he began crying desperately, and guilt poured from him in waves.

The big man began to lean again. *No*, she thought, *no more!*

"Cody! Cody, where do I go?" she shouted at him. "You have to tell me."

"What?" He seemed confused for a minute.

"Where? Tell me where to go."

"Go…he says go…to…to P-p-patrick's P…" Cody struggled over every word and even groaned at the end.

"We're going to find you. We're coming," she assured him to sooth his pain and panic. "Where Cody? Who's Patrick?" she questioned with a smooth, kind voice, despite feeling his trembling throughout her own body. Fortunately, the pain was muted. She knew he was hurting, knew where the wounds were and how bad, but it wasn't overpowering her like it had in the past. She attributed it to Jarrett and his focus techniques.

"The cliffs. Go back to the cl… The Point…" His words were mumbled now. He was losing consciousness.

"What cliffs?"

"Don't—" he started to say, but Collett could feel him drifting away.

"Cody, wake up. Which cliffs?"

"Go back…don't—go," he pleaded incoherently.

~ 317 ~

C.B. Haight

Collett felt herself losing the connection. Her clarity was wavering. "Hold on Cody, we'll find you!" she promised, hoping he could hear her. "Please, just hold on."

The next thing she knew, Collett found herself looking into Cade's compassionate eyes while her body shook.

"I know," Cade assured her before she could explain anything. "We saw." She looked around to see everyone staring at her with grim, sad expressions.

With tears streaming down her cheeks, Collett wrapped her arms around Cade. "We have to help him."

Jarrett knew, as did everyone else, that they were out of time.

CHAPTER 29

Everything moved swiftly after that. None of them could see the horror of something that terrible and ignore it. Within an hour, the group managed to figure out Cody's reference to Patrick's Point. He spoke of the cliffs in Northern California near the coastline. Within a day, transportation—via Darrin from Texas—was arranged.

Two days after Collett's connection to Cody, they all sat in a tiny hospital room at Fort Carson. They made the added stop in Colorado upon Cynda's insistence. Cynda refused to go to California without seeing her children and Jenny... just in case.

None in the group held any illusions about what they were going into. They recognized Niall's excuse of wanting to talk as the lie it was, and they knew this meeting could go badly as quickly as it could succeed. They hoped the latter would happen, and they all fiercely clung to the hope that it would.

In Colorado, everyone managed to think positively, and Cynda and Rederrick carefully instructed their children while maintaining the belief that they would see them in a few days. All three of their

~ 319 ~

grown children protested the choice to leave them behind and argued vehemently that their presence could possibly turn the tide. In the end, it was Rederrick's plea that they remain behind and be ready to fight should they fail at Patrick's Point that ended any further arguments.

During the trip, Collett noticed a few positive things and held them in her heart as closely as she could to try to replace the images of Cody's suffering. She watched how many times Nate stole Ashley away, and she considered the growing feelings that trickled from them as a good sign. She saw how Jarrett interacted with the others in the group, including James and Tracy, whom he'd never met. She noticed that Cade and Jarrett comfortably moved around and conversed with each other. The tense feelings they once shared were gone. All these things encouraged her in this desperate time, and she had faith that, despite the dangers, it all must have happened for a reason.

All too soon, she found herself watching Rederrick and Cynda embrace their children and offer tearful goodbyes. Both parents silently worried whether they would make it back to see them again. She felt the same feelings they felt, shared the same thoughts they had, and prayed that, no matter what, this family could be together again soon, whole and complete.

Three days after her vision in the woods, Collett sat in yet another rented SUV with Cade and Jarrett cruising down the winding curves of Highway One in Northern California, on their way to Patrick's Point. She was keeping herself as open as possible in an effort to connect to Cody again, and as a result, she could sense Cade and Jarrett's thoughts and impressions. She smiled at how close their thoughts aligned.

Jarrett kept thinking how great it would be to drive along this road on his bike. He imagined how he could open her up and race down the winding curves with the wind rushing all around him. Cade was thinking much the same, but his mind went to the little black Camaro that Rederrick kept for him instead. He thought about the speeds at which he could zip in and out of every turn and how, right now, it would be the perfect release.

Collett even let out a poorly-concealed laugh when, almost at the same time, they thought about how confining and rigid the SUV was. Cade and Jarrett both looked to her, but she offered no explanation for her chuckle and only waved them away with her hand. Though still curious, they both eventually went back to their own ponderings.

Before long, they drove into the campgrounds near the cliffs that visitors stay in during the summer months. Nearing the end of January, the campgrounds were empty. It was a relief that the group would not have to contend with large crowds. The only people they would likely see were the occasional hikers.

The temperatures were chilly, especially in the evenings, but not uncomfortable, and would suit their needs well enough. The rain was worse. During the winter months, rain here could be substantial; yet another reason the average tourist waited for summer.

Massive Redwood trees and different types of foliage surrounded the area in all directions, and fog came in and went out as well. The brothers worried those elements could trap them, but Collett saw both problems more as a source of protection than anything.

The afternoon they arrived was filled with a low fog that made it difficult to pick an ideal location. A few times, the group exited their vehicles and searched for a suitable spot, then decide to move on. On the fourth time, they deemed the area workable and began to settle in.

Planning as much as possible, they'd brought all the gear they deemed necessary, and everyone pitched in to set up for the undetermined amount of time. Making camp kept them busy and calmed their nerves.

The next morning was different. Smart enough to know this would be a setup, Jarrett, Cade, and Delphene spent the day as wolves scouting the vicinity around camp. While they did, Collett explored, following one of the many trails and taking in the sights.

The majesty around them was something one could not take lightly. She considered the natural beauty of every tree and flower. Before long, a midnight-black wolf materialized through the fading fog not far from her. She knew he was there and sensed his disapproval of her wandering alone.

It was heartening to know he cared at all. Jarrett watched her as she placed her hand gently on the trunk of a mighty redwood that stretched so tall it seemed as if it would reach upward to touch the sun before much longer.

"I think I've been here before," she confessed.

Jarrett cocked his head to an angle, listening carefully.

"I've wandered these woods before," she paused and looked around slowly.

Jarrett padded to her and nudged her hand with his head, urging her to continue.

"It was different then. These trees—I don't know, maybe it was somewhere else," she said, turning to meet his eyes.

He didn't move, she knew he didn't agree.

"Cody told me to go *back*," she said, as if in agreement. "But if I've been here before, it must have been a very long time ago," she told him, looking up at the giant tree.

Jarrett used his large wolf's head to indicate the direction of camp. She patted him softly and began walking, but she stopped after a few steps. Turning to look at him again, she confessed, "I wanted to save her, Jarrett." He looked away. She knew he didn't want to talk about it. "I don't understand much about who I was, who I am, but I know I wanted to save her." Collett looked to the sky above her. "I can't explain the feelings I have or what they mean. I know though, I *couldn't* save her. It wasn't meant for me." Looking back, she saw him staring at her again, and she met his soul-piercing gaze once more. "Somehow, I understand that I would have made things worse, but I'll forever be sorry for the little boy it hurt."

Jarrett kept eye contact with her for several heartbeats.

"With everything—in case I don't——I thought you should know," she said with a sigh.

She felt his sorrow as a result of bringing the subject up, but she also felt his acceptance wash through her. It offered her a sense of relief. He jerked his head in a form of assent and then padded off toward camp, indicating he was finished with the conversation.

That night was quiet, and it made everyone feel edgy. None of them could predict how or when Niall would find them, and not knowing was the worst part. After almost everyone settled in their respective tents, Jarrett sat outside by the small fire with Delphene to keep watch.

"Do you think the boy is still alive?" Delphene asked him quietly, with her thick accent more prominent because of her low tone.

Jarrett only shook his head. He didn't think Cody would still be alive.

"Maybe we've made a mistake. If he is dead, then what do we gain? She is not ready," she told him.

It wasn't anything he hadn't already thought about himself. "Because he'll find another victim and do it to her again," Jarrett answered, knowing Niall's threat was real.

Delphene said nothing for a while after that. "If he knows her so well, better than she herself, can we have a hope of outsmarting him?"

Jarrett did smile then, a wicked, cocky smile that sent a shiver down the she-wolf's spine. "We don't have to. All we need is an opportunity, and that arrogant bastard is going to give it to us." Jarrett looked back to the flickering flames in front of him and watched them dance and sway. "I'll find a way to end him. Even if it isn't this time. I fully intend to make sure that, one day, Niall will regret ever crossing my path."

"At this point, wolf, that is something I do not doubt he does already," she replied.

Early the next morning, the fog was once more thick and enveloped the area. Rederrick and Nate moved about early, collecting wood for the day. They stayed fairly close to camp for safety reasons, but it was still a good distance between them and the others. Searching for dead branches and fuel had them about 20 yards apart from each other and weaving in and out of trees.

Nate heard a shuffling emanate from behind a tree not 10 feet from his position. He covertly bent as if to retrieve wood, but instead he dropped all but one branch. He mimicked brushing at his pants, but silently pulled the dagger from his boot in the process.

"This wood's got ants in it," he called loud enough for all to hear. "Big ones. They must be crawling all over our camp." Luckily, Rederrick understood his meaning and moved his direction. He only hoped the rest of them heard.

Nate moved forward as if nothing changed, and as he passed the tree, the man struck. Or at least, he tried to. Nate dropped low and swung the fist-thick log around, making contact with the attacker's stomach.

He heard an audible grunt as the wood hit his opponent, but Nate wasted no time thinking about it. Commotion erupted around him. He ignored it. Using his momentum, he swung up and around, landing several blows to his victim's face and a heavy kick to the gut. Grabbing the attacker's arm, Nate yanked him forward and threw him off balance. As his enemy began to stumble, Nate forced him back with a jab at the man's throat.

The quick actions were a blur of movement and impressive by any standard. Over years of training, Nate had learned how to use every muscle as a weapon, a weapon so efficient that he could even make it past Cade's defenses on occasion.

Nate forced his opponent against the very tree the attacker had hidden behind. With his forearm bunched and pressed tightly against his neck, Nate assessed the situation. Cade stood, sword in hand, not far away. Demon remnants scattered the ground around him, and Jarrett stood nearby in much the same manner. Thick fog made it hard to see, but he managed to make out the rest of the group, alert and in defensive positions.

He turned his attention back to his would-be attacker, and realized it was the man from the warehouse where they found Jarrett. It took Nate a second to think of the man's name. "Victor?" he questioned, then his lips curled and he accused angrily, "You are Victor."

"I calculated you'd be the easiest and least likely to kill me," he rasped through his constricted windpipe.

Bringing his knife within the man's view, Nate replied, "You should recalculate, and fast."

"No, wait!" Collett shouted.

Nate made sure to display his disappointment. Even though he suspected someone would stop him, he figured there was no sense in letting Victor know that. Cade approached with Victor's imminent death displayed in his eyes, but Jarrett's expression promised much worse than death.

"On second thought, considering those two, maybe you were right," Nate implied.

"I have a message," he rasped out desperately.

"Well you better deliver it quick, otherwise you're not gonna get a chance," suggested Nate with dead seriousness.

Cade arrived first, and placing the tip of his sword against Victor's chest, ordered darkly, "Talk."

"You can't scare me. I've been around my master far too long to be afraid of you. Could someone retrieve my glasses please," Victor replied defiantly with a cool, snide tone.

C.B. Haight

Moving up to them, Jarrett nudged Nate aside and stood in his place in front of the prisoner. Nate only grinned knowingly as he shifted from view.

Victor tried to stare Jarrett down as he had Cade, but failed miserably. He swallowed hard at the promise of violence evident in The Hunter's eyes.

"Talk," he said with complete calm.

"My message is for her," he said, pointing to Collett. "I am to deliver it and return with her response. You can't kill me, or he'll kill the boy," Victor told him.

Jarrett lifted a brow. "That's unfortunate, because you won't be going back." He lifted his sword and eyed the length of it.

"Why should I tell you then?" Victor questioned.

"You might live if you do," Cade injected with venom.

"How do I know you won't kill me anyway?" Victor asked.

Bending in closer so they were practically nose to nose, Jarrett said in a low voice, "I suppose you'll have to calculate the odds. You seem to be good at that."

Victor heard the deadly threat lacing every word. "The cliffs not far from here," he started to say, but then he hesitated.

Jarrett gave him a hard look.

"The cliffs. Tonight, he will meet you on the cliffs. Right up that trail there," he said, pointing to one of the many trails. "If she comes to talk with him, then you can have Cody back."

"Yeah, right," Nate replied.

"He says to tell her he knows who she is. He can help her remember, but she has to come alone."

"That's not going to happen," Rederrick said from behind them.

"When?" Jarrett questioned in a low tone.

"Tonight."

"When?" Jarrett replied more firmly.

"After the sun is gone from the sky," Victor said.

~ 326 ~

The Price of Knowing

Jarrett tore his attention from Victor to look at Cade. Without any words, Cade understood Jarrett's intent. He hesitated, but seeing no alternative, he grimly agreed with a nod. Jarrett lifted his sword.

"No!" Collett shouted.

Cade and Jarrett both looked back to her as she ran to them. "No!" she repeated with a firmness that surprised them. "You can't do this."

Jarrett glared at her.

"Will you be like him then?" she accused, propelling Jarrett back to his memory of her standing proud and strong, dressed in white, between him and the preacher that ordered Rowena's death.

"He would have killed any one of us," Jarrett replied, wavering. "If we keep him here, he still could."

"Maybe, but you are not his judge. You have no knowledge of what his crimes are or what brought him to this point." She lowered her voice, taking on a softer tone, "You are not like him. Don't act as he would."

Cade and Jarrett felt guilt from her chastisement. "What would you have us do?" Cade asked. "We have no safe way to keep him, and if he goes back to Niall, he may have the chance to kill any one of us when our back is turned."

"There is always a solution. We only have to think of it," she promised. "For now, we'll have to keep him unconscious. It's the safest way to keep him. Jeffery, can you——" She stopped her request mid-sentence when she heard the awful sound of Victor's head smack into the tree.

"Unconscious," Jarrett confirmed, releasing Victor's shirt. The knocked-out Faction member crumpled as Jarrett strode away.

Cade couldn't help it, he grinned, but he quickly wiped it away when Collett glared at him.

Nate, smiling openly, moved up to the body and rolled him over. "That looks pretty unconscious to me."

As the day passed, the group spent time scouting and making plans. Cynda concocted a tea to keep Victor asleep for the rest of the night. When they tried to convince him to drink it, he obstinacy refused until Jarrett grabbed him, implying his alternative. After he was out, they tied him to a nearby tree. Secretly, Jarrett hoped a bear would happen by.

The plan they made was fairly simple. Collett would not face Niall alone as he wished. Cade and Jarrett would stay with her on one of the higher peaks of the cliffs they had decided was the best possible position. Jeffery insisted on coming along with them, but he would use his magic to stay invisible. Everyone else would stay in pairs and find lower areas out of sight. They sought out places that could give them access to each other in case the brothers needed backup.

They were anxious—everyone but Jarrett. Jarrett was eager for a chance to face and defeat Niall. They all walked in silence late that afternoon. As they were hiking up to the cliffs, everyone took time to mentally prepare for what was to come. Quicker than they wanted, the group arrived at the first trail that Nate and Delphene would follow to reach their position.

"Be careful," Delphene said somberly.

Jarrett nodded. "Watch your backs."

"I'll save a few for you," Cade told Nate, grabbing his offered hand in a firm, wrist-gripping shake.

"Make sure you do," he replied with a grin.

Collett hugged them both. "Thank you," she whispered to each of them.

"*Non fret une petite*," Delphene soothed.

Soon enough, Nate and Delphene were making their way down the path as the rest of the group moved on. A few minutes passed, then they all heard, "Radio check. Testing. Can you hear me?" Nate said.

"We hear you, Nate," Rederrick answered.

"Oh good, because there's something I've been meaning to tell you," Nate replied.

"What's that?" Rederrick asked.

"If we live through tonight, I intend to marry your daughter."

Rederrick grinned, and Cynda's eyes lit up. "Really?" she asked with excitement.

"Well, I figure I deserve something here since I put my life and limb on the line and all."

Cade smiled and grabbed Collett's hand. "What do you say, Rederrick? Is the risk of life and limb enough to steal your daughter away?"

"Not for the likes of that one," said Jarrett.

"Well, it's a good thing I don't need to ask you then huh, Cowboy?" Nate teased over the radio.

Cade laughed, and Jarrett turned to him with a quirked brow. "Cowboy?"

Still chuckling, Cade said, "What can I say, I admire his bravery. Not many would dare call you, 'Cowboy'."

"No, not many," Jarrett agreed.

Nate came through the ear buds again, "Well?"

Rederrick smiled at his wife. "I suppose if you manage to see the sun in the morning and are able to talk your way out of the 'cowboy' thing, you'll have earned my blessing."

"No pressure then," Nate joked.

Jarrett shook his head and actually smiled.

They reached the place where Jeffery, Jarrett, Cade, and Collett would wait to confront Niall. It was a big area with room enough to give Niall a good fight. Collett trembled when she recognized her surroundings from her dream of Jarrett's death. Cade rubbed her back with a comforting hand, unaware of what she knew. She squared her shoulders and swore to herself, *I will not let him die.*

~ 329 ~

C.B. Haight

"I guess this is where we split," Cynda said reluctantly.

Pulled from her thoughts, Collett hugged her friend as she had the others. "Be careful, okay?"

Cynda nodded. "You too."

Rederrick gave her a tight bear hug, lifting her, then set her on her feet. "Watch your back, little girl, and give 'em hell."

She nodded and stepped away so Cade and he could grip hands and share a manly embrace. "See you in a bit, Old Man," Cade said affectionately.

"Don't do anything stupid," Rederrick replied. They broke apart, and Rederrick put a hand on Jarrett's shoulder. "You either. I'm kinda starting to like you."

Jarrett gave a quick nod. "I'll do my best."

"You stay out of sight, Jeffery," Cynda admonished in a motherly tone. "You betrayed them just as Jarrett, and I don't want him to know you're here. I don't want to see anybody else like we saw Cody. Do you understand me?"

"Yes ma'am," he replied, warmed by her concern.

Dropping their supply packs near a tree, the four of them walked toward the center of the area, and Cynda and Rederrick continued to the other side. Collett looked at the people surrounding her and tried hard to think of ways to keep them alive. She knew that whatever occurred, it would not be an easy battle to win.

CHAPTER 30

Cold waves crashed against the base of the cliff where they stood. The violence of the ocean was a direct contrast to the descending sun that shone with exceptional brilliance and tinted the sky a multitude of reds, purples, oranges, and golds. The scene supported the myth of warmth and life.

When they reached the center of the bluff, the four of them stopped simultaneously and looked from one to another. Jeffery angled his head, taking in the sunset, then glanced back. He offered them a mock salute and disappeared.

Cade shifted his focus, soaking up the view. Green and yellow grasses as well as tall weeds grew spontaneously around the rocks and up through the packed dirt. They danced and swayed with the rhythm the breeze provided. Standing in his human form, Cade listened to the sound of the salty water batter relentlessly against a rock wall. He knew his own mood was one of violence, determination, and cold reality, much like the ocean.

This would be the place. Here is where they would try to end it. This man, Niall, whoever he was, must be stopped, no matter the cost. Cade knew that whatever Niall wanted with Collett, it wasn't good, and the time had come to confront him and end his reign over people with supernatural abilities.

Cade looked to his wife. She wasn't the same woman he'd met nearly three months before. Just then, she looked like an avenging hero from a storybook. She stood proudly with a wide stance; her hands rested on weapons strapped to her waist, and the picture she presented felt right.

What was left of the reddish sunlight glinted off the multiple golden highlights in her hair, and the same wind that stirred the waves into their rhythmic frenzy lifted and twirled her unbound locks about her perfect, ivory skin. Her long, scarlet coat stirred around her legs and showed off tall black boots that covered the tight jeans up to her knee. The entire scene was surreal and could easily lead a person to believe the wind surrounding her was under her control. For just a second, Cade thought of the storm from her memories and wondered.

Standing in this place, despite the impending confrontation, Collett appeared strong and confidant. Gone was the timid, confused woman he'd fought so hard to protect. Instead of vulnerable, she was vibrant. Instead of cowering, she was courageous. Even with so few of her memories restored, Collett was an entirely new woman, and by some miracle, she was his. Cade's heart swelled with love and pride for this woman and all she had become.

Distracted and unaware of his scrutiny, Collett closed her eyes, sensing the environment surrounding them. Cade had a sudden apprehension settle in the pit of his stomach. He didn't want her here. He didn't want her involved. He wanted desperately to pick her up and run, and keep running until he was sure she was safe. It was killing him to take this chance with her life. Fear, something he rarely felt, twisted in his gut.

She opened her eyes and smiled calmly at him. Her expression reassured him, and comfortable warmth settled into him. The knot in his stomach loosened. It amazed him that even here, in the worst circumstances he could imagine, Collett infused him with light and hope.

He released her gaze to look at Jarrett standing a few feet beyond Collett. Dressed head to toe in black; his long coat, battle gear, and the sword strapped to his back gave an air of danger to his image. The Oakley sunglasses that covered his eyes made him look even more reminiscent of the hunter he was.

Cade appraised the man he finally claimed as family. Jarrett's chin was covered with dark stubble, and his hair was loose and free, shading his face. That wasn't the only thing Jarrett kept shaded. He knew so little about his brother, and yet he finally felt connected to him. Sensing Cade's scrutiny, Jarrett gave his attention to his twin and inclined his head in solidarity.

Behind them, Jeffery took up his position. As promised, his magic kept him from being seen by everyone but Jarrett. Still, Cade knew he would be there as discussed, and he shook his head at the idea. He never would have guessed how much he'd come to rely on the young sorcerer. Collett was not the only one who had changed. One woman had turned his world upside down and created something so much bigger. There was a peaceful sense of purpose in that knowledge.

Rederrick's voice came through the ear buds, "Heads up boys and girls. It's almost time."

The moments before the encounter seemed to move slowly. At Rederrick's words, Cade turned his attention back to the sky. The sun had almost finished its descent, and the fiery sky had cooled, shifting into the purple and blue hues of night. Suddenly, distant thunder sounded from above and dark, angry clouds began rolling in.

"Show time," Cade said to everyone. Reaching deep and taking a fortifying breath, he readied himself for what was about to come.

C.B. Haight

Collett felt his presence. As thunder rumbled in the sky, a sharp but familiar sensation of emotions invaded her. Her blood cooled, and her stomach roiled. With wide eyes, she whipped around to face the other direction. "He's here."

Trusting her completely, they all spun. Jeffery, once behind them, was now in front of the trio, still unseen. Cade and Jarrett instinctively sniffed the air, but smelled nothing aside from the coming rain and salty sea. They both looked to Collett with identical expressions, as if they were mirror images.

"Be careful, there's magical energy in the air," Cynda cautioned.

Shortly after her words echoed in their ears, Cade and Jarrett caught the scent of burning cinder and flesh. He appeared out of nowhere and stood mere yards away from them. At his feet, lying face down, was a battered and bruised body that they all assumed was Cody.

The man standing before them was surprisingly handsome, well groomed, and completely normal looking. Cade half expected his appearance would reflect his evil reputation. It didn't. His hair was greyed, though he did not look older than 30. He was tall, broad, and perfectly manicured. He wore a tailored suit, as if he came to conduct a business meeting instead of the hostile confrontation they expected. He looked more like the Godfather than a powerful demon lord.

It was his strange eyes that gave him away as being otherworldly. When Cade focused on his face, he felt a chill run through him. Niall's eyes were an unnaturally dull grayish-cloud and looked as if they were sightless, or maybe glass. A simple glance from the cloudy orbs communicated deadly promises and malicious intent. Cade didn't even need empathic abilities to understand why Collett looked ill at the moment. This man was the very definition of evil.

Niall's lips turned up in a sickly, sinister smile, then he directed his full attention to Collett. Cade momentarily faltered when he followed Niall's line of sight to his wife. Raw emotions of anger and

The Price of Knowing

hate rushed through him in a violent surge. Red hot rage spread through him, and he almost pounced, but Collett, pale and drawn, stilled him with a single glance. Shaking her head, she mouthed the words, "Not yet."

Trusting in his wife, Cade regained his self-control. Doing so was more difficult to do than it had ever been for him. Anything that threatened Collett threw him off balance.

Jarrett's reaction to Niall's arrival was less subtle. A lot less. His eyes began to glow, and he actually snarled. Even though he lacked Cade's general temperament, his years of being The Hunter taught him control over the wolf inside. He made it clear he felt no need to disguise his disgust and intent.

"You're not alone," Niall said to Collett. Thunder sounded again, the wind picked up, and the temperature felt as though it dropped a whole twenty degrees in minutes. Niall spread his arms out wide and spoke with a voice that grated the nerves much like fingernails on a chalkboard, "Child, come to me. There is no need for such drama." The words were spoken gently and his gesture was almost fatherly, but it felt eerily unholy to everyone.

Both brothers growled, and deadly promises were reflected in their expressions.

"Oh, come on now, this is too much. Call off your dogs before they get hurt."

Collett was having a difficult time. An image of this man standing before her flittered across the recesses of her mind. In it, he wore armor and smiled as if they were friends. She closed her eyes in an effort to process it.

Seeing her struggle, Jarrett warned, "Block it, Collett. Don't let him distract you."

Shaking it off, Collett tried hard to quell the impressions she was experiencing. She couldn't even speak to reply. She was barely suppressing the physical reactions to the taint of his presence.

Evil poured from him in waves that battered her developing discipline like the ocean battered the rocks below. Collett could see mists of death and misery surrounding him like a hazy, black shroud. Using the methods Jarrett taught her, she tried her best to block him, but she was not entirely successful. Flashing images jumped to her mind but left before she could grasp onto them. She closed her eyes and channeled every effort into focusing and breathing.

Cade spoke for her. "Is he alive?" he ground out forcefully, indicating Cody with his head.

Niall's attention snapped to Cade, and his expression looked like one of annoyance and anger, as if speaking to Cade was beneath him. However, his words were still cool and calm, "Of course. I keep my promises." He directed his attention back to Collett, "Though, if you wait much longer, he might not be."

"You've never kept a promise," Jarrett accused with a growl.

Niall glared at him.

"He's alive," Collett confirmed softly, reassuring them. Even while he was unconscious, she could sense Cody's fitful pain.

"Is it Cody?" Cade asked her softly.

Niall answered before she could by viciously, yet dispassionately, kicking the heap at his feet. The body rolled over. "See for yourself."

Collett couldn't hold in her gasp at seeing Cody's abused appearance. His face was bruised and swollen. He was completely unrecognizable, and blood was caked and dried in various places all over his body.

Cade cursed. Jarrett ground his teeth. Both men were hoping to return the beating tenfold to Niall.

Unconcerned with their reactions, Niall examined Cody like a kid would examine a dissected bug. He was admiring his handy work. "You know—Cade, is it?" he began with disdain and pity lacing every word. "She was mine before she was ever yours. You cannot possibly imagine the intimacies of our relationship. If you would've only given her back, this," he gestured to Cody, "could have been avoided."

The Price of Knowing

Cade took a step forward and Niall's features brightened.

"Don't let him bait you, Cade," Cynda reminded him through the earbud.

"He lies!" Rederrick added at the same time.

Niall's grin widened. "Yes, I do lie, but not about this." His comment informed them that not only was he aware of *all* their presence, but he could hear their private exchanges through the coms.

"Don't listen to him," Jarrett ordered.

Cade felt his eyes burn. Little bumps rose on his skin, but he reminded himself Collett and Cody had to be his priority. Suppressing the transformation, he replied, "We get the boy. Then you can talk."

"Suit yourself. Come and get him. I am done with him anyway." Niall chuckled as if the whole situation was amusing.

Collett stopped Cade. "No," she said softly, "He wants you to come closer." Everyone turned their attention to her, but her focus stayed on Niall. "Don't go any further. He'll kill you. He wants nothing more than to see us all dead. Don't you?" she accused.

"Interesting," Niall replied, his smile diminishing. He was surprised she could read his thoughts so easily. The information he'd been given indicated she hadn't gained any control of her gifts yet. He realized Cody had miraculously managed to withhold that little detail from him and deceive him completely.

Ready to get on with the killing, Jarrett reached over his shoulder and drew the sword at his back. The sliding steel drew Niall's attention, and his eyes widened in surprise upon seeing the familiar weapon. "Where did you get that sword?" he demanded.

"It doesn't matter where I got it. What matters right now is what I'm going to do with it," Jarrett said, pacing from side to side to assess Niall's defenses.

Niall hadn't seen that sword in over four centuries, and seeing it now gave him pause. Jarrett popped his neck and began walking toward him. Niall grinned and shrugged the bitter nostalgia off,

~ 337 ~

because it hardly mattered at this point. He had a pretty good idea of who had given Jarrett the blade, and Niall resolved to pry his old weapon from the traitor's cold fingers after he'd killed them all.

The Faction's leader threw his arms out and used the stored dark energies within to summon reinforcements. The ground beneath them trembled as a bright light, much akin to lightning, flashed and struck the earth near Jeffery. Invisible, Jeffery barely escaped the strike because he felt the energy build around him and instinctively jumped out of the way. An extra dimensional doorway appeared in the same spot. From that iridescent opening came Niall's demon reserve.

Seeing what was coming forth, Cade valiantly dashed forward, changed from man to hybrid as he rushed to action, and before the first demon crawled free of the infernal doorway, he cut it down.

Jarrett pivoted and positioned himself to defend Collett against the creatures crawling up the cliff face at their back. Two vampiric leeches made their way to Jarrett, and with smooth practiced efficiency, they were beheaded for their trouble. The bodies turned to dust and revealed two more behind them. "I hope you can put all that practice to good use," he challenged Collett as he struck out at the next one.

Similar portals opened up below as well. The com link filled with chatter from Nate, Rederrick, and Delphene. "Incoming on the east side."

"They're all over here, Cade," Nate informed them.

"*Merde!*" exclaimed Delphene.

All hell broke loose, literally. The abyssal creatures rushed in to keep the friends from rallying. Surrounding them on all sides, the demons forced each group to defend their various positions.

On the east side, Cynda and Rederrick were pushed up the incline as the lesser demons advanced toward their leader. They weren't so hard to dispatch, being lesser imps and fiends rather than the massive greater-demons they'd encountered before. But there were simply too many of them. When one fell, two more replaced it.

The Price of Knowing

The couple fought with every step. Rederrick swung his sword with practiced efficiency. He used his strength and skill to slash and stab at anything that got near them so Cynda could concentrate solely on her magic.

He shouted to Cynda, "Were losing ground here. We've got to pull back and gather together!"

Nodding, Cynda chanted rapidly to cast her next spell, "With my will and my might, I ask the powers to steal their sight. Take from me to steal from these, rob them of what they can see." She felt the drain on her energy immediately, but she knew couldn't dwell on it.

Tingling magic collected around the demons. Cynda knew it would only buy them a little time. Grabbing Rederrick by the arm, she began pulling him along as she shouted above the noise, "We have to make a break for the bluff. They need us, and we can't stay here!"

Trusting her completely, Rederrick sprinted toward the bluff with her, but kept his eyes on the chaos behind them as he followed. The demons stumbled about blindly, bumping into one another, and a couple of them even wandered off the cliff, plummeting down to be grabbed by the cold, swooping waves of the ocean. His wife's creativity never ceased to amaze him.

On the west side of the cliff face, Nate and Delphene fought viciously against the sudden onslaught of creatures called forth by Niall. The demons pressed hard against them as well. They battled back with sword and claw, fist and tooth[BT2], but as one enemy fell there was always another to take its place.

They were surrounded and could not see a way to make it to the ridge where the rest of their friends were gathering. One demon let out a guttural growl and clawed Nate's leg as he made a sweeping kick toward it. The fiend's claws tore through clothes and skin alike, and Nate felt a sharp, burning pain that caused him to cry out. Delphene, who battled in her hybrid body, pivoted to defend him. Sweeping out with her long reach, she grabbed the offending demon by the head and used her supernatural strength to toss it over the cliff. While she did this, another winged imp leaped upon her and dug its claws into her back.

The advantage against her didn't last long. Nate quickly dispatched the creature with a dagger between the eyes. He caught the dagger as the imp turned to dust and moved on to the next one. Another demon that Delphene set upon screamed out as she ripped through its thin wings, and its dark ichor spilled on already slick earth beneath their feet.

Nate and Delphene continued to work in tandem for some time, taking out one demon after another, but their strength began waning. They could not go on like this for much longer, and the pair knew that they were only fighting now to give their friends the best chance possible.

The battle that Cade, Jarrett, and Collett faced was no better. Using fang and claw, Cade fought tirelessly at the doorway that Niall had created. Blocking the entrance, the close-quartered combat would not allow for his sword, but with his natural weapons, he wreaked devastation among the enemy in his effort to keep any more demons from entering the field. Blood trickled from various places on him, and the constant attacks were taking a toll. Even as a werewolf with extraordinary healing ability, Cade's body couldn't keep up with the constant barrage.

At one point, Cade was thrown back, and three of the hellish beasts made it through. They were immediately met with Jarrett's blade and blew to ash. Jarrett skillfully engaged any within range of his brother and Collett. More creatures made their way to the top of the cliff and fell to Jarrett's wrath. He almost seemed to relish in it, and the former demon hunter was so skilled, few made their way past him to Collett.

As they came at her, Collett battled ferociously, but she was struggling. The problem for her was not the few stray demons that made their way past Jarrett or Cade. Collett also fought a mental war

The Price of Knowing

against a sudden torrent of images jumping randomly through her mind.

There were bitter flashes in her mind of another battle, a different sunset, and a powerful storm. She kept getting pulled into the past while she battled fiercely for her future. Frustration plagued her. She wanted to remember so badly, knew it was coming back, but she had to push it away because it was so confusing, not to mention distracting. Collett needed to focus on staying alive and keeping her friends safe.

As Cynda and Rederrick made it to the top, they saw Jarrett yell savagely. His human voice turned to a growl as his back bent, cracking audibly as he shifted. His body twisted and morphed, his nose elongated, and teeth grew into deadly, sharpened points. Midnight-black fur spread to cover his entire form. Even in the throes of the change, he swung his sword wide and beheaded a creature coming at his back. When the metamorphosis into hybrid was finished, he looked directly at the running couple. His once golden eyes smoldered the bloody red of vengeance and rage. Despite knowing he was on their side, Cynda felt a chill run through her.

Jarrett felt the power and adrenaline that accompanied the change from man to beast course through him. He leaped into the fray, tearing through the enemy's ranks with cruel efficiency. He cleaved through the bloated form of one of the lesser underworld monsters, and he took off the head of another. Black ooze spilled to the ground as demons fell before him one by one.

Rederrick began to fight his way toward the half-man, half-wolf that was brutally beating back the enemy. He lifted his sword to attack the first one he met, but it was thrown away like nothing more than garbage by Jarrett. Without a glance at Rederrick, the black lycan moved on to the next demon. With a shrug, Rederrick merely moved in the opposite direction to vanquish another opponent.

~ 341 ~

Down on the western lower ridge, Nate and Delphene fought for their very lives. The demons began to encroach in on them more and more. They panted from extreme exertion. Shallow cuts and scrapes mottled both of them. A deep gash across Nate's forehead stung and trickled blood at a steady rate, and his body was slowing from blood loss. Delphene glanced at him, knowing at any moment they would be struck down. He could only smile at her with the same final truth reflected in his eyes.

It happened too fast for either of them to react. A behemoth sized demon came at him from behind and reached to grab him. Delphene's animal eyes widened with fear as she saw it coming, but two more swarmed her. Recognizing the warning for what it was, Nate knew he didn't have time to react properly. Instead, lunging forward with his sword, he ran it through the demon on her left to even the odds. He twisted the blade once, waiting for the ash, but he lost his grip before the demon fell to dust. The greater-demon yanked him from behind and dragged him away from her.

The nasty creature threw him to the ground and went back for Delphene, as two more monsters piled upon Nate. They began scraping and tearing at him. Suddenly, the soil beneath them vibrated. Grasses and weeds sprouted and shot from the earth like dancing vines. The living foliage wrapped around hands, feet, heads, and disfigured bodies, effectively restraining the monsters.

From out of nowhere, Nate heard Jeffery's voice, "You've got to get up to the others. Hurry!"

Delphene's breath heaved in and out as she searched for Jeffery, but she didn't see him right away. All the demons surrounding them were completely restrained by the entangling vegetation.

Finally, Nate pushed his tired body up and forced his weakened legs to move. He stumbled toward the top of the bluff, and Delphene didn't waste the reprieve. Getting a second wind, she ran full speed past him and reached the top just in time to see four more leeches scurry like spiders onto the top cliff to engage in the melee. Not even breaking her stride, she ran directly to them.

Jarrett had other ideas. He smelled more of the blood leeches coming and considered going after them, but pushed the instinct aside because he wanted someone else even more. He wanted Niall, and he intended to get to him first. He fought tirelessly, gaining ground with every creature that disintegrated in his wake. Blood and ash coated the ground. He locked eyes with Niall, and the sight revived his strength and renewed his purpose. He charged, forcing his way to the real monster.

CHAPTER 31

Niall surveyed the battle and ground his teeth. Unbelievably, and despite the odds against them, Collett's lap dogs were gaining ground against him. It was something he could not stand for. He locked eyes with the betrayer, the black wolf, who forced his way closer and closer. Even though he loved to feed off the chaos, such things must eventually end. Anger built within, and thunder overhead cracked like a gunshot.

Cynda knew she needed to close the demon doorways if they were to have any chance of ending this. She reached within herself and pulled magic from the depths of her resolve. She was tired already, feeling drained from the use of so much energy, and wasn't sure how she would find the strength to close the gates. However, she was determined to do what must be done. Despite all the noise and distractions of battle, she focused. Rederrick fought to defend her, and she went into a trance-like state as stinging rain poured from the sky.

"Powers from the east, west, north, and south, I call upon you at this time, at this place. Gates stand open from the darkest hole, and demon seed spill forth to challenge righteous grace. Close these gates, seal them tight, close the door, and stop this blight."

The door of light wavered, but the effort of trying to close the portal required too much energy from her, as she feared it would. She felt the drain and knew holding the magic could kill her. The realization that she could not close the gates with her will and strength alone stung, and she stubbornly refused to accept it.

Everyone would die if she didn't close the gates. In a war of numbers, they couldn't win—no matter how skilled they were. Sooner or later, they would tire. She refocused and repeated her chant, regardless of the risk. Her vision swam. She chanted tenaciously.

Something reached out to her then. No, not something, someone. She jumped back, almost losing her focus, until Jeffery shouted over the din of battle, "Hold the spell. Channel my strength."

She uttered her chant once again, feeling magic pour from her, and this time Jeffery chanted with her. He channeled his energies with hers as they had the night they created the unity pendants. Together, they began to feel the spell flow more freely.

The gate before them closed halfway. They chanted again and again, sacrificing more energy each time in the midst of chaos to force the magical openings closed. Already drained from before, Cynda felt her head spin. Feeling her waiver and knowing she controlled the spell, Jeffery forced more of his strength into her. The first doorway flickered, then faltered.

Cade moved away from the fading portal. The demons could no longer get through. For the first time, he turned toward the battlefield and assessed the dire situation they faced. His heart almost stopped. Delphene and Nate fought against four vampiric leeches, Cynda chanted her spell while Rederrick forced anything that tried to breach her circle back, and Collett battled fiercely against three demonsm while Jarrett left an oily, black trail on his way to Niall.

Cade didn't know which direction to go. It seemed everyone needed help. His heart wanted to help Collett, but she was holding her own. His head told him Rederrick would need backup the most, but Nate and Delphene were not looking great either.

As Cynda and Jeffery finished closing the gateways, they both felt depleted from the extended use of so much magical energy. Sweat dotted Cynda's brow, and her head pounded viciously. Her knees buckled, but strong, invisible hands kept her from crumpling. Her eyes widened when she saw what was heading for her. In that moment—a tenth of a second—she saw death approaching. A fiendish demon darted past Rederrick and charged toward her with a sharpened dagger raised. She watched, transfixed, as time slowed. The demon lifted the wretched blade to strike, and as it descended down, she knew no one could get there in time. She would die and readied herself for the final blow.

It never came. Instead of feeling the sharp sting of cold steel forcing its way into her chest, she heard a strange and terrible thump. She lost all thought as she stared into the demon's blood shot eyes. Her breath caught in her throat, and her heart clenched as the demon's perplexed expression was replaced by Jeffery suddenly materializing in front of her.

White as a sheet, pained shock covered his features. His chocolate brown eyes looked down at his body, and Cynda did the same. To her absolute horror, blood bloomed from the center of his chest where the dagger protruded. He jerked oddly as the demon viciously ripped the dagger free. Cynda screamed. Her cry was full of anguish and grief.

The two of them fell to the ground together, and Rederrick engaged the fiend. She pulled the young sorcerer into her lap and, cradling him, tried to offer reassurance as she wept.

Following his heart, Cade started toward Collett. Then he heard Cynda's tormented cry, and though it pained him, he changed direction. Grabbing his sword, Cade tore apart two demons in his path to them, but it was much too late. He reached them as Rederrick finished off the fiend that wielded the dagger. Looking down, he could see Jeffery lying in Cynda's lap as she pressed her hands to his chest, trying to staunch the steady flow of blood as it leaked through her slender fingers.

A smile curved Jeffery's lips as he sighed, "I did it."

"Did what?" she asked through her tears.

"I finally did something right—something good. Tell my mom, I love her," he begged with a strained whisper, and then he went limp.

Tears streaked down Cynda's dirty face as she held him. She wiped at them with blood stained hands, smearing it on her cheeks, and tried to think of ways to save him. She wouldn't let go.

"Please, Jeffery, stay with me!" she pleaded, cupping his face. "Please!"

From somewhere far away, she could hear Rederrick and Cade calling to her. She felt herself being dragged up to her feet, and she refocused her attention on Rederrick as he gently shook her. "He's gone, Cynda. He's gone."

"He saved me!" she sobbed.

"I know," he replied, crushing her to him. "I know, but I need you to pull it together. It's not over yet, and we need you."

Cynda looked around and saw Cade's dark shadow move and dance about them as he continued to fend off anything that might harm Rederrick or herself. She realized how her actions were affecting them all.

Grief turned to anger. She pulled it together and regained a small semblance of control. Sniffling, she met Rederrick's worried expression once more and nodded.

"That's my girl," he said kindly and kissed her forehead. Giving her arms a firm squeeze one more time, he said with a fierce gleam in his eye, "Pay them back!" He handed her the very dagger that struck the killing blow against Jeffery. The young sorcerer's crimson blood still stained the blade.

Having dispatched any immediate threat, Cade ran to them and encouraged, "For Jeffery." She saw in his glowing red eyes that he too felt grief over the loss of their new friend, but he knew there was no time to grieve. If they lived through this, they would do that later.

Cade saw determination enter her eyes. Cynda let her grief and need for justice fuel her, giving her new strength. She did exactly as Cade and Rederrick told her. She paid the hellions back. Cynda plunged the dagger into the first demon she encountered and sent magical flames through it. The creature screamed and writhed as it died. She sharply ripped the blade free and moved into the melee.

Cade fought with a weight in his chest for the loss of Jeffery, but he used that pain to fight on as well. He mutilated and thrashed through several more of the enemy ranks. He decapitated a vampiric demon, and it fell in a cloud of dust. The beast in him clawed and slashed as the man in him rushed to where he last saw Collett.

Cade began to hope they could actually win. The knowledge that they were turning the tide sent a rush of adrenaline coursing through him. He leaped upon another greater demon, bore it down, and tore through its neck with his powerful jaws.

The Price of Knowing

Jarrett was almost to his goal. Only a few more feet and it would be just him and Niall. His body hummed with excited energy.

He saw his target within reach and watched as Niall extended his hand. Niall's other arm lifted upward, and Jarrett felt his feet leave the ground. Surprise and indignation rushed through him.

He twisted and struggled against the force lifting him. It had been a long time since someone had been able to use magic against him. Instinctively, he reached for his amulet and found it hot and burning against his hide. The magic was too strong. It overpowered the effects of his amulet. In his life, he knew only one other person that had been able to circumvent the amulet's protection completely. He turned his head to find Collett on the battlefield.

He didn't have a chance to find her. His focus faltered when he felt the strangest sensation. His breath caught in his throat; a burning chill crawled through him. It snaked throughout his body, freezing and clenching the muscles within as it passed. He tried hard to fight against it.

The wicked cold burned as it touched him. He couldn't think beyond his shock, so his instincts took over. He locked his hate-filled eyes on Niall. He twisted and strained against the paralyzing hold on him.

His rebellious reaction did him little good. His growl immediately turned into a howlish scream that rent the air as a pain worse than any he had ever felt lanced through him. His body shifted and twisted against his will, becoming a man once again. Niall magically forced him back into his most vulnerable state. He felt the frigid spell move up and curl around his heart. He choked briefly, and his howling cry caught in his throat. The icy fingers tightened their grip on his heart and began to squeeze.

Everyone, demons, humans, and lycans stopped mid-battle when Jarrett's scream of pure agony reached their ears. Following the tortured sound, Cade stopped his rampage and looked up to find his brother, once more a man, hanging in mid-air and screaming out in pain.

His heart pounded against his ribs as he heard his brother's cry, and Cade watched as Jarrett twisted desperately in the air. He knew the tormentor immediately. His eyes flamed brighter. With little thought, he ran full speed toward Niall. Rage filled Cade completely, and Niall's attention moved from Jarrett to Cade. Displaying a sinister smirk on his face, he smiled with wicked pleasure.

In a distant part of her mind, Collett registered the melee resuming, but she couldn't see it. The dam had broken, and she was in a different place. The images, hidden for so long, slammed into her full force. No matter how she tried, she could not block the assault she suffered upon seeing Jarrett dying before her eyes. A tidal wave of memories flooded her mind, obliterating the subconscious wall that had been imposed on her as punishment. A punishment she willingly accepted, and one only Justice could have inflicted.

Image after image poured into her mind, each one clicking into place like pieces of an enormous puzzle. Memories and thoughts coalesced into cohesive pictures.

She staggered backward and would have fallen if not for Rederrick, who rushed up behind her. Catching her, he eased her down as she pressed her hands into her eyes, trying to quell the storm raging through her mind.

Jarrett cried out again, and the storm ebbed. As quickly as the bombardment began, it ended, and everything was clear. For the first time in almost three years, Collett understood her purpose.

Victory knew who, and what, she was.

The Price of Knowing

She stood. Rederrick spoke to her, but she didn't hear it clearly. His words were distant, tinny, and unimportant to her then. Looking up, she could see Jarrett, who was writhing in pain, and her stomach clutched. He was dying. She knew it. Felt it. Everything was happening exactly as she foresaw in her dreams. Only now, she knew what to do.

She searched for Cade, who relentlessly forced his way to Niall with only one intention in mind. Demon after demon fell before him as he desperately fought to reach his enemy and save his brother. Her heart pounded with fear. Letting go of the fear, and knowing she was not helpless, Collett reached within and felt her power surge.

She locked her eyes upon the betrayer and felt warmth spread as the power filled her completely. She shouted with a voice that magically carried and echoed, "Bellig! You will not have them!" She thrust her hand out.

Everyone watched white-hot power fly from her fingertips, harmlessly over Cade, and strike Niall directly in the chest. He was thrown back several feet but remained upright. The attack did succeed as she intended, and forced him to lose focus. As a result, he lost his grip on Jarrett, who fell to the ground, limp and lifeless, with a horrible thud.

Her brilliant power and amplified voice caused shock to ripple through the entire circle of friends. Cade pulled up short, gripping earth to quell his momentum, and turned to look back at her in wonder.

Rederrick and Cynda could only stand in complete disbelief with astonished expressions. The two remaining vampires fighting, Nate and Delphene covered their ears and shrieked as if the sound of her voice hurt them, but neither Nate nor Delphene took advantage of the opportunity to easily kill them because they too could do nothing more than stare at her.

Collett eased away from Rederrick, smiled at her stunned friend, and turned back to her enemy. "You are a traitor, Bellig."

~ 351 ~

C.B. Haight

"That is not my name, and it is you who betrayed me!" he spat back across the torn field.

"You have broken the rules and forsaken your purpose, betraying us all."

"You break them now; you interfere again. Have you not learned?"

She continued as if his accusation was nothing to her, "I will not allow this any longer. You will not take them! None of them! They are mine to protect. To have them, you will have to get through me."

She rapidly spoke words of protection in the most ancient language, a dialect only her enemy understood. "Gamentea sy! Senoa sy lethan!" Brilliant, blinding light surrounded her and expanded until it encompassed the entire bluff.

Everyone shielded their eyes, and any remaining demons caught within the radius of the glow screeched horribly before turning to dust.

Collett strode forward, and with each confident step, the light began to dissipate.

When he could finally see once more, Cade could barely fathom the sight before him. Collett met his eyes as she passed him, making her way to Niall. Cade perceived that hers were different somehow. The pale, blue eyes he knew so well conveyed her love to him with a single glance, but he also saw they were hardened, fierce.

What is happening? he wondered. His brows furrowed as he tried to process the event.

Her eyes were not the only difference. When the glow around her was bearable, everyone witnessed that Collett walked forward with the smooth, fluid strides of a warrior. Her once loose hair no longer flowed in the wind. It was bound in an exotic, complex braid. She had manifested armor that appeared to be made of gold and silver, but even that description did the brilliant, shining attire little justice. Intricate symbols were etched into the breastplate that covered a silvery mail shirt. Pristine bracers protected her forearms,

~ 352 ~

The Price of Knowing

and glistening grieves covered her shins. An aura of light radiated around her, and the metal glinted because of it.

Most impressive of all was the long sword she carried in her capable hand. The shining blade flashed as she spun it threateningly in her practiced grip. As if it was crafted by divine power, the forged steel shone like a ray from the sun that had been plucked from the sky. She gripped the stunning weapon with a firm, steady hand as naturally as if she had been born with it there.

The entire party watched as this stranger with Collett's face advanced across the empty battlefield.

Niall smiled with grim satisfaction and murmured, "Ah, there you are."

Black mists enveloped him and snaked across earth, weaving through the tall grasses and covering rocks on the ground. When the darkness touched Cade's feet, he felt as if icy fingers reached for him. As the frigid fog retreated back to Niall, it revealed a warrior that appeared to be dressed in the devil's own armor.

Niall completely contrasted Collett. His eerie, black armor blended with the darkness of the night. It also bore symbols engraved in the breastplate, but the carvings pulsed with a light red tint and gave the impression they carried a depraved, sinister meaning. He lifted his arm, and they could all see the massive, red-bladed sword. It too seemed to pulse, much like a heartbeat, as he wielded it in his hands. Cruel intent shone in his evil eyes.

With a battle cry, Collett charged. Impossibly, she leaped the final distance to reach him, and lifting her sword high, she swung down with the full momentum of her maneuver. As the magnificent blades crossed, sparks flew and an unearthly ring reverberated all around them.

The initial blow vibrated down both combatants' arms, and the long-awaited battle between the warriors commenced. Collett blocked and parried, slashed and spun. They danced to a deadly rhythm only they could hear. Their movements were so quick and fluid, it was captivating.

C.B. Haight

After watching for more than a minute, Cynda, Rederrick, Nate, and Delphene made their way to where Cade helped a weakened, but conscious, Jarrett to his feet.

Rederrick supported Jarrett's other side, and Cade ordered, "Get Cody." He nodded in the direction of the unconscious man still lying where Niall, or *Bellig*, dropped him on the cold earth.

Delphene nodded her wolfish head at him, indicating she would take care of it. She rushed to Cody and easily lifted him in her arms. Cody groaned but otherwise remained unresponsive, so she made her way back to the tree line where the others stood watching the battle unfold.

Collett's new friends watched in amazement as the swords rang out each time they struck. Collett glided around Bellig and swiped her sword out as she passed, cutting his arm and drawing first blood. Niall whipped around angrily and thrust out hard, but he met only air because she had continued her graceful motion to end where she began.

Jarrett finally gained his feet, though they were still unsteady, and seeing the combat, he began to ask, "What'd I—"

Cade looked to him with mixed emotions of confusion, fear, and worry. "I'm not sure."

"She remembers," Cynda said in awe.

CHAPTER 32

Searching for the each other's weaknesses, the two combatants pulled back and circled one another again.

"You have betrayed your purpose! We are the protectors, not the destroyers!" Collett accused.

"No, I have found my purpose!" he spat back with venom.

"Killing and manipulating the innocent—the very souls you were charged to protect?"

"There is no need for this," Bellig chided in a placating tone. "Join us, realize your potential. Take your rightful place at my side. We are as gods. We are perfection. We should not be enslaved to mankind. You must know the truth by now."

"How did you get so lost? How could you forget your promises?" she inquired sadly.

"Lost? I am not lost. I am found! I have shaken the bonds of my enslavement."

"This must end, one way or another. You know this!"

"Agreed," he said with an eager expression, and began his advance once more.

"I am as you once were, and should still be," she declared, her voice carrying across the field. Conviction sounded in her tone, confidence showed in her stance.

"You are as I *once* was, and you will die this night," he taunted as he struck out at her from the side.

She expertly blocked the impending strike and shifted away from the wicked red blade. "Maybe," she said, "but not before I take you with me." Using only her left hand, Collett sliced through the air with a backhanded maneuver. Her enemy twisted away, and she barely grazed his armor with the very tip of her sword.

Quick as a snake, Niall turned the opposite direction and swiped low at her feet with his leg. She jumped over it, and he came in with that wicked blade. She dodged, whirling left, but before she could counter, he threw his elbow back, smashing it into her face.

Collett reeled and tasted blood. "You're weak," he taunted as he advanced. She blocked his sword as it came down hard, and he let his weapon scrape against hers, sliding down its length. Niall cleverly struck at her side. Twisting her grip, she stopped him again, and colliding steel sang. "If only you would have listened before, you would be so much more," he said with disgust.

Collett kicked him hard. Light burst between them, and he stumbled back. She spat blood from her mouth and advanced on him again.

Jarrett had just pulled on pants from his pack when Bellig hit Collett in the face. Cade tried to surge forward. Leaving the shirt, Jarrett jumped on him, and they struggled. Feeling more animal than man, Cade growled, and a whine escaped his muzzle. "Stop, Cade. Think about what you're doing," Jarrett demanded.

The Price of Knowing

Irritation, fear, and bewilderment emanated from his brother, but Jarrett knew his twin could not stand against the being he'd known as Niall. He had felt the power himself and couldn't allow Cade to get himself killed.

"I won't stand back and do nothing while my wife battles that devil!" Cade countered as he pushed Jarrett away.

"What will you do? That is not your Collett out there! She knows him. She called him by a different name even. Look at her, Cade. Really look! She looks like Joan of Arc or an avenging angel. She cleared the battlefield of every demon and leech in less than five seconds. What could you possible do that she can't—bleed on him?"

He *was* looking. Cade saw what Jarrett saw, but she was still his wife, his everything. Even if he died tonight, he couldn't leave her alone in this.

"Trust me when I tell you that you can't take him. I've never experienced that kind of pain in my life," Jarrett admitted while rubbing his chest. "There are forces here we don't understand. I should be dead right now, but he arrogantly prolonged my suffering for his own pleasure."

The ring of swords pulled their attention back to the intense conflict between dark and light. Collett blocked blow after blow. Bellig forced her back step after step using brute strength, but she danced around him, making up for her weakness with creativity and finesse.

She twirled and spun, leaped and thrust, cleverly keeping his sword at bay while striking at him an equal number of times. Bellig thrust out with his red blade, and she narrowly avoided it by flipping backward. He swung his weapon in wide arcs as he pursued her athletic feats.

Despite her returned powers, Collett was at a disadvantage. Not only had Bellig always been stronger, but he also knew her—he'd taught her. He anticipated her every move. She struggled to keep up with him.

Collett's sweat-dampened hair stuck to her head, and her breathing grew more labored. Her arms ached while he was rested. She had fought with demons from his portals while he sat back and watched. The repeated blocks and parries against his strikes were costing her. Every time their swords connected, he weakened her further. She had to outmaneuver him, but she couldn't find an opening.

She risked a desperate glance back to Cade and the others. Collett knew they needed to get to safety in case she couldn't win the battle. The distraction cost her. Niall slashed his razor-sharp blade across her belly. She jumped back, barely avoiding the killing blow, but her reaction was still too slow. His enhanced blade cut through her armor and grazed her skin.

Stinging pain traveled through her, but she couldn't give up. Grunting, she kicked out and made contact with his thigh. He only stumbled back a few steps, and he advanced again with an arrogant smile.

Seeing the strike, Cade refused to stand idle any longer. Together, they would be stronger than she was alone. "Get them out of here!" he barked fiercely to no one specific as he charged toward Collett.

Feeling the same way, despite his earlier speech, Jarrett called forth the wolf once more. With a glance back to make sure Delphene was helping the others escape, he followed his twin to what he was sure would be their death. The brothers charged furiously toward the constantly clashing blades. As he drew near, Cade felt adrenaline surge through him and used it to increase his momentum.

When he reached the border of the conflict, Cade rebounded off of a strong magical barrier. His muscles jerked as he yelped in pain and fell back into Jarrett, who would have hit the invisible wall a second later if Cade hadn't crashed into him.

Cade felt as if he'd been electrocuted. His muscles twinged, but he stubbornly got to his feet. He tried to reach her from a different angle and found himself repelled once more. He howled and charged again.

She heard him growling and yelping in his efforts, but she couldn't help them. She cringed inwardly at the sounds but forced herself to focus. Her heart raced as she accepted the outcome that suddenly flashed into her mind. She knew if she deviated from the path before her Cade and Jarrett would die.

The brothers were not prepared to face Bellig. They weren't strong enough, not yet. Her old mentor had grown in power over the centuries, and he was even stronger than she realized. He sent waves of malevolent emotions at her and attacked her from every direction.

She had been undefeated in battle for centuries, but he'd had a millennium. She saw no gap in his defenses. Up, down, and to the side, he met her each time, and their swords sparked as they clashed.

She tried to retreat back and gain ground, but he made an attempt to disarm her with a circling motion. She barely managed to counter it. Collett spun and tried to come at him as she had before, but he anticipated the strike and went the opposite way, stopping her before she could come around. She shot him with her white fire. He jerked as it hit him in the shoulder, but he continued to press in on her.

She was losing. Cade could see it. It tore at him to see her struggle while he watched helplessly. She was so close! He tried penetrating the barrier for a fourth time and fell to his knees when the shock radiated through him. Every muscle in his body twitched at this point, but he refused to give in.

Jarrett grabbed him and pulled him to his feet. He jerked Cade around to face him. "Why did you marry her?" he demanded, referring to their previous conversation.

"I love her!" he pledged with his heart breaking.

"I see what it is now—love," Jarrett said, putting something in Cade's hand. Cade looked down to his clawed, beastly grip to find the green gem Jarrett always wore with a broken gold chain hanging from it. These last weeks, Jarrett watched Cade risk everything for Collett, himself, and their friends, and he finally understood selfless love. "It requires sacrifice and courage."

He'd tried the boundary twice himself and felt the rippling energy attack his body. The magic that created it was strong, but Jarrett believed that with the amulet combined with the power of Cade's love for Collett, his brother could pass through. "It was our mother's, given to Rowena. Now I give it to you. It can only help one of us. Don't stop till you're through! It's only a buffer to ease the shock," Jarrett explained.

Cade looked back up to his brother, surprised, and nodded once in gratitude.

"Go!" Jarrett ordered, but Cade was already moving.

Gripping the gem tightly in his hand and using all of his strength, Cade ran full force toward his wife. He felt the magical sting as he encountered the barrier. For a couple of seconds, he couldn't break through, but his desperation to reach the woman he loved and the enchanted amulet helped him defy the pain and conquer the mystical wall. Growling violently, he pushed through. Cade howled in satisfaction and rushed to save Collett.

They both heard Cade. Collett hesitated, and Bellig grinned. He swiped down at her with his red blade again and taunted callously, "Determined, isn't he? Let's be rid of him." He began lifting his hand as he had done with Jarrett, and feeling the cold brush by her, Collett recognized his intentions.

Everything around her cleared. Having her memories restored, Collett understood her purpose. She knew the time had come to finish this.

With regret in her eyes, she glanced at Cade charging toward them, and within a single beat of the heart, she conveyed her plan and her love.

The Price of Knowing

He ran faster. "No," he growled, "Collett!"

Resolved, Collett focused on her opponent, charged, and cried out, "You will not take him!" Her actions drew his full attention back to her.

The distraction worked as she knew it would. In the distant past, they had once fought side by side. In recent centuries, they had been at war against each other. The history they shared gave her enough insight to defeat him, but Collett understood the price required to accomplish her goal.

She used his arrogance against him. He had accurately predicted her in battle enough times for Collett to understand he could guess how she would react to a threat against Cade. As she charged, he thrust up high. She could have spun away, but it would have defeated her purpose. With their combined momentum, Bellig's red blade of death impaled Collett through her chest.

Time practically stopped for Cade, who was so close, yet still too far. He watched in horror as the wicked sword slid effortlessly into the woman he loved. Collett's body curled around the invasive steel. Cade cried out in agony, fear, and grief, "Collett!" He froze briefly, and his breath caught in his throat.

Her eyes widened at the sensation of the blade invading her body. She choked as pain erupted in her chest. Bellig grinned with satisfaction, but his grin was short lived as a strange awareness traveled through him.

Collett had out maneuvered him. He looked down, stunned to find the pommel of her weapon protruding from his middle, right beneath his ribs. He watched in horror as the ancient symbol on its hilt pulsed with light.

Lifting his chin, he locked onto her iridescent blue eyes—eyes that had always captivated him. His mind flashed back to a time, centuries before, when he still saw innocence in their depths—a time when he believed she could love him.

~ 361 ~

"Who are we?" Collett asked him. He found her youthful virtue and vibrance endearing.

"Silly child, I am Strength, you are Victory," he answered, smiling.

She laughed. "No, I mean what *are we?"*

"Ah, well then, we are the guardians, my dear."

"You are to teach me then? Teach me what it is to be a guardian?"

"I will teach you all you need and more."

The memory faded, and he could again see her as she was now. She stood as a fierce warrior before him, unafraid of her impending death. Blood trickled from her mouth, past her soft, pink lips, as she tried to speak.

Collett uttered her words with a gurgling whisper only he could hear, "I am..." she tried. Then, more forcefully, she said, "I am the Guardian Victory! A protector of all that is good and a beacon of hope. You will *not* have them!" As she finished, Collett used the very last bit of her strength to drive her blade deeper into him with a twisting motion, tearing and shredding his insides as she did.

Surprised, horror covered Niall's features. He gasped.

She grimaced.

He tried to breathe, but his breath would not come.

She closed her eyes and felt a light breeze on her face.

Desperate to free himself, Bellig stumbled back, pulling away from the burning blade embedded in his body. His backward movement violently ripped his own sword from her chest. He roared in pain, anger, and defeat.

Without so much as a whimper, Collett crumpled to the cold earth. Horrified, Bellig continued to backpedal. Suddenly, a heavy, black mist appeared and enveloped him. It carried him away before Cade arrived to fall beside his beloved Collett.

Raw emotion consumed Cade completely. He felt his heart shattering. His body reacted without any thought, and he changed

The Price of Knowing

into a man. With despair and grief clawing at him, he gently scooped her limp form into his arms. Pulling her close and rocking her, he cried, "No, no, no. NO!" He reached down and covered the wound with his human hand, much like Cynda did with Jeffery. "Please," he begged, "you can't go."

Collett tried to look at him, but she was too weak. A white space was pulling her in, and an airy feeling crept over her. Her hands felt so light it was as if they were no longer there. She wanted to tell him it was all right because it didn't hurt, but the words would not come out, or even form on her lips. She tried desperately to tell him she loved him, but her lips would not obey.

She felt his gentle touch as he brought her head to his lips. She heard his whispered plea, "Please, Collett. Please, I love you. Come back," but she could not heed his call. Her last breath shuddered out on a sigh, and Cade gave into sobbing as only a broken man could.

He didn't even register the sound of footfalls behind him. He didn't notice Cynda falling to the ground beside him to cry out her denial upon seeing Collett's sightless eyes, or see Rederrick drag Cynda up to envelop her as he shared her grief. He definitely didn't feel Jarrett's supporting hand on his shoulder or notice the bitter regret evident on his brother's face. For Cade, there was only pain—horrible, heart wrenching pain.

Nate watched Delphene, with Cody still cradled in her arms, quietly make her way to where the group gathered to mourn. He scanned what was once a peaceful place, but was now a bloody battlefield. He saw no sign of the demons that had rained down upon them so recently.

It was over, but not one of them felt victory in their hearts. Nate's eyes paused on Jeffery's body, which still lay where he fell. He looked to Cynda, sobbing into Rederrick's chest.

He felt the air around him stir, and he watched Delphene carefully lay the battered Cody on the ground. He could see sorrow in her wolfish features. Nate turned his attention to the grieving

C.B. Haight

Cade and then hung his head in lamentation. He thought, *No, there was no victory here.*

Minutes passed. No one moved. It was so startling, so final. The secrets that plagued them regarding Collett's powers, her past, and her connection to The Faction's demented leader would forever remain a mystery.

After a long time, Jarrett met Rederrick's gaze, and his new friend acknowledged him with a tight nod. Without speaking, they understood each other. Rederrick whispered into Cynda's ear. "Come on," he urged. Sniffling, she clung to him tightly as they began the long walk back to camp.

Nate left them and walked across the uneven ground to Jeffery's body. Shaking his head and bending down, he lifted Jeffery's shell up over his shoulder to carry him back so there could be a proper burial. He noted Delphene was also heading down to the camp with Cody in her arms once more.

Poor Cody, he thought. Despite the fact that The Faction's leader was gone, it was disheartening to realize they weren't even certain the kid would live. The sacrifices they made to save him may not even pay off. Lost in his own sadness, it was difficult for Nate to see any justice in the situation.

The twins were left alone to mourn. Two brothers brought together by one woman, who had irrevocably changed their lives. Cade continued to rock his wife and allowed his emotions to consume him. He tenderly caressed Collett's peaceful face, and pressed his lips to her forehead.

No, he thought guilt-ridden. *Not this way. Not so soon. We should have had an eternity together. It was my job to keep her safe.*

He stayed like that for a long time. He couldn't think. He couldn't move. He felt a sharp, crippling pain cut at him as if the blade had gone through his own heart. Even breathing was painful, and all Cade could do was hold her.

Jarrett retrieved their gear without Cade even noticing. He grabbed a coarse blanket that was for first aid purposes and laid it

The Price of Knowing

over his brother's shoulders. There was still no response from the grief-stricken man.

After donning his second pair of jeans and a t-shirt, Jarrett made sure to pull out his sunglasses to cover up his own suffering. He then stood over Cade, silently protecting and supporting his twin like never before. He waited, and he would continue waiting for as long as Cade needed.

Jarrett knew better than anyone the bitterness of having a life stolen from you. He imagined that, for Cade, the loss of his wife was debilitating.

The men stayed upon the peak for a long time. Hours later, Jarrett looked up and saw the blackness of the night sky begin to lighten through a heavy fog that blocked the sunrise. *Always darkness*, he thought. He'd endured centuries without caring, without hope, and now he could feel again—because of her. Jarrett cursed.

Cade looked up with raw pain evident in his eyes. Jarrett knew this would be the darkest day in his brother's life, and that more would follow. He regretted that lasting happiness eluded them both as if it was not meant for them. He said nothing to reassure his twin, because he knew personally there were no words to ease the deep ache.

Jarrett tilted his head to the pack sitting between them. "Let's take her back." Seeing the pack for the first time, Cade turned back to Collett and laid her down with a reverent gentleness. He barely took his eyes off her as he eased into the new shirt and pants provided. He thought he could believe she was sleeping—wanted to believe it. However, the violent wound through her shining armor and the crimson stain on the ground below her wouldn't allow him the delusion.

Cade bent to pick up the discarded blanket to wrap her in, but was distracted by an odd sound coming from Jarrett. He looked toward his brother as a strong wind descended upon them. The

~ 365 ~

waves began crashing more violently below, and the fog thickened around them as the sun continued to rise.

The brothers watched as an ethereal, white mist formed all around Collett's body. The armor she wore glowed subtly before fading away. She was left in virginal, white clothing marred by crimson blood that soaked her chest.

In the next second, mist spread over her entire form, and she began to dissipate, fading away to be pulled into the swirling wind. As soon as Cade realized what was happening, he dove for her and tried to pull her back into his arms, but his hands merely passed through the vapors.

Collett was gone. The brothers could only stare in disbelief as she was completely taken from them. The only evidence she had ever existed was a magnificent, silvery sword and a copper medallion once worn with pride.

EPILOGUE

One week later-

It all tasted bitter to him, the flowers, the music, the people. None of it was comforting or helpful. All of it was wrong. It was a beautiful service, but there should be no service. She should still be here with them. Cynda and Rederrick had made the arrangements, even insisting on a coffin for proper closure and to keep suspicions to a minimum. It hardly mattered to him. Let people think whatever they wanted. She was gone, and he felt sure nothing would really matter again.

He half-heartedly listened as Rederrick spoke of love, sacrifice, God and Heaven, but none of it helped. He only hurt more. His friends were all there with him, standing under the canopy of a darkened sky with a sad, drizzling rain pouring out from weeping clouds.

Jeffery's mother and a few of her friends stood together. A few members of The Brotherhood also came to offer support. They included Rory, who'd been undercover with The Faction, and Darrin from Dallas.

Ashley stood in the comfort of Nate's embrace with tears streaking down her cheeks, and James held his mother's hand on one side while Tracy grasped the other. Delphene, loyal and strong, stayed close to Jarrett, whom had remained with Cade since he had lost the best and most important thing in his entire life.

Cade could only stare absently at the empty, golden coffin next to the shiny, black one that held Jeffery's body. There were no words that could possibly ease the empty ache in his chest. He closed his eyes, trying to compose himself and remain strong.

He felt someone squeeze his shoulder. He turned his head and saw Jarrett holding out a white rose. His brother was the only one who didn't offer him empty words, and the only one Cade believed understood. The twins had finally forged the bond that Collett wished for them.

Cade looked down at the rose as Jarrett tilted his head toward the caskets, indicating it was time for final goodbyes. He'd been so lost in thought that he didn't even realize Rederrick had finished speaking. He looked back to his brother and wrapped his fingers around the fragile stem of the flower. "I'm not ready," he whispered.

"I know," Jarrett replied sympathetically.

Cade looked around to his friends and then moved toward the coffin. He ran his fingertips across the smooth, shiny surface. Then he brought those fingers to his lips and, kissing them, he transferred the kiss back to the golden casket. He stared at the engraving of the unity symbol from Cynda's and Jeffery's conjured medallion for several minutes. He decided the symbol was wrong; it should have two missing links in the circle. Their group was broken, and there was a hole in his heart.

With a trembling hand, Cade lay the first of two dozen white roses upon Collett's symbolic tomb.

He watched Jeffery's mother move up next, and with tears streaking her face, she bent and kissed her son's coffin. Then mimicking Cade, she placed a purple rose on the black and silver casket. *Cynda did a good job with planning every detail,* he thought. *Jeffery would have liked the colors.* He looked at the white rose again and knew Collett would have liked them as well. He felt pain overwhelm him once more.

The Price of Knowing

He swallowed hard, choking back the grief, but he missed a single tear that escaped before doing so. It made a path down his roughly whiskered cheek before he realized it was there and wiped it away. Finally, after several minutes, he stepped back so Cynda could follow him. He watched her place a rose on each casket, and then Rederrick did the same.

Others shuffled forward, repeating the gesture, each laying a single rose upon Collett's coffin, and then one on Jeffery's. Tracy stepped forward next, then Ashley and James, each one of them met his eyes with compassion and sorrow displayed within his or her own. Their mourning did not lessen his.

Cade couldn't help thinking that Jenny should be present too, but she still lay comatose. She was another victim of an unknown monster.

After everyone took their turn paying their respects, Jarrett stood alone. Behind dark glasses, his eyes roamed over the people around him. He still couldn't believe how recent events had led him here. He was surrounded by people that actually cared for one another, cared enough to protect and die for each other. Strangely, he was now a part of that team. He also finally understood the sacrifice that Rowena made for him all those years before. She died so he could live, not merely survive, as he'd been doing for centuries. She would want him to live, and he realized Collett had wanted the same for him all along. *No, not only me*, he thought. She wanted that for all of them. Collett had selflessly given her own life so they could have theirs.

Awkwardly, he stepped forward, and like Cade, he held only a single white rose. Jarrett took another hesitant step, feeling uncomfortable but not out of place. He reflected on all he had learned these last few weeks. In witnessing Collett and Cade's love and devotion for one another, as well as the loyalty and dedication within the family as a whole, Jarrett finally found the inner peace he'd sought for so long. For the first time, he was a part of

~ 369 ~

something good. Unfortunately, the cost of his discovery was much too high.

Looking down at the golden coffin, he laid the perfect white rose atop the others. "I didn't hate you. I hated me," he uttered softly. "Thank you for everything."

With his sensitive hearing, Cade was the only one who heard his brother's confession, and he understood its meaning perfectly.

When Jarrett looked up again, their identical gazes met. Cade inclined his head, and Jarrett mimicked the gesture. Staring at each other through dark glasses, they knew everything had changed. For they weren't simply men working together to seek vengeance against a common enemy anymore. They weren't only lycanthropes with common ancestry either. They weren't even merely brothers. In the most difficult trial they ever faced, they found understanding and forgiveness. They found each other. For the first time since birth, Cade and Jarrett bonded, and they were finally friends.

"It's not over," stated the dark-haired Selena, who watched the funeral unfold from a distance.

"No," agreed the other woman softly.

"Can it be done?" Selena questioned.

The woman in white smiled wistfully as she watched the two brothers and knew their thoughts. "Now it can." Her smile widened as she watched the scene play out before her. In a gesture of brotherhood and trust, Jarrett placed his hand on Cade's shoulder. "Yes, it definitely can," she said with confidence.

Looking over to the tree where the woman in white stood, Selena watched as she faded away. "I hope so, for everyone's sake," she muttered to herself.

The Price of Knowing

**Turn the page for a sneak peek at book three in
The Powers of Influence:**

THE TRUTH OF VICTORY

Only a few days after the private funeral of one Jeffery Garrison, in which the police department had not been permitted to attend, Detective Hall pulled his unmarked car up to a beautiful house situated within the beautiful Rocky Mountains of Colorado. Fairly new to Colorado, he still found himself struck by the majesty of the mountains here. He was new to the department, having recently arrived from Texas. He couldn't quite get used to the cold either. As he parked the car, he couldn't help but admire the grand estate owned by Rederrick James Williams and his wife, Cynda Esther Williams.

He came here in search of the truth.

His new partner, Detective Peterson, shook his head and whistled. "Damn. You got to give the guy credit. He sure knows how to pick a good spot."

"Stay focused, buddy. This house and the polish on it means nothing. It's just another way to pull the wool over our eyes. There's something off about their story, and I intend to find out what."

"You sure you want to do this? I mean, the guy's a lawyer. You may be asking for trouble," Peterson asked sincerely.

Hall considered the question, and his gut twisted. He knew he was toeing the line here, but the whole situation smelled to him. He wanted more, and he wasn't quite ready to let it go yet.

"I'm sure. We've got ourselves one body, one kid who took a worse beating than I've ever seen in all my life, and one housekeeper that has yet to wake up from a coma. There's more to this than they are telling us, and I want to find out what." He didn't mention to his partner that he had attended the funeral and seen two coffins. You didn't tell your new partner things that could get him fired if he knew. Looking into the funeral had been against orders. But the whole damn thing stunk of lies. Two caskets for one body was simply evidence of that.

"Could be as they said, a drug deal gone bad. The captain buys it."

Hall shook his head. "Well, I'm not buying it."

"All right, it's you neck. You want to stick it on the chopping block, I'm your partner, I'll try to keep the ax from coming down on ya."

They got out of the car and made their way to the front door together. It wasn't long after they knocked that a tall, young man in military dress came to the door. He had chestnut brown hair, and though he was lanky, he was clearly in shape. Detective Hall's mind automatically recognized him as James Randall Williams, the youngest of Cynda and Rederrick's three children. He began mentally ticking off facts he knew about James.

Twenty-two years old, almost twenty-three. Some sort of an electronics whiz. He was a sergeant in the U.S. Army and brother to two sisters, Tracy and Ashley.

James answered the door with a smile that Hall noticed faltered, ever so slightly, when he saw who was on the other side.

"Mr. Williams," Hall said with a nod.

"Detective. What I can do for you?" James questioned kindly enough, but there was a clear edge in his tone.

"Can we come in for a minute?"

"Of course you can," Cynda said coming into the foyer. She touched James on the arm. "James, go get some coffee for these gentlemen, will you? Then let your dad know Detective Hall and Detective Peterson are here."

The two officers stepped over the threshold as Cynda opened it wider and gestured them in. They followed her into the parlor where she sat primly upon the edge of her couch in a way that Hall had to admire her class. Peterson took one of the winged back chairs and practically flopped on it.

"I appreciate your time, Mrs. Williams."

"No problem, I assure you. What can I do for you?"

"Actually, I came to see Cade Werren. It's my understanding he stays here with you."

He saw a sharpness to her sea green eyes, but then it was gone. "Well, he does, on occasion, stay here."

Ah it is a problem, he thought.

"What do you need Cade for?" she asked, adding the right amount of sweetness to her tone.

"I just have a few routine questions for him. Is he here?"

"No, he's not," came a deep, menacing reply from the entrance to the parlor.

Hall turned. He first thought it was Cade speaking as Hall had only met him once before. However, when he looked closer, he knew it wasn't. He met angry, golden eyes belonging to the most intimidating man he ever saw. He kept his expression plain, not giving away a thing. Standing, he offered his hand, "Excuse me, I'm not sure we've met."

"We haven't," Jarrett said rudely and walked across the room to stand behind the couch where Cynda sat.

James brought in a tray and handed the detectives each a mug. He lifted a cup of tea for his mother and then sat with her on the couch.

Eyeing Jarrett carefully, Hall took his seat once more.

"Detectives, this is Jarrett. He's Cade's brother," Cynda explained, trying to keep things easy and normal.

"Ah that's right, Jarrett Hunter," Hall said easily, feigning ignorance.

"That's right," Jarrett replied.

"Strange that you two would have different last names, seeing as you're obviously twins," Peterson injected.

Tilting his head, Jarrett actually grinned with arrogance. "We were adopted."

"Ah, detectives," Rederrick said. He came in and shook both of their hands companionably. "What can we do for you today?"

"We were just discussing that," Peterson told him.

"We would like to have a word with Cade Werren," Hall added.

"Oh?" Rederrick answered with an easy curiosity, but Hall didn't miss the steel in his eyes either.

You're a cool one, Hall thought.

"Jarrett has informed the detective that Cade is unavailable," Cynda explained.

"While that's true, perhaps we can help," Rederrick replied.

"Do you know where he is at this time?"

"No," Jarrett said firmly, before anyone else could answer. Rederrick closed his mouth and swallowed his more diplomatic reply.

"Really? That seems unlikely," Peterson questioned skeptically.

"Well, it seems unlikely that you were smart enough to make detective, but here we both are—inconvenienced by circumstance," Jarrett answered with enough seriousness that Peterson had no reply.

Hall cleared his throat. "Do you know when we can reach Cade?"

"I thought this business was all finished, Detective," Rederrick stated.

"We're just clearing up a few details, shouldn't be anything to worry about."

Jarrett glared at him.

"Well, I will have Cade get in touch when he can," Rederrick supplied.

"That's fine. For now, would you mind going over the night of the break-in here and how you and Cade tried to save Jeffery and Cody from the," he pointedly looked at his small notebook, "Californian drug lord, was it? One last time. I want to make sure I remember it accurately for my report." As he pulled out his notebook, Hall observed Jarrett's jaw clench and anger simmered in his eyes. *Isn't that interesting*, he thought to himself.

OTHER POWERS OF INFLUENCE NOVELS

FORGOTTEN ENEMY
THE TRUTH OF VICTORY

Made in the USA
San Bernardino, CA
19 August 2017